SEEDS

ANGIE PAXTON

Text copyright © 2024 by Angie Paxton

All rights reserved. For information regarding reproduction in total or in part, contact Rising Action Publishing Co. at http://www.risingactionpublish-ingco.com

Cover Illustration © Nat Mack
Copy Edited by Marthese Fenech

ISBN: 978-1-998076-84-0
ebook: 978-1-998076-91-8

FIC010000 FICTION / Fairy Tales, Folk Tales, Legends & Mythology
FIC009030 FICTION / Fantasy / Historical
FIC009090 FICTION / Fantasy / Romance

#SeedsBook

Follow Rising Action on our socials!
Twitter: @RAPubCollective
Instagram: @risingactionpublishingco
TikTok: @risingactionpublishingco

To Nick
for the continual supply of support in the form of laptops,
writing software subscriptions,
hours of listening, hours of solo parenting,
and bottomless belief in me.
This book wouldn't exist without you.

SEEDS

1

PERSEPHONE

A scream shattered the early morning quiet of the village, penetrating the walls of the hut Persephone shared with her mother. Persephone jerked, nearly dropping the cup she held, and some of the barley water slopped out. The shrill cry sounded as though someone had taken a mortal wound.

Persephone set the vessel on the table. Then, wiping her hand on her tunic, she hurried to the door. The dried reeds clicked against each other as she pushed it open and peered out.

A short distance away, Thais darted out of her home and into her daughter's. A moment later, she emerged supporting Nadira. The two women took a few steps before Nadira curled over her distended belly and gave a short, sharp yelp, softer than the scream that had earlier startled Persephone but just as distressed. Thais tightened her grip on her daughter's waist, then spoke to her for a moment. The pair commenced stumbling toward the House of the Mother Goddess as Thais shouted, "It's Nadira's time!"

The two women disappeared into the temple. Moments later, doors all over Henna opened, and women spilled out. In groups and pairs, they moved toward the temple answering Thais's summons. Persephone slunk back inside her hut, pulling the door tightly closed behind her.

Her gaze went immediately to Doso's basket resting on its shelf. The older woman was gone. There was no one to help Nadira bring her child into the world, except perhaps, Persephone—if she had the courage to try.

With only a few strides, Persephone crossed the small space of the hut. Hands shaking, she took the basket down and sorted through its contents. Doso had filled it with supplies, leaving it in good order, just as she had her bed of blankets, folding and stacking them in the corner before disappearing in the dead of night with no word of farewell a handful of days ago.

Clearly, Doso had intended the basket be put to use again. As Doso had taught Persephone, and only Persephone, the various purposes of the basket's contents, it also seemed apparent Doso expected Persephone to step into the place the old woman had vacated. Yet how could she? She'd never attended a birth. Even if the women didn't hound Persephone from the temple the moment she entered, her failure still seemed likely. But if she succeeded, an enormous reward awaited her, something she wanted for as long as she could remember. For that reason, she had to try.

Hands still trembling, heart thundering, Persephone slid the basket's handle up her forearm and left the safety of the hut.

She had nearly reached the temple when a pack of girls darted across the path in front of her, all gangly limbs and tangled hair as they churned through the dust in one of those games peculiar to childhood. Persephone cowered back, but they didn't pay her any mind. Instead, they raced away, sharing a camaraderie Persephone had never experienced. So much of their lives were and would continue to be different than hers. By the time they reached Persephone's age of twenty years, the promise of their future, wedding, bedding, and ruling their own hearths, would

2

be fulfilled. Persephone, however, would never be taken to wife, not in this village where the men feared her curse would shrivel their man-parts. She was sentenced to languish in her mother's hut unless she carved out a different path for herself today, one that could lead to a surcease of the villagers' fear of her and the unkindness with which they treated her. Then, she might find a place among them and a home of her own.

Straightening her spine, Persephone closed the small distance to the temple. As she lifted a hand to pull open the door, a familiar voice called her name. Stomach plummeting, Persephone turned.

Her mother strode toward her. Demeter's presence in the village at this time of day was unusual as her work in the fields generally occupied her daylight hours. That, combined with Demeter's narrowed eyes and pinched lips, forecast an oncoming confrontation. Sweat slicked Persephone's hands.

Demeter stopped in front of Persephone then gestured at the House of the Mother Goddess. "Why are you here? This is no place for you."

"Nadira's babe is coming."

"So it is. What concern is that of yours?" Demeter asked.

"I mean to aid her." Though Persephone intended to convey confidence, the tremble in her voice betrayed her.

"No. I forbid it. Return to the hut."

Persephone drew in a breath, tilted her chin. "Mother, the woman labors unaided. I must—"

Demeter barked laughter. "Unaided? Every bedded woman in Henna is with her and most have at least a rudimentary knowledge of midwifery. If they weren't so addled by suspicion, Nadira would have more than sufficient help to bring her child into the world."

"But they won't settle enough to assist Nadira until one who has the Mother Goddess's favor attends upon the birth."

"Perhaps that's true, but you are not that one, Persephone. On the contrary—"

"Had I not broken Her image the villagers wouldn't be so afraid. As it was me who knocked her statue to the floor, it's my—"

Demeter waved a hand. "Nonsense. You were a babe. You can neither be blamed for your actions then nor the villagers' ridiculous suspicions now. Go back to the hut. There's more than sufficient work to do there that's within your abilities. Aiding Nadira is not."

Always the same argument. Persephone was too young, too foolish, too incapable to do any but the most menial of tasks. This time, however, her mother was wrong.

Persephone tightened her grip on the basket's rough handle. Pain shot through her fingers. It helped steady her, helped pluck the quaver from her voice as she said, "I won't return home. I'm going to help Nadira. I have the knowledge to do so."

"And much good will it do you," Demeter snapped. "Doso was a fool to teach you herblore and midwifery and you a fool to attempt to learn. None here in Henna will accept your help."

Blinking rapidly so the tears pricking her eyes wouldn't fall, Persephone said, "Doso wouldn't have passed on her knowledge if she believed—"

"Doso's gone!" Demeter shouted. "What she believed doesn't matter."

The tears escaped the dam of Persephone's eyelashes and spilled down her cheeks. Using the back of her hand, she wiped them away with quick, furtive motions.

Nostrils flaring, mouth tight, Demeter continued, "You grieve as though your mother abandoned you, not some old beggar woman."

Persephone couldn't deny the assertion and admitting to it would only further enrage her mother, so, instead of making any response, she turned to the door of the temple.

Demeter's hard hand closed on Persephone's upper arm, and she spun her daughter back around. "I'll attend the birth." Demeter released Persephone and extended her open palm. "Give me the basket. The Sicani believe I have the Mother's favor. That will settle them enough that surely one of the other women will recall that she has the necessary skills to aid Nadira."

Shaking her head, Persephone stepped back. "What if that doesn't occur? Please let me go. I can do this."

"You can't. Should you cross that threshold they'll drive you from the temple and beat you bloody to ensure you don't return." Demeter grabbed the basket's handle and tugged. "Quit your obstinance. Let me have this."

Something large and hard bumped Persephone's back, and she stumbled into her mother. Demeter released the basket to catch her.

Persephone turned in her mother's grip to see what had struck her. Thais stood on the threshold of the House of the Mother Goddess. Hands coming up in a warding off gesture, the woman staggered back, only halting when she came up against the door which had swung closed behind her. "Go! Go, Goddess Breaker! You must not be here."

Tears sprang to Persephone's eyes again. Always the loathing. Always the fear. It hadn't lessened one whit over the course of Persephone's life. Her chance to change the villagers' perception of her was now, and it was slipping away.

"You see?" Demeter reached once more for the basket.

Persephone jerked it away.

"Kore!"

Persephone twitched. Her mother's use of her other name was like the sting of a lash on her skin. Kore meaning 'girl' or 'daughter,' in the way a dog is only Dog, as a creature is only Thing.

Demeter took hold of the basket again. This time, Persephone allowed the rough handle to slide from her fingers and then it was in her mother's possession. A waft of lavender and sweetened oil curled up Persephone's nose. Doso's scent, the only thing Persephone had left of the older woman and all the love she gave.

"You mean to attend Nadira, Demeter?" Thais asked.

Demeter gave a curt nod. Thais's sweat-sheened face broke into a grin.

"Come. Come then." The woman opened the door of the House of the Mother Goddess and bustled inside. Demeter moved around Persephone to follow.

"Why won't you call me Persephone when the villagers can hear? They don't know it's meaning and even if they did, none here would dispute that 'destroyer of light' suits me."

Demeter stopped. Her head swiveled a bit. Her profile was shadowed by the crown of her golden braids, and Persephone could find no clues in her mother's expression as to what Demeter thought or felt. Perhaps, though, her question would elicit some kernel of explanation as to why her mother had chosen to name Persephone as she had. In that lay the mystery of why Demeter despised Persephone and what, if anything, Persephone could do to change her mother's opinion and, hopefully, treatment of her.

After a long moment of silence, however, Demeter turned fully from Persephone, her neck and spine rigid as she moved inside, the bang of the door swinging shut Demeter's only response.

The battle was lost. Persephone's position in the village and in her mother's estimation set as surely as the stone in the walls of the House of the Mother Goddess.

Shoulders slumping, Persephone walked back to the hut. Once inside, her muscles still quivering with pent up pain and anger, she found all of those mindless tasks for which her mother deemed her abilities fit—scouring the dishes, sweeping the hearth, carding the wool—waiting for her. But the hut was too close, too confined. She had to get out and away, at least for a time.

Persephone collected a basket of soiled clothes, moved toward the door, then stopped. She knew what awaited her at the washing place. Because most of the women were attending Nadira, there would likely be none to shift down the streambed away from her, lowering their voices as if even their conversation would be tainted should it reach her ears. The children would find her there, though, with stones in their hands and fear in their hearts, their taunts of 'Goddess Breaker' and 'cursed one' ringing in her ears as she hunched over her task.

She looked down, unsure what to do, and her gaze fell on a partially blackened blossom lying near the fire. It had been part of the garland Persephone crafted for her mother only the day before. Persephone had given her mother many such simple gifts, but this one enraged Demeter in a way none of the previous ones had. She'd taken it up in her fist, stood over Persephone where she sat on her bed, and shouted at Persephone to tell her where she came by the blossoms.

When Persephone explained she procured them from the Mother Goddess's Meadow, Demeter extracted from Persephone a promise that she *never* return there, then flung the garland into the hearth fire. Yet another of Persephone's tokens that wasn't enough to bring a spark to her mother's cold blue eyes, a smile to that severe mouth. However, this was the first time Demeter willfully destroyed one of Persephone's offerings. The burning of the garland had been unexpected and painful, giving rise to an ache in Persephone's breast that had been revived by the morning's confrontation.

With her toe, Persephone nudged the flower. It had survived her mother's rage, but it was still doomed. In the dry heat next to the hearth, the blossom would shrivel up and crumble to dust, just as Persephone would if she stayed any longer in this village where she was feared, in this hut where she was hated. She had to go, had to carve out a home in a place where the villagers didn't dare venture and her mother would never think to look for her.

A strange calm settled over Persephone. She turned from the door, put the basket of laundry back in its place, picked up one of Doso's blankets, and spread it out on her bed. Then she moved about the hut gathering the few belongings that were hers alone, set them on the blanket, and tied the four corners of it together.

With the small bundle tucked under one arm, she grabbed a stack of honey cakes then walked out the door. As she hurried away from the hut, childhood memories nipped at her heels: the many dolls made of grain Demeter crafted for Persephone when she was little, the colorful wooden tops Demeter set to spinning over and over again before Persephone's fascinated eyes, the saffron tunic embroidered with lilies that Demeter laid across Persephone's lap the night after Doso left—the tunic Persephone wore even now. Most haunting, though, was the remembrance of the feather-soft touch of Demeter's lips on Persephone's brow to which she woke that morning. No doubt meant in recompense for burning the garland the night before.

Persephone's step faltered, and she almost turned back to the hut. But no. That was Demeter's way: a slap, a lashing, cruel words, then a touch of kindness, some token of affection. Kindness followed cruelty but so would cruelty follow kindness. Always.

Brushing her hand across her forehead as though that could erase the memory of her mother's kiss, Persephone hurried to the scrap heap on the far edge of the village. The area was, as usual, deserted, the smell alone enough to keep most folk away. Stepping into the fringe of the forest, Persephone made a soft chirruping sound. After a few moments with no response, she tried again. She wanted to be well away from the village by the time Demeter finished with Nadira's birthing, but she would wait as long as necessary. Leaving without Phlox was unthinkable. He would be her only companion in the new life she meant to make for herself.

Persephone peered at the undergrowth, the deep shadows making it difficult to distinguish any movement on the forest floor. But, yes, there it was, a flick of vibrant orange in all the dimness and then another as Phlox drew closer.

Persephone crouched, a bit of honey cake in hand as the fox emerged from the underbrush just a few feet away. Phlox limped toward her, favoring the back leg from which Persephone pulled an arrow some years ago, the act that had begun her friendship with this wild creature. He was young then, barely more than a kit, and with Persephone's care had recovered well. In the last few months, however, the old injury seemed to be taking its toll.

The long trek to the Mother Goddess's Meadow promised to be a painful one for Phlox to make. And what could Persephone offer him should she succeed in using the honey cakes to lure him to follow her there? She had no warm dry den for the old fox to curl up in on cold nights, only a dank cave with a few dusty and worn furnishings. Persephone intended to subsist off the various plants which she knew to be edible, but Phlox wouldn't be able to do so. He needed meat to fill his belly. There was no scrap heap in the meadow from which he could scavenge leavings and his limp made it nearly impossible for him to hunt. Here, at least, he could spend the little time he had left to him in some comfort and ease.

With his sharp white teeth, Phlox carefully took the honey cake from her fingers, then sat, his bushy tail curling around his feet. Persephone went to her knees and put her arms around his neck. The coarse hair of his orange ruff pressed against her cheek for only a moment before Phlox, with a high-pitched bark, jumped back out of her arms. He watched her with his yellow eyes, black-tipped ears tilted forward, wary of this new and strange behavior.

With tears burning in the bridge of her nose, Persephone laughed and put a hand out. Phlox stepped forward, sniffed her fingertips, then licked them with his rough pink tongue. She was forgiven, but what would he think when she didn't come with honey cakes in hand to visit him as she did most days? He wouldn't seek her in the village. The arrow through his back haunch had taught him to fear all humans except Persephone, but would he believe she had stopped loving him? Would his wild mind even notice her absence? For her part, she would miss Phlox desperately. Without him, she would be utterly alone in the Mother Goddess's Meadow. And yet, even that was a better fate than the one which awaited her if she stayed in Henna.

Persephone rose to her feet. It was time to go. Delaying would only make this farewell more difficult. Persephone tossed the stack of honey cakes to the ground. Phlox immediately set up on them.

"Farewell, my friend," Persephone said. Phlox looked up, but his eyes were uncomprehending. After only a moment, he went back to his work on the honey cakes, the meal a touch of sweetness in the last fleeting days of the old fox's life. At least she could leave him with that much.

With tears sliding down her cheeks, Persephone set off on the downward sloping path through the woods. At the bottom of the hill, deep in the interior of the trees, she stopped at a forest pool. She lay on her belly and submerged her tear-swollen face into the cool, sweet water. She never would have dared this in the village where she always had to be on guard for one of her mother's harsh rebukes or the villagers' kicks, hits, and thrown stones.

After the water cooled her face, Persephone rolled to her back. The deep, rich scent of the earth under the trees and the distinct sweet smell of sap from the ash trees curled up her nose. The light from Helios's chariot high in the sky filtered through the branches. She put a hand in a beam and it glimmered, turning the pale reddish hair on her arm golden. Something in her chest loosened. She still had this, the peace and beauty of forest and meadow. No one could take that from her. It would be her solace in her new life.

Persephone rose to her feet and set out once again. She adopted a purposeful pace for the rest of her trek through the trees and soon emerged into the Mother Goddess's Meadow. Flower-dotted grass covered the vast treeless expanse. Some distance out, Helios's light gleamed on the surface of a lake. Beyond that, the forest took over the landscape again.

This place was forbidden to all but the Henna village elders. Even they only ventured here when in dire need and with no choice but to petition the Goddess on her own ground.

Persephone was perhaps ten years old when she realized that, as she was already cursed, the Goddess could do no more to her. One day, seeking a haven from her mother's wrath for some task not done or done badly, she risked visiting it and here found a sanctuary from her mother's unkindness and the drudgery of daily chores. Doso allowed her to play here but warned her—in the garbled language only Persephone could understand—not to tell Demeter. Demeter's ire when she had discovered Persephone had ventured here clarified why Doso counseled Persephone to keep her time in this place a secret. Persephone still had no explanation as to why her mother wanted her to keep away from the meadow and now, she would likely never get one.

Persephone stepped from the trees. The long grass and nodding blossoms brushed against her legs as she moved across the meadow to the cavern she had discovered on one of her many excursions here.

It was danker and darker than she remembered; however, the inexplicable furnishings present during her first foray into the cave still resided near its mouth. The depredations of time had hardly touched the table and chairs, which were constructed of dark, glossy ebony, and the pair of golden goblets on the tabletop still glimmered faintly under a thick coat of dust. The bedframe, however, canted to one side, most of the leather long since gnawed away by denizens of meadow and cave. Persephone would need to tie it together with cords of braided grass before she slept there, if she could sleep there. It was cold in the cave, and she only brought one blanket.

Instead of starting on the necessary cleaning and repairs, Persephone dragged a hand across her eyes, then pulled one of the dust-rimed chairs out and sat on it. She hadn't even had the foresight to bring sufficient bedding. Her mother was right. She was foolish, a dullard, not fit for anything but the meanest labor, certainly not suited for life on her own.

A thud came from within the reaches of the cave. Persephone peered into the darkness but she could see nothing there and the sound didn't repeat. Perhaps she'd imagined it.

She put a hand on the table to push herself to her feet just as the noise came again: a thump, this time followed by a snort and the jingling of metal.

Persephone rose and stepped toward the dimness. "Is someone there?"

For a moment, silence was her only response. Then came a soft repetitive scuffing, the same noise her feet made on the dirt floor of the cave when she'd entered it. The sound was close enough now she should have been able to see its source, but only darkness loomed in front of her.

The skin on the back of Persephone's neck prickled and her hands grew damp with sweat.

The footsteps stopped. Warm air bathed her face but still she could see nothing. Fingers trailed through a length of her hair.

A deep voice whispered, "Kore?"

2

PERSEPHONE

Persephone screamed and stumbled backward, tripping over the chair and nearly tumbling to the ground. Scrabbling at the edge of the table, she hauled herself upright, then raced for the safety of the light.

When she was some distance into the meadow, Persephone spun to look behind her. The blank, black eye of the cavern stared back, keeping its secrets as it always had. The rest of the day was serene; birds chirped and a breeze soughed through the trees as Helios's chariot raced through the cloudless blue sky.

Air concussed against Persephone's back in a soundless explosion. At the same moment, a violent gust of wind shook the trees. Persephone screamed again and whirled to face this new threat.

Among the long grass and nodding flowers stood a group of women unlike any Persephone had ever seen, save perhaps her mother. They all had long, graceful, well-formed limbs, smooth skin that seemed to capture Helios's glow, berry-red lips, and magnificent crowns of hair. Rather than tunics, they wore tops cut below their breasts that laced tightly to their torsos. Long skirts in every color Persephone had seen, and some she hadn't, fell in flounces from their waists. Jewelry draped their necks and wrists and hung from their ears, but the baubles couldn't compare to the brightness of their gaze as every pair of gemstone eyes turned to her.

One of the women said something in a low voice and the others laughed, a clear, ringing sound.

At their merriment, Persephone surveyed herself. Mud from laying on the bank of the pool still spattered her tunic. Dust from the chair and table in the cave filmed her hands and arms, and her feet were black from her trek through the forest. Scurrying away as she longed to do would only increase their amusement at her expense, and might even, as it did in the village, lead to a pursuit and a hail of stones.

Persephone brushed down her tunic and smoothed her hair back from her sweat damp forehead. "Good day to you."

"You can look upon us?" one of them asked in a voice as clear and lovely as her laughter.

The woman spoke in the language Demeter used with Persephone rather than that of Sicani, so they couldn't be of Henna. Perhaps Persephone didn't need to fear them. "I can. Should I be unable to?"

"Can it be her?" one of them whispered.

Another replied, "She does have red hair."

And then another, "She looks so very . . . mortal."

"As do we when in our earthly forms," one with kind brown eyes chided.

Another woman with hair like gleaming black water said, "Strange tastes for a strange God, I suppose."

Strange God. Earthly form. Their words were nonsensical, and Persephone wanted no part of their odd conversation.

She opened her mouth to take her leave, but before she could, the black-haired woman looked at her and asked, "Who is your mother, Little Sister?"

Persephone's brows drew together. "My . . . mother? Demeter of

Henna. Why do you ask?"

The women erupted into a furor of musical cries. Then the black-haired one broke away from the group, walked to Persephone, and took her hand.

Persephone gasped. This woman was the only person aside from Demeter and Doso to ever touch Persephone willingly and the warmth of her hand on Persephone's skin was a wonder. However, the woman seemed unaware of the magnitude of her gesture. She merely introduced herself as Ianthe as she drew Persephone toward the others.

When Persephone joined their circle, the women folded their legs beneath them and sank to the ground with the airy elegance of falling flower petals. Persephone's own descent, by comparison, was that of a branch crashing through the treetop canopy.

"Are you Kore, then?" one of the women with golden hair asked. Before Persephone could reply she continued, "For if you are, you're one of us."

Persephone looked from one lovely face to the next. "One of you? How can that be?"

They made no response to her but shared glances with one another, lips turning up and eyes twinkling.

Rolling to her knees in preparation to stand, Persephone said, "I know enough of mockery to recognize it well. I'll bid you good day now."

"No mockery, Little Sister. We only want to know you. Now, are you Kore?"

These women couldn't be aware of her reputation as an outcast in Henna. If they were, they wouldn't have welcomed her into their midst. Ianthe wouldn't have touched her. Perhaps she could trust they meant no offense by their words.

Persephone settled herself back on the ground. "That's what my mother calls me."

Ianthe laughed delightedly. "We thought to seek you out, yet here you appeared to us, Kore."

That name coming from such lovely lips was unbearable. "You may call me Persephone."

"Persephone? Did you give yourself such a name?" a flaxen-haired beauty asked.

Face heating in a blush, Persephone looked down. "I am twice-named by my mother."

"We need have no doubt as to how Demeter finds motherhood and mortality then," Ianthe said.

The women tittered.

Persephone raised her eyes, tilted her chin. "Though it's an unkind name, it's the one I choose to be known by."

"Very well," Ianthe said. "We welcome you, Persephone."

"Welcome, Persephone," the other women said as one, and in their ringing voices it sounded like a blessing and their names, when they gifted her with them, were like poems.

"Do you not know us now?" one of them asked when they finished their introductions.

The women were so alike in their perfection it was hard to recall who was whom, but this one had a bow and a quiver of arrows slung over her shoulder which set her apart from the others. She called herself Artemis.

"Should I know you?" Persephone asked.

A long moment of silence ensued as the women once again exchanged glances.

"Your mother has been neglectful," Artemis said.

"Bitter," Ianthe corrected.

"We are your dear ones," another said.

"Your beloveds," they chorused.

"Your sister Goddesses," added one with hair of burnished gold, similar to Demeter's, but her eyes were warm brown rather than austere blue. Her name was Aphrodite.

Persephone shook her head. "I don't understand. The only Goddess I know of is the Mother Goddess, yet you say you are Goddesses as well."

"I am," Artemis said. "And Aphrodite as well. Ianthe and the others are nymphs. They're free to come and go from Olympus as they like, but they have none of the power we Goddesses possess. All of us, however, are Immortals. The blood of the Titans, one of whom is Rhea, or the Mother Goddess, as you call her, runs in all our veins, including yours. If it didn't you wouldn't be able to look upon us without going mad."

Looking from Artemis to Athena, Persephone repeated, "I don't understand."

Ianthe reached for her. "Lay your head, Persephone, and I'll tell you a story."

Persephone hadn't been cradled in a lap and told a tale since she was a little girl curled up with Doso in her nest of blankets on the floor. It was an odd request for one grown woman to make of another. Much about these women was extremely strange, but they were offering her friendship, something that she had felt but little of in her life, and not at all since Doso's departure.

Persephone allowed Ianthe to tug her down until her head rested on the warm curves of the woman's thighs.

"We," Ianthe raised her hand and gestured, encompassing the circle of women, "live in a place called Olympus, in a realm few mortals can reach. It's a place passing fair, where everything is delightsome, lovely, and wondrous."

Ianthe dropped her hand, plucked a few blossoms, and began to twist them into Persephone's hair as she spoke. "In a place where beauty abounds, one Goddess stood out among all the Immortals. She had eyes as deep and blue as Poseidon's Sea and hair of such beautiful, glorious gold that even Helios wept with envy. Zeus, ruler of us all, Immortals and mortals alike, desired her greatly, in the way a man desires a woman."

"You'll have a lesson in that soon enough, Little Sister," Artemis interjected, her hazel eyes sparkling as she smiled at Persephone.

Persephone smiled back, but hers was quirked with puzzlement. "I don't—"

"Hush now, Artemis. You know we aren't to speak of that," Ianthe said, then continued. "Zeus favored this Goddess above all others, even his wife Hera. He plied her with music, food, wine, laughter, and kisses, but she spurned him. This Goddess's Immortal birthright included an affinity to plants. In a last attempt at gaining her affection, Zeus granted her dominion over all the green and growing things that spring from Gaia's flesh. In return, the Goddess gave herself to Zeus. They hid their love from Hera, but after a time the Goddess found herself, as a woman will when she lies with a man, expecting a child. Zeus promised the Goddess that, should she give birth to a healthy Olympian son, she would replace Hera as his consort. To keep the babe safe from the prying eyes and jealous heart of Hera, Zeus asked his lover to leave Olympus, take on her mortal form and live in a cave on an island near the barbarian Sicani, those who know nothing of we Olympians. Zeus spent much more time with the Goddess on her island than he did on Olympus. His heart had grown cold toward his wife, for she had given him only one healthy girl child. Their second child, a boy, was so malformed Zeus hurled it from Olympus. Hera felt his coldness, noted his absence, and suspected her husband had taken yet another lover. She found Zeus and the Goddess in their hiding place and worked a rite to steal from the

Goddess her immortality, trapping her in her mortal form. The Goddess gave birth to a girl. Zeus, in his disappointment, left the Goddess and her child in their exile."

Ianthe stroked Persephone's furrowed brow. "Can you guess the name of the cast-off Goddess, Little Sister?"

Persephone drew in a breath that coursed like flame down a throat gone tight and swollen. "Demeter."

"Our lost one," Aphrodite said.

"Our love," the other women chorused.

"My mother," Persephone said.

"And now you see how you are one of us?" Artemis said.

Persephone didn't see. She couldn't be one of them. She had nothing of their beauty, grace, or self-assuredness ... but her mother did. It was easy to believe Demeter belonged among them, easy now to understand why she was so different from the Sicani, easy to see why she resented Persephone.

No doubt when Demeter returned from Nadira's birthing and found Persephone gone, she would waste no time grieving her daughter's absence. Joy would speed her feet all the way to Olympus where she would regain the life from which Persephone kept her. The little hut where they'd lived together in Henna would be left to be reclaimed by nature, for no one would dare lay their head where the Goddess Breaker once slept. Even if the hut were habitable, the Sicani wouldn't permit Persephone to live among them without Demeter's mitigating presence. Persephone would have nowhere to go should life in the meadow prove too hostile.

Persephone tugged her hair out of Ianthe's grasp and sat up. "If I'm truly one of you, take me with you when you return to Olympus."

Ianthe's violet eyes widened. She looked beyond Persephone at the other Goddesses.

Artemis's warm hand encircled Persephone's. Her expression was earnest, eyes soft with compassion. "Though you are a Goddess, you haven't a place on Olympus. Zeus wasn't best pleased with your birth. He won't thank us for bringing you into his palace."

Persephone's heart was a hard, hot stone in her chest. The prickle in her nose warned of tears to come. She drew her hand out of Artemis's and stood. Even if she was a Goddess, as they kept claiming, she had no place with them, either. The threatened tears sprang to her eyes.

Aphrodite also rose. She crossed the circle of women and settled her hands on Persephone's shoulders. "Don't cry, Little Sister. Though we can't take you with us to Olympus, we'll come to you again in this place."

"We will," they all agreed.

Aphrodite smiled, and it was so lovely Persephone's heart cracked.

"You'll visit me here? You vow it?" Persephone asked.

Giving Persephone's shoulders a gentle squeeze, Aphrodite said, "You may soon find yourself resident in a different place, but until that day we'll gladly visit you here. And none of us needs depart yet. Come, let's make a game of the time we have left." Aphrodite tapped her cheek with one elegant finger a few times then said, "I want to know which of the blossoms in the meadow rivals me for beauty, but not by sight. I want to judge only by scent and texture." Removing her hands from Persephone's shoulders, she looked around at the other Goddesses. "I command you all to gather one of each flower in the meadow, so I can compare them and choose."

At Aphrodite's pronouncement, the Goddesses erupted into laughter and chatter.

As they got to their feet, Persephone asked, "This is how you mean to spend your time? Surely you have other duties to which you must attend?"

Persephone's life, from the moment she woke until the day was done, was a series of dull, onerous, and exhausting tasks. Immortals, with their duties stewarding humans, must have at least as much to accomplish. However, Persephone snuck away often enough for an hour or two to gambol in the forest with Phlox or to lay in the sun in the Mother Goddess's Meadow. Perhaps that's what this was, a small slice of time stolen from the arduousness of being an Immortal.

Artemis, still standing at Persephone's side, chuckled. "Ah, Sister, there's nothing we *must* do save please ourselves."

This wasn't then a bit of respite for them, but rather simply what it meant to be an Immortal. Is that why mortals toiled under so much strife? Because those who could lighten their burden chose instead to occupy themselves with seeking out pleasurable ways to pass their time? No, she had to be mistaken. These wonderful beings couldn't be so indolent, so selfish. She need look no further for proof of that other than the kindness they lavished on her.

"Bring me the loveliest, Persephone," Aphrodite commanded, her face robbed of its liveliness and individuality by the cloth now tied over her eyes.

"I shall," Persephone called and darted away as the others scattered in their search for the most beautiful blossom.

Though the undertaking put before her seemed simple enough, Persephone couldn't bring her mind to bear on it. Instead, her thoughts bumbled like a bee searching for more nectar. This strange day had exceeded all her hopes for a different life. She could be happy here in this place with the Goddesses' visits to look forward to. The time they spent with her here would alleviate her loneliness, though she would still sorely miss Phlox. And, surely, they would help her should she find herself in any extremity. Given time, they might even convince Zeus to let her join them on Olympus. Perhaps that was what they meant when they said she'd soon be resident in a different place.

A trace of laughter floated to Persephone on the breeze. The Goddesses flitted through the meadow, consulting each other as they plucked blossoms. Persephone hadn't picked so much as a single bud. It wouldn't do to disappoint in the first duty they'd charged her with.

Persephone moved through the grass, dissatisfied with each flower until her search for the perfect blossom took her back to the cavern's mouth. A lone narcissus bloomed there. It shone out startlingly white against the black of the cave at its back. Persephone stared. If it had been here when she arrived, she would have taken note of it. Yet, it must have been here. Flowers didn't spring up fully formed in the matter of half a day. Or perhaps they did. Perhaps it was tangled up in the mystery of the sounds she had heard within the cavern, the touch she felt, the disembodied voice.

Regardless of its origin, the narcissus was the most beautiful flower by any criteria. Aphrodite was sure to be pleased by it and flower or no, Persephone had to make her peace with the cavern before nightfall if she meant to spend this night and those hereafter in its shelter.

Persephone moved toward the cave but paused a short distance outside. All was silent and still. She took a few more cautious steps, stopping just inside the cavern's mouth. Then, after listening for some time more, she bent to pluck the flower.

She gave a gentle tug, but the stem resisted. Persephone doubled her efforts and still the stem refused to give. She didn't want to slay it, but needs must. She grasped its base and pulled. The entire plant came up abruptly in a shower of dirt.

Persephone grunted and lost her balance. She laughed a little as she landed on her backside. With her dirt-bespattered skirt, filthy hands, and clumsiness, no one, least of all herself, would believe she was the daughter of two of Olympus's chosen.

Holding the narcissus carefully, Persephone got to her feet. A sudden wind came up, howling over the meadow, flattening the grass, and churning the tree branches. Heavy thunderheads rolled in where only moments before the sky had been an expanse of serene, unbroken blue.

A boom ripped across the sky, strong enough that it shook Persephone's bones. When the growl of it died away, the vibration continued in her feet and legs. Its source, however, wasn't thunder but a low rumble which issued from the dark reaches of the cavern.

The sound from within the cave pressed on Persephone, growing more ominous with each moment. Sweat sprang from every pore, and her heart thudded in her breast.

Persephone turned and dashed away from the cavern back toward the Goddesses. They had gone far in the quest Aphrodite set them. Their mouths were open, in laughter or conversation, Persephone couldn't tell. The crashing thunder and screaming wind seemed not to concern them as they traipsed about, filling their hands with flowers.

Persephone opened her mouth to call out, but all that escaped her throat was a low, hoarse caw. The rumble behind her grew unbearably loud, throbbing in her ears. She looked over her shoulder.

The red, flaring nostril of a horse filled her vision. To one side and behind the animal's muzzle, a chariot wheel spun furiously.

Another boom split the sky. It mingled with the crack of a whip, and a man's voice exhorting his steed to go faster.

The beast was almost on her. Persephone would surely be trampled. She jerked her head around. Her legs churned. Her breath pumped in and out. The heavens roared. The wind howled.

Despite her desperate burst of speed, the horse quickly pulled alongside Persephone. She saw then that there were four of them, great, black, gleaming beasts. In less time than it took to blink, they passed her, and the chariot wheel rolled by.

A hard hand closed on Persephone's upper arm. Calluses rasped against her skin. Legs still pedaling, she was lifted into the air, swung around, and yanked backward.

The rear of her ankles slammed into the edge of the chariot basket. She sucked in a sharp breath. Her captor hauled her up. For a moment, she faced the cavern, before the man who had seized her once again spun her, his arm snaking around her waist.

The horses' heaving backs and bobbing necks came into focus. Beyond them, the Goddesses still frolicked under the looming sky, unaware of her plight. Persephone didn't waste breath calling out to them again. Her voice couldn't compete with the cacophony of wind and thunder.

Still pinned to his side by a granite arm, Persephone looked at her captor. A swath of blue-gray wool stretched across a broad, muscled chest. She tilted her head back. A black beard covered the lower portion of the man's face. Hair of the same color fell in curls behind the whorl of one pale ear. Turning his head, he looked down on her with slate-gray eyes that held not a spark of warmth or kindness.

Persephone twisted out of his grasp and lunged for the edge of the chariot. He grabbed her upper arm, halting her. Snarling, screeching, she clawed at his fingers but couldn't break his grip.

The chariot wheeled and Persephone was thrown hard against him. His arm came around her again, anchoring her to his side once more. She strained and struggled, but he held her so tightly she couldn't free either of her arms to fight. She spat at him all the Sicani curses that had been hurled at her over the years. He made no response. It was like doing battle with a stone.

The horses raced back to the cave. Without so much as checking their stride, they plunged into the darkness. Persephone craned her neck to look behind her as the light receded.

The churned earth of the meadow where the chariot had pursued her threw out tender shoots of grass at an astonishing rate. Inside the cavern, the dust resettled itself in their wake to fill in the indentations of hooves and wheels. Any who thought to find her would have no reason now to venture past the mouth of the cavern.

Persephone let the narcissus fall. The plant slid from the chariot's basket and landed on the floor of the cavern. The white star of its blossoms shone in the black of the cave for a moment. Then its blooms withered and crumbled into dust. At the destruction of this last sign of her descent into the cavern's depths, Persephone called on the God that the Goddesses claimed was her father, the all-mighty Zeus. If she was his child, surely he would come to her aid. If not, she was lost.

3

DEMETER

Opening her eyes, Demeter rolled in bed, the leather straps creaking beneath her as she turned. Pale gray light streamed through the smoke hole in the ceiling, lighting up the hearth and the tattered, blackened blossom that lay at its edge. Demeter's breath left her in a long sigh, and she shifted her gaze to where Persephone still lay in her bed on the other side of the hut. Even in sleep, a small groove marred the skin between the girl's brows.

Demeter threw back her covers, rose, crossed to Persephone and knelt at her side. When Persephone didn't stir, Demeter pressed a kiss to the small indentation on her daughter's forehead and waited to see if she would wake. Her eyes remained closed.

Sighing again, Demeter got to her feet, returned to her pallet and pulled the coarse wool blankets up over it. As she smoothed them down, the material snagged on her red, work-roughened hands. If their ache wasn't a constant reminder that they were indeed attached, she would scarcely believe they belonged to her. Her hands should be lily-white, petal smooth, free of pain, and capable of so much more than the dreary labor she used them to accomplish every day.

Bitterness, black and viscous, leached through her, driving out all her earlier contrition. She looked at her daughter once more. Persephone's eyes fluttered open. Demeter spun and hurried toward the door. With this mood on her, it would be best for both of them if she was gone before Persephone fully woke. Demeter had caused enough hurt the evening before. No need to risk another disagreement.

When Demeter exited the hut, she almost stepped on a basket containing a loaf of bread and a small wheel of cheese that had been placed outside the door. A smile turned her lips, but it wasn't a pleasant one. The villagers' simple offerings of gratitude were nothing compared to all Demeter would have now if Persephone had only been a boy. Leaving the items for Persephone to collect, Demeter made her way to the outskirts of Henna.

Although the day was still pale gray, Helios not yet riding the sky, some of the villagers already toiled in the fields. Despite their many shortcomings, Demeter could say this for the Sicani: they listened well when she showed them how to determine which soil was best for growing, how to irrigate it, and how to cultivate the crops. These bounteous fields were proof of that.

Before joining the villagers in their work, Demeter strode through the grain to check the health of the plants. A sticky, light brown substance coated some of them. She squatted to study it. It was, as she feared, the blight that displaced seed heads, leaving dark purple or black growths in their stead. Without intervention, it would spread to the entire crop.

Demeter's hands hovered over the infected stalks. She could cure them with a single touch, but it would cost her dearly, a depletion without repair, for she no longer had her Immortal essence or the power provided by her worshippers on which to draw.

Demeter raised her head and looked in the direction of her home. She looked back at the plant, at its fellows clustered around it also suffering from the same disease.

Demeter cursed. Her gaze traveled once again to her hut, but no. No matter the cost, Persephone must be kept from the knowledge of her Immortal heritage and abilities. Any use of them could draw the notice of those on Olympus. Then they would come here, fetch Persephone, and leave Demeter forsaken and utterly alone among the mortals.

Demeter called to two of the villagers. "These plants are diseased. This quadrant must be ripped up by the roots and the earth here left fallow for a year at least."

"But, Lady," one of the men protested, "surely there must be another way."

Demeter turned her chill blue stare on him and lifted one eyebrow.

Bobbing his acquiescence, he set to work pulling up the plants.

A scream rang out through the early morning silence, a sound of pain, of violence. Eyes wide, heart thumping, Demeter turned in the direction from which it came.

Thais bolted from her hut and ducked into her daughter's home. Moments later, she emerged again, supporting Nadira who wept and lolled against her mother's shoulder. The pair of them stumbled toward the House of the Mother Goddess as Thais shouted, "It's Nadira's time."

In answer to Thais's call, women came out of huts all over the village, grouping together as they moved toward the temple. Instead of the good cheer and camaraderie that was usual before a birthing, the women were subdued, hardly speaking to one another. No doubt they were frightened because Doso wasn't here to help the laboring woman, but at least Demeter wouldn't be called upon to attend. The Sicani women had learned better.

Demeter took up a hoe and hacked at the earth around the infected plants to make it easier to remove them. After much too short a time, her back protested. She winced, put a hand to it, and straightened. As she did so, she caught sight of Persephone striding purposefully toward the House of the Mother Goddess, Doso's basket over one arm. Surely, her daughter wouldn't be so foolish, but, after a short pause to let some children race past, Persephone continued on her course, walking toward certain disaster.

Demeter dropped her tool and set out to intercept the girl. She must be stopped before she came to harm.

When she was close enough that her daughter would hear, Demeter called, "Kore."

Persephone stopped, turned, chin tilted, lips set in a grim line that said she wouldn't be easily persuaded to keep away from Nadira's birthing.

As Demeter feared, Persephone proved to be unusually recalcitrant, insistent on moving forward with her ridiculous plan despite its risks. Demeter had no recourse but to offer to attend the birth in Persephone's stead. Even that wasn't enough to dissuade her. It was only when Thais emerged from the House of the Mother Goddess and reminded Persephone just how deeply the Sicani feared and loathed her that she at last relinquished Doso's basket.

Demeter meant to watch until she was sure Persephone was on her way back to their hut but then the girl asked why Demeter didn't call her Persephone when the villagers could hear. There was too much history, too many secrets and too much old pain wrapped up in why Demeter named her daughter as she had and why she kept that name a secret between the two of them. It wasn't a conversation Demeter ever meant to have with her daughter so she followed Thais inside, allowing the bang of the door to serve as response to her daughter's question.

The moment she found herself shut in the temple, Demeter gagged at the combined smells of smoke, unwashed bodies, and old blood. The stench, the rush-covered floor, and the dark red walls with their ominous, black figures were the same as they had been when last she was here.

Contrary to that night, however, a throng of women, their dark eyes expectant as they looked at her, waiting for her to guide them in one of the basest of mortal processes, one of blood and pain and sacrifice that had brought Demeter to depths from which she'd never risen. A pulse pounded in her temples. Sweat trickled down her back. She couldn't do this. Wouldn't do this.

She turned back to the door and put out a hand to push it open but paused. If she left, Persephone would once again attempt to take up this task, and there was no guarantee Demeter could again dissuade her. If Persephone entered this building, she wouldn't leave it unharmed.

Gripping the basket handle, Demeter forced herself to turn back around. The crowd of woman parted. Thais took Demeter's arm and led her toward the center of the room. Nadira lay on a pallet in the middle of the floor, writhing and moaning.

Sights, sounds, and sensations Demeter never wanted to revisit rolled over her. When she labored with Persephone she'd also lain on the ground, contractions racking her body, but she hadn't moaned. She'd screamed Hera's name when her traitorous sister left her laboring in the cavern in Nysa. Demeter also hadn't had a room full of attendants as Nadira did. Not at first. She'd been alone until a shadow had separated itself from the deeper darkness at the back of the cave and approached her.

Demeter thought it a creature sent by her sister to end her life. Far from being afraid, she welcomed it. Death would have meant an end to her suffering. As the shadow approached, however, the light from the cavern's entrance revealed it to be only an old woman.

The crone came to Demeter's side, rolled her to her back, and slapped her legs apart. The pain when the old woman stuck her fingers up Demeter's cunny and prodded at her had been excruciating, though only a fraction of the agony that was to come.

Nadira, too, was just taking the first steps down the long, arduous path to motherhood and she was managing them no better than Demeter had. With each contraction the young woman's eyes rolled wildly, as she wailed and thrashed as though she could somehow flail free of her suffering.

Thais turned to Demeter, eyes huge in her pale face. "Help her."

Demeter looked around. Surely someone else, someone with the necessary knowledge and skills would answer this woman's plea, but the other Sicani only blinked back at Demeter out of faces wrinkled with worry. They truly expected her to act as midwife. The fools.

"Chant. Pray," Demeter snapped, flapping a hand. After a moment, Thais began a litany. The other women soon joined in, their voices gaining in certainty and volume as they voiced the familiar words.

Demeter wasn't sure what more to do. She set Doso's basket on a nearby table and pawed through packets of herbs and small stoppered jars. She plucked up container of oil scented with mint and lavender, the only thing in the entire basket she knew the use of. She should. Doso had used it often enough on Demeter's aching hands.

Demeter held it out to Thais. "Knead this into Nadira's lower back. It will help loosen the muscles there and ease her pain."

Thais thrust out her palms and shook her head. "It must be you, Lady."

Nadira sobbed and moaned. The other women's chanting grew ragged, the young woman's distress affecting them. If Demeter couldn't calm Nadira the others would soon give way to hysteria. The absurdness of the situation maddened Demeter. She shouldn't be here. Persephone and her foolhardiness bore all the blame for Demeter's current predicament.

Demeter pursed her lips and huffed out an impatient breath through her nose. "Very well. Help Nadira kneel and rest her upper body on one of the benches against the wall."

Thais did as Demeter commanded. Demeter went to her knees behind the young woman, raised Nadira's tunic above her waist, poured a measure of oil onto her lower back, and began to work it in.

During her next contraction, Nadira whimpered, but gone were her earlier hysterics. The other women formed a semi-circle behind them, their chanting regular and in unison once again.

Demeter's hands were cramped and aching from ministering to Nadira by the time the young woman's moaning and shifting indicated that, not only were her contractions coming closer together, they were also gaining in strength and length. Surely now, one of the Sicani women would take over, but they, it seemed, were content to chant while Demeter bungled the birth.

Demeter had no choice but to harken back again to her labor in the cave as it was the only birthing experience she had. At this point in the process, Doso had hauled Demeter to her feet and chivvied her to make the long walk across Nysa through the forest to Henna. It made for a brutal journey, Demeter cursing and weeping every step of the way, but it had helped her progress in her labor.

Demeter addressed Thais. "Nadira needs to walk."

Thais stepped forward out of the circle of women, reached for her daughter's arm, and pulled her upright. Another woman hurried to Nadira's other side, tucked in next to Nadira, and drew the girl's other arm over her shoulder. Demeter rose from her knees. The chanting women moved back against the walls to make room for Nadira to pace. As much as she hated to, Demeter slotted herself in amongst them.

Nadira sobbed and pleaded to be set back down at first, just as Demeter had done. Eventually, however, the girl settled as she shambled in slow circles around the perimeter of the room.

Though the walk was difficult, the hardest work was yet to come. There would be no rest for the girl at the end of her trek to nowhere, just as there hadn't been for Demeter when she and Doso had finally reached Henna. Doso had dragged Demeter up to and through the doors of the House of the Mother Goddess. Soon after, the village women trickled in to attend Demeter.

Doso again subjected Demeter to the indignity of having her nether parts bared to strange eyes, though by that time Demeter hadn't cared. Indeed, she begged them to pull or cut the thing out before it killed her. Nadira would likely feel the same in her extremity.

Nadira's walk turned into more of a shuffle. The women holding her arms paused more frequently to allow for her contractions. Her moans carried over the Sicani's prayers. Finally, the trio came to a stop in front of Demeter.

"Is it time to see how her labor's progressing?" Thais asked.

"Yes, I think that would be best," Demeter responded, her voice confident, though she wasn't so sure. When would these dolts realize she hadn't the necessary skill to deliver this child?

Thais and the other woman lowered Nadira back to the pallet on the floor, then encouraged her to bend her legs, draw them up, and part them.

After Nadira complied, the women looked at Demeter. Making a small sound of dismay and disgust that reached only her own ears, Demeter sank to her knees in front of Nadira. She extended a hand toward the juncture of the girl's legs, but before Demeter even touched her, Nadira cried out, arched, and bucked. A small dark moon appeared for a moment, nudging at the threshold of the world.

Demeter gasped, and in her shock reverted to her native tongue. "I see the head." The other women stared at her blankly. She repeated the phrase in Sicani.

"She labors quick," Thais said. "Time for the stool now, I think."

At last, the woman seemed to have comprehended Demeter wasn't suited for the role the Sicani wanted her to play here. Obligingly, Demeter moved out of the way as Thais helped Nadira to her feet and led her to the birthing chair. Thais lowered her daughter onto its low, narrow seat so Nadira's nether regions were framed by the empty circle of wood. Then she moved around to the seat back and reclined it until Nadira was in a position to best facilitate her child's emergence.

"Will you catch the babe, Demeter?" Thais asked.

Sighing, Demeter nodded, then went, once again, to her knees in front of Nadira.

When the next contraction tightened the muscles of the young woman's belly, Thais commanded her daughter to push. Nadira shook her head and sobbed that she couldn't.

Demeter had said the same words as she'd squatted on the same stool, the scent of her own blood in her nostrils, certain she would die there because she could fight no longer to expel the child from her body. In a misguided attempt to give Demeter strength, one of the women had put a simulacrum of the Mother Goddess in front of Demeter. With its bared breasts, flounced skirt, and upraised hands twined about with serpents, it looked so much like Hera, Demeter wanted to strike it to the floor. She had been so exhausted, however, she only slumped on the birthing chair and sobbed, no better than any other weak, puling mortal.

Gods, she wanted to be free of this place, free of these memories.

Demeter grabbed Nadira's hands and bore down until Nadira

groaned and focused her rolling eyes on Demeter's face.

"You must do this. Hold to me and push."

Seeming to take strength from Demeter's determination, Nadira drew in an enormous breath, tightened her grip on Demeter's hands and, with a grunt, bore down. She ended the push with a shout that quavered up to a high keening note.

The cry of another female voice, low and harsh with fear, mingled with Nadira's scream. Cold fingers traced their way down Demeter's spine. She looked around. The cry certainly hadn't been Nadira's but none of the other women showed any signs of distress.

"Demeter?" Nadira panted.

Demeter gripped Nadira's hands again, snapping, "Save your breath to push, girl. No more screeching."

As Nadira grunted her way through another contraction, the call came again: a throbbing cry of abject terror. This time there was a word in it, but Demeter couldn't make it out.

Half rising to her feet, Demeter looked once again around the room, "What was that? Which of you called out?"

"Nadira, of course," Thais said.

"No, the other cry. Didn't you hear it? The low ..."

The women began to shift and mutter, their eyes moving quickly around the room, peering about for omens and portents. Their suspicions would soon get the better of them, and the temple would descend into chaos, delaying the birth and Demeter's departure.

Demeter smoothed the worry from her face, then turned once more to Nadira and said, "Bear down now, with all your might."

Demeter had received no such niceties from Doso. Instead, the old woman slapped Demeter and, with burning eyes, commanded Demeter give into her body's demands. So, Demeter pushed until it felt like her eyeballs would burst from their sockets and her teeth would crack. Past the point of utter exhaustion, she strained and cried out into a void that seemed to have no beginning and no end.

A void, it seemed, Nadira wouldn't descend into. With just one more push her babe entered the world, sliding into Demeter's hands as neatly as an egg into the nest. A hush settled over the room, waiting for the cry of a living child to break it.

Nadira's babe was as well formed as Persephone had been, all his limbs and fingers and toes present and in the correct number, but he was silent, still. Thais snatched him from Demeter, laid him belly down over her forearm and vigorously rubbed his spine. The infant began to cry, a lusty, healthy sound. It was quickly followed by the laughter and chatter of the Sicani women. They could celebrate now it was apparent this child wasn't affected by the curse they believed Persephone had brought on their town.

Persephone had cried in the same full-throated indignant way: ugly, purple-gray, and howling in Doso's hands. A healthy child hadn't been enough for Demeter though. She sobbed when Doso showed her what was between the babe's legs.

Ignoring Demeter's obvious distress, Doso deposited Persephone into Demeter's arms. Rather than curling her babe to her body, Demeter held Persephone away from her, sure she couldn't have produced something so hideous.

Her cries spiraling higher, Persephone flung out both slime-covered arms. One of them dashed the statue of the Mother Goddess out of the hand of the woman who held it. It fell to the floor and shattered. It had given Demeter great satisfaction, but the village women screamed and cowered away from the babe. That was the origin of Persephone's status as a blight on Henna, a blight which, according to the villagers' ridiculous superstitions, could only be held at bay if the laboring mother was attended by one they thought had the Mother Goddess's favor. One such as Demeter, inept as she had proven herself to be.

Persephone, rejected by her mother, reviled by the villagers, was accepted by only one after her birth. Doso stepped forward and reclaimed the infant from Demeter, a beatific smile on the old woman's face.

Nadira reached for her child just as Doso had reached for Persephone, and Thais passed him into his mother's arms, then prepared to attend to the afterbirth.

Nadira's tears dampened a face already wet with sweat. She smoothed a hand over the little head, pressed a kiss to his brow, and looked up with shining eyes. "He's beautiful."

This girl comprehended more quickly than Demeter what a miracle her child was, but Demeter had realized it eventually. Doso presented the infant to Demeter again once she was cleaned and swaddled. This inclined Demeter to hold the child no more than right after the birth, but a dangerous glint in Doso's eyes convinced Demeter to cooperate. Once Doso settled the babe in the curve of Demeter's arm, she pushed back the blankets so Demeter could see her child's face.

From the curl of eyelashes on Persephone's rounded cheek to the opening of her little hand, like the blossoming of some rare and precious flower, this child was painted with the brush of perfection. She was Goddess born, though fully encapsulated in her mortal form.

Tears had pricked Demeter's eyes. "My *kore*."

Doso patted the babe on the head, and ground out with her stump of a tongue, "Kah."

Demeter wasn't naming the babe, only stating what she was, girl, daughter. Eager to correct the old woman's misunderstanding, Demeter had said, "No, I mean to call her ..."

It was a cruel name, though, one that seemed especially harsh for such a tiny being. It was also a name that made it clear how unkind Demeter's feelings had been toward her own child. No one need know she thought of her daughter in such a way and so she'd finished the sentence with a whisper for her ears alone. "Persephone."

But it seemed her daughter heard and understood, for she opened her mouth and wailed.

Someone jostled Demeter, pulling her from her reminiscing. It was Thais. She pushed in front of Demeter, shouldering her away from the birthing stool. With abrupt, jerky motions, Thais plucked her grandson from Nadira and passed him off to another of the women. Then, grasping her daughter's arm, she barked, "Help me lay Nadira down."

A woman hurried to Nadira's other side. She and Thais pulled Nadira from the birthing stool then settled the girl back on her pallet on the floor. Blood oozed from Nadira's nether part and soaked the rushes around her.

"What's happening? What's wrong?" Demeter asked.

Thais looked up. "She's bleeding too much. We must stop it."

Thais commanded the women to pack Nadira's cunny with cloths, then said to Demeter, "Doso has a tincture for this. Look in her basket,"

Demeter gave the woman a hard, cold look. She wasn't to be ordered about like some slave, but it was wasted. Thais paid no attention, just returned to frantically packing more rags around Nadira's lower body. They became saturated at an alarming rate, and Nadira had gone as pale as the limestone walls of Zeus's palace. Her eyelids fluttered and her eyes rolled back in her head. The girl was dying.

"Demeter, please!" Thais shouted as her grandson began, once again, to cry.

Demeter moved to the basket. She picked up jar after jar in her shaking hands but there was nothing to indicate any of their uses. That knowledge was lost with Doso's desertion and Demeter's banishment of Persephone.

The women began to keen, a wild ululation of grief, Thais's voice spiraling higher than all the others. Demeter turned.

Nadira, head lolled to the side, arms outflung, lay pale and motionless on the floor. The cloths were soaked with blood and still it continued its slow, lethal ooze.

There was no doubt the girl had died, her shade likely falling out of her body, sinking through the ground to the Underworld. There she would stand on Styx's bank and wait for the inexorable ride across those dark waters, a journey Demeter had set her on in her zealousness to protect her own child. No, the blame for this couldn't be laid at Demeter's door. The Sicani should have seen Demeter didn't know what she was about here and taken over.

Thais, on her knees at Nadira's side, clutched her hands to her chest. Her long, graying hair dragged back and forth over her daughter's torso as the woman rocked in a paroxysm of grief. Nadira was Thais's youngest child and only daughter, the child her heart had longed for, as she often said.

Thais's pain at the loss was unbearable and yet bear it she must, as would Demeter if Persephone was ever taken from her. Though death would never steal Demeter's Immortal daughter, Zeus could choose to reclaim her at any time should he be reminded of her existence. These thoughts were ridiculous, of course. Persephone was safe at home, completing her daily tasks, but still Demeter spun away from the grieving women, flung open the door of the House of the Mother Goddess, and hurried toward her hut. She wouldn't feel easy again until she looked on Persephone's face.

As Demeter walked, memories cascaded over her: Persephone sitting up by herself for the first time, screeching for the sheer joy of hearing herself; Persephone wobbling about the hut on unsteady legs, undaunted in her determination to walk by even the most painful falls; Persephone's sparkling green eyes flitting from Demeter's face to some wooden tops spinning on the table between them which Demeter set to turning over and again merely for the reward of Persephone's little girl laughter.

For every good moment, however, there were thousands of bad ones: so many nights when Persephone refused to settle to sleep and Demeter could scarcely refrain from shaking the child until her teeth rattled, and so many days when Persephone whined from dawn until dusk and beyond. Then, as she'd grown older, Persephone proved herself unable to accomplish many of the tasks so necessary to survive in the mortal world or completed them so shoddily Demeter had to set to rights what Persephone had done wrong then do the rest of the work herself. More recently, it was disagreements like the one this morning, when Persephone needed to be argued out of some foolish plan that would result in danger to herself and inconvenience to Demeter. On nearly all of these occasions, rage rose up to choke Demeter, and she wasn't able to stop herself from striking out at Persephone, sometimes just with angry words but other times with a pinch or a slap.

Guilt burrowed like a tick into Demeter's mind. She had to find some way to quell her bitterness, to quash her anger. Now that Doso and all the comfort she gave Persephone was gone, Demeter needed to be kinder to the girl. If those on Olympus tried to lure her daughter away, Demeter's love would be all she could offer to tip the scales in her favor. Thus far, that love had tussled with resentment and most often came up the loser. That had to change. Demeter had to show Persephone it was going to change. Perhaps she could give Persephone some token of her resolve, something akin to the many little favors the girl had showered upon Demeter over the years.

Demeter stopped and looked about. Flowers grew just off the village path. Demeter dropped to a crouch to pick them. She could weave them into a garland for her girl and perhaps undo some of the hurt she caused by burning the crown of flowers Persephone had given her the previous night.

Persephone had never seen a Goddess-woven garland before. Its intricacy and beauty were sure to please her. It would be better if it were made with blossoms from Nysa, that place Persephone knew only as the Mother Goddess's Meadow. The blooms there were almost as beautiful as those that grew on Olympus. It was no wonder Persephone sought them out for the crown she made for Demeter. It had been a beautiful gift, but its destruction was necessary to make Persephone understand she wasn't ever to visit Nysa again.

The burning of the garland had likely been what led to Persephone's uncharacteristic disobedience that morning. An uneasiness slithered under Demeter's skin, but she was being foolish. Persephone wouldn't dare break her vow to Demeter and visit Nysa again. Even if she had, Demeter had no reason to believe her daughter was in any danger. Except those cries, the low terror-filled cries she'd heard not once but twice while helping Nadira bring her child into the world, chilled her. The chaos of the birth and all that followed had driven them from her mind and yet, now, thinking of them, she felt sure it had been Persephone's voice she'd heard. Some harm had come to her daughter.

Heart stuttering in her chest, Demeter hurled herself down the path toward Nysa.

4

PERSEPHONE

If it hadn't been for her captor's arm around her waist, the bobbing of the chariot beneath her, and the occasional jingle of harness or snort from the horses, Persephone would have been utterly unmoored in the vast blackness of the cavern. Along with robbing her of sight, the dark was so deep it muffled sound, muted touch, and could, she felt, stop her breath if it so wished. She ceased struggling against her captor long ago and his grip had slackened. She could try for escape now, but even if she managed to get free there was nowhere to run in this never-ending night. It would absorb her into its depths as easily as a snake swallowing an egg.

The chariot bore to the right and the silhouette of the horses' ears appeared against a barely discernible illumination some distance ahead, their black bodies finally contrasting with the darkness around them. The light didn't necessarily mean safety. That land beyond the cavern could be as deadly as the dark. No, Persephone would bide her time until she had someplace safe to which she could escape.

"I'm Hades."

Persephone jerked as the deep voice splintered the silence. It was the first time her captor had spoken since taking her.

His words gave her the courage to ask the most important of the questions battering her brain. "Why have you abducted me? And where are you taking me?"

Hades made no response, only tightened his hold.

Persephone pushed back against his restraining arm. He eased his grip, and she stopped struggling. A small victory, but a victory nonetheless.

The chariot finally passed out of the cavern, its stony roof replaced by a baleful red sky. A short distance away, a river stretched to the horizon on both the left and the right. There were scores of people standing between the cave exit and the water's edge, all of them silent, all of them staring across the wide, black waters.

"You must be silent," Hades commanded as he carefully steered the chariot into their midst.

In response, Persephone cried out, "Help. Help me!"

"Be silent," Hades repeated, his tone emphatic.

Persephone wrenched away from him. "Please, help me."

He dragged her back to his side. "You must cease that. Now"

Struggling against his grip, she called, "Please, he's taken me from my home. Please help me. I must get away."

Some of the people nearest the chariot turned toward it.

Persephone reached out to the closest of them, a woman who looked to be about Demeter's age. She reached back, grasped Persephone's fingers. Her hand was ice cold, her flesh rigid and unyielding. A lurch of revulsion moved through Persephone. She drew back, but the woman refused to let go. She trotted alongside the chariot, face turned up, gripping Persephone.

"I need something with which to pay passage," the woman said as Persephone continued trying to free her hand. "Please, have you anything you can give? I've been waiting so long."

The woman's pleas drew the attention of many of her fellows on the riverbank. They began to move toward Hades's chariot, amid a rising cacophony of pleas, threats, sobs, and screams.

Persephone wrenched her hand loose. The woman cried out as though Persephone had pierced her with a spear.

"I told you to be silent," Hades said. "See how you've upset them?"

"Who are they?" Persephone asked, her voice deep with loathing and fear as she surveyed the desperate crowd.

"My subjects. And yours."

Persephone's gaze flew to his face. "Mine?"

His gray eyes met hers. "Yours. You are to be my queen and consort."

Before Persephone could formulate a response, Hades cracked his whip over the heads of the crowd and bellowed, "Silence!"

Persephone's ears rang with the instant quiet that followed his command.

He cracked his whip again, though this time with less force. "Move away. Get back."

The people did as he commanded, the only sound that of their feet shuffling through the dirt as they cleared a path to the river's edge.

A large flat-bottomed boat was drawn up to the bank there. In a matter of moments, the chariot reached it and rolled aboard, the horses' hooves booming against the wood of the vessel.

Persephone surveyed the boatman. Dirt streaked his face, obscuring most of it except for his red, wet lips. They peeked out at her from his long, tangled beard which hung almost down to his waist. His garment was unlike any she'd seen. It only covered from hip to knee, and it was so filthy she could scarcely tell it had originally been red.

It appeared he hadn't properly cared for himself in an age, but still, he might be an ally, someone who could help her get free. She raised her gaze once more to his face and met his eyes. Those deep, black orbs burned with a hungry fire. His lips twisted in a lascivious smile, then his tongue darted out of his mouth, as though he were a serpent, testing the air for her essence.

Persephone recoiled, pressing herself into Hades's side. Hades twitched and muttered a wordless exclamation. The arm around her tightened, but this time she didn't fight it. She was caught between two men, neither of whom she was safe with, neither of whom she could trust, but Hades at least didn't appear as though he longed to devour her whole.

"This her then?" the boatman asked, his voice sounding as though stones broke it to bits before casting it out of his mouth.

"This is Persephone and mark her well, Charon. She doesn't ride your ferry unless it's with me."

Charon grunted acknowledgement as his eyes roved over Persephone's face and body. Persephone crossed her arms over her breasts and looked back toward the cave.

Wood scraped on rock. The ferry lurched as the river's current grabbed it, whirling it away from the cavern. If Persephone lost sight of it, she might not be able to find her way back home. The distance to the bank wasn't far, and she was a strong swimmer. Once she was across, she could hide herself in the darkness of the cave while she contrived some way to navigate it. The horses had managed it. Surely, she could too.

She twisted free of Hades's grip and leapt from the chariot. A bolt of pain shot through her ankles, reminding her of the injury they'd taken when Hades abducted her. She staggered toward the ferry's edge and the night black water.

Hands gripped her arms, yanked her back, and spun her about.

Hades's eyes were wide, his grasp painful. "You must never go in this river. If even a single drop of Styx's water enters your mouth, it will cause you unspeakable agony. Do you understand?"

Frightened and confused, Persephone could only stammer. "I-I..."

Hades turned her again, extending his arm over her shoulder to point at the riverbank. "Look at them."

Some of the people there tore at their clothing and beat their breasts in a maelstrom of despair. Others held up earrings, necklaces, bars of copper, or small statues made of gold, silver or some metal that appeared to be a mixture of both. All of them pleaded for the ferry to return. It was apparent they wanted to cross the river and yet, not even one braved the water.

"Do you understand?" Hades repeated.

Persephone nodded.

Hades released her.

The despair of those at the river's edge was too close to the feeling that trickled through Persephone's blood and seeped into her bones. It would drown her if she let it. She turned her back to them.

Hades moved toward the chariot and offered Persephone his hand. It was a petty rebellion, but she ignored him and climbed back into the chariot basket unaided. He followed.

Shivering in the cold, dank air, Persephone stood as far from him as she could and stared at the bank to which the ferry was carrying them. Though it was shrouded in a fog as thick and impenetrable as the darkness of the cavern had been, it might still be possible on that side to find a way to convey herself back across these deadly waters and safely home.

Once they reached the shore, Hades clucked to his horses. They moved off the ferry and into the mist with no hesitation. Hades didn't try to secure Persephone to his side again. It seemed he was now sure of her inability to escape, but she must not let hopelessness take her. There had to be some way to get free of him, get free of this place, whatever it was.

They traveled only a short distance before Hades again halted the horses.

"Be silent and keep still," he said.

Persephone opened her mouth to ask why. Then, recalling what had occurred on the riverbank when she called out, pressed her lips together and nodded.

Hades jumped to the ground, put his fingers in his mouth, and whistled.

Now that there was some distance between them, she could see the man clearly for the first time. His features were well-formed, with a straight nose and a generous mouth framed by a neat black beard, but there was no warmth in his face, no light in his gray eyes, nothing to indicate he was anything other than an unkind man who had taken her by force to do with what he wished. He was also tall, taller than any of the men in Henna, and broad-shouldered. His arms and calves, though pale, were thickly muscled. She would be at a distinct disadvantage in any physical contest with him.

A rhythmic thudding came from somewhere off to her right. Persephone peered in that direction but could see nothing through the fog.

Hades moved so he was between the chariot and the unseen source of the sound. Then he crouched, his fingers flexing on the whip handle.

At this slight show of nervousness, the first emotion Hades had displayed despite the horrors they'd already passed through, Persephone's upper lip and armpits prickled with sweat.

A creature broke through the mist. Its body was doglike, but it had three heads. Ropes of spit dangled from its mouths. All six eyes settled on Persephone. All three heads barked, slightly out of sync, giving the sound a strange, rolling echo, and its legs churned faster.

It took every ounce of Persephone's will to keep her scream locked behind her lips, to stop herself from leaping off the chariot and hurling herself away from the beast, but she managed. She had no desire to find out what would happen if she disobeyed Hades's instructions this time.

Hades cracked his whip. The creature slowed but didn't stop.

Hades took a few steps forward, snapped his whip again and roared, "Cerberus, halt!"

The animal dug in its hind feet and came to a sliding stop. Hades closed the distance between them and bent to pat the creature.

Persephone expelled the breath she was holding in a gust that sounded like a soft sob. Skin still twitching with fear, she watched the monster quiver and squirm under Hades's hands. The creature's behavior wasn't unsimilar to Phlox's happy frolicking when, as a young fox, he would greet Persephone, but this creature had nothing else in common with him. The fox's wild beauty had been a blessing. This beast was an abomination.

Three tongues lolled out to lap at Hades's face. He laughed and ruffled the creature's fur. No, not fur. Serpents. The thing had a nest of serpents behind its head.

Persephone clamped down on her scream so hard this time that she bit the tip of her tongue. The coppery tang of blood filled her mouth. She choked and struggled to swallow without making any noise.

Hades turned from the beast and gestured. "Come."

Persephone looked from Hades to the creature, then at Hades again. She gave a slight shake of her head.

"Come." He held out his hand. "He must learn how you smell. I've told him you're precious to me and he must not harm you, but he must have your scent to truly know you."

Persephone blinked. *Precious to him?*

"Come," Hades said again. "It's the only way I can ensure he won't do you any injury."

The trembling in Persephone's body made it difficult to climb from the chariot. Her legs shook so violently once she reached the ground, she couldn't move any closer to Hades and the beast.

Hades stretched his arm to its fullest length, grasped her fingers and drew her forward. Then he put her hand directly under the nose of the central head.

One of the serpents on the beast's neck hissed and struck at her. Persephone jerked her hand back. The creature made a low growling bark in the back of its throat.

As though punishing a disobedient pup, Hades, using one forefinger, tapped the animal between its center set of eyes. "Hush and meet your mistress."

The creature stopped growling. The serpent's nest calmed. Hades drew Persephone's hand forward again.

Persephone tried to hold as still as possible so as not to antagonize the beast, but she could no more calm the quivering in her hand than she could have found her way through the thick fog back to the riverbank.

All three noses sniffed at Persephone. Then the tongue on the central head lolled out and licked her fingers. It was rough and wet, quite similar to Phlox's. The comparison seemed a sacrilege. She could never love this creature the way she had her fox. She could never love anything that was a part of this terrible place.

Hades released Persephone and dismissed the creature with a *thwack* on its rump. A serpent's tail lashed the beast's haunches as it ran away. Persephone shuddered and wiped the spittle from her hand on her tunic.

"That was Cerberus. He won't harm you now that he has your scent, though I advise you to go carefully should you encounter him. He can't kill you, for you're Immortal, but the contents of the snakes' fangs will cause you such agony you'll wish your life could end."

Persephone held herself rigid. If she opened her mouth, even a little, she would begin screaming and never stop.

"Come. We must continue on." Hades reached for her hand.

Persephone snatched it away. He gestured her toward the chariot. Spurning his help again, she clambered aboard. She had no choice. A three-headed venomous beast, a disorienting fog, an unswimmable river, and a cavern with blackness so thick it would consume her whole now stood between her and home.

As they continued, the fog lightened. Its absence would, no doubt, only introduce further horrors. However, when it finally dissipated, it revealed a vast meadow full of asphodels. Mingling among the tall, light-green, spiky plants were scores and scores of people.

They rocked slightly, leaning more in one direction than the other, their motion similar to that of underwater plants moving in response to a slight current. They also seemed to be going through the common rituals of daily life. Here, one lifted his arm as though to swing a hammer, but he held no tool. There, a woman scrubbed at a piece of dirty laundry, but her hands were as empty as her eyes. They weren't frightening in and of themselves, but their utter silence and repetitive motions were unsettling.

"What are these folk doing?" Persephone asked.

"Their work," Hades said.

"But they don't—"

Hades gave her a dark look. She said no more.

The asphodel meadow looked to be endless, but eventually the plants dwindled and then disappeared altogether as the chariot climbed a slight rise. On the other side of the hill, a group of people congregated on either side of the road. Some wept and tore at their clothes. Some strode about beating on their breasts. And others knelt and rubbed dirt all over themselves in what appeared to be a frenzy of grief.

A cry of mingled pain and horror burst from Persephone's lips. She clapped a hand to her mouth, but none of the people took the slightest notice.

"Tenants of the Vale of Mourning. They waste themselves in longing for things they can never have," Hades said, his voice low and rueful.

Persephone couldn't take her eyes off the tormented souls. Their agony echoed so perfectly what she felt now. She didn't turn away from them until the chariot climbed another hill and the Vale passed out of sight.

From the top of this second rise, Persephone could see a crowd of people who appeared to be waiting for admittance into a large building at the juncture of the road.

In its careful construction and obvious importance, it reminded Persephone of the House of the Mother Goddess. This edifice, however, was easily two or three times the Sicani temple's size and it had an enormous eye carved on the lintel stone.

Hades drove the chariot down the hill. The crowd made way for them, but buzzed with low angry mutterings, their faces twisting with hatred.

Persephone shrunk away from them and bumped into Hades. The warmth of his body leaped into her chilled skin. She could stay there, absorb his heat, take some little comfort, but no, he was the enemy. Whatever reassurance she found in him would be false and short-lived. She moved back to her previous spot.

They were almost past the building when the door swung open and a figure exited. Perhaps here, at last, was someone to whom Persephone could turn for help. She craned her neck around as the chariot pulled farther away. The figure had its back to her as it looked out over the crowd. Judging by their height and broadness, the person was likely a man, and one who looked to be a match to Hades in strength.

As though sensing her gaze, the man turned his head toward her. The hollows of his eyes were as dull and black as old blood. Yet, somehow, in that crusted, opaque stare, Persephone saw all the things of which she was most ashamed: flinging rocks at a lamed village dog when she was a small child in hopes of gaining favor with the other children; raging at Doso and scratching her hard enough to draw blood in a fit of temper; her own face contorted with hate and a lust for revenge after Demeter lashed her for some chore she'd done poorly.

Gasping as though she'd been immersed in a deluge of icy water, Persephone yanked her head back around, breaking the hold the terrible gaze had on her.

"Who is that man?"

"Aecus. He never leaves the temple. He speaks only the sentences of those he judges."

It was apparent even before Hades's statement that the man at the temple wouldn't aid her, but there had to be somewhere in this wretched place to which she could run. "What lies down the other road, the one to the left at the juncture?"

"Tartarus and eternal punishment. You may visit there if you wish. None of this land is denied to you, but I warn you it's hideous, and its keeper, in her blood-soaked robes, doesn't welcome company."

Persephone slumped, hope draining from her as though her skin was a sieve. Hades drew her to him. This time she didn't fight. The chariot rattled on, now heading toward an enormous black hulk of a building. It wavered before her tear-wet eyes, but she could still see it clearly enough to know it was somewhere she didn't desire to go and yet, go she would.

She had no choice.

The building was constructed in much the same style as the judge's temple. Blocks of dark stone, wider than Persephone was tall, fitted tightly together to form the walls. It had been built into an enormous black rock, the surface of which was pitted and uneven. It looked as though the building had sprouted a diseased growth that was slowly consuming it, determined to turn it all into an undifferentiated mass with no form or purpose. It was hideous and terrifying, but the day had wrung from Persephone any capacity to be further horrified.

When they reached the building, Hades drove the horses through a set of open gates and into a courtyard. He stopped the chariot in front of a pair of doors that gaped wide under a lintel stone carved with Cerberus's likeness. The beast's jeweled eyes winked malevolently.

Hades gestured toward the doors. "Your palace, my queen."

It seemed as though he expected some remark from her. Congratulations on the beauty of his home or, thanks, perhaps, for doing her the honor of taking her captive and making her his consort. She would give him no such thing for she felt nothing of the kind. She drew away from him and shivered as the cold, dank air touched the parts of her body that had been warmed by contact with his.

Sighing, the chariot creaking and shifting under his weight, Hades climbed out of the basket then turned and reached up for her.

She wanted to spurn his help again, but her ankles still throbbed with pain that would only increase with the leap. She stepped forward and put her hands on his shoulders. His hands came about her waist. He lifted her down and set her gently on the ground. She stumbled as she stepped away from him, eager to escape the heat of his grasp.

"You're tired. Go inside. Take refreshment and rest. I shall join you when I've cared for my horses."

There was nowhere to run, nothing to do except obey. Persephone nodded and walked to the entrance, but this place was alien to her. She had no idea where to find rest and refreshment though she was in dire need of both. She turned to ask Hades, but he was already walking away, his horses striding alongside.

He reached up and fondled the ears of the animal closest to him. After a moment of that, he slid his hand down to pat the big round bone on the side of the beast's face. The horse nipped at him with loose, rubbery lips. Hades laughed as he pushed its muzzle away, then stroked the horse's muscled neck. The obvious affection between the two was so similar to what Persephone had shared with Phlox. She likely would never know anything like it again, most assuredly not so long as she was trapped in this terrible place. Tears smarted in her eyes, and she looked down. Let the horses have Hades's attention. She certainly didn't want it. She'd find her own way.

She walked through the open doors into a hallway with a set of stairs at either end. Directly across from her was another pair of doors. She walked through those, entering a chamber which could easily hold the entire village of Henna within its walls.

In the center of the room was a large circular hearth, the circumference of which could have circled the trunk of any one of the ancient trees in the forest that ringed the Mother Goddess's Meadow.

Behind the hearth, a large stone chair sat on a small, raised platform. Four horses were painted in profile on the wall to the rear of the platform, two on one side of the chair, two on the other. Their necks were arched, hooves lifted high, tails and manes fluttering as though stirred by a breeze.

A hand settled on the small of Persephone's back at the same moment a deep voice said, "This is my megaron."

Jerking away, Persephone cried out. Her heart thudded and she put a hand to her breast.

Hades didn't react to her obvious fear of him. He merely gestured to encompass the room. "It's here I'm meant to banquet with my guests."

"Do you have many guests?" Persephone asked. Her voice was too eager, likely betraying the hope that there might be one among his guests who would aid her to escape.

Hades looked at her, cold eyes staring out of an expressionless face, and that was all the response Persephone received. Yet, it was sufficient to send her plunging into despair once again. She would find no help in this place either.

"I'll show you to your chambers. Come this way," Hades said, once again putting a hand on her lower back.

Persephone twitched away from his touch. Mouth settling in a grim line, he turned and exited the megaron. After a moment's hesitation, Persephone followed, limping along behind him as he walked toward the staircase to the right of the entrance to the big room. At the top of the stairs, he turned down a long hallway lit by oil lamps on low tables. At the end of the hall, Hades stopped outside a set of doors and gestured her forward.

Persephone's entire body ached, but her ankles hurt the worst, throbbing in time to her heartbeat. Perhaps here she'd find a place to sit and tend to them. She pushed open the doors on a chamber that was a replica of the megaron below, only much smaller and possessing a few more furnishings.

On the walls, blue-winged swallows cavorted over a field of lilies and little hunting cats prowled through the flowers. On another wall, a group of women that greatly resembled the Goddesses danced among the blossoms. On a third wall one of the little hunting cats stretched out on the lap of a maiden with hair like flame and eyes as green as grass. A fire roared in the hearth, providing a welcome warmth, and there was a small table heaped with food and flanked by two chairs.

It was a lovely chamber, warm and welcoming and completely at odds with all the horrors Persephone had experienced in this place thus far. A small smile touched her lips.

"Come," Hades said.

The smile slid from her face and, wrapping her arms about herself, Persephone reluctantly approached the table.

A man emerged from an inner chamber and walked toward the door through which Persephone and Hades had just entered. He was old, frail, bent nearly double, but even if he had been young and hale, Persephone wouldn't have thought him a possible ally. His eyes and face were blank and there was something off-putting about him. His trajectory placed Persephone squarely in his path, but he seemed to be unaware of that fact.

Before Persephone could move out of his way, Hades grasped her arm and jerked her aside. "You mustn't touch them. Never touch them." His voice was harsh with insistence.

Eyes wide, Persephone nodded startled acquiescence.

Hades released her. "He's one of the shades that care for my household needs. There are a number of them, and you'll see them about the palace often. You must not interfere with them in any way."

"Why mustn't I?"

"It ... upsets them. Best to avoid doing so."

Persephone wanted to ask what would happen should she upset one of them, but Hades made an expansive gesture to the table as though eager to change the subject. "Would you care to take some refreshment?"

Persephone looked at the banquet laid out there. She should be hungry. She hadn't had the chance to break her fast that morning before rushing to aid Nadira. Could it have only been that morning? It felt like ages had passed since then. Yet, like the serving man, something was wrong with this food, something Persephone couldn't quite name. Her stomach knotted and nausea clambered up her throat at the thought of consuming it.

Hades sat and motioned toward the other chair.

Though Persephone didn't intend to eat, she could at least sit and take the weight off her ankles. She limped to the seat and settled herself into it.

"You're in pain?"

Persephone nodded. "My ankles. I struck them on the edge of your chariot basket."

Hades rose and walked around the table.

She stiffened and pressed back into her chair. He dropped to a crouch which brought him eye to eye with her, but he didn't look into her face. Instead, he reached down, grabbed her foot, and lifted it.

Her ankle was swollen and marked with deep purple bruises.

Hades turned her foot first one way and then the other and gently flexed it back.

Persephone hissed in pain but didn't draw away. Pulling free of his grasp would have been more painful than his examination.

He assessed her other foot. Then, with the tip of one forefinger, he lightly traced the curve of her ankle. Goosebumps erupted all over her body.

He raised his eyes to Persephone's. A strange expression flitted across his features, a small breach in the fortress of his face. Then it was gone.

He lowered her foot, released it, and stood. "They're only bruised. They'll heal soon but they wouldn't pain you at all if you would rid yourself of your mortal shell. Such a slight hurt wouldn't affect your Goddess form."

The words echoed something the Goddesses had said earlier in the meadow, but Hades's statement was no clearer than theirs had been. "What do you mean, my mortal shell?"

He gently plucked at the skin of her forearm. "This form. This outer layer. You may pull it inside and let your Goddess-self come to the fore."

Persephone drew away from his touch, put a hand over the spot he'd pinched. His words made no sense. Her current body was the only form she knew. She had no wish to change it, especially if he desired her to.

He regarded her a moment more before turning away.

As he walked back to his seat, Persephone asked, "What is this place? Where have you brought me?"

He settled himself in his chair, met her gaze. "You truly don't know?"

Persephone shook her head.

His eyes were as gray and flat as the heavens before a storm as he said, "This is the Underworld. You're in the realm of the dead, Kore."

5

DEMETER

Demeter yanked the door of her hut open and staggered inside. Her legs refused to support her weight any longer, and she sank to the floor. She pressed her forehead to the cool, packed dirt, her despair too deep and all-consuming for tears. She had failed.

Hands gripped her arms, tugging, yanking, hauling her to her feet. A face that was somehow familiar loomed for a moment. Then the hands settled Demeter into a chair before her own table. A cup was pressed against her mouth. Demeter opened her lips. Warm broth, rich and salty, splashed over her tongue and cascaded down her parched throat. Demeter wrenched the vessel from the hands that held it and gulped.

"Slowly. Slowly, you fool, or you'll vomit it all back up."

Demeter emptied the cup in three long gulps then held out the vessel. "More." What was left of Demeter's voice after calling her child's name for days on end, emerged as a hoarse whisper.

"That's enough for now."

Demeter slammed the cup on the tabletop. "More."

"No."

The woman who dared deny Demeter sat across the table, knobby hands folded over a breast flattened by age. Though the wizened face was unfamiliar, Demeter recognized something in the woman's dark eyes and serene expression.

"Doso?"

"Try another name, Sister."

Only another Goddess would address Demeter as sister, but this hag wasn't one of the Olympians. She could think of only one Immortal who looked so aged. "Hekate?"

The old woman nodded.

"But you ... you were Doso?"

"I was. Hera bade me come to you in disguise."

"Hera? Why? Why would she send you to me? And why did you leave?"

"Time for all that later." Hekate reached across the table and wrapped her crooked fingers around Demeter's scratched and bleeding hands. "I heard our Kore cry out. Where is she?"

Demeter slowly shook her head. "I don't know. I heard her, just as you did, but Nadira was also screaming, and I didn't recognize my daughter's voice. I thought she'd gone to Nysa, been harmed there somehow, so I sought her there but found nothing except a field of flowers beheaded by one of Zeus's storms. For nine days I've searched for Kore, and I can tell you with certainty that she is neither within the boundaries of this island, nor in the sea surrounding it, nor in any land that touches on that sea."

"How can you know? In nine days, no mortal, not even you, could search all of that."

"I didn't achieve it on my own. I was aided by the birds, the naiads and dryads of the forest, and the Neredai in the depths of the sea, every step of my journey illuminated with torches made by Hephaistos."

"Hera's malformed boy? The one Zeus hurled from Olympus?" Doso asked.

Demeter drew her hands out of Hekate's to toy with the cup on the table. Before her daughter's disappearance, every day when Demeter returned home for her midday meal this very vessel waited for her, filled to the brim with barley water and pennyroyal. And every day she failed to thank Persephone for this small service, taking it as only her due, but her daughter wasn't the only child who had been injured by Demeter's pride.

Demeter set the cup aside, forced herself to meet Hekate's gaze. "Yes, the very one. Did you know Kore was to be Zeus's vindication, his proof that he could sire a healthy fully Immortal son with a fellow Olympian?"

"Our Kore was to replace Hephaistos so you could displace Hera?"

Demeter nodded, added quickly, "I didn't ask for Hephaistos's help in my search. He lives near Etna. The dryads there heard my story from their sisters in Nysa. They told it to Hephaistos, and he insisted the birds bring me to him. He fashioned for me torches of Etna's fires, made them so cunningly even my mortal hands could carry them and not be burned. By their light, I searched everywhere, sea, land, and air, and asked all manner of creatures who live in those realms. I scarcely drank or slept, and I took no food in the nine days I searched, but it was no use."

Demeter drew breath. Her throat was clenched as tight as a fist, and it burned all the way down. When she went on, her voice was thick with unshed tears. "Kore is gone, Hekate, and no one knows where. I'm near the end of my strength, and I can't think what more to do."

Hekate took Demeter's hands again. "You can't, but I can. And I'm not bound by mortal limitations. Together, we will seek her out."

Hope flooded Demeter with renewed strength. "Yes. Yes. Let's go now." She rose and tried to pull Hekate out of her seat.

"No, Demeter. We'll not leave until after you rest."

Demeter doubled her efforts to get the older woman to rise. "We leave now. She's been gone nine days. We can't waste another moment."

Hekate remained unmoved. "Listen, child, to one both much older and wiser than you. Rest, and when you wake, we shall go visit the one who sees all and will surely know where our lost one is gone."

Demeter ceased tugging at Hekate. "What do you mean?"

Hekate said nothing, only pointed up at the smoke hole through which early morning light streamed.

"Helios?" Demeter asked.

Hekate nodded. "I ask only that you sleep this one day. Then I shall take you to him, and you may discover Persephone's whereabouts almost as soon as you wake. She could be with us again two days hence."

"She's been gone so long already. Every moment she's away means further harm could be done to her. We must go now."

"There's no way to reach Helios other than the God Road. You can't travel that way without me, Demeter, and I won't take you until you've rested. You're mortal, and you must recover yourself if you're to live to see your daughter's face again."

Yes, Demeter was mortal, weak, pitiable, and if she forced her frail form to do any more without sleep and sustenance, she'd find herself in Hades's realm rather than in Helios's presence. She could rage and cajole at Hekate all she liked but none of that would give her more strength for the search. The older Goddess was right. Demeter needed rest.

Demeter crossed the small space of the hut and lowered herself to her bed. She would sleep only until midday and that would have to be enough to satisfy Hekate's demand. She closed her eyes and abruptly fell into a deep, black abyss where nothing, not even dreams, existed.

When Demeter woke, the slant of the light coming in through the smoke hole told her she'd slept much longer than she intended. She threw back the blankets. She was naked and clean, the cuts and abrasions she accumulated in her search for Persephone, bound up. Hekate must have attended to her while she slept.

Demeter rose from her bed and hurried to the chest in the corner. She pulled out the only clean tunic inside, Persephone's old one. The girl had set it aside after Demeter gifted Persephone with a saffron tunic embroidered with lilies by Demeter's own hands. At least Persephone had that token of Demeter's love wherever in the world she was now.

The cast-off tunic was worn and patched, but it had once been Demeter's so at least it fit. As Demeter drew it over herself, her fingers brushed the loose, slightly crumpled skin of her lower abdomen.

How she'd despised it, this reminder that she would never be the glorious Goddess she once was. Now she smoothed her hand over it. She couldn't recall precisely how it felt to be prodded by a hand, an elbow, a foot from the inside, but she could remember the yielding softness of Persephone's baby cheek under her lips and how that same butter-smooth skin flushed hectic red after being struck by Demeter's open palm.

Demeter clenched her hand on the edge of the chest lid and bit back a cry. She had to find her daughter, to hold her fast and tell Persephone she loved her, had always loved her.

Hekate padded into the hut and, dashing the tears from her eyes, Demeter straightened.

"Good, you're awake. Sit. Eat." Hekate placed a pot of honey on the already laden table.

"Hekate, I've rested. We must away now."

"You can go nowhere without me, and I won't leave until you eat. Sit and take refreshment while I plait your hair."

Demeter made a frustrated sound in the back of her throat, but she had no choice. She sat and shoveled in food while Hekate fussed about behind Demeter.

Demeter stuffed the last bite of bread in her mouth and tried to stand. Hekate yanked viciously on her hair. Demeter sank back down, fidgeting as Hekate continued her attentions. Finally, after pushing and prodding at the heavy plaits on Demeter's head for what seemed an eternity, Hekate lowered a round piece of polished bronze before Demeter's face.

"Fit to walk among the Gods," Hekate said as Demeter looked at her reflection.

The woman in the mirror had a web of fine wrinkles at the corners of both eyes, a deep crease between her brows that gave her an ill-tempered look, and a slight sag at the jawline. Demeter's hands crept to her breasts and her touch told her they weren't nearly as pert or round as before Persephone's birth and subsequent breast-feeding.

Demeter gasped out, "I can't go to Helios like this. I've aged so. They called me Loveliest. I'm ..." She swept a hand over her face, her fingertips pausing next to the furrow in her brow, the wrinkles near her eyes.

Blowing out a puff of air, Hekate put down the mirror and crossed the hut. She was back at Demeter's side in only moments, her fingers working once again at Demeter's hair.

She finished her task and raised the mirror again. "Just as the Goddess you once were."

Hekate had worked a garland in among Demeter's braids. Demeter raised her hand, plucked out the blossoms one by one, and dropped them to the floor. They withered as soon as they left her hand.

"Demeter, what are you doing?"

Demeter looked at the brown, dead blooms. They were the flowers she'd picked for Persephone the day her daughter had disappeared. Somehow, she'd carried the garland she made of them with her through her nine days of fruitless searching. Her God Touch must have kept them

65

alive. It was no wonder she looked so aged. She'd used up so much of herself.

Demeter turned to look at Hekate. "I won't wear flowers again until I put a garland of them in my daughter's hair."

Demeter rose from the chair and crossed again to her clothing chest. She pulled out a long, dark length of cloth, draped it around her shoulders, and drew a fold of it up over her head like a hood, throwing her face into shadow. "Thus will I return to Helios."

"Then let's go to him." Hekate took Demeter's hand, led her into the forest behind the hut and not even the slightest stir of air marked their crossing to the God Road.

6

PERSEPHONE

Through the door of Persephone's bedchamber came the muffled thumps of food being set on the table in her megaron. If she didn't go out, Hades would come in to collect her, putting his hand on her back, her arm, using any excuse to touch her as he ushered her to her seat. Not wanting to give him any reason to subject her to his grasp, she rose from the chair in which she had thus far spent the better part of the nine days she'd dwelled in this Underworld. As she came upright, her head spun and the room around her disappeared in a haze of sparkling, spinning silver dots.

She swayed, then gripped the back of the chair until her hands ached and the pain brought her back to herself. She couldn't lose consciousness, couldn't allow herself to be unwary for even a moment. She learned the consequences of that on her first night here. It wouldn't happen again. It wouldn't have happened that night if she hadn't been distracted by her own misery. Weeping in the dark, she had huddled in the nest of blankets on the floor of her chamber, apparently the only bed she would have in this place. Hades's voice, when it came out of the blackness asking for admittance, had deceived her. It changed somehow into something softer, kinder, perhaps because she was unable to see the storm cloud gray of his eyes. Foolishly, she allowed him to come to her side.

His hands had been gentle, almost tentative at first as he strove to soothe her. Her weariness and the warmth of his body conspired to make her submit to his touch. Eventually his caresses, the kisses on her hair, her cheeks, her lips turned ravenous. He seemed not to hear her pleas for him to stop, not to realize she was struggling to free herself from his grasp. Eventually, however, he ceased kissing and stroking her but hadn't let her go. Instead, he held very still for a time, his breath rapid and hot on her face, the proof of his desire pulsing against her thigh. Then, making a low, angry noise, he released her, got up, and strode from the room.

Persephone had heard and seen enough among the Sicani to know she only narrowly avoided the violence forced upon most captive women. Though Hades hadn't entered her bedchamber since that night, she lived every moment in fear he would, and that this time all her exhortations for him to stop would fall on deaf ears. This very terror made her cling to consciousness with all her might, made her join him in her megaron every evening, so he had no reason to seek her out in the dimness of her bedchamber.

Limbs trembling, Persephone released the chair back and moved toward the door. She'd been without food the entire time she'd been in this place. Her Immortal birth would likely keep her from dying for lack of nourishment, but she wasn't sure how much longer she could continue to move about in her enfeebled state.

As Persephone reached the doorway separating her bedchamber from her megaron, she drew herself straight and hid her shaking hands in the folds of her tunic. Then, she entered the room.

Hades stood by his chair. When Persephone's eyes met his, he took a step toward her. Though it took all her will, she held his gaze, trying to inject into her stare the forbidding chill she'd seen so often in her mother's eyes. Hades's gaze didn't falter from hers but neither did he move any closer.

As Persephone crossed to her place, she heard the scrape of the other chair being dragged across the floor. Hades had taken his seat without trying to escort her to hers. Hidden within her tunic, her clenched fists loosened. She sat, keeping her attention on the food, not wanting to look into Hades's face though she could feel his eyes on her, like the heat on her skin from the fire burning in the hearth.

After Persephone took her seat, she realized her plate, which had remained empty throughout every meal in this place thus far, was heaped with food. She contemplated it, then lifted a loaf of bread. Her throat didn't clench. Her belly didn't heave. With no further hesitation, Persephone tore off a great chunk, barely chewing before swallowing it and returning for another bite. After she finished with the bread, she worked her way through everything on the plate save one strange reddish-pink globe which she wasn't entirely sure was edible.

"The pomegranate isn't to your liking?" Hades asked, reaching across the table.

Persephone held herself stiff as his hand loomed closer. She wouldn't shrink back, no matter how much she wanted to, wouldn't let him see how he terrified her. Knowing that would give him more power over her than he already had. Showing fear only invited more violence. She had learned this from the Sicani children.

Plucking the globe off her plate, Hades's fingers passed within a hairs-breadth of Persephone's breast. At this, she did pull back, an involuntary spasm of movement that Hades surely noticed, though he gave no sign as he drew his hand away.

Hades gripped the sphere in both hands, his fingertips turning white as he did so. The pomegranate split down the middle with a sound like splintering wood.

He held half out to her. "The seeds are edible."

Persephone looked at the pomegranate but made no move to take it.

Hades put half of the globe on the table then drew back. After a moment's hesitation, Persephone reached forward, keeping her gaze on Hades. He remained expressionless, motionless. Still eyeing him, she delved into the fruit and separated a cluster of the little red globules from the outer shell. As she moved back, she placed some of the seeds in her mouth. Even as full as she was, her eyes widened in pleasure when the sweet, tart sacs exploded on her tongue.

A smile flitted across Hades's face. Moving slowly, as though Persephone were a skittish horse he didn't want to frighten, he, too, liberated some of the seeds from the rind. They sat in silence eating the pomegranate, which stained their fingers, lips, and tongues a brilliant red.

As Persephone plucked the last seed from the fruit, Hades said, "Would you care to walk with me? You've seen little of the palace, nothing of Elysium—"

Persephone shook her head. Leaving the confines of this room, especially in this place, would be too much, *far* too much, for her to bear. Terror would consume her from the inside out. The tenuous safety she felt here in her chambers was the only thing keeping her whole.

Hades made no response to her hasty refusal, merely turned away, presenting her with his profile. His face was hard as his eyes roved over her megaron, but there was something in the set of his shoulders, the tilt of his head that spoke, not of anger or even disappointment, but of a man who looked as though he were attempting to recover from a hard blow. After a moment, he looked back at her and stood.

Persephone swallowed and a chill sweat sprang from her pores as he crossed to her side.

When he reached her, he said, "Shall I escort you to your sleeping chamber then?"

Her stomach threatening to disgorge all she had eaten, Persephone rose. She held herself tall, spine straight, chin tilted, but her hands were once again clenched, and her legs shook so badly it was all she could do to place one foot in front of the other.

When they reached the door of the bedchamber, Persephone's legs would no longer obey her. She stood, jaw tight, breath a high whistle as it pumped in and out of her nostrils.

Hades opened his mouth, reached for her. Every muscle in Persephone's body went rigid in an effort to hold herself still, as his hand drew closer to her arm.

"Kore, I ..."

She regarded him, once again summoning the same cold gaze Demeter had turned on her so many times. "I would ask that you call me Persephone."

It seemed Hades thought the name suited her for he made no remark about it nor asked any questions, only dropped his hand back to his side and said, "Very well, Persephone." Then he turned and left her chamber.

Persephone covered her face with her hands, but no tears came. Her eyes remained as dry as a drought-stricken stream. Perhaps if she could fold herself into Doso's arms or bury her face in Phlox's soft ruff, the dam that held back her emotions would break. Then she could have some release and relief, as had happened so many times when she sought those comforts after Demeter doled out some punishment. But neither Doso nor Phlox were here—Persephone was utterly alone in this place.

Persephone dropped her hands, lifted her head, and regarded her bedchamber with weary eyes. Her fingers crept to the hem of her tunic. She clasped a lily between her thumb and first finger and began to roll the soft threads of Demeter's embroidery between them. It was the only bit of home, of safety, of comfort she had left to her, all she would ever have if she didn't find some way to free herself.

Continuing to stroke the lily on her hem, Persephone took up her seat in the chair again. She drew a blanket over her, tucked it around her to protect her from the chill of the stone, and stared into the fire. Now she had taken nourishment and her strength was returning, flight from the Underworld, from Hades, was a possibility, nay, a necessity. She needed a plan of escape.

She shifted in the chair, trying to find a position where stone didn't grind against bone. The blanket moved, and for a moment Persephone smelled lavender. She pressed the wool to her nose, seeking the scent again, but couldn't find it. However, it was enough to free the tears she'd longed for earlier.

They rolled off her face as images of Doso, Phlox, her mother, their hut in Henna, and the Mother Goddess's Meadow flashed through her mind. Did anyone note her absence? Had the Goddesses wondered at her sudden disappearance? Had Demeter sought her at all or, even now, did her mother banquet on Olympus with those Persephone had kept her from? And what of Doso? She was the only one who loved Persephone well enough to mount a search, but if she never returned to Henna, she would never know of Persephone's absence from it.

Persephone pressed her face into the blanket. "Why did you leave me? I wouldn't be here if you hadn't left me."

After a time, her tears abated. She wiped her face on the blanket, catching again the telltale whiff of lavender. Though her longing for home had, for the time being, retreated to a dull ache in her breast, she continued to ponder the mystery of Doso's desertion. The older woman had been with them from Persephone's birth, with never so much as a night spent outside the bounds of the village. Then, one day,

Doso decided to leave half a lifetime's worth of living and slink off like a mortally wounded animal tucking itself away in its warren.

Sitting up, the blanket slipping from her shoulders, Persephone said, "To die." Then she leapt from the chair, rushed out of her chambers, sped the length of the hall, and hurried down the stairs. At the bottom she stopped, considering.

On her third day here, Hades had taken her to a room containing a deep pool that, though warm, made her eyes water with its scent. There she had bathed, trying to scrub away the memory of Hades's hands and mouth on her. She knew from that trip that the hallway she stood in now continued around and past the stairs, which mirrored those leading to her chamber. It then turned to run alongside Hades's megaron before terminating in the room with the bathing pool. She didn't think Hades's chambers would be found that way.

His rooms had to be either up the stairs on the opposite side of the entryway or behind his megaron. She thought it likely that, as the staircases reflected one another, so did that which they led to. Persephone crossed the entry then mounted the stairs on the other side, her pace now tempered by uncertainty and fear.

At the top of the staircase, a hallway stretched away to her left, and she turned down it. There were no doors off this corridor, save one at the end. Persephone walked toward it, but her steps grew ever slower as she proceeded.

The door stood ajar, and she stepped forward to knock. Through the crack, she saw Hades stooped over a table at one side of the room. The sound of soft snuffling intermingled with an occasional grunt reached Persephone's ears.

She pushed the door open. "Hades?"

He whirled. He held one hand under his nose, sniffing at some white rounded things. His other hand was fisted at his side and thick browns strands poked from between his fingers. The mingled surprise and shame on his face was as shocking to Persephone as if she had stumbled on him unclothed.

Hades swung back around to the table behind him. When he turned to her again, he held nothing and his face was expressionless, but his eyes skittered away from hers and his right hand flexed spasmodically at his side.

"I'm sorry. I didn't mean—"

Hades waved a hand, still not meeting her eyes. "This is your home. You may go where you like." He paused, cleared his throat. His eyes finally found hers. "May I be of aid?"

Persephone dared a step farther into the room. "Is there a way to find the shade of a particular person?" Without waiting for an answer, she continued, "There was an old woman who lived with my mother and me. Her name was Doso. She had no tongue, and—"

"Was she buried with some precious trinket or treasure?"

Persephone blinked at the strange question but replied. "I'm not of a certainty she's dead, but if she is, I doubt she was buried at all and certainly not with any treasure. She had nothing to call her own."

"If she has nothing with which to pay the toll for Charon's ferry she'll be on Styx's far bank."

"I must go there and find her then. She'll answer if she hears me calling. I'm sure she will." Persephone paused then asked, "She will know me, won't she? She does remember her mortal life though she's dead."

Hades nodded. "Those who await the ferry haven't yet partaken of the water of the River Lethe and can still remember their life before death."

Only understanding that Doso would recognize Persephone if she saw her, Persephone turned to go, ready to run all the way back to the

River Styx. Then, remembering Hades's instructions that Charon not let Persephone on the ferry unless Hades was with her, she turned back. "Will you take me to her?"

Hades closed the space between them and took her hand. She wanted to snatch it back, but she needed his goodwill. If tolerating his touch led to a reunion with Doso it would be worth the way her skin clung to the memory of his caress, long after the warmth from it had faded.

"Even if you find your old woman, she can't join us here. The laws Chaos set to rule this place are absolute. With no way to pay the toll, a soul must wait a hundred years before Charon can ferry them across. If the body wasn't given some kind of death rite, treasure or no, there's no crossing Styx. The soul waits for eternity on the opposite bank. I can't change the laws, even for you."

Persephone did pull her hand away from Hades at this, though she nodded her understanding.

"Did she know you well, this Doso?" Hades asked.

Persephone nodded again, struggling to choke down the hot stone in her throat. She would not weep again in front of this man. "She helped my mother bring me into the world. She was—is—as a mother to me."

"When did she die?"

"I don't know. A score of days at least has passed since she left us, but I don't know for sure she is dead." Persephone clenched her jaw, then burst out, "Why do you torture me with these questions? Whether she's dead or not, she's beyond my reach."

"I'm sorry. I didn't mean to cause you pain, but I don't believe your Doso is dead. Nor do I believe her name is Doso. It may be what you called her, but I knew her by a different name."

"What do you mean?"

"Nearly a month past, the old Goddess Hekate visited her cave in my realm. When I heard of her return, I sought her out only to find her weeping as though she meant never to stop. When I finally coaxed her from her mourning, she spoke to me of a child she loved as her own, a child she had to leave. A child with hair the color of Helios in his last glorious blaze of the day, a child with delicate and lovely ankles, a child with a heart open enough to love any creature no matter how wretched or undeserving."

Again, Persephone didn't understand all Hades said, but she gathered enough to realize that Doso, or some form of her, was here in this place.

"May I see this Hekate?"

"She departed my realm some days ago. I don't know when she'll return." Hades's eyes held a wealth of sorrow in their depths, but he couldn't be mourning for Persephone's pain. Surely, no such sympathy existed in him.

"If she returns, will you take me to her?" Persephone asked.

"I will, but it could be months, years perhaps, before she does."

Persephone turned. She had to flee the room before her tears fell.

The weight of Hades's hand came down on her shoulder. He spun her back to face him.

Persephone struck out at him. "Don't touch me."

"I only meant ..." Despite her struggles, Hades held her with one hand, while with the other he scrabbled behind him.

Persephone lunged against his grip. She wanted no part of whatever horrors he meant to procure.

"Take these." He pushed something warm, soft, and yielding into her hand, closed her fingers around it, and released her.

Opening her hand with a cry of revulsion, Persephone fled the room, leaving whatever foul thing Hades had given her on the floor of his chamber.

7

DEMETER

Gaze lowered, Demeter stood next to Hekate in the woods on the western bank of the great river Oceanus. From the corner of her eye, Demeter glanced at the older Goddess. Her eyes were fixed on Helios. Demeter returned her gaze to the ground. She would be blinded if she caught so much as a glimpse of him before his glow was doused by his descent. Still, it might be a price worth paying, but no, she would be useless to Persephone if she lost her sight. She mustn't give in to temptation.

Closing her eyes tightly, Demeter conjured Helios in her mind's eye as she'd last seen him; the radiant crown he wore on his golden, curling hair, his face as smooth and hairless as a maid's, eyes the color of honey, shimmering skin stretched taut over the muscles of his perfect body.

The memory of his beauty made her recall again the worn and weary face she'd seen reflected back at her in her hut. Would Helios recognize her in spite of her cloaking cloth? If so, what would he think of the desiccated thing she'd become?

Demeter's heart began to pound. Her fingers moved to the hem of her tunic, and she plucked at the loose threads that dangled there.

The rumble of Helios's chariot wheels told Demeter he had completed his descent and she could safely gaze upon him. She raised her head then drew in a sharp breath. He was even more glorious than she remembered.

Though her eyes could bear the sight, her heart couldn't. She dropped her gaze to the ground again.

His chariot wheels rumbled past as he made his way to the stables where he would rub down, brush, and make a fuss of his four steeds before putting them on the ferry that would float them to the eastern edge of the world, while Nyx dragged her black cloak across the sky.

"Come, Demeter," Hekate said and set out.

Demeter's feet felt mired in Gaia's flesh, but she couldn't leave this up to Hekate. She had to push past her fear and shame for her daughter's sake.

Demeter shifted the fold of her shawl, so her face was completely in shadow. Then she hurried to catch up Hekate, and they walked side by side to the stable.

Though she trembled with fear, it was far from the first time Demeter had entered this place. When she'd still been part of the glorious cohort of Olympians, she and her sister Goddesses visited Helios often to ride his steeds. Her mount of choice had always been Pyrois, the biggest and boldest of Helios's horses. Yet, she had been a Goddess then, powerful, lovely, perfect. Now, she was nothing.

Demeter turned to leave. Even for Persephone she couldn't bear Helios to set eyes on her in her current state. Hekate banged the stable door shut.

Before Demeter could open it again, she heard Helios say, "Hekate, good Sister, I'm gladdened to see you've emerged from your hole in the ground to grace me with a visit. And with a guest. What brings you both to my stable today?"

Demeter turned back, but kept her chin tucked to her chest, ensuring her shawl obscured her face.

Hekate took a few steps forward. "Helios, I come to beg a boon of you. Ten days past, in the Plain of Nysa, a young woman dear to my heart cried out as though in pain or fear and hasn't been seen since. Did you, from your lofty perch, see why she cried out or whither she went?"

Demeter raised her head just enough to allow her to see Helios. His face was drawn, his forehead furrowed as he removed the last bit of harness from his horses.

He raised his eyes and his gaze locked on Demeter. She dropped her head, so the shawl covered her once again.

"Who is your dark and silent friend, Hekate?"

"A nobody, a beggar woman. Did you not hear my question, Brother?"

"I did, but I won't satisfy you with an answer until you satisfy me with an honest one. Who is the cloaked lady?"

Their dithering would bring Demeter no closer to finding Persephone and neither Helios nor Hekate were likely to yield to the other. Demeter would have to reveal herself.

Trying not to see the work-roughened skin of her hand as she raised it to her head, Demeter pulled back her shawl and stepped forward. "You knew me once as Loveliest. Now I'm known as Demeter, mother to Kore. I ask you, if my grief may sway your heart, tell me where I may find my daughter?"

Helios dropped his handful of leather straps, ducked under Pyrois's neck, and gathered Demeter to him, nearly crushing the breath from her body. She gave an involuntary cry of pain. Her damnable mortal frame was so frail, so incompatible to life among these Immortals with whom she once belonged.

Looking chagrined, Helios loosened his hold and said, "Demeter, Sister, in the time since Hera told us of your fate, I searched for you as I made my way across the sky, but I never found you. Where did you hide yourself?"

Demeter would say nothing that even hinted at the slovenly existence she'd eked out over the last twenty years. She pushed out of his embrace. "I come seeking my daughter, Helios. I'll speak of nothing else. Now, please, tell me if you can, where is she?"

Helios's eyes slid away from Demeter's. He was treating her as all Gods treated mortals, looking aside from her anguish, ignoring her plea. She would find no help here. A sob escaped her. She pressed a palm to her mouth and turned away.

A hand dropped on her shoulder. Helios pulled her back around, put his other hand on her other shoulder, and looked into her face. "Zeus bade we Immortals not to speak of it, but as I'm a Titan, and not subject to him as the Olympians are, I can tell you. It was Hades's doing."

Hekate gasped. Demeter looked at her. She wouldn't meet Demeter's eyes, but this was no time to question the older Goddess about her sudden unease. The solution to the mystery of Persephone's disappearance was nigh.

Demeter looked back at Helios. "What do you mean it was Hades's doing?"

"Though I know not how he came by his knowledge of her, Hades traveled to Olympus and asked Zeus for permission to court your daughter. Gaia helped him in his suit by putting forth a narcissus to tempt the lady to the mouth of the cavern in Nysa. After Kore pulled the narcissus from Gaia's flesh, Hades sped out of the cavern in his chariot. He captured her and disappeared into the cave with her tight in his grasp. Gaia concealed all signs of their flight so none would know to seek her in the Underworld."

Demeter clutched at Helios. Never in her worst imaginings had she entertained the notion her daughter might have been taken to the realm of the dead. It wasn't a thought to be borne. Hades, with his strange gray eyes, and stern and joyless countenance would terrify Persephone. He would also surely put her to hard and abominable use. But the worst aspect, the very worst, was there would be no reclaiming Persephone. Demeter could never comfort her daughter, never assure her of her love. The Underworld never gave back that which it took. This was a fact known by mortals and Gods alike. Another sob broke from Demeter's lips.

"Still you grieve, Demeter?" Helios chided, gently shaking her. "Now that you know where your daughter is, your heart must be at rest. Hades begged Zeus's consent to have Kore as his queen. Zeus agreed. Hades is a God. Your daughter is a Goddess. She will be queen in her own realm. You could ask no more for her. Zeus dispensed with her as he saw fit, as is a father's right. I would have done the same were she my child."

Blood pounded in Demeter's temples. Rage pulsed red at the edges of her vision. She knocked Helios's hands from her shoulders then darted around him. Something caught at her shawl. Demeter shook free of its folds, leaped onto Pyrois's back, and spurred him forward. Hekate called her name. Helios commanded her to stop. She heeded neither of them.

As Pyrois pushed through the stable doors, the cool night air brushed Demeter's face, drying the tears on her cheeks, but it did nothing to chill her rage. Shifting her weight, Demeter turned Pyrois toward Olympus. At her urging, the great horse gathered his legs beneath him and with all the strength and speed that allowed him to convey Helios over the great arch of the sky every day, he bore Demeter to the place her heart had yearned after for twenty long years.

When they passed into the forest that Zeus had claimed on the skirts of Olympus's peak, the power of the place whispered in Demeter's ears, plucked at her skin, sang along every nerve, and raised the hair all over her body. Without her Immortal essence to protect her, staying here too long would drive her to the brink of madness and perhaps beyond, but Demeter only urged Pyrois to greater speed.

The pale walls of Zeus's palace rose out of the gloom before her. Demeter leaned back, bringing Pyrois to a snorting, rearing halt. Even in the weak light cast by Selene's rays, the limestone building shimmered and winked. Demeter's gaze moved to the entrance and came to rest on the huge lintel stone. A single lightning bolt graced its face and it said all it needed to about the God who dwelled here.

Demeter urged Pyrois forward. His hoofbeats echoed in the still night as they passed under the lintel stone. She glanced at the doorway to her right, but the room was dark and empty.

In her time as an Immortal, Demeter had gone to the door of that chamber countless times, the meager pile of offerings Hermes conveyed to her from her few shrines and one temple in her arms. One day each month, Zeus would be there seated at his tallying table, stylus in hand. His precise markings filled tablet after clay tablet as the other Gods' and Goddesses' offerings filled up the baskets and storage jars in the room behind him. Though it was an onerous duty, the kind Zeus usually shunned, it was one he allowed no other to take on. He wanted to ensure he received the percentage due him of each Immortals' offerings and, more importantly, the power that went along with those offerings. He recorded and hoarded each item received with more zeal and tightfisted-ness than that gold glutton Midas.

The first time Demeter went to that room after she and Zeus lay together, Demeter had been sure he would take a bit less from her than usual. She was sorely mistaken. He totted it all up with the same cold precision and, not even gracing her with a smile, plucked what was owed from her arms and gave it to a satyr to be put in its proper place.

A snort of bitter laughter broke the silence. Demeter startled, then realized the laughter was her own. Such a fool she was then, but somehow, this time, she'd find a way to wrest what was rightfully hers back from Zeus.

Pyrois plodded past the tax room through the large courtyard beyond. Demeter stopped the horse outside a wide set of doors thrown open to the cool night air.

She could see across the hallway through another set of open doors into Zeus's megaron, a large, high-ceilinged room constructed of the same spangled limestone. It needed no decoration for its occupants were adornment enough. Within its walls, Gods and Goddesses mingled with satyrs, dryads, naiads, and even a centaur or two. The room was aglow with the light of countless oil lamps, loud with laughter and talk. Long tables groaned under a great burden of food, all at its peak of ripeness.

Seeing them there in all their glory, Demeter recalled again the mark her time as a mortal left on her face and form. She was absent the disguise provided by the shawl. She had left it behind in Helios's stable. She should turn back. She couldn't bear for them to see her brought so low. As if in mockery of her thought, Zeus's laughter boomed out, loud enough to obliterate all other sound spilling from that vast, brilliant room.

The rage she felt inside Helios's stables returned, coalescing in the pit of her stomach, throbbing behind her eyes. Demeter urged Pyrois forward, digging into his sides with sharp knees and heels until the horse plunged through the doors, across the hallway, and flung them both into the midst of the banqueting crowd.

Disquieted by the light and sound and slick plaster underfoot, Pyrois neighed and rose up on his hind legs, front hooves slashing the air. Demeter leaned forward and twined her fingers in his mane. If she lost her seat on the big horse's back, she lost whatever chance she had of reaching Zeus.

The heavenly company immediately sent up a cry. Shouts of confusion, anger and panic echoed and reechoed in the huge chamber. A satyr stepped forward, hands in the air, trying to calm the horse.

Shouting Pyrois's name, Demeter struck him on the neck with the flat of her palm. The animal immediately dropped to all fours. Demeter kneed him into a trot, then a canter, jerking her legs away from the hands that reached for her as she went, never taking her eyes from the raised platform at the far end of the room. As she rode toward the dais, her eyes flicked from Zeus to her sister Hera's face.

Like a voice calling from another room, Demeter remembered the words her sister had flung at her in the cave in Nysa on the day she stole Demeter's Immortality, 'One day you too shall feel the pain of having your child wrenched from your arms just as my Hephaistos was, and you too shall have no way of knowing if it is cared for or if it weeps in vain for the comfort only a mother can provide.'

Zeus may have given Persephone to Hades, but Hera had likely been the viper whispering into his ear that he should do so.

When Pyrois reached the dais, Demeter used her knees to guide him into a turn. Without signaling her mount to slow his pace, she leaped from his back and landed on the platform. The moment her feet touched the ground, Demeter darted toward Hera, hands hooked into claws.

8

DEMETER

With an exclamation of outraged surprise, Zeus caught Demeter by the waist with one hand and turned her seeking fingers away from Hera's face with the other. He accomplished this with the ease of a mortal waving away an insect, but this didn't slow Demeter in her attack. She darted her head forward, mouth wide, ready to use her teeth since no other weapon was available to her. Zeus yanked her hard against his chest and enclosed her in the prison of his arms.

"You!" she screamed, still fighting against Zeus's grip. "You did this. You poured your poison in his ear until he agreed to give my child to Hades. Why? Why? Your loss of Hephaistos was none of my doing. And he yet lives in the bosom of Mount Etna. He's well within your reach while I may never hold my daughter again. Your punishment far exceeds any wrong I ever did you."

Hands pushed back the hair that had fallen over Demeter's eyes. Hera's face loomed large in Demeter's vision.

Demeter met her sister's gaze and flinched back, ceasing her wild struggle, for it was not a woman who looked out of those burning sockets, but a ravening creature held tight in madness's teeth.

It wasn't just in Hera's eyes. Demeter saw the decay of insanity everywhere; in the dirty, frayed state of Hera's flounced skirt, in hair gone dull that was once as soft and shining as a mink's pelt, in the small scabrous wound at the corner of Hera's mouth that wept yellowish fluid, in the ragged nails chewed down to the quick. These were desecrations of her own body that Hera had to engage in almost every moment to prevent her Godbody from healing itself. The thing that shocked Demeter most of all, however, was Hera's Godlight. The corona that surrounded her, once the purest and brightest of all the Immortals, now had the sluggish, sullied look of silty water.

"Hephaistos yet lives? In Etna? Do you speak true, Demeter?"

Before Demeter could respond, Zeus turned her in his arms. Demeter felt the wind of Hera's passing as she rushed past Demeter off the dais, but Demeter couldn't bear to look away from Zeus's face long enough to see where her sister went.

Zeus's eyes, as warm and deep and blue as the heavens he ruled, pierced Demeter's heart. A great bruising ache of wanting poured out of the wound and seeped into her entire being. She turned her face away. She must not lose her rage. It was the only weapon she had in this battle. He wasn't blameless in this. He forsook her and Persephone to the fate Hera meted out, leaving her as a mortal in Henna and giving Persephone away as though she were no more than chattel.

"Demeter," he said and clasped her close again. Her heart pressed against his, though hers beat fast, much too fast.

He released her, surveyed her face. "It's been long since last we met. You are most welcome." Zeus gestured at the table piled high with food. "Sit. Eat."

Demeter shook her head. She must speak for Persephone now or forever be lost to the spell of being in Zeus's arms in this place surrounded by such exalted company. "I come seeking my daughter. I know Hera swayed you to do so, but I'm told you gave her to Hades as his queen. I ask only that you command him to return her to my care. Then I shall go from this place and never come again."

In a familiar but long forgotten expression, Zeus drew his brows together and pushed out his bottom lip, looking like nothing so much as a petulant child. "Hera had no hand in it. Hades asked for Kore. I consented. I believe him to be a worthy consort for our daughter. There's no more to be said on the matter."

Demeter's eyes widened. "*Our* daughter?"

Zeus nodded. "Our daughter."

Demeter laughed, a cold sound that shattered against the stone surfaces of the room. "Where were you then during the bloody travail of her birth? How many nights did you walk the floor with her while she wailed with colic or pain in her gums or sickness in her belly? What part did you play in feeding, clothing, and keeping her? You spilled your seed into my womb and then let your wife dispense with me and the child within me as though we were chaff, yet you call Kore 'our daughter.'"

She moved closer to Zeus, head thrown back, eyes sparking with rage. "Summon Hades to this place now. Tell him to return Kore to me. If he has put hands on her, I—"

"Be silent!" Zeus roared and from around the room came the sharp report of limestone cracking.

Demeter clapped her hands over her ears, the volume of Zeus's shout making them ache. She cowered. There was no other word for it. For a moment, here in this shining place, among this heavenly company, Demeter forgot she wasn't one of them, forgot she no longer had their power and beauty, forgot Zeus could destroy her with no more thought than she gave to uprooting a weed.

Zeus folded his arms, raised his brows. "Make no demands of me, Demeter. Should you wish a boon, you'll petition for it as all mortals do."

Demeter lowered her hands from her ears, her eyes searching Zeus's face. Surely, he wouldn't force her to beg.

He motioned with one hand. "You may begin, or you may be gone. It makes no difference to me."

Demeter would beg then. If that's what it took to secure Persephone's return. There was little enough of her pride left after this night of humiliations, but she would sacrifice what scraps there were for her daughter's sake.

Moving slowly, deliberately, as though her bones pained her, Demeter extended her arms from the shoulders, palms up and open. She drew in another breath. It scored her throat as it traveled downward. Then she dropped her head, chin to chest, eyes on the floor, the perfect semblance of a humbled supplicant.

An astonished gasp went up from the occupants of the room behind her.

Demeter swallowed once, twice, forced her lips to form the words. "Please. I beg you. Bade Hades to return Kore to me. She loves Helios's light, this daughter of ours, and flowers, and birds, and beasts, and all the beauty of Gaia. Kore is tender and kind and will wither in that place cut off from all the things she cares for."

Demeter stopped, drew in another jagged breath. "She doesn't know how beautiful she is because I never told her. She won't understand how he wants her, why he took her. She'll be frightened and hurt if he has her in the way a man has a woman, because I never told her how it would be, or how it should be. I never told her so many things."

Demeter's voice turned ragged and rough as she tried to speak through a throat that swelled and burned. She was pleading now like the lowliest, most desperate of mortals, but it didn't matter. All that mattered was seeing Persephone again. Demeter had so many regrets, so many things she needed to make right. "I didn't love her as I should have. Instead, I longed for all the things I lost when my Godhood was stolen from me and let the thought of them turn me bitter. I blamed her for all my misery. I-I named her Persephone, not Kore. I named her Persephone."

Demeter crumpled to the floor, her legs folding beneath her. She fell forward and pressed her face to the cool plaster, completely prostrate now, weeping. "Please. Please."

"That's sufficient, Demeter. You may rise," Zeus said.

Wiping her face, Demeter hastily stood. She would be biddable in everything if Zeus would only grant her this request. The expression on his face slayed the burgeoning hope in her breast. At the same moment any remnants of affection she had for this God fled from her. Only the ashes of it, dry and acrid, remained in the back of her throat.

"Persephone shall stay below. However, I can restore to you those things which you've longed for all these years, your Godhood, your place among us, your stewardship over the green and growing things which spring from Gaia's flesh."

A lightning strike of exultation pulsed through Demeter, and she sucked in a breath. It wasn't what she'd come here for, but a restored Godhood would mean many things which weren't possible before would be, including Persephone's rescue.

With blue eyes bright and a smile curving his lips, Zeus flicked his fingers. At his small motion, a golden light cloaked Demeter, then sunk through her skin in a slow, delicious trickle. Her heart slowed so that one beat required the span of several moments. The blood in her veins came to a near halt. The time needed between breaths seemed an eternity. All her bodily processes ceased rushing at a mortal's breakneck pace toward the void of death and slowed to an infinitesimal crawl, something so close to eternal life that there was no reason to make any distinction.

After this great change was wrought internally, the power spread outward. The million small aches and exhaustions that Demeter had accustomed herself to dissipated. Demeter sighed, tipped her head back and raised her arms in ecstatic enjoyment.

With her arms still above her head, she spread her fingers. The scabbed over scratches on her arms, obtained in her abortive search for Persephone, healed before Demeter's very eyes, sinking into the skin as though they never existed. The few scars that marred her skin also faded away, the puckered edges lightening to match the creamy paleness and smoothing down into it as Demeter's mortal shell sunk, shrunk, and finally reduced itself to a tiny core inside Demeter's body. Her Godlight sprang from her skin and a golden shimmering flowed over her entire form.

The life of all the green and growing things around her filled Demeter. Somewhere nearby, a wind soughed over meadow grass. Ants traipsed over the bark of the great elm in front of Zeus's palace. Dew collected within the cup of Olympus's flowers and their roots ground down through the soil. It was a lullaby that had sung itself in Demeter's head from her earliest memory.

Though she thought she had accustomed herself to its absence when she lived as a mortal, in its restoration she realized she had missed it every moment of every day during her time in Henna. She closed her eyes and ears to the sights and sounds of Zeus's megaron, the better to relish the song the plants sang only to her.

"Loveliest, indeed," Zeus murmured.

At Zeus's words, Demeter opened her eyes. Zeus's gaze roved over her body. She looked down at herself.

Her breasts were pert and round again, her waist supple and trim. She put a hand to her lower stomach, seeking through the cloth of her tunic for the loose, crumpled skin of her abdomen, the only token of motherhood she had left. Her searching fingers found only the taut, smooth skin of a woman who had never known what it was to carry a babe beneath her heart.

"No. No." Ever more frantic, her fingers plucked and picked at her stomach.

"Demeter, what ails you?"

She looked up as he reached for her. The light of the lecher shone in his eyes.

Her earlier wrath returned, spawned, multiplied. She drew back her head and spat. The gobbet of her abhorrence landed on a cheek that was babyish in its pinkness. The look of injured surprise on Zeus's face caused a bark of laughter to erupt from Demeter. How had she never before seen what a child he was?

Zeus's brows lowered and a wind rushed through the megaron, casting aside platters and dashing goblets to the ground.

Demeter flung back her head. "Do you think I fear you now?"

Thunder shattered the night. Screams and panicked cries erupted behind her. The crash of chairs being overturned as Olympus's inhabitants rushed to escape Zeus's fury filled the room. Demeter remained unmoved as the maelstrom raged around her.

A claw grasped Demeter's forearm, gnarled fingers digging into her skin.

Demeter swung her head around to see who gripped her. Hekate stood there, Demeter's shawl held in her other gnarled fist. The older Goddess must have intuited Demeter's intentions when Demeter fled on Pyrois and followed her here via the God Road.

"You *should* fear him," Hekate said, "for he still has the power to break you. And then who will save our Kore? Now move, you fool."

The reminder of Persephone's plight plunged Demeter into a sudden acute awareness of her own. She allowed Hekate to pull her off the dais, and they fled Zeus's megaron.

When they reached the relative safety of the forest beyond Zeus's walls, Hekate, breath rasping loudly, stumbled to a halt.

Demeter pulled her hand from the older Goddess's, closed her eyes, and summoned her power. Surprisingly, the well of it contained more than mere dregs. Then, a smile turned her lips; it was all those small offerings from the Sicani, none of which she'd had to share with Zeus. It was little enough to reap from those lost years, but something nonetheless.

She opened her eyes. "I take my leave of you, Hekate."

Hekate, still struggling for breath, gasped out "What do you mean to do?"

"To go to the Underworld, of course, and reclaim my daughter from Hades."

"That's ill advised, Demeter."

"What do you think it best to do then? Leave her there because Zeus commands it, because Hades desires it? I refuse to be subject any more to the demands and desires of these Gods. Ill-advised or no, I mean to venture to Hades's realm and bring Persephone home."

Hekate cocked her head. "Do you wish then, Sister, to spend an eternity in Tartarus, chained perhaps next to the very Titans you helped defeat and imprison there? Such will be the fate of any who venture to that place intending to take Ko—Persephone back. Hades's will dictates the actions of all the creatures in the Underworld. Cerberus will hunt you without thought, question, or mercy. It will be an easy matter, after the contents of his serpents' fangs does its work, for Hades to collect your insensible body, transport it to Tartarus, and let its keeper have her way with you. She's very inventive. And I think she'll exercise all her ingenuity to come up with a punishment befitting such a particular threat to her master's happiness."

"He wouldn't dare imprison a fellow Olympian." Demeter began to pace. "If I go to him and demand he return—"

"See sense, Demeter. Hades hasn't left the Underworld in a decade. He emerged for the sole purpose of gaining Persephone as his wife. He isn't a man to go to such lengths without great inducement. He means to keep her. I have no doubt he'll use all his resources to achieve that end."

Demeter ceased pacing and looked at Hekate. "My Godbody won't be so easily defeated as the mortal he still believes I am."

"Which is why, instead of simply using Lethe's water to wipe your mind clean of any memory of Persephone and returning you to your life on Henna, which he most likely would have done had you sought her as a mortal, he'll inter you in Tartarus forever, so you can never threaten him again."

"It doesn't matter." Demeter resumed her pacing. "I mean to try. Zeus won't have his way in this. I shall regain my daughter."

Hekate grabbed Demeter's arm, arresting her movement, and forced Demeter to turn and face her. "I too wish for Persephone's freedom, for a more particular reason perhaps even than your own."

Demeter thrust her face close to Hekate's. "You dare imply your love for her exceeds mine?"

Hekate stepped back and brought her hands up. "Calm yourself, Demeter. That wasn't my meaning, though I do love her at least as dearly as you. That you must concede."

Drawing back from the older Goddess, Demeter gave a grudging nod. "Yet for all your love of her you still counsel me to forsake her in that place?"

"I don't mean for you to forsake her," Hekate snapped. "I'm simply wise enough to know some obstacles are better overcome with patience and planning. Would that you have same wisdom." Hekate drew breath. Her voice, when it emerged again, was absent some of its previous ire. "There are other ways to gain Persephone's freedom that won't result in the loss of your own."

"What ways?"

"There's an old rite, practiced shortly after I came into the world, but even then, parts were lost. When worked on a mortal it made them impervious to the laws that govern the Underworld. I mean to seek it out, the whole of it. Then we can perform it on a willing mortal and send them to the Underworld as our emissary."

"Why a mortal? Perform the ritual on me. I'll go."

"No rite, no matter how potent, can cloak one Immortal from another. Hades will know of your presence in his realm the moment you step within his borders. Before Zeus's generosity, working the rite on you would have been possible. Now ...." Hekate made a gesture encompassing Demeter's Godbody.

"Yes, his *generosity*." Demeter swallowed a flood of hate-riddled saliva. "Yet, had he left me mortal, it would have been useless to send me to the Underworld, rite or no. No human has strength to match Hades's or enough power of their own to employ against him. If we must use a mortal as our emissary, then we're defeated before we've begun."

"Do you truly think me such a fool? I don't suggest we send our ambassador to Hades's door with the intent of wresting Persephone from his very arms. The rite will give our chosen emissary the ability to traverse Hades's realm without detection or impediment, taking much of the danger from the task. However, we must find a mortal with wit enough to take Persephone from Hades by cunning and stealth."

"I believe you're misled in your estimation of humankind's abilities. I doubt there's one such as that among them."

"Tell me then, what do you mean to do to gain Persephone's freedom and still maintain your own?"

"Very well," Demeter snapped. "I'll aid you in seeking out the rite."

"Yes, you shall, for I mean for you to go to your mother."

Demeter shook her head. "I can't. She's gone. She took herself out of this land when the Titans were defeated."

"This land, yes. This world, no. I believe we'll find her among the Phrygians, who worshipped her as Cybele long before she was known to the Achaeans as Rhea."

Demeter looked beyond Hekate into the darkness of the trees. "I wish not to see my mother."

"Then you wish not to save Persephone. Rhea is the only being not imprisoned in Tartarus who's old enough to remember the portions of the rite that I can't. Come." Hekate extended her hand.

Demeter lifted hers, held it in the air above Hekate's for a long moment, then clasped hands with the old Goddess. A moment later, they were on the God Road bound for the land of the Phrygians.

9

PERSEPHONE

The sound of a man calling Hades's name startled Persephone awake. She flung herself from among the fleece and cushions on the floor that comprised her bed in this place, cursing and kicking as they entangled her legs. She flailed free, staggered upright, dashed from her bedchamber through her megaron, and out the door into the hall beyond.

"Help!" she cried, hurling herself down the hallway toward the stairs.

"Hades?" the voice called.

"Help! Help me!" Persephone shouted as she came to the head of the stairs.

At the bottom of them, a tall, lean man with curling chestnut hair and a long, dusty brown cape hanging from his broad shoulders turned and looked up at her. His berry red lips peeled back from his teeth in a smile.

There was something about the expression that curdled Persephone's pleas for aid in her throat. She checked herself in her headlong rush.

"Where's your husband then, Kore?"

"I'm Persephone," she said.

"That wasn't the name Hades gave Zeus when he asked if he could have you." His eyes slid over her body. "Though I now understand Hades's desperation to claim you for his own."

When the man said nothing more, only stood and devoured her head to foot and foot to head with his eyes, she asked, "What name do you go by?"

"Why, I am Hermes, messenger of the Gods," he told her breasts. "Do you not know of me?"

"No."

"You should." He motioned to her. "Come down that we might speak as civilized folk instead of bellowing at one another like barbarians."

Persephone descended the stairs slowly, assessing Hermes as she walked. Though he looked young, strong, and certainly able to aid her in her escape, he didn't seem any more trustworthy than Hades. As he had known of Hades's plan for her abduction and did nothing to prevent it, she doubted she would find much help in him.

She stepped off the final tread and stayed there, a good distance from Hermes.

"Was Hades not above stairs with you?"

Persephone shook her head. "He hasn't made himself known to me this morning."

"There's only one place he loves enough to tempt him from the bed of such a wife. Follow me, and together we'll seek out your wayward husband." Hermes held out his hand.

Persephone looked up the staircase that led back to her chambers. She could return, but to what end? Only to curl into the stone chair and torture herself by conjuring and discarding plan after plan to elude Cerberus while the day stacked itself upon her shoulders, each moment heavier and harder to bear than the last. Spending another day like that would almost be worse than bearding all the horrors of this place at once.

Spurning Hermes's offered hand, Persephone said, "Lead on. I'll follow."

Hermes inclined his head, then pivoted on his heel and traversed the palace to the front doors. When they entered the courtyard, Hermes turned to the right. As Persephone followed him, she noticed his sandals glinted even in the red glow that passed for daylight here. Then, she looked closer. The movement she saw wasn't light reflecting off the gold of his shoes, but the occasional twitch and flick of small wings.

She opened her mouth to question Hermes about his strange footwear, but at that moment, he turned once more and pulled open a pair of large wooden doors which sat in a recess in the palace walls.

Persephone followed him inside but at a cautious pace. What she saw beyond the doors drove the questions about Hermes's sandals from her mind. In front of her was a long aisle flanked by stone rooms whose walls reached only partway to the ceiling. In each of these rooms stood one of Hades's horses. Hades was in the aisle between the rooms, back to Persephone, stroking and patting one of the beasts over the wooden rails that served as doors.

Hermes called Hades's name just as one of the other horses lifted its head from where it nosed in its hay and neighed.

At the dual sounds, Hades spun and looked toward them. The horse he held wheeled away in startlement. For a brief moment, Hades looked after the beast, his expression as bewildered and bereft as a small child who has been deprived of a loved toy. Then, his usual stony expression settled over his face as he strode forward to greet them.

"A banquet of delights from the Upper World awaits in your bed-chamber and still you find your way to the stable," Hermes said as he clapped Hades on the shoulder.

At Hermes's words, Hades turned his gaze on Persephone. Under his perusal, she recalled that she had dashed from her bed without so much as belting her tunic or plaiting her hair. It stuck to her face now with soft tenacity. She reached to draw the strands back. Hades's eyes went to her breasts. The skin on her chest prickled and her belly erupted in a nervous furor. Persephone dropped her arms and crossed them over her chest, tilting her chin up and injecting frost into her gaze. Hades looked away.

"I wouldn't have left such a feast for any reason," Hermes said, his eyes also moving to Persephone. "Indeed, I believe I would have stayed until I was sure I had sampled every delicacy, perhaps twice."

Putting a hand on the whip wrapped around his torso, Hades said, "Gluttony hasn't served me well in the past. I warn you against engaging in it while within my walls. A price must be paid by those who partake of the fare here, as you well know."

"What price?" Persephone asked, her voice emerging higher pitched than she liked. She'd eaten a great deal the previous evening.

Hades looked at her. "You don't know? Truly?"

"I don't. Is it one I must pay? For what I ate yestereve?"

Hades, brows drawn, studied her face. "I thought you ..." He shook his head. "There's no toll for the food of which you partook."

Hermes, eyes lingering on the whip, said, "And I vow I'll not so much as brush my lips over a morsel so long as I'm belowground. But I beg you grant me one small boon to ease my body's hunger."

"What boon?" Hades asked, finally looking away from Persephone.

"Let me ride one of these magnificent creatures at long last." Hermes swept his arm in a wide arc, encompassing Hades's four steeds.

Hades's face creased in a smile. Persephone thought the expression sat strangely, wrestling for position among the somber lines of his countenance.

"I shall let you help me loose them in Elysium, but no more than that."

"Bah." Hermes waved a hand, then bent to tug at the wooden rails across the doorway of one of the rooms.

Hades turned back to Persephone, his face absent the smile. "Now that you've found your way to my stable at long last, I would have you meet my horses."

He moved toward the animal he had been stroking when Persephone first entered the stable. After a moment's hesitation, she followed him. When Hades reached the beast, he extended a hand to it. The creature put its head over the wooden rails and pressed its nose into Hades's palm.

Persephone studied the horse. Its night-black coat gleamed in the dull light that came in through slits in the walls. It was thickly muscled, and Hades's head came only to the top of its shoulder. The beast could crush her if it wished, but its large brown eyes were calm, almost friendly.

Persephone put out her hand. The horse moved its muzzle to blow a hot breath across her palm.

"This is Lethe," Hades said.

Lethe lipped at her skin. It wasn't unlike Phlox nipping at her fingers to ask for more honey cake, but she had no idea what delicacy to offer an animal such as this.

Gesturing at the horse stabled next to Lethe, Hades said, "The one which Hermes is freeing from his stall is Akheron." Hades turned and pointed at the beasts in the stalls across from Lethe and Akheron's. "That's Styx, and the last one is Phlegethon." He turned back to Persephone. "You needn't fear Lethe. He's high spirited, but of an even temper. Akheron and Styx will tolerate you. But I warn you to stay away from Phlegethon. He would trample Zeus himself had he the opportunity."

Persephone nodded and went back to studying Lethe. The horse returned her scrutiny, ears flicking, sometimes both toward her, sometimes both away, sometimes one flicking forward while the other rolled back. Then it turned its head to the side, still regarding her with one liquid, brown eye and bobbed its head.

The gesture was more human than anything Persephone had yet seen in this Underworld. A smile turned her lips. She stroked a hand down the flat of Lethe's face. When he tolerated her caress, Persephone reached up to scratch at the base of his ears as though he were indeed a large version of the little dog fox she'd left behind in Henna. To Persephone's amusement, Lethe's ears lolled as the horse leaned into the caress. After a moment, his bottom lip drooped and began to wobble as his eyes rolled in ecstatic enjoyment.

Hermes called, "I'm taking Akheron to Elysium."

Hades replied, "Take Styx as well. Leave Phlegethon for me. We'll join you soon."

"Aye."

Persephone slid her hand down to Lethe's neck. Hades grabbed her wrist, arresting her movement. She flinched and tried to jerk away.

Hades pressed a brush into her hand and released her. "He enjoys being groomed."

Persephone rubbed her hand on her tunic yet she couldn't rid herself of the lingering heat of Hades's flesh, the sensation of the calluses on his palm rasping against her skin.

To put herself out of Hades's reach, Persephone slipped between two of the wooden rails that made up the door of Lethe's stall, stood for a moment eyeing the horse, then stepped forward. Hades came into the stall after her. Moving away from him, she raised the brush, trying to show no sign of the fear that shuddered through her at being caught between such a large animal and Hades.

When Lethe only lipped at her again, then returned to nosing in his hay, she ran the brush along his back, spiking the hair up as she went. Lethe snorted and sidled.

Persephone backed away, but was halted by the broad terrain of Hades's chest. She went rigid. The brush dropped from her nerveless fingers. From the corner of her eye, she saw Hades collect the brush from the floor. Then, he walked past her to Lethe's side.

He fondled Lethe's ears for a moment and murmured, "Hush now. Shh. All's well. All's well."

After Lethe settled, Hades moved the brush over the horse's back, smoothing down the small spikes and ridges Persephone's brushing had raised. "You must comb in the direction in which the hair grows. To go against it unsettles them."

Hades turned away from Lethe and held the brush out. After a moment, Persephone took it from him, taking care her fingers didn't touch his. She stepped past him and began grooming Lethe's shoulder, making sure to follow the whorls in his shining coat.

As Persephone continued brushing, her timidity dissipated and she began using firmer, longer strokes. The horse shifted his weight, leaning into Persephone. His bottom lip began once again to waggle, looking oddly disconnected from the rest of his head. Persephone laughed aloud, then jumped when Hades's laughter echoed her own. She'd forgotten in the soothing monotony of working the brush that Hades was still with them.

Hades moved to Persephone's side and patted Lethe's neck. "Enough for now, Old Man. Outside with you."

Hades turned from Lethe and removed the wooden rails that enclosed the animal. Tail held high, the big horse trotted out of the stall, down the aisle and through a door at the back of the stable which stood open to the outside.

Persephone placed the brush on a shelf and joined Hades in the aisle between the stalls. He reached as though he meant to take her hand.

Persephone stiffened. Hades paused in his movement, extended his fore-finger, drew it over the back of Persephone's wrist, then turned and walked toward Phlegethon's stall.

Flattening the small hairs on her arm that had come upright at Hades's touch, Persephone walked out the door through which Lethe had exited.

She stopped, blinking, hardly daring to believe her sight. A meadow, a true meadow, with long waving grass that was dotted here and there with the misshapen cousins of Upper World flowers stretched out before her. Granted, the light was still the same sullen grayish red, like the sky in the morning just before a storm. The grass was such a pale green as to be almost white and the flowers were strange indeed. Despite that, it was so beautiful Persephone let out an inarticulate cry of almost painful joy.

Some distance out, Hermes gamboled with Akheron and Styx. The horses pranced and trotted, shook their manes and kicked their heels while Hermes laughed and grabbed at their tails. Beyond them, on the far horizon, stood buildings of some sort, not many and spread very far apart, but still most definitely buildings. Perhaps the people who lived there might be the sort who would help Persephone to escape from this place.

The stable door banged closed behind her. Persephone flinched and looked over her shoulder. Hades, leading Phlegethon, walked toward and then past her. She followed as they moved farther into the meadow. Lethe soon joined her, ambling at her side.

Hades stopped walking, removed the rope from Phlegethon's head and fashioned it quickly into dual loops. Then he bent, slipped them over Phlegethon's front hooves, and slid them up his ankles. "There that should keep you," he murmured to the horse as he straightened. "I'll not chase you the length and breadth of Elysium today."

"Is that what this place is? Elysium?" Persephone asked.

Hades turned to her. "It is. I thought you would seek it out when you first arrived."

"Why would I?"

"It's Elysium," Hades said again as though that were some sort of explanation.

Persephone looked at him blankly.

Hades moved closer. "You're the daughter of a Goddess. Surely, you've heard of Elysium."

A furor again erupted in Persephone's belly at Hades's proximity. She shifted her weight to her heels to widen, if only slightly the distance between them. Her fingers brushed a warm, hair-covered something. Persephone looked down. In his grazing, Lethe had positioned his neck directly under her hand. She buried her fingers in his mane and her pulse stopped thrumming quite so wildly.

She looked back at Hades. "I lived among people who didn't worship the Olympians. Indeed, I don't think they even knew of the Olympians. My mother didn't speak to me of anything dealing with the Gods, save to tell me Chaos created our world as well as the laws that govern it. She also told me the Goddess who lightens the sky in the morning is called Eos. Helios is the God who rides the sky throughout the day. Nyx brings the night with her cloak and Selene illuminates the darkness of it with her rays. I didn't know anything of the Gods or Olympus, or that I was Godborn until the day I met Ianthe and the others in the Mother Goddess's Meadow."

"Nysa," Hades said, his face and voice softening.

"What?"

"The place that was known to you as the Mother Goddess's Meadow. Its proper name is the Plain of Nysa. A place frequented by the old Gods, especially Rhea, or the Mother Goddess as you know her, but the knowledge of it was lost when Zeus defeated the Titans. Your mother and Zeus rediscovered it, named it Nysa, and now it's a stopping place on one of the God Roads."

So much in Hades's statement made no sense to Persephone so she seized on what she thought to be the easiest matter for him to explain. "Is that what this place is?" She gestured to the meadow surrounding them. "A stopping place for the Gods?"

"The Gods don't stop in the Underworld," Hades said, his face hard again, his voice low and harsh.

He grabbed Persephone around the waist. A high thin sound escaped her as he lifted her. He placed her on Lethe's back and his hands dropped from her. It was strange looking down on him from this great height. He wasn't nearly so frightening.

"Elysium is paradise. The great heroes come here when they die." Hades jerked his chin toward the buildings on the far horizon. "Those are their homes."

Just then Hermes yelled, "You allow her to ride?" He strode toward them, brows lowered, lips in a hard line.

Persephone thought she saw a smile flicker over Hades's face, but he drew back so quickly she wasn't sure. A moment later he flung himself onto Lethe, straddling the big horse behind Persephone.

Persephone scrambled up Lethe's back, almost onto his neck. Hades wrapped one arm around her waist, pulling her snug against him.

The warmth of his breath stirred the hair at the nape of her neck. The heat of his upper thighs burned into hers. Even the hard bones of his ankles knocked against her heels. Nearly every inch of her body was touching his.

She pushed at his arm. She must put at least some small space between them. This closeness was overwhelming, unbearable. Her actions had no effect on Hades. He kept her pinned against him.

Hades said something that sounded like 'tcha' at the same moment his legs moved against Lethe's belly. With a great lunge, Lethe moved into a gallop.

Persephone's body jerked with the motion and she shrieked. If not for Hades's restraining arm she would have been flung from the horse's back. Now Hades's grip on her made sense and she almost welcomed it as they thundered past an indignant Hermes. Then the whole of Elysium stretched before them.

Hades's thighs tightened on Lethe's body. His arm dug into Persephone's midsection as he strengthened his hold on her, drawing her even closer. She clenched every muscle in protest. As she did so, her legs drew tight around the barrel of Lethe's ribs. Her body, which had been hitching and jerking in wild discordance, fell into concert with Lethe's movements.

Persephone felt the power of Lethe's body beneath her, the big muscles bunching and then elongating as he flung himself forward. For a moment, it was as if it were her feet on Elysium's earth, her body flowing sleek and powerful over the meadow. She forgot Hades behind her, the Underworld before her, everything but the sense of speed and strength coursing through her. She let out a cry of exultation.

Then Hades laughed, recalling to Persephone where she was and who she was with. Her muscles went slack, shaking from the effort of clinging to Lethe, but Hades's laugh continued to ring in her ears even after he resumed his silence. There was no mocking in it, nothing cruel. It sounded with the same wild exhilaration Persephone felt when she cried out to the day, the same triumph at having, for a moment, found a way to shed all the uncertainty and fear of her current circumstances. There was something else in that laugh, something that caused Persephone to recall the indulgent smile Doso gave Persephone when, as a little girl, Persephone found something, a toy, a trinket, a pretty stone that delighted her.

Nothing about this man should call Doso to mind. Doso loved Persephone. Hades merely wanted to possess her, another treasure to ferret away in his cold, austere palace.

As though in sympathy with the ponderous misery of her thoughts, Lethe slowed his pace until he was moving at a walk. They had traversed a great distance during his wild gallop, however, and had almost reached the buildings Hades told her were the homes of the heroes. There was a river just beyond them, its waters rolling with a friendly sounding burble.

Hades slipped off Lethe's back. As Persephone lifted a leg in preparation to dismount, Hades shook his head. "I'm going to teach you to ride."

In her mind, a small, redheaded girl, tears of frustration and fear pricking at her eyes, sat before a loom while a bitter-eyed woman bent over her, screaming, "Ruined. You've ruined it, you clumsy dullard. All that work, all that wool gone to waste. I should never have let you try. You wonder why I won't allow you to help in the fields. This, this is why. You can't learn anything."

If her own mother could show such rage over Persephone's stupidity, how much worse would the anger of this cold, distant God be when she failed to learn the skill he wished to impart?

Sudden fear dampened Persephone's palms. She swallowed to moisten her dry throat. "I can't—"

Hades interrupted her protest. "Nudge Lethe's sides with your heels."

Persephone didn't move.

"Only a small nudge. No harm to either of you," Hades encouraged.

Lethe craned his head around as though desiring to know the reason for Persephone's hesitation. Though his eyes were brown, the expression in them reminded Persephone of Phlox, beseeching her to run and gambol in the forest with him. A request she could never deny.

Persephone lifted her heels a bit then tapped them against Lethe's ribs. The big horse immediately swung his head around and stepped out. A smile broke over her face. She'd done it.

Hades, keeping pace at their side, said, "When you want him to stop, lean back."

The instruction was clear and simple, just as Hades's previous one. She had achieved that. This should be no more difficult. She leaned back. Lethe continued plodding along.

"Fool," Persephone muttered under her breath, tears burning behind her eyes. She had to do this correctly. Hades was frightening in his regular state. Angry, he would be utterly horrific.

Persephone lifted herself a bit, then sat down hard. Lethe stopped so abruptly Persephone's buttocks once again left his back, but involuntarily this time. Persephone laughed a little as she resettled herself.

"Well done," Hades said as he moved closer. He grasped Persephone's ankle and pushed her leg close to Lethe. Lethe's ribs pressed against her own bones but that sensation wasn't enough to override the feeling of Hades's callused palm rubbing against her skin.

"Keep your legs close to his side and bent at the knee rather than hanging loose. Then, you'll be able to use the muscles in your legs to both control him and hold you on his back."

This Persephone knew she could do. She already achieved it accidently during their wild ride over the meadow. Perhaps riding horseback was a skill she could master. "What else?"

"If you want to move at a quicker pace, urge him into a walk as you did before, then tighten your knees against his body," Hades said.

Persephone nudged Lethe with her heels. He stepped out. Hades's hand fell away from her ankle but the warmth from his touch lingered there.

Eager to widen the distance between them, Persephone squeezed her legs as Hades's had instructed. Lethe moved into a joggling trot that nearly jounced Persephone off his back. Persephone made a sound that was part groan, part laugh. She hurriedly signaled the horse to stop.

"I don't like that one at all, Lethe." She patted the big horse on the neck as Hades jogged to their side.

At that moment, a drawn out, baying cry rent the air, raising the hair all over Persephone's body.

10

PERSEPHONE

Hades flung himself onto Lethe's back behind Persephone. She had no time to react to his presence before they were hurtling back toward the palace at the same earth-ripping pace they'd left it.

Persephone opened her mouth to question Hades about the sound she heard, but the wind whipped her breath away. She clamped her mouth shut, clenched her leg muscles, and leaned low over Lethe's neck. Any beast in the Upper World or Under would be hard-pressed to match the big horse for speed, even a three headed dog with serpents on its back. Perhaps Persephone had finally found her way home. She twined her fingers in Lethe's mane and leaned lower over his neck as though he already sped her there.

As they approached the palace, Hades slowed Lethe to a jarring trot.

Hermes ran to meet him. "Hades, I heard—"

"I know." Hades's voice was grim. He inserted his hand between Persephone's thigh and Lethe's body. In one fluid movement, he lifted her leg and swung it over Lethe's neck. "Get Persephone and the horses inside, Hermes," Hades commanded as he nudged Persephone from Lethe's back.

Then Persephone was in Hermes's arms and Lethe was galloping away, Hades still mounted on his back.

Persephone pushed out of Hermes's embrace. Though she was wary of the God, his touch didn't disquiet her in the same way Hades's did. That, for some reason, was more unsettling than if it had.

Hermes didn't seem to notice her discomfiture. His gaze was fixed on the point where Hades and Lethe had disappeared from sight.

Persephone asked, "Where have they gone?"

Hermes's gaze left the horizon and found her face. "To join Cerberus in his hunt."

"What do they pursue? Surely there are no hinds in the place."

Hermes chuckled. "Hinds? No, there are no hinds here. The only quarry in this land are shades."

An image of the three-headed beast fast on the heels of one of the mind-blasted folk in the asphodel meadow appeared in Persephone's mind. She shuddered.

"Ah, come now, he's only a dog. He merely has a few more eyes and teeth than most."

The statement surprised a laugh out of Persephone.

Hermes grinned at her. "Let's get these horses inside. Then to the feast."

The smile left Persephone's face, Hermes's comment causing her to recall his exchange with Hades in the stable. While Persephone hadn't understood all that had been implied, the conversation had certainly been about more than feasting.

Hermes flung back his head and laughed. "Food, my dear lady, food is all I mean to share with you. I have no wish to feel the sting of your husband's whip."

Persephone looked away from Hermes. Hades wasn't her husband, only her captor, but debating that with this God would likely do no good. She caught sight of the buildings on the horizon and gestured toward them. "Hades says those are where the great heroes go when they die."

"So they are." Hermes approached Phlegethon. Lips drawn back, the horse darted its head forward, obviously intending to bite. Hermes danced back out of the way. "I think I'll leave you for Hades. Those hobbles should keep you from any mischief until he returns."

"Can you tell me the names of those that live there?" Persephone asked, eager to direct his attention back to their conversation.

Hermes moved toward the other horses, making shooing motions with his arms. As they ambled toward the stables, he said, "I can't, for none dwell there yet."

"Then why ...?"

"The Moirai predict a great war. A war over a woman whose beauty must be at least a match to yours, else I can't see men dying for her otherwise." He offered Persephone a lecherous grin. "During that war, many heroes will be killed. Hades had those built for the time of their coming."

"The Moirai?"

"Surely you know of the Fates?"

"I don't," Persephone said. Here was yet another Immortal to cast up her ignorance to her. Why had her mother told her nothing of these things?

"They are those who know the moment a man will draw his last breath before he has even taken his first. Zeus himself isn't immune to their power."

"They foresee even the lives of the Immortals?"

Hermes nodded, but said nothing more as he continued to drive the horses toward the stable.

Persephone opened her mouth to ask if that meant the Moirai foresaw

Hades's abduction of her. If that meant that this Underworld was where the Fates meant her to be. But Hermes would likely no more know the answer than Persephone herself. She closed her mouth on the question, keeping her silence as they walked toward the palace.

There was a small building only a short distance from the rear of the stable that Persephone hadn't noticed earlier. Likely her fascination with Elysium was to blame for the oversight. It was built of small, rounded, multi-hued stones rather than the massive black blocks which made up Hades' palace. A golden glow spilled from underneath and around the edges of the door to the hut. It couldn't be firelight. It didn't waver and dance but stayed steady almost like the light from Helios's chariot. A curious little structure, much more inviting in its appearance than any of the larger buildings in this land below. It almost seemed to draw her to it. Persephone veered away from Hermes, intent on exploring it.

As Persephone moved toward the hut, the air around her grew warmer. The little building emanated heat. With tentative fingers, she brushed the wooden doorhandle. It was hot, but not so much that it would burn. Taking a firmer grip, she pulled and the door swung open. The light that poured out was much brighter than that of the Underworld day. The source seemed to be a triangular thing hanging from the ceiling, but her eyes filled with moisture from the unaccustomed brightness so quickly she couldn't make out any details. Her impression of the rest of the room was similarly blurry. Large rectangular containers filled with a dark substance sat on long tables. A few large pots, filled with the same sable material, were scattered around the floor. Water burbled quietly and the air was thick with the smell of dirt.

"Ah, I see you've discovered the folly," Hermes said from behind her.

Persephone looked at him over her shoulder. "Folly?"

Hermes crowded beside her in the doorway and peered around the small room. "That's what Hades calls it, though folly seems too light a term for the failed experiment of a madman."

"And is Hades the madman?"

Hermes laughed. "How astute you are. Yes, Hades is the madman in question. Since he took up governance of this place, he's been determined to find a way to bring some small piece of the Upper World here. He thought a bit of a broken wheel from Helios's chariot, some water, dirt, and seeds would be enough to make overland plants grow here, but as you can see, he found no success. Nothing that grows under the sky can flourish down here."

Persephone moved into the small room. It was wonderfully warm, especially in contrast to the relentless chill of the Underworld. There were small piles of seeds heaped about on the tables. A few of the long troughs and a couple of pots bore the ragged remains of plants that hadn't made it much beyond a first sprouting. Most of the containers, however, were empty even of that, but they did hold rich, black dirt. It looked like soil that should have nurtured whatever seeds were placed within it but something had evidently gone wrong. Perhaps, if Persephone had been intelligent enough to learn all her mother's lore about the living things that grow from Gaia's flesh, had been allowed to work alongside her mother in the fields, hadn't been too clumsy and foolish to trust with such precise and delicate matters, she could achieve what Hades had failed to do here. It could be a place of comfort and contemplation while she planned her escape, but she hadn't the wherewithal to puzzle it out for herself. Surely, she couldn't succeed where a God had failed.

Hermes broke into her thoughts with another laugh. "Or rather, I suppose he did find success. For here you are, his own little piece of paradise, plucked straight from the Upper World."

Spit gathered at the back of Persephone's throat. It would give her no end of satisfaction to launch it at his face and obliterate his insufferable grin, but he didn't seem the sort to let such an insult go unpunished. Instead, she pushed past him, pulled the door shut nearly in his face, and said, "We should see to the horses."

Persephone's movements were stiff with anger and pent-up frustration as she moved toward Akheron and drove him into the stable. By the time she wrestled the wooden rails into place to enclose him in his stall, her ire had calmed enough so she could trust herself not to do something ill-advised.

"Now we dine," Hermes said.

Careful to keep some distance from Hermes, Persephone walked with him to the palace entrance. Once inside, she hesitated before the doors to the great megaron. Hades had said that was where he meant to banquet with his guests. Before she could enter the big room, however, Hermes turned to the staircase that led up to Hades's chambers. She followed, stomach churning with uncertainty. Hades would surely be angry with her if she failed to treat their guest with due respect, but she had no idea how to go about summoning the shades that served Hades's household. She had also seen nothing to indicate where food was stored or prepared in the behemoth building

Hermes walked to the door of Hades's chambers, opened it, and went in. Persephone stopped on the threshold. The horrors Hades held in his hands last night might still be on display within and it might anger Hades if they entered these rooms while he wasn't here to give permission.

"Come." Hermes gestured her forward. "This is where Hades and I always break bread during my visits."

Persephone's discomfiture eased somewhat and she stepped through the door. A generous repast was spread on the table where Hades had stooped over his grotesqueries the night before.

Hermes seated himself and took a swig of wine. He spat it back into his goblet. "Horse piss. They should have put out the wine I brought last night." He pushed back his chair and rose from the table. "I'll return shortly."

After Hermes quit the room, Persephone moved closer to the circular hearth where a fire crackled, and tried to chafe some warmth into her upper arms. The Underworld seemed colder now than before her short time spent in the folly's interior. She would visit it again if only to warm herself fully through. Being within its walls now would certainly be preferable to this cold, impersonal chamber. Hades hadn't even decorated his megaron with any of the frescoes that adorned almost every other wall in the palace. It was fitting; a chill, severe place for a man who seemed frozen from the inside out.

Persephone turned to warm her backside at the fire and saw a door set in a recess in the wall. It must lead to Hades's bedchamber. Perhaps that was where he'd tucked away the monstrosities he'd been poring over when she stumbled upon him the previous night. The door was ajar. She could risk a look.

She stepped forward and pushed the door open a bit more. Her eyes widened as they took in the room. The frescoes in her own chambers were lovely, but they were nothing compared to the beauty that embellished the walls of Hades's bedchamber. It seemed every flower that ever blossomed, every tree ever grown, every animal that had ever set foot on Gaia's surface was represented in the bounty of vibrant pictures, and Helios rode above it all, a golden vision in his chariot. The panorama was stunning but also frightening. The brilliant color and sheer volume seemed to speak of a kind of madness.

The furnishings throughout the rest of the palace, including those in Persephone's own chambers, were made from various stone material: rock crystal, marble, quartz. Most were inlaid with shining metals and jewels. Here in Hades's bedchamber everything was constructed of gleaming wood ranging from the deep black of ebony to the near white of polished willow. Woven cloth of many different colors graced the backs of the chairs, the couches, and the surface of the tables, but there was no black, brown, gray, or any other somber hue included in so much as one embroidered edge.

On a small table nearest the bed was an odd sort of collection. A bouquet of Upper World flowers drooped in a wooden vase. A pile of crumpled leaves lay next to the vase. Yellowing grass littered the tabletop and the ground beneath it. Strangest of all, a number of willow branches that had been peeled of their bark languished on the table amidst the leaves. Persephone cast her eyes about to make sure she was still alone and unobserved. Then she entered the room and crossed to the table.

Once there, she picked up a willow branch and lifted it to her nose to see if any fragrance lingered in the tender wood beneath the bark. In that instant, the reason for their presence became clear. It had not been hair and bone as she thought when she saw Hades with them in his hands the previous night, but branch and bark.

It was such a small trove of twigs and every one had been laid bare. Had Hades had parceled them out one by one to make them last through the night? Or, in a frenzy of longing, had he feverishly stripped them all and inhaled their perfume until he was dizzy with the heady scent of life and light? It was a bleak consideration.

Persephone dropped the willow branch back onto the table and turned her attention to the leaves. Dark green seeped through the outer layer where they had been broken and crushed. She picked them up, and squeezed them in her fist. Last night, she'd thought the thing Hades closed her fingers around felt like flesh, but no, it had felt like this, only warm as though the leaves had been held in another hand first.

This then, after his failed experiment in the little hut, was how Hades kept a meager connection to the Upper World. How many years had he resorted to this? And how long before she was reduced to such straits? Persephone dropped the leaves back on the tabletop and, wiping her hand on her tunic, hurriedly quit the room.

Hermes entered Hades's megaron just as Persephone banged the door to Hades's bedchamber shut behind her. He raised his eyebrows, but said nothing as he crossed to the table and put a wine jar down on it.

As he seated himself, he said, "Come. Join me. It's not good for the guts to eat alone."

Persephone approached the table, waiting for nausea to swell in her belly. It didn't. She took her seat and reached for a pear.

Hermes lifted a date between thumb and forefinger. He brought it to his mouth, caught Persephone's eye, and extended his tongue to enfold the morsel.

Persephone pointedly turned her attention to the pear and took a bite of the deliciously ripe fruit.

"I'm pleased to see you enjoy the food I brought." Hermes plucked up another date. "I must congratulate you on your cleverness in avoiding the trap Hades set for you. Yet, I wonder how you knew he wouldn't let you starve yourself into insensibility if you continued to refuse the food he put before you?"

A flush of anger passed over Persephone. "Must you continue mocking me? I didn't avoid his trap. I was most successfully caught."

Hermes narrowed his eyes and cocked his head. "You truly don't know. I thought you must be jesting in the stable." He shook the date at her. "I speak of the food, Persephone. The food Hades offered you prior to yestereve was libations from the graves of the dead. The food belongs to the dead. The dead belong to the Underworld. If you partake of the food of the dead, you belong to the Underworld, and, as he is its ruler, to Hades."

Persephone nearly choked on the pear. She'd been so close to eating the fare Hades put before her, a hairsbreadth from unwittingly chaining herself to this place and its master forever. One more night, perhaps, could she have withstood the gnawing in her belly, no longer able to mollify it with the wine. The wine. She'd already imbibed a great deal of it in her time here.

Persephone leaned forward and seized Hermes's hand. "What of the wine? Will it bind me to this place?"

"I don't know why, but drinking the wine doesn't have the same effect. Although you've no doubt noticed the bitter taste it leaves on the tongue? It's the tears, shed into it as it's offered on behalf of a loved one who has died."

A shadow of the cloying aftertaste of what she'd drank last night rose up in Persephone's mouth. She gathered spit and swallowed, but that didn't dispel the phantom flavor on her tongue.

Persephone moved to draw her hand away, but Hermes gripped it. Eyes locked on hers, he stroked Persephone's wrist with one finger. Her skin didn't warm under his touch. The small hairs on her hand remained flat. With a sharp jerk, she freed herself.

Laughing a little, Hermes settled back in his seat, lifting his arms and crossing them behind his head. "How did you manage it then? Did you weep? Did you barter your favors? What trick did you use to convince Hades to provide you with food that wouldn't fetter you to this place?"

"I used no tricks. I couldn't eat what he put before me. It made me vomitous even to contemplate it, but I didn't ask for different provender. He simply gave it."

Hermes waved a hand. "Very well, keep your secrets then, Persephone. I hoped for a tale to give those on Olympus when I return, but it seems you will send me away unsatisfied in more ways than one."

"Do you reside on Olympus?" Persephone asked, the jibe about his being unsatisfied unworthy of any response.

"It's where I spend what time I have when not engaged in my duties."

"Do you travel there by the ...." Persephone paused, trying to recall Hades's words. "God Roads?"

"Your ignorance continues to astound." Hermes shook his head, but in negation or disbelief, Persephone wasn't sure. "No, I don't travel here by the God Roads. Those paths all terminate in the living world." Hermes bent, head disappearing behind the edge of the table for a moment before reappearing with a sandal in one hand. The wings on the heels fluttered as though agitated. "These bear me from the Upper World to here and back again."

Persephone stretched out a finger to touch one of the tiny feathers. The wing stilled under her caress. "How fortunate for you. They must carry you high over the River Styx so you needn't be subjected to the desolation of the souls on its banks."

Hermes twitched the sandal out of her reach and replaced it on his foot as he said, "Styx? I avoid using that entrance as much as possible. I only alight there when I have stray souls to put on its banks. The Underworld has other entrances and, while none is pleasant, they're certainly less dreary than that particular byway."

Persephone shot forward in her seat. "There are other ways to access the Underworld?"

The ruddiness in Hermes's cheeks receded. "I-there ...."

Persephone leaped to her feet, went around the table and pulled at Hermes's arm. "And you know where they are. You *can* help me. Please,

Hades frightens me and … and I fear he means to … harm me, and this place—this awful place—I must get free. I must go home. You could carry me in your arms. We could go now while Hades is away."

Hermes yanked free of her grasp. "Don't be foolish. I wouldn't take from Hades that which he claimed. I've no wish to spend an eternity in Tartarus. He means to keep you as his wife, and keep you he will."

Persephone shook her head, hands coming up as though she could ward off his words. "No. It can't be! If you won't help me, I'll find a way to free myself. I can't bear …. He can't hold me forever …. I must …." Persephone covered her face with her hands.

Hermes pulled her hands down and grabbed her chin, tilting her head up. "Your husband comes. Stop this. I won't have him thinking I'm the cause of your distress."

Persephone jerked out of Hermes's grasp. Did none of these Gods possess a shred of pity, of kindness? Did they think only ever of their own comfort? It was no wonder Demeter had been so distant and unkind, exposed to such beings as these. Taking a few deep breaths, Persephone wiped her wet eyes and reclaimed her seat.

Hades entered the room and stopped, his gaze flicking between Hermes and Persephone. The corners of his mouth drew down, and his hand settled on the handle of his whip still wrapped about his torso.

Persephone dared a glance at Hermes. Though his teeth showed in a grin, his face was pale. He looked desperate to escape Hades's wrath. To do so, he might report to Hades that Persephone had asked his aid to escape. There was no telling how Hades might react to that information.

Hades stepped closer to Persephone. "Are you well?"

Persephone dared another glance at Hermes. She could accuse him of some violence, turn Hades's anger upon him but in any confrontation, Hermes might reveal the true reason for Persephone's disquiet. It would be best, in the current circumstances, to say as little as possible.

"I am well," Persephone said, holding Hades's gaze. The concern in his eyes changed to relief at her response.

Hermes tossed a date at Hades. It hit his shoulder and tumbled down until fetching up against Hades's hand on his whip. Hades turned his attention to Hermes.

With a widening of his forced smile, Hermes said, "Villain. Knave. I can't number the times I asked, nay, begged to sit the back of one of your horses. And today, without even a request, this *kore* gained the privilege for which I've long petitioned."

Hades collected the date and flung it back at Hermes, a laugh lurking at the back of his words. "Calm yourself, Hermes. It was a grievous wrong I did you, but I wanted only to gain favor with my wife. Surely you can't fault me for that."

Rather than wait for a response from Hermes, Hades looked instead at Persephone. In his eyes, Persephone saw the reflection of a girl, heart brimful of hope, holding out a crown made of flowers meant to make her mother love her. She could negate the gift Hades's had given her, douse the hope in his eyes, wound him as cruelly as she had been wounded by Demeter time and again. It was what he deserved, but she wouldn't. She understood that pain far too intimately to inflict it on another, even this God.

Persephone drew breath, held it for a moment then pushed the words through her lips. "I thank you. Riding Lethe was a true pleasure."

Hades scanned her face, emotion lightening and darkening his eyes like clouds across the sky on a windy day. Then he nodded and turned away to take his seat at the table.

11

DEMETER

Demeter examined her mother from the top of Rhea's tall, cylindrical hat to the bottom of her long, belted robe. Though the lion curled at the side of her throne gave Rhea an undeniable aura of power, under the veil, which covered her head to foot, Rhea looked diminished, aged, almost ugly, nothing like the small-breasted, trim-waisted, youthful Goddess that Demeter remembered. Rhea's dim dusty throne room also spoke to how far she'd fallen since coming to the land of the Phrygians.

"I apologize my exterior is so appalling that you can't seem to take your eyes from it, Demeter. However, it is this form which the people of this land recognize, and so it's how I appear here."

"I don't find you appalling, Mother. I'm only eager for your answer to our inquiry."

"And you believe gaping at me will speed my response?"

"My daughter has been in that place nearly a score of days," Demeter retorted. "I very much desire her return. I'll do any and all things I can to speed your response."

Rhea grunted, shifted, picked up a blackened metal rod that rested against her throne, and began poking at the fire burning in the hearth before her.

Demeter could almost hear the ponderous working of the Titan's brain as Rhea sorted through her eons of memory, questing after knowledge of the rite which Demeter sought.

"So much to hold onto," Rhea mumbled, stroking at her forehead. "It began by paying homage to the three realms, flesh into the sea, blood into the ground, smoke into the sky. I recall that much."

"As did Hekate, Mother. Can you remember any of the parts she can't?"

"Patience, Child."

Demeter looked at Hekate where she squatted in the shadows near the wall just outside the ring of light cast by the fire. They might have more success if the older Goddess would join Demeter in her attempts to chivvy Rhea along, but Hekate only gazed silently into the flames.

Rhea sighed, shifting. "No, no it won't come. Give me rest and time, and perhaps I'll recall it."

"Time and time and more time. There is no time. Think, Mother!"

Rhea pointed to a chair. "Sit and be silent, Child. You weary me."

Demeter took a step toward her mother rather than toward the chair to which she'd been directed.

The lion extended one paw, unsheathing his claws.

Demeter sat.

"Perhaps tomorrow after I've slept, I'll recall something." Rhea settled back in her throne, stroked the lion's mane. "Now tell me, how goes it on Olympus? Are you all steadfast and conscientious in your stewardships? Do you govern and keep mortals in the fashion we Titans did?"

There was a scuffing sound. Hekate emerged into the light. "No, Lady, I fear in the time I spent with your daughter and granddaughter, the Olympians care of mortals deteriorated a great deal. Zeus is displeased by how many of them still subscribe to your worship. In his efforts to induce your followers to his temples instead, he's used violence, subterfuge, and various other tactics, some quite vile. When he's garnered all the power he can, he intends to destroy humans and fashion a new race, one Zeus hopes will do great deeds in his name and so increase his following even more. He's gone so far as to speak with Prometheus about it."

"Oh, my son. My golden-haired boy." Rhea shook her head. "And what of Hera? What does she say to this scheme?"

Demeter exchanged a quick look with Hekate before speaking. "Hera is—she's mad, Mother. Her power is Zeus's to do with what he likes."

Rhea shifted in her seat to look at Demeter. "Well, Daughter, what reason have you for not opposing him?"

Demeter put a hand to her chest. "I? I've been a mortal for the past score of years."

"Now you are a Goddess once again."

"And my daughter has been taken by Hades. I won't play shepherd to those pathetic creatures of your creation and leave my child to languish in darkness for eternity."

"As you think I did you?"

"Didn't you?"

Rhea flapped a hand. "I'm too weary to trip down that oft-trod path with you, Demeter." Rhea turned to Hekate. "Do any contest Zeus's plan?"

"Prometheus does. And I've joined him in his attempt to dissuade Zeus since my return to Olympus. We are, however, too weak to prevent him should Zeus decide to proceed in this course."

Rhea lapsed into silence and her metal pole found its way into the heart of the fire again, causing it to snap and flare in a way that was maddening to Demeter's senses.

After a time, Rhea looked up. "Daughter, what if I charged you to return to Olympus?"

"I wouldn't go."

"You have no desire to aid the mortals, though you lived amongst them as one and know well the trial of their existence?"

"No."

"You must be an icy thing indeed, if that experience couldn't stir you to pity," Rhea said.

"As the travail of our time in Kronos's belly stirred you, Mother? When we called out to you unceasingly night and day from inside that dark place, what answer had we from you then?"

Rhea erupted from her throne, the lion at her side roaring as she shouted, "I did what I could when I could!"

Demeter surged to her feet, her fury matching her mother's. "You forsook us there for time out of mind, then bound us as veritable servants to your golden-haired boy by choosing him as the one to rescue us. Hera stole my Godhood and Zeus left me to fend for myself and my child in the mortal world for twenty long years. Now you chide me because I find no pity in my breast for those who call out to me for aid. This icy thing I am, you created—you and Hera and Zeus."

Rhea's bosom heaved as she sucked in breath to retort. She opened her mouth, closed it. Her shoulders slumped, and her head drooped. She clutched the arm of her throne and lowered herself clumsily back onto it.

"Tell me of the rite, Mother, so I may go. We, neither of us, find any joy in this visit."

"I can't recall it."

"You won't aid me?"

Rhea passed a hand over her eyes. "I cannot."

Demeter clenched her fists until she felt blood oozing over her fingertips. "Very well. Goodbye, Mother. I hope not to see you again. Hekate, come."

Hekate rose, moving toward Demeter.

"The Achaeans suffered much in the time you spent with my daughter and her child, did they not, Hekate?" Rhea asked.

Coming to a halt, Hekate responded to Rhea. "As I said."

"Though you know Zeus plots their destruction, you would leave them without an advocate once again, while you strive to free Demeter's daughter?"

Hekate looked from Rhea to Demeter then back at Rhea.

"You won't give me your aid, Mother, and now you seek to wrest from me the only one who will?" Demeter asked.

"There are more weighty matters than the loss of Persephone, Child. As I've abdicated my power in the land of the Achaeans, and you won't work for their benefit, I must have one on Olympus who will. Hekate has long been partial to mortals. I know she'll guard their interests against Zeus's ambition. Will you not, Hekate?"

"All you say is true."

Demeter opened her mouth, but Hekate held up a hand. "Patience, Demeter."

Demeter subsided.

Hekate turned to Rhea. "As I said, I have a particular reason for desiring to see Persephone freed. I ask only that you give me time to accomplish this task. Then I'll return to Olympus and take up my role as advocate for mortals."

"What reason?" Rhea asked, leaning forward.

"A reason none need know but myself."

Demeter said, "As Persephone's mother, I believe I have a right to the knowledge of your reason, Hekate."

Hekate shook her head. "I made an error, but I intend to do all I can to make recompense for it."

Demeter moved toward Hekate, eyes narrowed. "An error that led to Persephone's abduction?"

Hekate looked down, tangling her gnarled fingers together. "Yes."

"Tell me."

Hekate was silent for a long moment, the only sound that of her harsh breathing. Finally, she looked up. "After I left you and our *kore*, I went to the Underworld to shelter there for a time."

Hekate's fingers tightened on each other, turning into bloodless twigs. "I told Hades about her. He wouldn't have known of her otherwise. I believe my words inspired him to take her."

Demeter rushed forward, gripped the old woman by her upper arms. "Why didn't you tell me this before?"

"Demeter," Rhea barked. "Cease that. Loose her."

Demeter shook Hekate. "How could you betray her? I thought you loved her."

"It wasn't my intent," Hekate said, tears dampening her withered cheeks.

"Demeter!" Rhea shouted.

"You were meant to protect her." Demeter pushed Hekate backward. The older Goddess stumbled but caught herself.

Demeter moved toward Hekate again. "Why would you betray us that way? Why did you go to him at all?"

Hekate wiped at her damp cheeks, her eyes opaque with misery. "Because I already perpetrated a greater betrayal against you and Persephone than the one I performed in speaking to Hades of her."

Demeter stopped. "What betrayal could be greater than that?"

"Some days ago, you asked why I came to you and Persephone. Do you remember?"

Demeter nodded.

"It was at Hera's bidding. She removed my tongue so I wouldn't forget myself and speak to you of Godly things. She meant for me to aid you in your labor then leave you in Henna so the Sicani could teach you how to care for yourself and your child in the mortal world."

Hekate paused. Her fingers found their way to one another once more. "I came into being as you see me now, a fruitless, hideous hag. I have never and will never know the love of a man nor bear a child, but I loved Persephone as my own the moment she entered the world. Rather than leaving as intended, I decided to stay to ensure she was taken care of, watched over, loved. And she was. You were so fond, so affectionate with her as a babe."

"No," Demeter protested. "I was angry, frustrated, exhausted by her constant needs. The nights she called me from my sleep, kept me awake, the days she wouldn't settle, only whined to be held, to be carried about, I wanted to shake her until her teeth rattled. I wanted to strike her until she stopped her unceasing demands."

"Did you?"

"You know I did."

"When she was a babe, did you?"

Demeter began to nod then paused, her mind traveling back over the years of Persephone's infancy. "I didn't," she said at last, her voice quiet.

"You were as any other mother, Demeter. Loving, tender, but worn at times. Caring for a babe is no easy task and none comes through it without feeling the frustration and anger you experienced. It was only after Persephone grew some, after the time she fell mostly under my care while you labored in the fields, that you became impatient and unkind."

"Why then did you stay? When you saw I was caring well for Persephone as a babe?"

Hekate hunched forward, and her face seemed to blur and crumple. "I wanted her for myself. I envied that you had her love, every moment of it. Every smile she bestowed on you, every kiss, every laugh. It twisted like a knife in my heart when she turned in my arms to reach for you."

Hekate clutched at Demeter's hand with both of hers. "I didn't mean to, Demeter. You must believe me. I didn't intend it. As soon as I became aware of what I was doing, I left in hopes that, without me standing between the two of you, you would find your way to each other once more."

Demeter pulled herself free of the older woman's crooked hands. "What didn't you mean to do? Of what are you speaking?"

A harsh and broken breath escaped Hekate "I allowed Persephone to perform badly those household tasks you most hated so you would have to take them on yourself and be reminded of how onerous the yoke of your mortal life was. I encouraged her to leave you tokens that by their very simplicity would remind you nothing you possessed in the mortal world could compare with the gifts you left on Olympus. I applauded her simple, unsophisticated manner, so at odds with those you knew in your existence as a Goddess. For years, I stoked your bitterness at your mortal existence and your longing for Olympus through Persephone's actions. And I accomplished what I wished. I turned your heart from her to all you lost."

Hekate looked down, clasped her hands together. "But I couldn't turn her heart from you and therein lays my greatest shame. She wanted your love so badly, and I made that impossible. Of the pair of you, my actions inflicted deeper wounds on her than any that scar your heart."

Hekate's sad eyes lifted, settling on Demeter's face. "We believe we're better than mortals, but even we Gods have a way of keeping our deepest thoughts and darkest desires hidden even from ourselves, especially from ourselves. The moment I discovered the truth in myself I left, vowing to never look on Persephone's face again as punishment for my sin against her." Hekate bowed her head. "Do what you will with me, Demeter. I deserve all your fury for my sin against you, and I'll submit to any punishment you see fit to mete out."

Rage unfurled its burning wings in Demeter's belly. She felt her power uncoil with it. Her Godlight sparked and crackled.

Hekate looked up, but true to her word didn't back away as Demeter advanced, only stood, tears tracking down the deep creases in her face.

With a roar, Rhea's lion came to its feet. It leaped at Demeter, its massive paws landing on her shoulders, bearing her to the ground. Her head cracked against the floor. Points of pain erupted in her shoulders and legs where the lion's claws pressed into her skin. Something hot and wet dribbled down her neck. Demeter struggled in vain to fling the creature off.

"You'll not harm a fellow Immortal, Demeter. Not where I can prevent it," Rhea said.

Demeter could only grunt in response, the great weight on top of her making it impossible to do anything else.

"Leander, loose her."

The lion stepped off Demeter. She clambered to her feet, clapping a hand to her neck. It came away, not smeared with blood as she expected, but coated with lion spittle. Wrinkling her nose, she wiped it off on her tunic, then sidled away from the great beast whose tawny eyes tracked her every movement.

Looking at her mother, Demeter said, "Why did you prevent me from punishing Hekate? Surely you can't dispute she wronged me and my daughter greatly."

"Don't presume to tell me what I can't do, Child. Hekate couldn't know speaking to Hades of your daughter would lead him to abduct her."

Demeter gestured at Hekate. "Did you not hear? She worked to turn my affections from my daughter?"

Rhea raised her eyebrows. "Surely, Demeter, as Goddess of the Harvest, you must know, as none other can, you only reap that which you sow. Had you no bitterness to stoke, Hekate would have been unable to turn your heart from Persephone. Your cruel treatment of your daughter is no one's fault but your own."

"Liar," Demeter screeched, lunging forward only to be brought up short when her arm was caught within the confines of Leander's teeth.

Panting, Demeter fell back. "I will free my daughter. She'll know the truth of Hekate's treachery. She'll see I'm the one who truly loves her, who never betrayed or forsook her the way I was betrayed and forsaken by so many."

Tears started in Demeter eyes. After bearing up under so much shame this day, this was the final, ultimate humiliation, to weep before her mother who had never had any regard for Demeter's suffering.

"Demeter," Hekate said. "I would still aid you in freeing Persephone if you'll let me."

"No," Demeter spat. "I've had a bellyful of Immortals and their games. I wish to have no more truck with any of you." Demeter turned to Rhea. "Call off your creature, Mother, that I may take my leave."

Rhea opened her mouth.

"Wait, Rhea," Hekate said and took a step toward Demeter. "Be wiser than me, Demeter. I know you desire to free Persephone, but be sure that's your only intent. Dark deeds and much harm can be done in the name of love. I know you believe Zeus and Hera and perhaps even I have much to answer for, but—"

Demeter sliced her hand across the air. "Enough. I've had enough from both of you. I go to do what I must to save my daughter. Call off your beast, Mother."

"Cease, Leander."

The lion released Demeter.

Rubbing at her arm, Demeter turned and walked toward the door.

"Daughter," Rhea called after her. "Just as rites can be forgotten, they can be made new again by one with enough determination and power."

Making no response, Demeter crossed the threshold of her mother's temple.

Rhea continued. "I hope you have more success in liberating your daughter than I did mine."

Demeter clasped her shaking hands in front of her until they stilled. Then, chin tilted, shoulders squared, she walked down the steps of her mother's palace. Once outside she looked up at the night sky, replaying Rhea's words. Determination she had. Power she would get. Success she would have. She would go to the city of Eleusis. Her only temple and what followers she had left were there.

12

PERSEPHONE

Coming to a halt, Persephone looked over her shoulder. Hades's palace appeared to be the same distance away as it had the last time she'd looked. The daylight of this Underworld never changed until night arrived with the suddenness of a thunderclap. Because of this, Persephone couldn't tell how much time she'd been walking, but she knew it was long enough that the palace should have been farther away and the heroes' homes on the far horizon closer.

Facing forward once again, she began walking at a faster pace, her goal the river that meandered through Elysium. She hoped to find one of the other exits from the Underworld along its banks.

There was no reason to believe she would find a way out there. It was simply the least frightening place to begin her search. If she didn't find an egress in this land, she would next search the asphodel meadow and then the area behind the temple where the judge held court. If there were no exits in any of those places, she meant to seek out Tartarus and ask its keeper to allow her in. Then she would search there also. She didn't relish the thought. Indeed, it made her sick with fear, but she would do it if necessary to escape this blighted realm and its ruler. Her knowledge that there was a way home, and her hope that she would find it, were the only things keeping her from going mad in the narrow sphere of her chambers, bathing room, and stable.

She shouldn't look behind her again. She hadn't traveled any great distance even at her increased pace, but still, she had to see. She turned once again and made a sound of frustration. The big black building seemed to be closer, if anything. She turned away from it, tucked the skirt of her tunic into her belt, and ran.

The high meadow grass whipped against her legs and forearms as she rushed through it, a sure sign she was making progress. Soon, she began to gulp for breath, pulling it in through a throat that felt hot and abraded, and her muscles protested the unaccustomed exertion. Finally, gasping, legs quivering, Persephone staggered to a halt and looked over her shoulder once more. This time she was sure of it; the palace was closer instead of farther away.

She shook her head in negation of what that meant. There had to be some means, other than on Lethe's back, to get away from the palace, because using Lethe to facilitate her escape was no longer an endeavor in which she could succeed. She wasn't sure if Hades had somehow intuited her intent, but in the five days since she had first ridden Lethe, every time she checked the stable doors they had been locked. She was only allowed entrance when she was with Hades, and could only ride Lethe in Hades's company.

The previous day while riding in Elysium, Persephone had, in desperation, urged Lethe into a gallop thinking to simply ride away too fast for Hades to keep pace. She looked behind her and was flooded with grim satisfaction when she saw Hades dwindling to a dark speck in Elysium's grasses. Then a piercing whistle, not unlike the one Hades used to summon Cerberus, split the air. Lethe turned so fast Persephone was nearly unseated and the horse pounded back toward his master at the same swift pace he had run from him.

Lethe's betrayal had wounded her almost as much as if it were Phlox who was the traitor, and so she no longer took as much comfort in the big horse's presence. It was apparent where his loyalties lay. If she meant to break free of this place it would have to be under her own power.

Persephone looked at the high black walls of the palace, considering. Perhaps if she ran toward it, the building would have the opposite effect and repel her.

With the thought still burning bright and new behind her eyes, she once again dashed forward, her abused legs and heart and lungs crying out in protest. It was to no avail. The walls of the palace loomed larger as she got closer. Persephone slowed to a jog, then a walk, then stopped altogether, chest heaving, lungs burning.

It seemed no matter what direction she ran that foul building drew her to it. The only way to escape was on horseback and Hades's precautions ensured that was an impossibility.

Persephone dropped down in the meadow grass, heavy with despair. The bridge of her nose prickled. She made a disgusted sound in the back of her throat and dragged a hand over her eyes. Tears accomplished nothing. They wrung no pity from Hades, no help from Hermes and brought her no closer to her goal of escaping.

The urge to cry abated, but she was still weary, aching and cold, her body gritty with dried sweat. The bathing pool would clean, warm, and ease her, though she would have to make use of it quickly. There was always a risk Hades might venture to the pool while Persephone was making her ablutions, and there was no telling what he would do if he saw her there unclothed.

Persephone rose to her feet and trudged toward the palace. The light from Hades's folly spilled from around the door and beamed its steady glow over Elysium's grasses. Though Persephone couldn't clean herself in the little building, she could get warm within it walls, without fear of Hades intruding upon her. It had become apparent in the time they'd spent over the last few days near the stables and in Elysium with the horses that Hades avoided the hut.

Persephone made her way to it, this time narrowing her eyes before opening the door. She waited until her vision had accustomed itself to the illumination before stepping inside and pulling the door closed behind her. Her entire being seemed to expand. Even the heaviness in her heart eased some in the warm golden glow. She peered up at its source. Four jagged spokes thrust from a small curved piece of wood which was suspended from the ceiling by a thick chain. Even such a small piece of Helios's chariot wheel was almost unbearably bright. If it stayed illuminated all day and night it was no wonder Hades hadn't had any success cultivating his seeds. Persephone didn't need any of Demeter's teaching to know plants needed their rest in the same way every other one of Gaia's living creatures did. It seemed unthinkable a God would make such a simple miscalculation.

Persephone picked up a handful of dirt from one of the troughs. It was, as she'd thought upon her first glimpse of it, dirt from the Mother Goddess's Meadow, rich, black, fertile. However, it was very wet, almost muddy. It fell from her fingers in thick clumps. The seeds which were in little hummocks here and there on the tables looked as any other seeds. There was no telling what kind they were, though judging by size and color, it seemed a fairly large variety.

The trickle of water from the back of the hut drew Persephone's attention. A small hole in the wall at the rear of the hut with a series of cleverly angled, wooden tubes delivered water from there to the troughs. That was what made the dirt so replete with moisture.

Persephone cupped a hand under the spout, then brought it to her nose. The liquid was cold, clear, and with none of the slight scent of rot present in the bathing pool. The problem wasn't with the quality of the water then, only the quantity. While it was true there were plants that grew well in the wet soil on the banks of streambeds or shores of lakes, most needed far less moisture than what Hades had provided here. And much less light.

Persephone more closely inspected the wooden tubes which carried water to the troughs. It wouldn't be too difficult to temporarily disconnect them or design a way to dam up the source at the wall so she could control both when and how much water reached the different containers. She would also need to contrive a screen of some kind to shade a portion of the room. There were myriad chests in her bedchamber containing an assortment of clothes, none of which she had any intention of wearing, but she could stitch some of the skirts together and fashion a way to hang the resulting drape. She could make it large enough so, if necessary, it could cover the chariot wheel at night. There was no way to tell what seeds would produce which plants or what conditions they would do best in, but she could imbed a few of each into all the troughs and observe which flourished and where. Then she could plant a larger portion of seeds with their fellows and before long have a prospering population of plants, all grown by her own hand.

Her own hand. Was that even possible? Likely not. Persephone's earliest memory of her mother was of Demeter hounding Persephone from the fields, shouting, "Begone from here. This isn't for you." Never had Persephone been allowed to toil in the dirt at Demeter's side. Though it was no wonder Demeter hadn't wanted Persephone's aid. As Demeter was wont to observe, Persephone made a muddle of everything that required any skill; cooking, spinning, weaving. This would be no different. Persephone would no doubt leave the hut in more of a shambles than it was now, only succeeding in depleting the precious stock of seeds in her ill-advised attempts to nurture them. No, better not to make the endeavor.

A bang came from outside the hut. Persephone let out a little cry and spun around to face the door, hand going to her thumping heart. On the other side of that door lay Hades and all the horrors of his realm. Somehow, Persephone had forgotten that, forgotten where she was, how she had come to be here, what little hope she had of escaping. Her brain's plucking at the problem of how to bring Upper World plants to life in this place had been a kind of sorcery almost, a rite she worked on herself. She could do it again. She could come to this place every day, experiment with the water, sew a drape, sort the seeds and plant them. She could try. She could learn. Just as she had learned to ride Lethe. And she could puzzle out the problem of how to escape while her hands were busy with the work here. It would, at the very least, make her time here less dreary and dull. Likely, she would fail, as she had in nearly everything else, but her failure here would make no matter to anyone except herself. Hades had already given the place up and Demeter would never know.

More noises came from outside the hut: thuds, thumps, and then a high-pitched neigh. Persephone knew that sound. It was Phlegethon protesting the prison of his hobbles while the other horses ran free. Her breast twinged in sympathy. The bang that had so startled her had been nothing more than the stable door closing after Hades loosed the horses in Elysium.

So long as the horses ran, the stable would be unlocked. Persephone could go through it to access the palace's front door, rather than walking all the way around the big building and the hideous rock on its west side. If Hades's attention was fixed on the horses, she should be able to slip inside the stable without him seeing her. Hades might make some objection to her working in the folly should he become aware of her presence there.

She moved to the door of the hut, pushed it open only far enough so she could peer out. Hades, his back to Persephone, was a good distance out and walking farther away. Lethe strode behind Hades, his muzzle touching the top of his master's shoulder, following him through the Elysium like Phlox had followed Persephone so many times through the forests around Henna. Her fingers twitched, seeking the soft ruff of fur they would never feel again.

Persephone eased the door of the hut open far enough to let her pass through, then shut it carefully. She had crossed almost half the distance to the rear stable doors, when Hades's voice drew her to an abrupt halt.

"Where do you suppose your mistress is, Old Man?"

Heart pounding, Persephone dropped to her knees in the long grass and looked toward the pair. Lethe snorted and shook his mane.

"I haven't seen her about either. I thought she'd be waiting by the stables, eager for a chance to ride you. Would she had the same enthusiasm for spending time with me."

Lethe whickered and lipped at the shoulder of Hades's tunic.

Hades turned to face the horse then. Persephone stiffened. The grass hardly obscured her, especially the vibrant yellow of her tunic. Surely, he would catch sight of her now, but he only pressed his forehead against the broad flatness of Lethe's forehead and put his hands on the big round bones on either side of the horse's jaw. "I am lost, Lethe. I was lost from the moment of my birth, but never so much as when I saw her face. And she turns from me. She turns from me to you, from me to her hope of escape. She loathes this kingdom I formed, hates and fears me and pines for her home. I know all this and yet I don't have the strength to give her up. Give me the strength, Lethe. Give me some of your great heart, so I can face the thought of an eternity with you as the only thing with which to share my withered soul. Then I can let her go."

He passed his hands up Lethe's face to entwine them in the horse's mane. Lethe remained still, his ears pricked for the sound of his master's anguished tones.

Persephone rose to a crouch, then crept toward the stable, Hades's words repeating in her mind. He had seen how unhappy she was here and how much she hated him. Did he truly mean to let her go?

Hades's voice rose again into the stillness of the day. "I've lived my life in darkness. I cannot give her up."

Persephone staggered and fell to her knees as the hope within her died a swift and brutal death. She took deep breaths. She wouldn't weep. She wouldn't let this defeat her. She would get free. She must. She repeated this to herself until she calmed. Then, she rose into a crouch again and made her way toward the stable.

Would she had not been here to witness all of this. Then she could continue to deny the thought that, since Hermes's visit, prodded at the edges of her mind every time she woke in the night. She and Hades were akin, seeking for heart's ease in any wretched little way they could, living on the barren edge of the world of which they were supposed to be a part, pitiful in their desperation to be loved by one who wanted only to flee their grasp and return to a better life.

There was no way to be free of that knowledge now. She would never be able to cleanse from her ears the sound of Hades's agonized voice or remove from her mind's eye the desperate way he clutched at Lethe.

She finally reached the stable. Without glancing behind her, she straightened and slipped inside the already open door. Her own sweat was a pungent counterpoint to the sweet smell of hay and horse that filled the air. She needed the bathing pool badly and she should have sufficient time to use it since Hades was with the horses. With that as her goal she hurried through the stable across the courtyard and into the palace.

When she reached the bathing room, she removed her tunic. Little wonder Hades hadn't spotted her in the meadow. The garment was soiled, more gray than yellow and the embroidery around its hem had lost all its brightness. Still, she wouldn't wear the clothes Hades had provided. It would be yet another way he could lay claim to her. The tunic was the only proof she had of her mother's love, the only bit of her life aboveground left to her. She would continue to clothe herself in it until it went to shreds and fell from her body.

In preparation for washing it, Persephone placed the garment out of the way of the steps that led down to the pool so it was closer to the shallow part in the dimness at the far end where it would be easiest to cleanse it. Then she lowered herself into the warm water. She released her hair from its plait. It fanned out around her head as she sunk below the black surface. She luxuriated in the feeling of the current carrying the sweat and grime from her body.

If only the water could enter her head and heart and sweep away these new thoughts and feelings regarding Hades, but no matter how long she stayed beneath the surface, cleansing her interior landscape wasn't possible. She would simply have to learn to reconcile the similarity between herself and Hades, though how to accomplish that, she wasn't sure.

When her lungs began to beg for air, she shot to the surface. As she emerged, the rush of water plastered her hair to her skull and it hung over her face in long wet ropes, obscuring her vision. She pushed it out of her eyes then stopped, breath clogging in her throat.

Hades stood at the edge of the bathing pool. He was in the act of pulling his tunic over his head and it obscured most of his face. The rest of his body, however, was bared to her gaze. Curling black hair covered his chest but couldn't disguise its musculature. Below his chest, the hair narrowed to a thin stripe that bisected his entire abdomen, trailing down past his bellybutton to his loins where his manhood dangled, pale and unassuming, from the nest of curls there. His legs were long, as thickly muscled as the rest of him, and his skin was so fair he almost seemed to glow even in the dim light.

Unease sliced through Persephone as swiftly as a hawk dropping into a flock of doves to clutch at one with its cruel talons. It was undeniable this God she feared, this God she hated, also possessed the same fierce and sometimes frightening beauty that she saw in his horses, in his palace, even at certain times in this Underworld. It exerted a pull on her, one she didn't at all understand.

Her gaze traveled back up. Her eyes met Hades's. Everything in her body paused, then resumed its operation at a breakneck pace, shouting 'Beware. Danger here,' but he made no move toward her. Indeed, he held himself so still, had his tunic not still been swinging in his hand, he could have been mistaken for a statue. Only his eyes moved, tracing the lines of her body almost as closely as the beads of water that trickled down her neck, breasts, and belly before they disappeared into the bathing pool at her navel.

Hades took a step forward. The motion galvanized Persephone. She spun and splashed her way to the rear of the pool where the water was shallow. He wouldn't find her such an easy victim this time. She would make her stand here where she had the best chance of defending herself.

13

PERSEPHONE

With the water lapping at her ankles, hands already curling into fists, Persephone spun. Her gaze darted around the bathing room. Surprise flashed through her. It was empty. He had left. Still cautious—this could be some ruse—she climbed out of the pool. Then she grabbed her soiled tunic and drew it over her head.

She stood in the dimness of the bathing room, listening. Perhaps Hades waited for her outside the entrance, but the only sound was the quiet gush and gurgle of the water as it flowed through the pool. Finally, she exited the bathing room and hurried through the palace.

Inside her bedchamber she huddled into the pile of fleece, drew several blankets over herself and shook as though taken with a palsy. Eventually, eased by the cocoon of warmth, her body relaxed, but in her mind, the scene in the bathing room played over and over, each time Hades getting closer to the pool's edge, then stepping into the water, then moving to her side.

His rough palm passed over her breast and her nipple hardened in response. His tongue and teeth teased her ear. His other hand grasped her buttock, pulled her near. The muscles in his thigh flexed against her. She moaned. The hand at her breast slipped lower, trailing down her stomach, past her navel, then lower still.

Persephone came bolt upright in the dark, the sound of her own cry echoing around her. From out of the dark, a hand gently grasped her upper arm while another soothed back the hair from her forehead, just as Doso used to do whenever Persephone roused in the night from a bad dream. But here, now Persephone woke into a nightmare, and these weren't Doso's hands.

She turned her face away from the touch and wrenched free from Hades's grasp, but before she could move away, Hades put both his arms around her and gathered her in close.

Persephone tensed, her muscles trembling with the effort of holding herself rigid. Now he would lay her back the nest of fleece and demand more from her than she wanted to give. However, instead of pressing her down, Hades's hand found its way to the nape of her neck and began massaging the tight muscles there.

He began a litany of words in a low tone that were soothing in their monotony, "Hush, hush now. Shh. All's well. All's well. Shh."

He moved his hand to Persephone's ear where he rubbed and tugged for a time, still reciting his stream of comforting nonsense. His other hand moved in circles on her lower back. This wasn't the behavior of a man who meant to do her violence. The tension in her muscles eased some, and her breath slowed.

Hades slid his hand from her ear down the line of her jaw to her chin and tilted her face up. "Are you well?"

His warm breath passed over her lips. Heart still thudding, Persephone pulled away from him. Astonishingly, he let her go.

She moved out of his reach before she replied, "I'm well. I have no more need of your comfort."

Hades looked down, dragged a hand over his lower face, then got to his feet. "Dinner has been served. Do you wish to eat or return to your slumber?"

Eating meant spending more time with Hades. The memory of being with him in her dream as well as the reality of him here in her bedchamber were more than enough exposure. However, it had been hours since she broke her fast and her ventures in Elysium had caused her to miss the midday meal. The demands of her stomach couldn't be ignored any longer.

Persephone also stood. "I wish to dine."

Hades gestured for her to precede him into her megaron. She walked past him, careful to make sure even her tunic didn't brush against him as she passed.

Once seated at the table, Persephone shifted against the back of her chair but the rough contact didn't scrape away the memory of Hades's touch, the heat of his hands.

Hades placed half of a pomegranate on her plate. "I thought to find you at the stable today, yet you were nowhere about."

There was a question in his words, in his gaze. Persephone eyes skittered away from his. There was much she'd done today she didn't wish him to know about and he might see the perfidy in her face if he looked too long. Perhaps she could appease with a partially true response. "I went for a walk. I wanted to see more of Elysium."

"You should have come to me then. We would have taken the horses. You can go nowhere in this land on foot."

"Why not?" Persephone cried then pressed her lips together. The anguish in her voice had surely betrayed to him at least some of the purpose in her explorations that day.

Hades surveyed her, his face expressionless, his eyes unfathomable before he said, "You know, of course, of the rock on the west side of the palace."

Her throat was too thick to allow her to speak. She could only nod.

"It's a lodestone. It draws everything in this land to it. That's the reason I made my palace a part of it, so any who run from me are instead brought to my door. It exerts only a subtle pull on those who are content to be here, but those who actively try to escape my kingdom find themselves instead drawn ever closer to its heart."

Gripping the table's edge, Persephone rose partially to her feet. "No. No! Surely no stone, even one so monstrous as that, can have such power?"

"It isn't the rock but what's within it that draws those in my realm."

Lowering herself back into her chair, Persephone shook her head. "I don't understand."

"Those in the Upper World pour libations of blood into the ground to restore to those in the asphodel meadow memories of their mortal existence. The lodestone is the conduit by which that blood enters my kingdom. The blood carries the desire of those who pour it into the earth to be reunited with their dead. Though most of the shades in my kingdom have little mind left to call their own, they're still captive to the blood's pull, as are any who dwell within my kingdom."

"Why then can the horses leave and you with them?"

"The horses aren't subject to it because they're simple beasts with simple desires. When they travel across this land, it's only for the joy and freedom of movement. They care not for how far they can get from my kingdom . . . or from me."

Dropping her eyes to shield the desperation in them, Persephone asked, "Then if one could empty their mind of the desire to be free of this place, the stone would exert no pull...."

"You may be able to empty your mind of your wish to escape, Persephone, but could you absent that longing from your heart, for that is the desire the stone acts on?"

Persephone held herself rigid, each breath a careful sip of air as though her stillness could somehow repel the truth of his words. If they were true, she was lost for she couldn't remove her longing to be free, to be in the Upper World, from her heart.

Finally, looking up she asked, "When you first brought me to this place, you insisted I allow Cerberus to accustom himself to my scent so I could roam without danger from him. You knew then of the power of the lodestone. You knew no matter that Cerberus recognized me, I still wouldn't be able to move about this land. Why did you allow me to believe I could?"

"As I said, the stone exerts very little draw on those who are content to be here. If you could learn to be happy here, you could travel the Underworld as you wished, as I do. I thought when I first brought you here, it wouldn't take long for you to accustom yourself to the Underworld and my—my presence. I believed within a matter of days you would be in such a state of content that the rock would never hold any sway over your movements."

Keeping her voice soft as though that could lessen the blow she meant to deliver, Persephone said, "Why would you believe I could ever learn to be content in this place?"

This time it was Hades's eyes that faltered down from hers. His voice was low, almost inaudible as he said, "I thought to go from the arms of one who cared very little for you to the embrace of one who loves you as his own flesh would give you a measure of happiness." He paused, cleared his throat, his voice regaining some of its volume as he continued. "Hekate or Doso, as you call her, spoke to me of Demeter's cruelty and coldness to you and how you, instead of turning from her, remained a loving daughter. I believed if you could care for one who doesn't love you, your heart would open easily to me." He raised his eyes to Persephone's face at last. "And I believed my affection for you would be enough to overcome the monstrosity of my realm."

"It isn't....This place is full of horrors I can't accustom myself to, but ..."

But the greatest horror was Hades himself. Yet, after what she'd seen and heard today in Elysium, the way he'd clutched at Lethe and poured his pain in the big horse's ear, how could she tell him that? How could she inflict further anguish on one who wanted, as she wanted, only to belong, only to be loved?

"But?" Hades prompted.

"But I find myself curious, if the rock draws all who try to escape this land, why then do you have Cerberus? Surely you need no further assurance since the dead can't escape your grasp."

Hades blinked a few times, as though Persephone's question wasn't the response he expected. Then he straightened in his chair, his eyes and face closed to her once more. "Cerberus's duty isn't to keep the dead in, but the living out."

Persephone shuddered. "Why would the living ever come to this place?"

"To take back those whom they love, those whom I have claimed."

Those who he had claimed, such as she. He would never let her go, no matter if Demeter herself braved these depths. Hades needn't worry himself on that account. Still, Persephone conjured the unlikely image of her mother entering the Underworld seeking Persephone only to be brought down by Cerberus; the horror of the hunt, the terror of being attacked, the serpents' heads on the beast's back fastening onto her mother or some other poor mortal who ventured to this place out of love and loss. Persephone put the back of one shaking hand to her mouth.

"And Cerberus has one other duty which does regard the shades who are our subjects."

Persephone turned her face from Hades. She couldn't bear any more terrible truths about this place where she dwelled.

"At times, a shade may come in possession of mortal blood. That's why you mustn't touch those who've drunk from the River Lethe. When your flesh comes in contact with theirs, they sense the blood beneath your skin and will do anything to obtain it. The shades don't often succeed in acquiring blood, but when one does, it restores the memories of that shade's mortal life, and they try to flee my realm. A bite from the serpents on Cerberus's back removes those memories and allows the shade to return to its former contented state as my subject."

Persephone dropped her hand, looked back at Hades. "But you said the venom would cause great agony. Why must you hurt your—"

"For you, for any living being, it does. The contents of half the serpent's fangs is merely water from the River Lethe. It's the only mercy I can offer my subjects in the asphodel meadow, a surcease of all memories of the life they had before death. While the bite itself is painful, the hurt lasts only moments and then the shade is content in oblivion again. The other half of the serpents carry water from the River Styx. It causes any conscious creature the greatest of agonies. For you, as one of Olympus's chosen, the bite would be followed by nine years in which you would remain utterly insensible, not speaking, not moving, only clinging to the fringes of life. The same would happen if you drank even the smallest amount of the water of the River Styx. It's why the shades on its bank don't dare cross. It's why I exhorted you to not attempt swimming it."

A tightness gathered in Persephone's chest. There were so many obstacles to her freedom. It was impossible to escape. Clasping her shaking hands together on the tabletop, she drew in shallow breaths through her nose. Hades reached across the expanse of table, hesitated a moment, then put his hand atop hers.

Persephone met his eyes. "Let me go."

Hades looked down at the heap of their hands. "I can't."

Persephone remained silent until Hades looked up once more. As his eyes found her face, she said, "There's no air here not tainted with wrongness, no drink that doesn't taste bitter, no light that doesn't steal the hope from my breast." She shifted her hands from underneath Hades's. "No touch that provides me comfort. Please let me return to my home."

Hades rose from the table, his chair clattering against the floor, and quit the room. After the sound of his footsteps died away, Persephone stood and walked into her bedchamber. She wouldn't weep. She would do nothing to provoke him to try to comfort her again. Even his kindness was a trap and a lie.

14

DEMETER

Only a few more steps and Demeter would crest the small rise upon which the people of Eleusis had built her temple. It had taken her days to reach it. Something went awry in her use of the God Road, and she emerged from it in Thorikos, all her power depleted by the trip. She had to walk the rest of the way here, each step stoking her rage.

She topped the hill and her temple came into view though it hardly deserved the name. It was a small building made of a mixture of dirt and straw smoothed over a wooden framework. A thatch roof badly in need of repair topped the structure. *This* was her seat of power? It was scarcely better than her hut in Henna.

Pulling open the door, Demeter stepped inside. It took a moment for her eyes to adjust to the dimness within. Better she had stayed blinded. The cracked and faded frescoes on the wall, the crude altar made of piled stones, and the rodent carcasses and dead leaves that littered the floor filled her with inexplicable hilarity. Demeter rode the wave of laughter, shrieking with it. When it finally left her, she walked to the altar, aimed a vicious kick at its base, and toppled it. The Achaeans would never dare dedicate such a hovel to Zeus's worship.

Demeter strode from the building and returned to the edge of the rise. She surveyed the land. What she saw did nothing to ease her anger at the

Eleusinians. Fields surrounded the rise on which her temple sat and all of them abounded with different grains and grasses. Such fertile soil was rare in the hilly, forested country which, for the most part, made up the land of the Achaean people. Yet her followers had allowed everything to grow how and where it liked. No consideration was given to soil quality or water supply or separating the food crops from the choking grass. These fields could produce much more if only they were brought under a skillful hand. That, however, was something to be dealt with later, much later, if at all.

Her first task here was to create the rite that would make it possible for her to send an emissary to the Underworld. Each step must be carefully planned, bound to its purpose, and sealed to the other parts of the rite. It would then coalesce into a whole that should allow a mortal to pass through the Underworld undetected by its master or any of his minions. However, recreating the rite would require an immense amount of power which Demeter didn't, as yet, have.

When Demeter turned back around, a man bent nearly double with age was hobbling toward her temple. Thankfully, she never need experience what it was to live in such an ancient, withered husk. Looking down, she stroked her fingers over the supple skin on her arm. Even her mortal form had regained the youth and beauty it lost during her time in Henna. A small smile on her face, Demeter looked up as the aged man wrestled open the heavy wooden door of her temple.

Demeter quietly slipped in behind him and leaned against the back wall. He looked as though he barely possessed the strength to support his own meager frame, but stone by stone the man reassembled the toppled altar before he laid his meager offering of wheat sheaves on it. Arms extended, palms up, he made proper obeisance. Though the words he mumbled in his gravelly voice were too low for Demeter to hear, the power his worship provided her tingled through her veins even as he spoke.

He finished his petition and turned from the altar, jumping a bit when he saw her. Giving her a nod, he hobbled from the temple. Demeter waited a few moments then followed him as he made his way toward Eleusis.

Scattered buildings flanked either side of the road Demeter traveled. They were mostly hovels squatting next to small parcels of land in which listless crops slumped. The old man entered a hut next to one particularly wretched plot.

Once he was inside, Demeter entered his garden and moved through it, stroking each plant as she went. As she touched them, she encouraged them to sink their roots deep and find the rich damp soil beneath the thin, chalky stuff they clung to now. Each stalk came upright. Curled leaves unfurled and stretched upward. Soon, the little plot boasted a flourishing yield of onions, lentils, beans, and cabbage.

"You there, what are you about?"

Demeter turned at the shout. The man shambled toward her, waving his arms. He stopped abruptly and his eyes widened as he took in the lush plants filling his garden. He shifted his gaze from his crops to her face. This was her moment.

Demeter allowed her Godbody to spring free and encompass her mortal form. Transforming this close to the man would ensure he see her as blazing forth brighter than Helios in his chariot above. Hopefully, he would have the sense not to look at her directly lest he be driven mad.

She pitched her voice to carry above his frightened cries. "I, Demeter, Goddess of Olympus heard your petition and revived your garden so you may live in plenty. Tell all you know of my kindness. Bid them visit my temple, and I shall reward their worship of me in kind."

Then, while the man's eyes were still dazzled by her Godlight, Demeter contracted her Godbody, holding it tightly within the core of herself. The man lay prostrate on the ground, weeping and calling out his thanks. His renewed worship coursed through her veins. Demeter's lips curled in a satisfied smile as she turned and left him.

On the road once more, she paused, looking back at her temple then toward the tightly clustered buildings at the center of Eleusis. Any power she garnered for herself would need to be used on the rite, not on paltry things like food and shelter. She wouldn't reduce herself to slinking about and stealing as she had when she dwelled in the cave in Nysa. She had to find a place for herself here in the mortal world so humans could provide those necessities for her. Turning toward the city, she began walking.

A short distance down the road, a group of people approached. She called out that she saw the Goddess Demeter appear to a man in his garden just up the way. She exhorted them to go and hear the story for themselves. They went, their excited chatter causing those who inhabited the other hovels to peer from their windows or step from their doors. The moment they saw the miracle she wrought, they'd join their worship to that of the man's in hopes of receiving her next boon.

Demeter hadn't gone much farther when her legs went weak, and she staggered. Tingling heat traveled up her limbs into her groin, belly, and chest as wave after wave of power surged through her. She clutched at the low stone wall at the edge of the road for a time before mastering the flood within.

Slightly bloated with her burden of power, she finally straightened. She'd gained a surprising amount from those few mortals' petitions for a boon. The thread of the older man's gratitude for her miracle was a mere trickle by comparison. It seemed mortals worshipped most fervently when in want.

The fields and orchards around Demeter were rife with abundance. There wasn't much lack in this land, and Demeter needed the mortals' most ardent worship to achieve her ends. So she would make them want.

She was too exposed here at the edge of the road to do what she meant. She ducked into the shelter of a nearby orchard. Tucked away in the dimness of the trees' shadows, Demeter closed her eyes then hesitated.

In this pursuit of hers, she would bring grief upon these people akin to what she felt when she learned Persephone had been taken to the Underworld. Yet, what choice did she have? It wasn't to be borne that she, an Olympian, be ravaged by sorrow while these mortals went about their lives untouched by, no, not merely untouched by, but wholly unaware of her plight. She needed their pain and privation in order to ease her own. She would end their suffering when hers ceased.

Eyes still closed, Demeter spread her arms. The sensations of the world around her disappeared. She hung suspended in a cocoon that, while mostly black, glimmered here and there with hints of golden light. With each deep inhale, she drew the essence from the green things around her.

Though it roiled and churned within her, unsettling her stomach, making her heart pound and head ache, Demeter drew life from the plants until, at last, her reservoir of power was depleted, and she could do no more. The plants' essence swirled inside her, its once soothing lullaby now a wailing cacophony.

Demeter lowered her arms and opened her eyes. The trees around her which had been hearty and hale dropped their burden of figs from now wizened branches. A moment later, the trees' leaves fluttered down to cover the fruit. Demeter smiled.

As the trees no longer possessed their leaves, and the plants at the road's edge were all yellowed husks, the remainder of her walk to Eleusis was a hot and dry one. Thankfully, Demeter happened upon a well at the city's edge. Ignoring the mortals who congregated in clusters around it, she hauled up the bucket, scooped a dipperful, and slurped the cool, sweet tasting water. Though her thirst was lessened, it wasn't slaked, and she returned to the bucket for more. As she leaned over the dark pool, she startled and the dipper dropped from her hand.

She whirled. "Hekate?"

Some of the mortals nearest her gave Demeter odd looks before returning to their business.

Demeter turned back to the bucket and looked in. Staring back at her out of her own wide, cerulean eyes was a white-haired, hump-backed crone. Demeter put out a shaking hand, lightly touched the reflection. It wavered, then coalesced once more into a face crisscrossed by wrinkles and marred by brown spots.

Demeter's hand, which still hovered over the water's surface, was also wrinkled, dotted with age spots, and her fingers were gnarled and swollen at the joints. It appeared as withered and depleted as the vegetation along the road to Eleusis. But she had been youthful, resplendent when she'd stood outside her temple not so very long ago.

Demeter peered once more into the bucket. The old woman, blue eyes blinking rapidly in consternation, stared up at her. With a cry, Demeter shoved the bucket off the edge of the well.

She spun away. At the abrupt motion, her hip spasmed. Demeter sank down on a nearby rock. She shouldn't be in such pain. Only a crone such as she saw in the well would experience this kind of agony from such a simple act.

Something deep inside Demeter began to quake. She clenched her gut, pushing her fists against it. The trembling moved to her limbs, her face, her lips. The hollow where her heart rested throbbed, raw and hot. She pressed a fist to her chest, but the pulsing heat simply swelled around it. If she couldn't contain this agony, her mortal shell would be forced to give ground, revealing the Goddess under her mortal flesh. She couldn't show her true self, not here, not now. She had to release at least some of the anguish or be exposed before she could accomplish what she must in this place. She flung her head back and called out, a wordless, wild, ululating call of pain and grief as tears coursed down her face.

"Old Mother. Old Mother."

In her storm of grief, Demeter hardly heard the voice. Soft hands touched her arm, her face. "Old Mother?"

Demeter looked in the direction of the voice. A pale oval face framed by red hair shimmered at Demeter through the veil of her tears.

"Persephone?" Demeter struck the moisture from her eyes, tried to get to her feet but her hip spasmed once more, and she sank to the ground.

Eyes now clear, she sought her daughter's face.

A thicket of maids stood in front of her. Had her sister Goddesses heard her cry and come to render aid? No. This one had a nose too long for her face, that one cheeks like a squirrel with its pouches stuffed with nuts. The tallest of them was too broad through the hips and the one who appeared to be the youngest much too slim. Though they were lovely young women, they lacked the cohesive perfection of Olympus's creatures. And none of them was her Persephone.

"Are you well, Old Mother? May we aid you?" the one with the too long nose asked.

Clutching at the side of the well, Demeter gathered her legs beneath her. A flock of white hands fluttered around her, settling on her forearms, elbows, waist, and back, and helped Demeter stand. Once she was on her feet, the young women released her and stepped back.

Demeter straightened her tunic, and grunted a grudging thank you, but the maidens didn't move off. Instead, the long-nosed one said, "I am Kallithoe and these are my sisters, Kleisidike, Kallidike, and Demo. We're glad we were able to be of service to you, Old Mother."

"Are you a nursemaid?" Kallidike asked.

"You do have that look about you, Aged One," Kallithoe agreed. "One who hasn't children of her own, one who has never worn garlands in your hair in hope of finding love. My father Keleus employs many such women in his palace."

Demeter dropped her gaze. The water in the well hadn't told her an untruth. She did look like a crone, forsaken by both love and childbearing. Well, and so should she. She was betrayed in love by the one who took her child from her.

The quaking began again, low in her belly. Demeter clenched her jaw and breathed deep, bringing it in check. Kallithoe's words, though cruel, provided a possible way for Demeter to obtain a reliable source of shelter in Eleusis. Demeter couldn't risk losing the girls' goodwill by indulging in any more wild displays of emotion.

"Who are you and where are you from, Old Mother?" Kallithoe asked.

Demeter had to answer these questions most carefully if her plan was to work.

In Henna, the Sicani had no reason to recognize Demeter's name, and so she used it freely. Here, in this city, among the only people who had erected a temple in her honor, if she gave the maidens her true name, they would know her for who and what she was. She wanted the power her followers' worship would provide, but if it became known she was in the city in the flesh they would seek her out personally to beg boons of her. She had no intention of being mired down in their endless pleas and petitions while she strove for Persephone's freedom.

Since Demeter meant to play the role of a beggared crone in disguise and make a life out of caring for someone else's child, she would take the name of another who had done the same.

"Greetings, maidens. My name is Doso. I pray our meeting brings you pleasure and happiness. I hail from ..." Demeter paused. She had to provide a place far enough away that they would understand why she wouldn't wish to take upon the rigors of a return journey. The hazy expanse of the sea drew Demeter's gaze. Surely, they wouldn't expect a woman so aged to wish to sail to a far-off island. "Crete," she finished.

If Demeter wanted a position at the palace, it wouldn't be enough to provide only her name and where she was from. She needed to give a good reason why she came to Eleusis with no family or friends to take her in. If she didn't, the girls would likely assume she was a used-up concubine or runaway slave, unsuitable for anything but the meanest work in their father's palace.

Demeter continued. "I was taken from my home by pirates."

The girls gasped.

"They didn't land near this place," Demeter hurried to add. "But at Thorikos. I stole away from them so they couldn't sell me as a slave and traveled overland. That's how I came to be here, though I know not where I am or who lives in this land."

Kallithoe took Demeter's hand in her own, her eyes shining with unshed tears. "I'm sorry for your plight, Doso, but be assured your travail is at an end. You're in Eleusis, which is under the rule of our father, Keleus."

Demeter hid her wince of pain at Kallithoe's grip behind a tremulous smile. "You spoke of many women, nursemaids like myself, who are employed in your father's house, but surely four such fine young maidens need no looking after. Is there, however, another household that does have children to care for, a babe perhaps, new to this world?" Though it was a falsehood, Demeter added, "I'm wise in the ways of herblore and know many things to make a child grow straight and strong. I also spin and weave, launder and cook. I know much of women's work."

It wasn't Kallithoe but Demo who replied. She smiled shyly at Demeter before saying to her sisters, "The wives of those who manage the palace, most especially our dear mother, Metaneira, wouldn't deny one as aged and wise as this woman a position in our household. Sisters, let us go to our mother and tell her of Doso's troubles. Surely, she'll give Doso a place."

Demo turned back to Demeter, her timidity leaving her as she warmed to her subject. "Our mother has a dear son, born very late to her. If you raised him well using your herblore to ensure he grows strong until his coming of age, our mother's generosity in thanking you for doing so would make you the envy of every other servant in Eleusis."

"Come, Doso," Kallidike said. "And we'll away to our father's palace."

Demeter struggled to keep pace with their youthful legs as they walked. The plants' essence roiled in her gut and every part of her body ached and twinged with each step. The heat made it all even more intolerable. Thankfully, they only had to travel a short distance. The cool interior of the palace was a welcome relief.

Demeter followed the maidens, whose laughter and chatter now echoed off high stone ceilings, up a staircase, and down a long hallway decorated with brightly colored frescoes, a gratifying number of which depicted Demeter granting boons to her supplicants.

The maidens turned into a room near the end of the hallway. Demeter paused on the threshold. A number of women sat inside, some carding, some spinning, some doing embroidery, and one seated at a great loom that clacked as she wove. At the rear of the chamber sat a woman in a high-backed chair. Her masses of auburn hair indicated she was the mother of the four maidens who showed Demeter such kindness. This was Metaneira, then.

The woman cradled a babe to her breast, her head bowed over it. A tuft of red-gold hair was just visible above the edge of the blanket in which the infant was wrapped. A tiny fist emerged from the blanket, unfurling against the milk-white skin of the woman's breast. Pain carved through Demeter like an undammed river loosed into its former course. Demeter had to contain it. This was no better place to let it overwhelm her than in the city square next to the well.

Ignorant of her struggle, the maidens babbled to their mother all the reasons Demeter would be well suited as a nursemaid for their brother.

Metaneira turned her eyes on Demeter. "I'll give you my very throne, Doso, if you can keep my boy in the way you claim."

Her boy. Not my girl, Demeter told herself, but it did nothing to ease the throbbing ache in her breast.

"I'll do what I can," Demeter gasped out.

"You're ill, Old Mother," Metaneira said.

"The heat, only the heat," Demeter managed. If Metaneria thought Demeter unwell, Demeter would be turned out of the palace immediately.

"Of course. I'll have Iambe show you your quarters and you may rest there for a time before attending upon Demophon." Metaneira turned her head and called, "Iambe."

Bare feet slapped unevenly against the plaster floor. Demeter looked toward the sound. A small, dark-haired woman with a twisted torso and legs of uneven length hitched her way to Metaneira's side. Demeter shuddered. This woman was more malformed than Hephaistos.

"Iambe, take Doso to the women's quarters. Show her where she may rest."

"Yes, Lady," Iambe said and turned to Demeter. "This way."

Iambe led Demeter through several corridors and into a long narrow room crowded with rows of low beds. All were unoccupied, but from the items placed upon and around them, all looked to have been claimed by one or another of the palace's women servants.

"I haven't a bed ready for you yet. Do you wish to sit while I make one up?" Iambe asked.

Demeter nodded. She was weary and so burdened by grief she could scarcely stay upright.

"Wait here," Iambe instructed. "I'll return momentarily."

True to her word, the woman came back quickly with a low stool in hand. After placing it at Demeter's side, she opened one of the chests that sat against the wall, withdrew a fleece, and draped it over the seat.

Demeter sank down onto the cushion of wool and put a hand to the ache that still throbbed within her breast.

"Have you need of anything more?" Iambe asked. "Wine? Water? Some food perhaps?"

"Barley water with pennyroyal," Demeter requested, her voice cracking.

The little woman limped away, and Demeter was alone. At last. She hunched forward. Her grief took her then, surpassing the capacity of her mortal form. Her Godlight spewed forth, pulsing to the rhythm of her throbbing heart. From without the room came startled cries.

Demeter wouldn't be alone for much longer. She had to master herself and quickly. She drew in her breath, over and over, her Godlight dimming with each inhale. As running feet approached the room in which Demeter sat, the golden illumination ebbed, shrank, then winked out altogether. When Metaneira, her daughters and the other women from the throne room burst in on Demeter, she turned a baffled face to them and their enquiries about the blaze of brilliance they'd witnessed. The women soon moved on in their search for an explanation of the radiance.

After they left, Demeter curled forward, forehead to knees, and wept once more for all she had lost and all that had been taken from her.

15

PERSEPHONE

Over the thudding of Lethe's hooves and the bellow of his breath, Persephone heard Hades calling her name. She tightened her thighs on Lethe's body and leaned forward, urging him to greater speed.

A whistle pierced the air, one short, sharp note, different from the long tone Hades used to call his horses back to him. Lethe bounced to a halt. Even with her legs clenched around the barrel of Lethe's belly, Persephone's buttocks rose at the quick stop.

Huffing out a frustrated breath, Persephone shifted her position as Styx drew up to them, Hades on his back. In the nearly thirty days since Hades revealed to her the power of the lodestone, perhaps in an effort to curtail any further escape attempts, he had restricted their daily rides to the area directly behind the palace. Today, at last, he suggested they venture farther and so, for the first time since her first ride on Lethe, Persephone was again at the river that flowed through Elysium.

A ride along its bank could reveal to her another exit from this place. She wasn't sure how she could use that knowledge once she had it, as the lodestone and Cerberus were obstacles still to be dealt with, but knowing the way out would be a step, at least, on the road to freedom. Yet, here was Hades, once again, to thwart her. Persephone twined her fingers in Lethe's mane until the thick, coarse strands bit into her flesh.

"We've been a-horseback for a long while. It's time to rest and eat." Hades flung his leg over Styx's back and slid to the ground in one fluid motion. Then he walked to Lethe's side and reached up.

Persephone drew a leg over Lethe's withers, her momentum carrying her from Lethe's back into Hades's waiting arms. Since the night he had come upon her unclothed in the bathing pool, she no longer feared he would do her violence. What did disturb her were the thoughts that came to her on occasion as she drifted between waking and sleep. Memories of the way Hades's callused palms rasped against her skin, of his somber smiles, of his patience when he instructed her in the finer points of horsemanship, of laughter they shared over Lethe's antics, turned into dreams in which Hades touched and tasted Persephone in ways she hadn't yet experienced. She would wake from these nighttime forays, breathless and needful and despising herself for feeling that way.

It was this that made her too hasty as she stepped away from Hades, breaking his grip on her before she was entirely steady on her feet. She stumbled as she stepped back, then tripped and fell.

Hades reached for her, but she scrambled up before he could assist her.

"Is my touch still so loathsome to you?" Hades burst out. "You won't even allow me to aid you. Though this land I rule is monstrous, I am not a monster, Persephone. Can you not see that?"

Taken aback, Persephone blinked rapidly. Almost involuntarily she put a hand out, reaching for Hades, but he was already moving away from her. He lifted a small pack from Styx's back then walked to the river.

After a moment's hesitation, Persephone followed him, Lethe plodding along at her side. At the river's edge, Hades hunkered down on a log which lay on spit of rock and sand extending into the water.

Persephone sidestepped down the bank, her feet clacking on the stones when she reached the small peninsula. She paused and Lethe continued past her, over the rocky beach and into the water.

"I have food should you desire it," Hades said, his gaze never leaving the river.

Persephone picked her way to him then paused, rubbing at the soft embroidery on the bottom of her tunic. The length of the log necessitated that, should she sit there, parts of her would touch parts of Hades.

Hades glanced up at her, looked down, shook his head and then stood, leaving the small packet of cheese, bread and apples where they lay.

"Sit. I'll not molest you, though you seem determined not to believe me."

"Why should I...?" Persephone began then though better of it. She would likely only anger him if she explained how his actions her first night in his palace gave her every reason to question his veracity.

Ducking the sharp look Hades gave her, she sat and reached for the cheese, though she wasn't in the least bit hungry. She toyed with the food, every so often glancing up at Hades as he watched Lethe pawing at the water with one hoof.

"What river is this?" she asked when the silence between them spun out far too long for her comfort.

"Lethe," Hades responded, gaze still on his horse.

Persephone contemplated for a moment, then said, "There's a River Lethe, a horse Lethe, a River Styx, a horse Styx. Is there also a River Akheron and a River Phlegethon?"

Hades nodded. "There's a fifth river as well. A God much older than the Olympians dwells there. He's called Kokytos and the river bears his name, just as the other rivers bear the names of the Immortals who rule them, though none dwell belowground save Kokytos."

"Do you associate with him? Could I meet him?" Persephone asked, trying to keep from her voice the sudden surge of hope she felt at this revelation that another God lived in this place, and perhaps one with power of his own to aid Persephone in her escape.

Hades's attention remained on Lethe. "Kokytos and I were friends for a time but things ... went ill between us and I haven't seen him for many a year. He doesn't welcome my visits now."

Like wine pouring into a cup, despair filled Persephone. If she indulged in it, however, Hades would retreat behind his wall of reserve and they would spend the rest of their time at the river in silence. The quiet in this place under the looming red sky weighed heavily, so she asked, "Why did you choose to call your horses by the rivers' names?"

Hades finally looked at Persephone, his voice warming as he spoke of his steeds. "Lethe, so named because the relief I take in his company matches the mercy that river's waters afford my subjects; Styx because he's steady, but possesses lethal strength; Akheron, the river of sorrow that matches the melancholy that seems always to be in my mount's eyes, and Phlegethon, for the river of fire is the best match for a burning soul that refuses to be tamed.

"Did you catch the horses in this place or did you bring them with you when you first arrived?" Persephone asked.

"Neither."

"How did you come by your steeds then?"

A slight smile curved Hades's lips, and his eyes lost their shadowed depth, lightening to a clear gray. "Helios brought them to me after I had been here for some time. They're sons of his chargers, though only half Immortal. He also provided me my chariot."

"And how did you come to be in this place?" Persephone asked.

Hades's eyes darkened again. His gaze traveled over Lethe, then the river before moving to the opposite bank. Finally, he said, "It was allotted to me."

"By whom?"

Hades stooped, picked up a handful of rocks from the beach and began hurling them one-by-one into the river. "Zeus, Poseidon, and I, with our mother's help, overthrew our father and his cohorts, beings known as the Titans, who ruled this world before us. When the battle was over and those of the Titans who refused to accept our reign were safely ensconced in Tartarus, Zeus decreed we should draw lots to decide which of us would rule the different realms. He believed the Moirai would direct our hand to choose the domain to which we were most suited. He put three stones, one blue for the sea, one white for the heavens, one black for the Underworld, in a pouch. As the eldest of my brothers, I put my hand in first and drew out the black stone. Three stones for choosing, and I drew the dark one. There was no denying it was my fate. So, I came to this land while Poseidon plucked out the blue stone and departed for his watery depths leaving the white stone and the sky to Zeus."

Hades didn't seem to share Demeter's reticence when it came to the Immortals. There was so much Persephone could learn from him, so much she longed to know. "What of the other Gods and Goddesses? What of my mother? Was she part of this battle against the Titans? Why did she not draw lots with you?"

"Six of us, including your mother, battled the Titans. We were the first and founding Olympians. After we brothers drew lots, Zeus granted Hera, Hestia, and Demeter dominion over different aspects of the mortal realm. The others who dwell on Olympus now are, for the most part, my siblings' children. Zeus has given most of them various stewardships also."

"Why do you not dwell on Olympus with them?" Persephone asked.

Hades said nothing, only flung his last stone into the river. It soon became apparent he didn't mean to answer her. If she pressed him on the matter, he would likely retreat even further behind his stony wall of silence. Best to ask about a different subject. "Why does Zeus decree all these things? And why do you obey? Surely, he has no more power than you or Poseidon or any of the rest."

Hades remained silent, but just as Persephone decided he didn't intend to answer this query either, he said, "When he was born, Zeus, like the rest of us, possessed only the Immortal abilities inherited from our parents. Our mother Rhea, however, favored Zeus as her youngest child and plotted to allow him to remain free from the..." Hades paused and bent to collect another handful of stones. He lobbed one of them into the river before continuing, "confines in which our father Kronos kept the rest of us. Zeus later freed us and for that, we were grateful. Our gratitude gave him dominion over us, and so we must all bend to his will."

"In what confines did your father keep you?" Persephone asked. Demeter had, as one of the six original Olympians, been in that captivity with Hades. Being imprisoned by her father had surely influenced her.

Just then, Lethe flung up his head and curved his neck to look in Persephone and Hades's direction. He neighed so vigorously his entire body shook. Persephone turned to see what so excited the horse. Near the palace, a flash, like her father's lightning, but a rich golden color, streaked across the red haze of the sky.

"His stomach," Hades said, as he entered the river and splashed his way to Lethe's side.

It took a moment for Persephone to realize the cryptic comment was Hades's response to her question, but the words made no sense. *His stomach*? Kronos had kept his children in his stomach? Held them in his grumbling guts, like a birth turned horribly backward? Though it seemed incomprehensible, the stark expression on Hades's face, the flatness of his voice when he said it, testified to the truthfulness of his words. And her mother had been kept there, too. It was almost too horrific to contemplate.

Out in the river, Hades murmured to Lethe while rubbing at the base of his ears, though it didn't appear the horse was the one in need of soothing. After a time, Hades turned back to face Persephone. "We should return to the palace. It grows dark and, though he'll like as not leave before we arrive, Hermes is there and may need to speak to me."

The gold flash she'd seen must have informed Hades of Hermes's arrival, but it was a mystery how Hades knew nighttime approached. The light had changed not one whit from what it was when Persephone woke that morning.

With Lethe at his side, Hades emerged from the river, his wet tunic clinging to his loins and the muscles in his upper thighs.

Persephone's gaze lingered there for a moment before she looked up. Heat prickled across her chest and rose into her neck and face when she found Hades's eyes on her.

"Shall I aid you to mount or would you prefer to do so on your own?" he asked.

Persephone looked down at her palms, the scrapes from her earlier fall still stinging a little. Her lips quirked. She looked up at Hades. Something like a smile tugged at the corners of his mouth as well.

Persephone rose from the log. "I would welcome your help."

Hades stepped forward, put his hands about her waist, and lifted her. Usually, he allowed his hand to linger on her upper thigh or ankle before moving away. This time, however, he released her the moment she was safely aboard Lethe. As he always should have done. There was no reason for him to delay, no reason why, in the absence of his touch, her belly should plunge and the smile slide from her face.

She touched her heels to Lethe's sides, then twined her fingers in his mane and tightened her legs around his belly as the horse lunged up the riverbank. A few moments later, the clomp of Styx's feet behind her told her Hades followed.

Their earlier conversation had been so fascinating. She hoped Hades would continue it on the ride back to the palace, but he didn't urge his horse forward to ride next to her as was his wont. Instead, Persephone signaled Lethe to slow until Hades came even with them. Then she asked, "Did you speak much to my mother in the time you were together in your father's stomach? Did she say how she felt? What she thought?"

Hades's profile was stark against the red sky as he said, "I would gladly answer any of your other questions regarding your mother or the other Olympians, but I won't speak of the time before Zeus freed us."

Persephone looked down. She shouldn't have asked. It had been apparent on the riverbank his memories from that time were painful ones. Yet, his remonstrance had been gentle. He hadn't shouted at her for inquiring or told her to get out of his sight as Demeter had so often when Persephone asked what she believed to be an innocent question about her own or her mother's origins. He hadn't lost his temper a single time over the past month as he'd instructed her in how to become a better rider. He even tried to comfort her with his own strange methods when he thought her distressed. This God, this man, had in many ways, been kinder and more patient than her own mother. And yet, he'd still taken her captive, still made her submit to his hands and body her first night in his realm. The contradiction didn't bear thinking about. Not now. Perhaps not ever. Easier to let him fill her head with the knowledge of the Immortals that had been so long denied to her rather than these confusing thoughts, but she would allow him to choose the subject matter so their talk wouldn't distress him.

"I would like to know anything you'd care to tell me about the Immortals, my mother especially."

This time he did look at her as he responded. "The only things I know firsthand of your mother are those I learned during the war with the Titans and my infrequent visits to Olympus after coming to live in this land. All further knowledge I have of her and the other Immortals is what I've heard from Hekate and the tales Hermes sometimes provides. Occasionally, I come by information from other sources, though not often. Will secondhand accounts satisfy your curiosity?"

Persephone nodded eagerly, and Hades obliged her with story after story about her mother; Demeter's beauty, her wit, her power, her relationships with the other Olympians. His responses led Persephone to ask more questions about the Immortals and the place where most of them dwelled. He answered each one in great detail. She soon found herself riding the swell of Hades's words far beyond the dank land she traversed, even to the very heights of Olympus.

At his completion of the tale of Zeus's seduction of Leda, Persephone asked, "Do the other Gods and Goddesses spend as much time among mortals as Zeus?"

Hades gave her a smile edged with the indulgent look that always called Doso to Persephone's mind. "It would please me if you took as much of an interest in my realm as you do in the Olympians. Surely, if you came to know as much about it as you seem intent on learning about the Immortals, you couldn't help but find yourself content here, for in understanding it, you would lose your fear of it."

As swiftly as night arrived in the Underworld, gone was Persephone's enjoyment of their conversation. The sky seemed to press down, the far reaches of its horizons contract until she felt she could touch them should she so wish. She struggled to draw breath.

Hades continued speaking, but his words passed over her like mist. She worried at his comment as Phlox so often gnawed at his fleas. Then, as though some clever weaver climbed in her ear and drew the threads of her thoughts together into a bright cloth of hope, a plan came to Persephone.

She would encourage Hades to take her over all of this land, and as he did so, she'd seek out an exit. She'd feign interest in his realm in hopes he would think her to be striving for contentment. When she gained his trust, and he believed her to be happy here, she would ask him if she could take Lethe out unescorted. Then she would ride for the route of escape she found and hope that Lethe's great heart and long legs were enough to outpace Cerberus.

It wasn't a perfect plan, nor a quick one. It would take a great deal of time to get Hades to fully trust her. She would have to be patient but her work in the folly would make the days pass faster. It already had. Her hours spent working there seemed to go by in but the flicker of an eye.

She'd already ascertained the light from the chariot wheel did indeed fade to nothingness during the night so that was one problem taken care of. Varying the water flow was proving to be a bit of a challenge. She'd reconfigured the wooden tubes, blocking some, detaching some, and rerouting others to facilitate differing conditions in the various troughs, but she wasn't yet satisfied with the results. In the evenings after she and Hades dined, she worked on piecing together the drape. Once it was finished, she would still need to contrive a way to hang it in the hut. So much work to accomplish and no way to know if any of it would result in living plants.

Her stomach knotted at the thought. It was entirely possible she could fare worse than Hades had in making this experiment. Though she would be the only one to know of her failure, it would matter very much to her if she didn't succeed. Very much.

The same pulse of golden light Persephone had seen earlier pulled her from her thoughts. A dark object, which looked as though it had been propelled from the palace roof appeared in the sky, dwindled, then disappeared altogether.

"Hermes departs," Hades said.

"He didn't wish to keep company with you?"

Hades laughed, a short harsh sound. "Hermes seldom stays long in my realm. He made an exception at his last visit in order to meet you. As his curiosity regarding you is now satisfied and he's never taken much pleasure in my presence, I imagine it shall be some time before he finds reason to linger here again."

"You've less companionship in this place than you did in your father's belly," Persephone observed.

Hades jerked as though she had struck him.

Persephone put a hand to her mouth but there was no catching the words, no way to unsay them.

Hades tightened his legs about Styx's belly, leaned over the horse's neck and whispered 'tcha.' Styx sprang into a gallop. Lethe followed suit.

She had offended Hades, hurt him, and he had retreated from her, but for how long? How long before he raged at her the way Demeter would when Persephone said something imprudent? And would he only use words to wound? Or would he also strike her as Demeter sometimes had? She would soon find out. There was no escaping him in this realm he ruled. She must face her punishment, no matter how harsh. Sweat dampened Persephone's palms and she had to tighten her grip on Lethe's mane so the strands wouldn't slip through her fingers.

When Persephone brought Lethe to a halt at the rear entrance of the stables, Hades had already alighted from Styx's back. He came to her and lifted his arms. There was no anger in his expression, nothing to indicate he intended any kind of retribution.

Persephone slid from Lethe's back into Hades's waiting hands. He touched her carefully, let her go the moment her feet were steady on the ground, then turned away, his movements jerky, stiff, not with anger but with pain.

Persephone grasped his hand, arresting his movement. "I beg pardon, Hades. I shouldn't have been so thoughtless."

He turned back, his gaze fixed on her hand which still held his.

Then he raised his eyes to hers. They were alight with amazement. The wonder in them was a reflection of all Persephone felt when Ianthe had touched her in the Mother Goddess's Meadow.

"I thank you for the apology." He gave a small laugh. "I believe it's the first I've ever received."

From inside the stable, Styx gave a demanding stomp of his hoof. Hades looked over his shoulder, then looked back at Persephone. "I'd best attend to him."

Persephone released Hades, and he moved inside. The memory of the awe in his face, the clear gray of his eyes, like the sky just before dawn, the way the ridges of his knuckles felt against her palm would visit her as she slipped into sleep tonight, would perhaps chase her into her dreams. What would she do with him then, when there was no Styx to break the moment?

Lethe nudged her shoulder, impatient for his hay. Giving her head a rueful shake, Persephone patted him, then walked into the stable. As she entered, a glimmer of light in a small alcove at one side of Phlegethon's stall caught her eye. Persephone peered into the tangle of leather straps hanging from the wall there. The bronze head of an arrow winked at her from the shadows.

Persephone reached forward and drew it from the midst of the jumbled harness pieces. As she did so, something clattered to the floor. She looked down. A bow, its stave resting just beyond the tip of her sandal lay at her feet. She bent and picked it up. Putting the arrow aside, she traced the sinuous curve of the wood, twanged the string with one finger.

She reclaimed the arrow, touched the tip, and a spot of blood welled immediately. The bow seemed to be in good condition and the arrow was sharp, sharp enough to pierce anything, perhaps even the hide of a three-headed dog. Not lethal, not for that animal, but perhaps potent enough to discourage pursuit.

Recalling what she could of the archers in Henna, Persephone nocked the arrow, lifted the bow and drew back the string.

"I'd forgotten those," Hades said from behind her.

Persephone flinched, the feathered shaft dropping from her fingers as she turned. "They're yours?"

Hades bent to collect the arrow then offered it to her. "Rhea gave them to me during the war. I've little use for such things here. I put them away and never thought more about them. Do you hunt?"

"I never learned. Such weapons were forbidden to Sicani women."

"You aren't Sicani, and we aren't in Henna." Hades said, then reached behind her, his chest brushing hers. She drew in a sharp breath. He stepped back quickly, begged her pardon, and asked her to move aside.

After she did, he put a hand into the alcove, extracted a quiver full of arrows, and handed them to her.

Persephone riffled through the shafts, the feathers at their ends pricking her fingertips. Her lips curved into a smile. She handed Hades the bow, put the quiver strap over her head, and adjusted it until it rested comfortably between her breasts. She reclaimed the bow from Hades and walked out of the stable into the long grass of Elysium.

A good distance from the rear of the palace, Persephone stopped, nocked the arrow, and lifted the bow so the arrow's fletching was in line with her cheek. She sighted down the shaft at an asphodel then released the string. It twanged against her inner elbow, sending white-hot agony racing down her arm. She jerked and cried out in pain. The shot went wild, and Persephone dropped the bow from a hand gone numb.

"Such a fool," she muttered through clenched teeth as she bent to collect the bow.

"May I offer instruction?"

She looked at Hades over her shoulder, hesitated, gave him a brief nod.

"Nock the arrow and draw back the string as you did before."

Looking forward again, Persephone did as he asked. Her hands shook so the arrow wavered and danced against the string. She wasn't a fool. She wasn't. With Hades as her teacher, she had learned to ride. She could master this, too. Her hands stilled and the arrow settled into position.

Hades circled around until he was in front of her and surveyed her with narrowed eyes. "You need to remove your littlest finger from the string. That's likely what sent your last shot astray."

Persephone curled her pinky away from the bow.

Stepping out of the way, Hades said, "Select a target and aim, but don't shoot."

Persephone sighted down the arrow at the same asphodel.

Hades moved to her side. He grabbed the stave of the bow and pulled it down a bit. "Is the tip of the arrow at the base of your target now?"

"It is."

Hades nodded. "Always aim slightly low. You have to compensate for the difference between your eye and the level at which you hold the arrow. Now let fly."

Persephone released the string. It moved smoothly past her inner arm without impacting it, but the arrow still flew wide of her target. She made a frustrated noise in the back of her throat and lowered the bow.

"It's no simple thing to learn archery, Persephone. Be easy with yourself."

"What did I do wrong?"

"I can show you but it will require that I touch you. May I?"

He'd never requested permission before, simply put his hands on her as if it was his right. It was odd to be asked, though very welcome. She nodded, but her heart still sped up, thundering against her ribs as he circled behind her.

He aligned himself with her, reached around and adjusted her fingers on the bowstring. "Ease your grip. When you let the arrow go, simply open your fingers. Holding too hard and too long sends the tip of the arrow astray."

He moved her hips, turning them slightly. Her buttocks were pressed against his groin. His hands at her waist anchored her there. His warmth radiated through the cloth of her tunic. She shifted against him, and his breath, which stirred the hair at her temple, ceased for a moment. A pulse of heat shot through her at the catch in his throat. She pushed herself more firmly into the cradle of his hips. He made an odd sound. His hands slid forward, snugging her in even tighter. Her breath came short. She wanted him to do ... something, but she wasn't sure what. Instead, his hands fell away, and he stepped back.

Cloth rasped against skin. Then he cleared his throat and instructed her to pick a target.

Persephone's attention had shifted completely from the task at hand. She had to gather it back in like a skein of unspooled yarn, reclaiming it from the parts of her body that still blazed from contact with his.

Finally, focused once more, she adjusted her grip on the bowstring and sighted down the arrow. She lowered the bow a bit and, without tightening her grip, opened her fingers to release the string. The arrow grazed the side of the asphodel she was aiming at. It rocked from the contact. She turned to look at Hades.

The smile on his face echoed her own. "Better. Try again."

Persephone took another arrow from the quiver and nocked it. She waited, but Hades made no move to adjust her position as he had before. Finally, releasing a small sigh, she aimed.

The arrow flew from the bow and her target exploded into a shower of velvet petals. She let out a shout a triumph. It was a good hit, but one of Cerberus's six eyeballs would be likely prove a harder target. And a bloodier one, much like the wound that had maimed Phlox. Her mind recoiled, and she lowered the bow.

"A pity Artemis couldn't be the one to teach you," Hades said. You seem a student worthy of her skill."

One corner of her lip curling up, Persephone turned to face Hades. "I proved a poor pupil to my mother. Artemis would likely find me lacking as well."

"Perhaps the lack was in the teacher, not the student."

Persephone's throat convulsed. The breath she drew burned as it traveled to her lungs. For a moment she couldn't speak. When she finally did, it was only to say, "I should attend to Lethe now."

She extended the bow toward Hades.

"Keep it if it pleases you."

Hades would be the one to extract any arrow with which she hit Cerberus. It would be he who would have to hear the crack of bone, the grinding of gristle, the howl of agony as he tore the head free from his friend's hide. Continuing to hold the bow out to him, she shook her head. "I thank you, but no."

Hades passed a hand over his eyes, said softly, "Do what you will with it then. Put it with the clothes you refuse to garb yourself in and the jewelry you won't wear. It makes no matter to me."

Then he turned and, head lowered, walked toward the stable. Persephone watched him go. There was nothing she could say, no explanation she could give for her refusal of his gifts that wouldn't wound him more.

16

DEMETER

Using her toe, Demeter nudged the body on the floor of her temple. The man flopped to his back, eyes turned to jelly by the heat of the fire, skin blackened and smoking. Another failure. She bent, heaved the corpse over her shoulder, and grunting, straightened.

Carrying the body, Demeter strode to the door of her temple, opened it, and stepped into the night. At the edge of the rise on which her temple sat, she stopped and pitched the corpse over. It landed with a loud whump. Quieter thuds and thumps told Demeter it was rolling its way to the bottom.

It had taken her a month to create, bind, and seal the ritual as well as seek out three men she thought would do as emissaries. All had balked when she instructed them to step into the fire. All had burned to death when she forced them to it. Her rite, or at least this portion, it seemed, could not be performed on an unwilling participant.

Demeter looked down the slope into the darkness. Now that the third man had failed, Demeter had very little hope that a fourth or a tenth or a hundredth would put himself into the heart of the flame with no coercion on her part. Despite Hekate's belief to the contrary, there was no mortal who possessed the necessary courage, wit, and strength to pass through Demeter's rite, to say nothing of passing through the

Underworld to bring Persephone safely home.

Weary and aching from the constant strain of keeping the plants' essence contained within, Demeter turned and slogged her way to Keleus's palace. Once there, she went to the women's quarters, settled onto the creaking leather straps of her bed, and drifted into a haze of sleep.

"Lady?"

Iambe was the only one in the palace that called Demeter 'lady.' Demeter sighed and kept her eyes closed as she said, "Yes."

"Do you require anything before I take my rest?"

Demeter shook her head.

"No barley water with pennyroyal, then? I swear to you this time I'll not take a drink for myself. I learned better the first time I brought you that awful concoction."

Demeter opened her eyes and gave Iambe a wry smile. The day Demeter arrived in the palace, Iambe had stayed silent and unseen by Demeter's side until the worst of her storm of grief passed. Then Iambe turned all number of tricks and made all number of crude jests, including bending over and baring her buttocks, to jolly Demeter from her sadness. None of it affected Demeter in the least. Finally, conceding defeat, Iambe gave Demeter the drink she had requested. When Iambe proffered the cup, she took a sip to show Demeter the drink wasn't poisoned. Her face twisted into an expression of such unadulterated disgust at the bitterness of the draught that Demeter burst into peal after peal of laughter. Since then, Iambe had been Demeter's constant companion, trailing her, asking after her needs, always ready with a jest or a riddle when Demeter felt her heavy heart begin to show on her face as it likely did now.

Iambe settled herself on the stool next to Demeter's bed, cocked her head, and regarded Demeter with her bright brown eyes. Demeter prepared herself for some sally, but Iambe only said, "Why do you prefer that drink above all others?"

Demeter considered the woman. There was no harm in telling her the truth. "To remind me those things we find sweetest can turn bitter in but an instant."

Iambe laughed, a short, harsh sound, then leaned forward and clasped Demeter's hand between both of her own. Demeter tried to pull away, but Iambe held fast.

"I've watched you this last month, Lady, and I believe we are akin in our suffering. Trust me. Let me be your friend."

Iambe hadn't the speed, strength, or stealth necessary to spirit Persephone away from the Underworld, and surely hadn't the courage to walk through fire. Yet, she might prove useful.

Demeter put her other hand on top of Iambe's. "I seek an emissary. One who is strong, fearless, and has his wits about him. One who would let flames consume him should I ask. One who would brave the depths of the Underworld if I commanded. Can you find me such a man?"

Iambe regarded her for a long moment, then said, "I don't know, Lady, but I would try, for you."

"Doso!"

Demeter started at the summons, looking toward the door.

Kallithoe stood there, eyes wide, hair in disarray. "You must come. Quickly. Demophon is dying."

"Dying?" Demeter got to her feet and approached the girl. "How can that be?"

Kallithoe waited for Demeter to reach her before saying, "Mother hasn't been able to take proper sustenance. There simply isn't enough food because of the famine. Her milk has ceased to flow and there are no wet nurses in Eleusis with any to spare. Demophon will perish for a lack of nourishment. I thought you with your knowledge of herblore would have a draught of some kind to sustain him. Can you make such a thing?"

"I can, yes," Demeter lied.

"Gods be thanked. Let us hurry then. Hurry!"

When Demeter reached Metaneira's chambers, a bevy of weeping nursemaids clogged the doorway. Demeter pushed through them and stopped. Metaneira held Demophon to her breast but his head lolled there, lips slack, eyes lusterless, so weakened he no longer even attempted to nurse from Metaneira's empty pap.

Demeter huffed a sigh of irritation. If the boy died, she would be turned from the palace, possibly hounded from the city. Even if she wasn't, none would employ the woman who let the queen's son perish. Demeter would have no choice but to use her power to clothe and keep herself. After squandering so much on the men who went to their deaths in the fire, she had none to spare for such paltry concerns.

Demeter strode forward, and reached for the babe. "Give him to me. I'll set him to rights."

Metaneira surrendered the child with great reluctance. She called out a protest as Demeter turned and walked back to the long narrow chamber where she and the other servants slept.

After ascertaining the rest of the room's occupants were slumbering, Demeter sat and laid Demophon's slack body across her knees. Lifting her hand, she closed her eyes and summoned her power. The air above her palm rearranged itself, solidified, and settled.

Demeter opened her eyes and pushed the neck protruding from the side of the small golden vessel that had appeared in her hand between Demophon's lips. Golden liquid bubbled out of his mouth and dribbled down his chin and cheeks. Fear fluttered in Demeter's breast. Then

Demophon gave a tiny gurgling wail, swallowed once, twice, and began to suckle.

Demeter shifted him in her arms. "This is ambrosia, boy. You sup like a God tonight, like my Persephone should have been able to."

She studied the babe as he drank. He was finely built, apt to be a strong, capable man. He took the ambrosia from her hand so trustingly, though it could have just as easily been poison as physick. Were she to kneel and place him in the fire this very moment he would make no sound of protest, no motion of rebellion. If there were a way to preserve in him, as a grown man, the faith he had in her now, he would undoubtedly be the best candidate on which to perform her rite.

Demeter straightened in the chair, almost dropping the ambrosia. Demophon loosed a wail that faded into mumbled complaint as Demeter pushed the vessel between his lips again.

"Fifteen years before you're a man grown. Can I wait so long?" Demeter murmured. "And yet how else to get a mortal to willingly brave the flame?"

"Oh, Gods be praised."

Demeter looked up. Metaneira stood in the doorway, clutching the wall for support. When she met Demeter's eyes, Metaneira staggered forward before sinking to her knees on the floor in front of Demeter. She raised a shaking hand and smoothed it over Demophon's hair.

"Gods be praised," Metaneira said again. "I thank you, Doso, and bless the day my daughters brought you to us."

Demeter nodded in acknowledgement and went back to watching Demophon. He blinked slowly once, twice. The mouth of the vessel slipped from between his slack lips. He turned his head to Demeter's breast, babbling a bit of nonsense as his eyes slipped closed.

Metaneira reached for him, and Demeter gave him up to his mother.

Settling Demophon's sated body against the curve of her own breast, Metaneira asked, "What did you feed him?"

"An herbal infusion."

"An infusion? How did you make it so quickly?" Metaneira asked, reaching for the vessel in Demeter's hand.

Demeter jerked the container out of Metaneira's reach. "It's a special concoction of mine I keep always on hand."

"Whatever it is, I thank you and the Gods you had it ready. You've done much this night, Doso. Take some rest. I shall ask one of the other women to attend Demophon should he have need in the dark hours."

"No, I must do it." Demeter half rose from her chair.

The look Metaneira gave Demeter was sharp and suspicious.

"Demophon's strength isn't replenished yet, and this draught is the only source of nourishment available to him now."

Metaneira held out an imperious hand. "Give it here. I can feed him."

The woman would never believe the ambrosia was a simple herbal infusion if she saw so much as a drop of the golden liquid. Demeter would be revealed, all her plans set awry.

Demeter shook her head. "Nay, let me attend him. It's my pleasure."

Metaneira once again scanned Demeter's face. "Very well. Come to my chambers when you've rested."

With those haughty words, Metaneira quit the room, Demophon nestled against her. Demeter watched them go. It would be difficult to perform the rite on the boy without further arousing Metaneira's suspicions, but Demeter would contrive some way to manage it. She must if Persephone was ever to be returned to her.

17

PERSEPHONE

Narrowing her eyes against the brightness, Persephone pulled open the door of the folly. According to the notches she made in the frame, thirteen days had passed since she'd planted a variety of seeds in the various troughs and pots in the little hut. It had been a little over twice as much time since she'd decided to facilitate her escape by gaining Hades's trust. Neither course of action had come to fruition. That wasn't unexpected; she knew the plan to secure her freedom would take time. As for the seeds, she hadn't enough knowledge to decide when she should admit defeat, but it seemed if something green didn't emerge within the next few days, it likely meant she had failed.

Persephone crossed to the troughs on the table in front of her. Nothing in them except dark, moist dirt. The bridge of her nose burned with threatened tears. She bit her lip to drive them away. It was only soil and water and dried, husks of potential plants. If she accomplished nothing here, it would have no impact on anything of importance but the thought of failure still made her heart ache. All might not yet be lost though. There were still the troughs on the other side of the room, the ones shaded by the drape she constructed and hung from the ceiling before she planted the seeds.

She lifted the swath of material and ducked under it. Even from afar, little dots of green were visible against the soil in the troughs. Persephone let out a cry, then hurried to the closest one. There were only five or six tiny sprouts in it, but they were undeniably there, undeniably alive. She'd done it.

Persephone stretched out one forefinger and stroked a miniscule leaf. Something behind her navel lurched. It was similar to what she felt when Hades touched her now, a sensation that was almost pleasant but still somewhat unsettling. The plant under her finger doubled in size. That was wholly disquieting. Gasping, Persephone drew her hand back.

How had this occurred? It was her mother who had dominion over Gaia's green and growing things. Persephone's only skill seemed to be her ability to mismanage all but the simplest undertakings. And yet, here were these plants, all of which she'd nurtured herself, one of which had grown because she'd merely brushed it with a fingertip. Such a thing had never happened before and she'd touched all manner of flora in her life, though, perhaps, not any seedlings. The only place those were found in abundance were in the fields where her mother purposefully bared the ground so she could cultivate the grain she wished to grow there. Had that been why Demeter denied Persephone access to the fields, not because her mother was concerned Persephone would destroy the crops with her bungling, but that she would be too successful in aiding their growth? No, such a thing couldn't be. Surely, her mother hadn't known of this ability any more than Persephone had.

Persephone reached out to stroke another seedling just as a knock sounded on the door behind her.

"Persephone?" Hades called. "I can ride with you now if you wish."

Persephone turned to look at the door. Hades might have some explanation for why the sprout responded in such a way to her touch. She could bring him in, and show him what she'd achieved here. He'd long been aware of the time she spent in the folly and hadn't barred her access to it. Neither, though, had he asked her what she was about in the little building. His discomfiture when she mentioned it, or when, like today, he summoned her from it was apparent. Likely, his failure within its walls was a source of pain to him, a feeling she understood all too well. No, she wouldn't involve Hades, but she would return later, after their ride, for further experimentation.

With one last glance at the plants, she passed under the drape to the door and pushed it open. "I'm ready."

Hades made no effort to peer behind her, simply spun on his heel and set off for the rear entrance to the stables as he asked, "You're certain the asphodel meadow is where you want to ride today?"

"It is," Persephone answered. It was fortunate he had his back to her. Otherwise, he would have had no trouble discerning the apprehension that was likely inscribed in every line of her visage.

"Then that's where we'll go." He pulled the door to the stable open and disappeared inside.

Stomach lurching, Persephone followed Hades into the stable and approached Lethe's stall. Now she was committed to riding in the asphodels. Would that she could have found the exit she sought in Elysium, but their near-daily rides there hadn't revealed any such thing.

She'd seen many other things, though. Hades took every opportunity to show her what was beautiful in the Underworld: a flock of oddly formed, yet graceful, winged creatures landing on the River Lethe, a strange flower that bloomed only in one shadowed nook near the rock that made up the west side of the palace, a sheer cliff veined with gold, pockmarked with rough gems. His characteristic quietude was hardly in evidence except one notable occasion when they happened upon a white poplar grown tall and strong, very unlike the few other stunted trees that dotted Elysium's grasses. When Persephone wondered aloud about its difference, Hades said only it was a farewell gift from a dear friend. It was clear from his expression that inquiring further would elicit no more information so Persephone refrained.

True to her plan, however, Persephone asked all manner of other questions as they rode about, all the while keeping alert for any sign of a possible route of escape. There was very little to learn about Elysium beyond what Hades already told her and it was, at times, difficult to formulate credible queries but Persephone did her best.

As though inspired by her inquisitiveness, Hades took to inquiring about Persephone's life aboveground. She told him about Doso and Phlox and the things she loved about her life in the Upper World, but she shied away from stories that included some unkindness on either the Sicani or her mother's part or both. Speaking of such harshness felt not only disloyal to Demeter, but to the entirety of Persephone's existence in the Upper World. When she found herself without a happy memory to relate, Persephone would turn the talk from herself by asking Hades about those on Olympus.

He always answered with lively and, at times, amusing stories about his fellow Gods and Goddesses. And so many other tales, accounts of the Titans, notable deeds of the half mortal bastards of those on Olympus and even some anecdotes about the Achaeans; an entire history of a land and people and Gods Persephone had known nothing of in her narrow existence in Henna. Knowledge her mother could have shared with her but had chosen to withhold.

On occasion, when Hades wished to show her something far afield from the palace, the rides lasted days, beginning at first light and ending where Persephone and Hades happened to be when darkness fell. Those nights, with nothing but pale grass and a blanket separating their bodies caused Persephone no little anxiety, but her dreams were the only things that unsettled her sleep. She was grateful that Hades, as he softly snored at her side, had no reason to suspect the role he played in her nocturnal imaginings.

The previous day, when they'd come upon the white poplar once more Persephone realized they were revisiting parts of Elysium. This had forced her to a conclusion she'd been avoiding. If she wanted her freedom, she had no choice but to ask Hades to take her to the more forbidding parts of his kingdom.

Lethe put his head over the rails of his stall and bumped her shoulder. Laughing, Persephone shook free of her thoughts and put a hand on one of the big round bones of Lethe's jaw while rubbing the flat of his forehead with the other hand. He lipped at the top of her tunic.

"You may ride Styx or Akheron if you wish. You needn't always use Lethe as your mount," Hades said.

Persephone kissed the downy skin on the big horse's nose before saying, "If I left him behind, I would surely break his heart and I couldn't bear that."

A great maw of silence opened behind her. Persephone turned to see Hades giving the easy task of removing the rails from the front of Akheron's stall an undue amount of attention.

She'd hurt him with thoughtless words yet again, for she'd made it abundantly clear that, given the chance, she'd leave Hades with no thought for his broken heart. Shamed by the wound she'd unintentionally inflicted, and angry at that shame, she wrestled the rails of Lethe's stall out of their notches then shooed the horse into the aisle.

Persephone went to retrieve the mounting block from the alcove by Phlegethon's stall just as Akheron trotted into the hallway. Persephone flattened herself against the wall to let the big horse pass, but his shoulder still brushed against her, pulling her tunic and belt askew. After he moved clear of her, she looked down and tugged her clothes straight. When she raised her head, she found herself pinned by Hades's gaze.

He stepped across the space between them and lifted his hand as though he meant to brush away a lock of hair that the wind of Akheron's passage tugged free of Persephone's plait. She ceased breathing as she waited for his fingers to graze her skin. If he touched her, it would be the first time he did so purposefully and without permission since the day she'd spurned his gift of the bow.

A rueful smile turned his lips but didn't reach his eyes. He dropped his hand and moved to Akheron's side.

Persephone's guts settled heavily inside her as the buoyancy of anticipation and uncertainty fled. Sighing softly, she fetched the mounting block and brought it back to Lethe's side.

After Persephone climbed aboard Lethe, she and Hades rode out of the stable and made their way toward the judge's temple.

Persephone had to play her role of inquisitive queen well if she was to convince Hades she wanted to discover the mysteries of his realm and so learn to content herself with living in it. She could find nothing in her muddled thoughts, however, except the memory of the sad smile Hades had given her before dropping his hand and turning away from her.

Finally, gesturing to the crowd milling in the distance in front of the judge's temple, she burst out, "Why are all these shades here?"

"Because their mortal bodies have perished," Hades replied. His mouth twitched slightly as he spoke.

He had never teased her before, but it was a gentle jest and wholly unexpected from this somber man. Persephone waved a hand as though that could negate the foolishness of her inquiry. "Not here in the Underworld, but here in front of this temple? Why must they go in front of the judge?"

"I know that was your meaning." Hades's lips still trembled suspiciously. After he gained sufficient control of his expression, he continued, "Aecus must review their lives . He then decides how they deserve to spend their eternity. Some he sends to Tartarus; those whose great wrongs earn them great punishment. Some few are sent to Elysium. There have been heroes in that land in the past, but their shades faded and, for now, it's empty. Most go to the asphodel meadow or the Vale of Mourning."

When they were nearly upon the horde of shades in the road waiting their turn to be judged, Hades admonished Persephone to be still. Remembering all too well from her short time on the banks of the River Styx what happened when the shades there became aware of her and Hades's presence, Persephone held her peace. Even so, as they drew closer the shades began to shift and dart glances at them, their attention lingering especially on Persephone.

With dark mutterings, the crowd parted to allow them through. Hades went first. Persephone drew herself up and kept her eyes locked on the far horizon, not glancing at the shades even as they shifted closer to her. The cold emanating off their flesh chilled her to her very marrow and she shuddered.

When they'd put the mob behind them, Persephone asked, "Why do they hate me so?"

"To their eyes, you're a mortal. They likely see you as a traitor. You're here, alive and unharmed, and yet you do nothing on their behalf or attempt to better their existence in any way "

"In what way do they think I could better their existence?" Persephone asked, paused, and glanced back over her shoulder. "I would aid them if I knew how."

When she looked at Hades again, astonishment glimmered over his face, but it was quickly replaced by his accustomed somber expression. He shook his head. "There's nothing you or anyone can do for them, Persephone."

By this time, they'd reached the juncture of roads. Persephone shifted her weight to one side and pressed her leg against Lethe's ribs to urge him to turn left. They crested the small rise and made their way down into the Vale of Mourning.

As they rode through the Vale, Persephone took in the misery of its occupants in darting glances. Their visible despair clawed at her heart. It was the same feeling she did battle with almost every moment of every day here in this Underworld, but she couldn't let Hades suspect that, not now.

She swallowed past the tight, stretched feeling in her throat and asked, "You say Aecus sentences most shades to the asphodel meadow or the Vale of Mourning. What is it that determines to which of those places they're sent?"

Hades's gaze roamed over the pitiful souls before he turned it on Persephone. "The River Lethe takes from each shade who drinks of it all memory of their mortal existence. Once a shade releases its grip on that which was most significant to it in the Upper World, it slowly fades, eventually ceasing altogether to exist. Aecus informs the shades, those whose eternities are to be spent in the asphodel meadow, of this. The choice is left to them whether or not to drink of Lethe's water. I believe it's a mercy to be unable to remember all they experienced while they lived, especially as they are forever bound to this place which doesn't and can't bear any resemblance to their life in the Upper World. It's a mercy not extended to those sentenced to Tartarus or Elysium, though those in Elysium eventually choose to drink of Lethe's water and I don't turn them from that purpose. Eternity, even a peaceful one, perhaps especially a peaceful one, can become a heavy burden to bear."

Stroking a hand down his bearded chin, he continued, "Yet, there are many who don't drink. They are those that now dwell in the Vale of Mourning. In my time here, I've found those who choose not to partake of Lethe's mercy are those who spent their lives in the Upper World pursuing something they could never have—wealth, power, beauty, another person—while spurning those things that, with time and effort, could have brought them joy. The shades that inhabit the Vale of Mourning are in death as they were in life: clinging to an impossibility in hopes it will give them substance and meaning. They are, I believe, the most wretched of all my subjects."

It was a relief to leave those desolate souls behind as they entered the asphodel meadow. The shades didn't cluster nearly so thickly there, though each one they encountered worked at some mindless task, their hands absent the necessary tools to perform it, their minds absent the necessary consciousness to realize they accomplished nothing.

Persephone turned her head to look at Hades. "If those here in the asphodel meadow have no memories of their mortal existence left, why do they continue in these menial duties?"

Hades shrugged. "They do that which took up the most part of their time in the Upper World. I know not why, but it consumes them and to question them about it or attempt to turn them from it only enrages them, so I leave them in peace with their work. And some continue to serve a purpose of a sort, for it was shades from this place who aided me in building my palace and the other structures here. They also perform the necessary tasks for the running of my household."

"They're so numerous. Surely among all these souls," Persephone began as she swung an arm to indicate the whole of the asphodel meadow, "there were some who did good in their lives, some who deserve to go to Elysium?"

Hades followed Persephone's gesture with his eyes. "You see for yourself that which their mind or heart clings to after partaking of the River Lethe isn't great love or great beauty or even great sorrow or great hate. It is the minutiae of their day-to-day life. They went about their lives in an unremarkable fashion and influenced the world not a whit for either good or ill. Why should their eternity be any different?"

While Hades's words were convincing, the shadow in his eyes as he looked over the shades that populated the asphodel meadow belied what he said.

"Were there so many here when you first arrived?" Persephone asked.

"When I arrived, the shades ...." Though Hades looked at Persephone, he wasn't taking her in at all. Instead, he appeared to be searching his mind, struggling to remember, or perhaps trying to forget the memories her question called up. After a time, he continued, "All the shades of all the dead since the beginning of time were congregated on the far bank of the River Styx, and I had to pass through them when I first came. They—"

"Did they all know this place?"

"What do you mean?"

"The Sicani whom I lived among in Henna knew nothing of the Underworld, nothing of you. They thought death was but a sleeping and the time beyond it an endless dream in which they would dwell with the Mother Goddess. I believe it would shock and frighten those folk to find themselves here. Is none dismayed to discover this afterlife is so different than expected?"

A smile twisted Hades's lips. It wasn't a pleasant expression. "Very few, for in death as in life, most mortals see only what they wish. The glamour of this place works on that willingness to be deceived. In some eyes I'm the Mother Goddess. To others, I'm a being known as Osiris. Some call me Ba'al. And there are other names, too many to tell. No doubt they'll find their own titles for you as well. And once they partake of the River Lethe. they perceive nothing anymore and so it matters not if they see me or my realm true."

Persephone searched Hades's face. "Do I see you true?"

"Do you?" he responded, returning her look of out flat, opaque eyes.

She waited for him to say more, needed him to say more, but the silence ate up the space around them until Persephone couldn't break its confines to ask for the reassurance she so desired. Finally, she looked away from him.

Hades spoke then, but only to take up his tale again. "The shades on Styx's banks attacked and forced me into the river. During the struggle, I inadvertently drank of Styx's water. I was in terrible pain by the time I escaped, but I managed to drag myself onto the opposite shore."

"Where was Charon when you reached the River Styx? What of the ferry?" Persephone asked. Allowing herself to be drawn into the tale was a distraction, something to blot out the consideration of whether she saw Hades as he truly was. She knew too much of him now to simply say he was a monster who had taken her captive and dragged her to his monstrous realm and, yet, how could she define him as anything else?

Hades responded, "Together Helios and I built the ferry the day he brought me my horses, the day I learned I had slumbered for nine years. Charon didn't come to this place until later."

"Is Charon not a shade? Didn't you simply select him from those on Styx's banks?"

"Charon isn't and never will be a shade. He's Immortal. Zeus made him so at my request, but Charon was mortal and alive when first he came to me."

"Did he come here seeking a loved one?" Persephone asked, horror coating her voice.

"Don't waste your pity on that man. He wasn't of those who seek the shade of their beloved in my kingdom. Those who venture to my realm with such an intent are returned to the Upper World, though no memory of their time here or the one they sought remains with them. As a mortal, Charon was as he is now, warped, cruel, full of dark thoughts and desires such as you could never dream. He was spurned by every community of which he thought to become a part. Starving and desperate, he forever bound himself to me by eating the food off the graves in the Upper World before Hermes could collect it to bring to me. From that moment Charon became my tool to do with what I chose."

Hades's gaze fixed on the dark line of Styx on the horizon. "And I chose that he should pilot the ferry across the River Styx."

"Charon ate the food of the dead out of necessity?"

"He did."

"As I would, had you not provided me different fare."

Eyes downcast, Hades toyed with Akheron's mane. "I thought, as the daughter of a Goddess, you would know what it means to eat of the food here. I put it before you because I believed when you partook of it, it would be to show me that you found some pleasure in my company and were content to stay." Hades's lips quirked with a bitter little smile that disappeared as quickly as it had come. "When I saw that, like Charon, you would eat of it only out of necessity, I chose to give you an alternative because I ...." Hades lifted his head and turned his face away so she could see only the jut of his cheekbone, the curve of one pale ear, and the dark hair that fell in loose curls behind it. "I'm a God, Persephone, with a realm full of subjects who, if they have any mind left, long each moment of every day to flee beyond the boundaries of my kingdom. My subjects who are content here are those who chose to remove all consciousness. They're no better than animals, indeed worse for they have no finer emotions left to share. Were I not Immortal, Charon would put his hands about my throat and gleefully stop the breath in my body. Aecus is judge here only because that service appealed to him more than an eternity of tedium in Elysium. The few who spend their time in my company willingly are but dumb beasts and, of those, only Lethe and Cerberus have a true affection for me."

Hades turned back and met Persephone's gaze. "Do you wonder that I long for one . . . that I long for you to live with me in this realm because you find pleasure in my company and joy in the sight of me, not because I bound you to me against your will?"

Hades searched her face for a moment with eyes that pled for understanding. Then, looking away from her, his voice lower, harsher, he said, "I should never have brought you to this land, but now that you're here I find it beyond my strength to give you your freedom. For that, I'm sorry."

Before Persephone could respond, Hades bent low over Akheron's neck, shouted 'tcha,' and the horse leaped forward in a gallop.

Lethe lunged after Akheron. Persephone clenched her buttocks and leaned back. Lethe snorted, tossed his head, and danced under her in agitation but he did obey. Persephone held him in check until Hades and Akheron were out of sight.

18

PERSEPHONE

Just as she hoped and planned, Persephone was, for the moment, on Lethe's back and unrestricted by Hades's supervision, but there was no freedom to be found here. The silence of the Underworld pressed down on her, ringing in her ears. The shades around her, with their blank eyes, their mindless motions, were infinitely more eerie now she was on her own. It seemed as though they crept closer to her, the motion disguised by their continual swaying. She desperately wanted to leave this realm, but she didn't yet know of any way to escape, save on Charon's ferry, which was closed to her. Riding back to the palace would remove her from the shades' horrific presence but it would also necessitate she pass alone through the crowd of angry souls outside the Temple of Judgment. There was no safe place to which she could flee.

Snorting, Lethe spun in an anxious circle. When he again faced the direction in which Hades had gone, Persephone tapped the horse's ribs with her heels. With a shrill neigh, he plunged down the road after his master.

Persephone's pursuit of Hades had nothing to do with the plea in his eyes, the heart's longing in his voice when he told her he wanted her to stay for love of him. She wasn't chasing him because of the urge she felt, in the moment of his anguish, to smooth the pain away from his face with a touch, to ease the ache in his breast by laying her head upon it. It was fear, only fear, that prevented her from taking this opportunity to search for a way of escape.

Sometime later, Lethe neighed and slowed to a lope. His call was answered by Akheron. Persephone straightened and looked about.

Hades stood on Styx's bank talking with Charon. As she approached them, Hades turned to her. Like a herald of dawn, his gray eyes lightened and a smile curved his lips. Persephone swallowed and looked away. His heart was in her keeping and she didn't know how to hold it, didn't want to learn.

When she looked back, Hades was speaking to Charon again. After a moment, Charon nodded, then pushed away from the bank and poled his way into the river's current.

Hades mounted Akheron and rode him to Lethe's side. "Given your freedom on Lethe's back, I thought you might . . . return to the palace without me."

It was evident from the pause Hades hadn't meant to end his statement that way. What had he thought Persephone might do? Had he meant her to take the opportunity to escape? What did it mean, what message had she conveyed by following him, rather than running?

"Do you wish to go back now?" Hades asked.

Persephone nodded. The warmth of the folly would be welcome after the day's chill and perhaps she could find a bit of peace there with her little plants, sequestered from Hades's presence and the contradictory feelings to which he gave rise.

She turned Lethe in the direction they'd come and kneed him into a walk but brought him to a halt when she realized Hades wasn't following. She looked over her shoulder to see him doing the same. She followed the direction of his gaze to Styx's opposite bank and gasped.

The quantity of shades there had easily doubled since the day she first came to the Underworld.

Hades faced forward again and urged Akheron into a walk.

"Is all well?" Persephone asked as he came even with her.

Hades jerked his chin toward his shoulder indicating the riverbank behind him. "There are too many."

"Why have their numbers increased so?"

Hades shook his head. "It isn't the amount that concerns me. It's their lack of grave goods."

"Why is that worrying?"

"Without the means to pay the passage, Charon can't ferry them across," Hades said, returning his attention to the opposite bank. "They wait there tormented by memories of their mortal life, but unable to move forward into this plane of existence. Their pain would be eased by a single sip of the River Lethe. It's a respite I can't give them, not until they've paid the toll by waiting on Styx's bank for a hundred years. And for those who weren't buried at all, it's a mercy I can never provide them. They linger in agony for eternity and it—it's difficult for me to contemplate their suffering."

"What does it mean that so many are being buried without goods to pay the passage?"

"Or not buried at all," Hades added, then continued, "I believe whole families, perhaps entire villages are perishing at or nearly at the same time, with none left to ensure the dead are being cared for properly. The possible causes of such a thing are myriad, but none is good. Something very wrong is happening in the Upper World."

"What can be done about it?" Persephone asked, her heart writhing with pity. How awful to pass through the travail of a mortal life only to find endless suffering on the other side.

"Nothing."

"I don't understand. You're a God. You rule this land. Can't you simply—"

"No. I cannot," Hades said, his voice as sharp and stinging as the crack of his whip. "There are laws that were set in place by Chaos to govern this realm just as any other sphere. I must abide by them."

Persephone flinched. She reached down and began to roll the threads on the hem of her tunic through her fingers. Her other hand entwined itself in Lethe's mane. Surely, Hades only spoke as he had because other thoughts weighed on his mind, but that didn't remove the smart of his harsh rebuttal. It was the first as such she'd ever received from him, and it stung all the more because of that.

Hades kneed Akheron into a walk. Persephone followed, though this wasn't the direction she wanted to be going any longer. Home wasn't ahead. It was behind, across Styx, through the mass of shades on its bank, at the other end of ineffable darkness. Her entire being ached with the desire to be there.

When Persephone noticed the shade standing at the side of the road, hands moving as though vigorously scrubbing dirty cloth with a rough stone, she thought it was her homesickness that imposed a likeness to one of the villagers on the shade's visage and movements. As she passed, however, the shade looked up, fully revealing itself to her.

"Nadira?"

The woman didn't react to the name. Indeed, she didn't even acknowledge Persephone's presence, but it was Nadira. Persephone was sure of it. She halted Lethe, swung a leg over his back, and dropped to the ground.

Approaching the shade, Persephone said. "Nadira, it is I, Perse—Kore. You needn't be afraid."

The woman continued her motions unchecked. Persephone reached out.

"Persephone, no!" Hades shouted.

Persephone's fingers closed on Nadira's forearm. The black orbs of Nadira's eyes focused suddenly, fastening on Persephone's face. The village woman's lips peeled back in a soundless snarl. She lunged forward and snapped at Persephone, her teeth closing within a hairsbreadth of Persephone's cheek.

With a cry, Persephone jerked away, scrambled backward.

In utter silence, Nadira advanced. Her cold fingers scrabbled for purchase on Persephone's tunic. Persephone stumbled, lost her balance and fell. Nadira leapt. Persephone lifted her hands in front of her face to protect herself, but the attack never came. Hades had struck the village woman aside. Nadira hit the ground, rolled to a crouch, and propelled herself toward Persephone once again.

Hades stepped in front of Persephone and caught Nadira in his arms.

Persephone scrambled to her feet. "Don't hurt her, Hades. Please, she—"

Hades pressed a hand to Nadira's forehead. Eyes closing, she slumped against him.

Hades knelt and, with care, laid Nadira's shade on the dirt of the road. Persephone dropped to her knees at the Sicani woman's side.

"Oh, Nadira." Persephone lifted a hand to push the wild tangle of the woman's black hair off her face.

Hades caught her by the wrist. "Don't. Please. If you touch her, you'll rouse her to violence again."

Persephone let her arm go limp. Hades released her, and she folded her hands in her lap.

They trembled there with the force of her longing to brush Nadira's hair back, to straighten the woman's tunic, to return to her some semblance of humanity. "She shouldn't be here. If I'd been stronger, if I hadn't let my mother dissuade me from attending her in childbed, she wouldn't have died. I could have saved her."

"You have no way of knowing she died while giving birth," Hades said, quietly, gently. "Some other misfortune could just as easily have brought her here."

Hades spoke sense. Persephone couldn't know for certain the manner of Nadira's death, but her heart felt the truth of it. Her cowardice had brought this woman to the Underworld as surely as if Persephone had plunged a knife into her heart.

Nadira twitched and rolled her head to the side.

Hades stood. "Come, it would be best we're gone before she wakes."

"What will happen to her?" Persephone asked, unable to take her eyes from the village woman.

"She'll remember nothing of what occurred here and will return to how she was when you first saw her."

Persephone looked up at Hades. "She's no older than I. She has a babe waiting for her in the world above."

"I told you of the laws of the Underworld, Persephone. They rule me as well as my realm."

"There's no way to circumvent them even this once?"

Hades dragged a hand over his mouth, then down his beard and swallowed heavily. "There is."

Persephone held his gaze, a mute plea in her eyes.

"Her loved ones in the world above won't be glad to see her again. They performed funerary rites on her body, or else she wouldn't be here. They know she's dead. Her return will only frighten and confuse them. They'll surely spurn her, or worse, their fear may inspire them to violence against her."

Hades spoke only the truth. The Sicani feared Persephone merely because she'd broken a statue. Their terror of one returned to them from the dead would be much greater unless they could be persuaded her reappearance was a blessing, not a curse.

"Have you a statue of any of the Goddesses amongst the treasures in your palace?" Persephone asked.

"I believe so."

"If we sent it with Nadira and made sure she approached the village from Nysa, they would believe her return a gift from the Mother Goddess. She and the statue would be seen as a blessing, a lifting of the curse they believe has afflicted Henna since... since my birth."

"Persephone—"

"Please, Hades. Nadira's restoration would right so many wrongs."

Hades's back hunched and his body tightened as though in anticipation of a blow, but he only said, "Very well."

Then, one motion flowing into the next, he drew the bronze dagger from his belt, slashed it across his wrist, dropped to his knees, and pressed the oozing wound against Nadira's mouth.

The shade's eyes remained closed, her face slack as though in sleep, but her jaws clamped closed on Hades's arm. A horrible sucking, slurping noise filled the air. Blood so red it was nearly black ran out both sides of Nadira's mouth.

Persephone gagged, choked, and turned away.

A moment later she heard a sort of gurgling, bubbling croak. She turned back just as a rosy flush like the rays of Eos's dawn light raced over Nadira's skin. Hades pulled his arm from Nadira's mouth.

The normal pallor of Hades's skin was now chalky, with no luminescence to it at all. Even the pink of his lips had paled. He tried to get to his feet but staggered and fell back to his knees.

"Hades?" Persephone reached for him.

She heard another gurgle and turned her attention instead to Nadira. The woman, who was sitting up now, blinked, then stared with wide eyes at Persephone. Turning away from Hades, Persephone moved closer to Nadira. In an echo of Persephone's earlier action, the woman scrambled back.

Persephone stopped moving. "You needn't be afraid, Nadira. I won't hurt you. I vow it."

Eyes still wide, Nadira's lips moved, but no sound came out. She put her fingers to her mouth as though she could pluck the words she meant to say out of it and fling them into being.

From behind Persephone, Hades said, "You won't be able to speak for some days, Nadira. You've been ill. Your family entrusted you to me and my lady wife while you recover. When your voice returns to you, we'll return you to Henna. Now, I imagine you're frightened and cold and hungry. May we convey you to our home for some rest and refreshment?"

Confusion and terror still battling in her face, Nadira gave a slow nod. Persephone extended a hand. After a moment's hesitation, Nadira took it, and Persephone pulled her to her feet. Nadira looked down, pressed her hands against her flat belly, then looked up at Persephone, eyes wide with worry.

"Your babe is well and in your mother's care. You'll see your child when you return home." Persephone hoped she spoke true, but she had no way of knowing. However, if Nadira arrived in the Upper World and found her babe had perished, she would at least have her mother and the rest of her family to welcome her and comfort her in her mourning. It would be more of a homecoming than Persephone would receive if she ever made good her escape.

Nadira nodded her understanding, but her face was still full of fear, and she continued to clutch at her stomach with one hand.

"Are you in pain?"

Nadira shook her head.

"Do you think you can ride?" Persephone gestured to Lethe who stood, head lowered, cropping grass at the side of the road.

Some of the anxiousness left Nadira's face and she stepped toward the horse. Persephone had worried the woman might be frightened of him. He was larger than the horses in Henna, but it seemed his placidness and beauty cast the same spell on Nadira as they had on Persephone.

Lethe stood patiently while Persephone worked to get Nadira on his back. It would have been but a moment's effort for Hades, but he didn't come to her aid. Once Persephone got Nadira mounted, she looked about for him.

He leaned against Akheron, arms crossed over his chest. He was still pale, the flesh under his eyes like a bruise, and the creases that ran from his nose to either side of his mouth were carven and deep.

"We should return to the palace now." He straightened, winced, and fell back against Akheron.

Persephone hurried to him. "Are you ill?"

Hades stopped her with an uplifted hand. He brought himself to standing but pain still etched deep lines in his forehead and around his mouth. "You won't see me about the palace over the next handful of days. You must keep Nadira inside until I emerge from my chambers. Cerberus will be eager to reclaim her. Indeed, he'll likely be on the hunt soon and you haven't the means to dissuade him from his purpose. Nor will I for some time. I would ask that you care for the horses, for I'll also be unable to carry out those duties."

"Why?"

Hades swiped at the sweat dewing his forehead. "There's a cost for Nadira's return to her mortal existence. As it's my blood in her veins that price will be mine to pay."

"How? What price?"

"Flesh for flesh. Even now her mortal body is using mine to regenerate around her shade. When that process is complete, I'll be myself again." Hades's jaw clenched, and his lips thinned into a hard line.

Blinking rapidly, Persephone asked, "Your blood can accomplish such a thing? How is that possible?"

"As it's your mother's gift from our parents to slay or sustain the growing things of the

Gaia's flesh, so it's my inheritance to cut short or prolong the life of any mortal even against the decree of the Moirai." A bitter smile lifted one corner of his mouth. "You see how I'm uniquely suited to my role here."

Persephone didn't see. To have such a gift and to be barred by the laws of the Underworld from using it would constitute an exquisite form of torture especially for one with the depth of feeling she was beginning to suspect Hades harbored.

"Does it cause you a great deal of pain?" she asked.

Hades gave a curt nod. "In a few days it will reach its peak. Then it will ebb and go completely when Nadira is fully mortal again."

Persephone thought of the lurch behind her navel when she touched the little leaf earlier that day. It hadn't been a wholly pleasant feeling. If her entire body had been affected that way, the sensation would have left her writhing. Hades, it seemed, would be experiencing that for days.

"I didn't know her life came at such a cost. You could have denied me. You should have denied me," Persephone cried.

"And what kind of foul thing would you think me now if I had?"

"You could have explained."

"Would you have allowed me the opportunity?"

Heat crept up Persephone's neck and into her face.

"It's done, Persephone. Let it be. Come, I would return home now."

She'd sentenced Hades to this, the least she could do was return with him to the palace and what little comfort he could take there as quickly as possible. Persephone hurried back to Lethe. Before she could clamber on behind Nadira, Hades rode up on Akheron. He hunched over, one arm held tightly to his midsection.

She looked up at Nadira. "Lethe will follow Akheron to the palace. All you need do is remain on his back. Can you manage that?"

Entwining her fingers more tightly in Lethe's mane, Nadira nodded.

Persephone moved to Akheron's side and reached up to Hades. "Give me your hand."

"What?"

"Nadira doesn't need my assistance. You do. Give me your hand."

Hades dropped his arm from his stomach, tried to straighten. "The pain isn't constant yet. I can manage until it eases."

"And if you can't? I haven't the strength to get you back on Akheron's back should you fall. Best you let me on now so I can hold you there."

Hades looked out over the asphodel meadow, his eyes dark, his mouth drawn in pain. Finally, not meeting her gaze, he reached down.

Persephone gripped his forearm and pulled herself up behind him. She put her arms about his waist. His muscles were corded tight in pain.

Calling out to Nadira to hold on, Persephone tapped Akheron's ribs with her heels. The horse moved into a walk.

They were almost back at the Vale of Mourning before Hades's muscles finally unknotted. He settled back against Persephone with a gust of expelled air. The muscled terrain of his back shifted against her breasts. His hands dropped to his sides. They brushed Persephone's thighs with almost every step Akheron took. The heat his touch set to simmering in her belly and her groin was undeniable, unignorable.

Her hands, which had been clenched on his tunic in the effort to keep Hades upright, splayed open against the hard planes of his abdomen. For a moment, his belly ceased rising and falling. Then, Hades brought one hand up, placed it over top of hers, and began making small revolutions on her wrist and the back of her hand with one finger.

With his other hand he stroked the length of Persephone's thigh once, then again. The fire in her body was stoked by each pass. As they turned toward the Temple of Judgment, Persephone's gaze strayed to the white vulnerability where Hades's neck and shoulder met. The skin looked soft, smooth, as delightful to touch as a flower petal.

Heart pounding, breath shallow and short, Persephone leaned forward and pressed her lips there.

Hades's thighs flexed, and Akheron came to a halt. Persephone lifted her head. Hades turned his upper body, tilting his face down to hers. His breath played over her mouth. He murmured her name, his lips almost brushing hers as he spoke. Her stomach churned and her heart thudded. She drew back, pulling her hands from his body.

Hades remained as he was for a moment, but Persephone couldn't bring herself to meet his eyes. A sigh gusted from him, his breath stirring the hair about her face. Then he turned from her and signaled Akheron to walk. The horse had taken only a few strides when Hades groaned and leaned forward again. Sweat popped out on the back of his neck.

"Hades."

He made no response.

Persephone touched his shoulder blade, a brief skim of her fingertips.

"Hades?"

"Home," he moaned.

Persephone wrapped her arms around his waist once more, lifted her heels, and brought them down hard. With a snort, Akheron started forward in a lope. Persephone looked behind, assured herself that Lethe was following with a wide-eyed Nadira flattened to the horse's neck, clinging to it with all her might.

As they pounded their way toward the palace, Persephone's muscles quivered with the effort of keeping Hades on Akheron's back. He was very nearly limp in her arms. The enormity of his pain frightened her, this man she had thought was made of stone, impervious to hurt of any kind.

Persephone sorted through the healing knowledge she had learned at Doso's knee, though she wasn't sure if earthly remedies could heal Godly ailments. There was so much she didn't know about the Gods. So much she didn't know about Hades. Then, a cold wave of fear shivered over her as she recalled what he said about those in his kingdom seeing him as they wished, not as he really was. Who was the true Hades? The kind, compassionate man who gifted Nadira with her life, or the cold, cruel God who abducted Persephone, forced his attentions on her, and still showed himself now and again in brief glimpses? Which stoked her desire? And to which would she be wedding herself if she failed to escape this place?

19

DEMETER

Demeter stood on the threshold of Keleus's palace with Demophon in her arms. Not even the slightest of breezes stirred the starlit darkness and the heat shrouded her like a cloak. The only sound that reached her from the sleep-soaked city was an occasional ululation of grief from those mourning the newly dead, likely slain by her famine. As though in protest of her thoughts, a tempest erupted within as the plant life churned under her skin. Demeter winced, grunted, then mastered it once more,

After turning away from the doorway, Demeter made her way to Keleus's great megaron, the only room in the palace grand enough for the act she meant to complete this night. She would have preferred her temple, but Metaneira hovered so that taking the child out of the palace unnoticed was a nearly impossible task. It was late now, however, the queen slumbering. Demeter would be able to complete her rite on the babe without fear of observation or obstruction.

Once in the megaron, Demeter seated herself on Keleus's throne and placed the sleeping Demophon so he lay across her knees. She unwound the swaddling that enclosed his limbs, taking care not to wake him. She studied his firm, flushed little body, stroked one finger over his cheek. The past month of feeding on ambrosia had restored him completely.

Two nights ago, she bathed him in the seawater Iambe had hauled to the palace for her. The cut she'd made on his inner elbow the previous evening to drip his blood into the ground had nearly healed. There was nothing left to do now save the final step of the ritual.

Drawing her finger away from Demophon's face, Demeter opened her mouth and exhaled a long breath, encompassing his body in a pearlescent globe of air. She lifted him to her breast, her hands slipping easily inside the thin membrane, and crossed the deserted expanse of Keleus's megaron.

When she reached the circle of the hearth, Demeter kneeled on its rim. With one hand, she cupped Demophon's head while the other supported his buttocks. She extended her arms and carefully placed the babe into the heart of the leaping flames.

"Doso! Gods! No!"

Demeter whirled as Metaneira, eyes wild, arms outstretched, hurled herself from the doorway of the megaron toward the fire. Evidently, Demeter's precaution in waiting until the palace was deep in slumber to perform this final step was wasted for here was Demophon's mother to wreak her havoc. Demeter grabbed the woman by the waist and yanked her back from the flames.

Metaneira strained against Demeter's grasp, her mouth open in a soundless scream as she reached for her son. As the blaze flared up, obscuring the babe from sight, Metaneira turned from the hearth, attempting to scratch, bite, or rend any part of Demeter she could reach with nails or teeth.

Demeter flung Metaneira to the ground, sat on the woman's chest, slapped her twice across the face as hard as she could, and bellowed, "Be still!"

Demeter's Godvoice echoed throughout Keleus's megaron.

Metaneira went as motionless as death.

Sweating, Demeter climbed from atop the woman.

Metaneira's mouth worked. Surprisingly, she was able to say from between clenched teeth, "Please, I beg you, spare my Demophon. I know not who or what you are, but don't take my boy from me."

"I do your child good. You're a fool that you don't see that. Lie still and leave him be. The fire doesn't harm him." Demeter gestured at the hearth where Demophon's sleeping form, whole and hale—though surrounded by flames—was visible once more.

Metaneira's jaw worked again, her teeth unclamping. "As your mistress, Doso, I command you to remove my son from the fire or I vow I shall destroy you."

Flashing through her mind like clouds covering and revealing Helios's chariot on a windy day, Demeter remembered all the times over the last months she played the part of humble servant. The many times she bowed her head and acquiesced to this woman's demands, the nights she walked the floor with Demophon while Metaneira slumbered, only to take him from Demeter's arms in the morning and dismiss Demeter with a flick of her fingers.

A cold serpent of anger uncoiled itself and slid through Demeter's veins. She stepped over Metaneira's body, which now twitched and spasmed as the woman attempted to buck Demeter's decree.

Demeter reached into the fire, plucked Demophon up, and tumbled him into Metaneira's jerking arms. Metaneira cried out as she struggled to keep Demophon from falling to the floor. Her limbs wouldn't obey her, and she was unable to hold the babe. He rolled the short distance from his mother's breast to the floor, woke, and immediately began wailing.

As Metaneira regained control of her limbs and pulled herself into a sitting position, Demeter said, "You should have heeded my words. Better yet, you should have kept to your chamber and allowed me to continue caring for your son unwatched and unmolested. A few moments more sheltered by my breath in the heart of the fire and your son would have been exempt from all that makes death such a misery to mortals. Now the rite has been disturbed and it's a disruption without remedy. Foolish woman!"

Unable, as yet, to stand, Metaneira crept toward Demeter on her hands and knees and grasped Demeter's skirt. "Please, Lady, I knew not what I did. Please is there nothing . . . I would give much . . . I would give everything to keep my son from Hades's clutches."

Demeter took in Metaneira's distraught face and abject posture. Likely Demeter had appeared this wretched, this pitiable when she begged Zeus for Persephone's return. An unexpected pang of sympathy darted through her.

Demeter crouched down in front of the weeping woman. "The rite has been disrupted and must forever remain incomplete, but take heart. Because your son slept in my arms and ate of the food I gave him, he'll be protected from disease, have good fortune in his life, and father many children. Surely this is a fate any mother would wish for her child."

Metaneira continued weeping and refused to be consoled. Demophon's wails grew louder, but Metaneira continued sobbing into her hands, so involved in her own wretchedness she was utterly unaware of her child's. It was a wonder that a mother who would do anything to save her son from the Underworld's misery couldn't take on the simple task of comforting him in his current distress.

Demeter scooped the babe up and patted his back until he stopped crying. She looked him over. She had squandered a great deal of power on this mite of a human. She likely hadn't enough to perform the rite again, even if she did find a mortal on whom to work it. She needed more power, and she needed it quickly, yet all those who would willingly worship her were already doing so. She didn't know what more she could do to draw additional devotees to her temple. She did, however, have the queen of the Eleusinian people groveling at her feet. Demeter nudged Metaneira with her toe.

Sobs hitching in her chest, the woman raised her swollen red eyes to Demeter's face. Demeter handed her the babe, and this time Metaneira gathered him to her breast.

"I wish you to build a temple, one constructed of stone as this palace is so it will last for all time. Tell Keleus he must command the entire city to participate in its construction. It must be done quickly and even as they build, you must command all peoples in Eleusis to worship me."

"But, Lady, a temple for whom?"

Demeter released her Godbody from its tight knot in her center. Her spine straightened. Her limbs lengthened. She reveled in the surcease of the thousand aches that plagued her every day in her aged mortal form. Her Godlight burst out in a blinding flash that Demeter was sure lit the whole palace, if not the entire city. "For me, Demeter, Goddess of Olympus."

Metaneira's cry as she threw her hands up to shield her face was lost in a hubbub of voices coming from without Keleus's megaron.

Demeter glanced at the main entrance to the room. She must depart this place soon or be beleaguered by humans and their petty concerns. "Do as I command, Metaneira."

"To save my child, anything," Metaneria replied.

"It isn't to save your child, but mine. The things I ask of you won't benefit Demophon in any way, but if you don't do as I order it will not go well with you or your family. You must obey me."

Metaneira ceased weeping and gave Demeter a wide-eyed nod. Then her eyes rolled back in her head, and she slumped to the floor.

Satisfied Metaneira would do as commanded, Demeter turned and walked to the doors. As she crossed the wide hallway leading to the palace's front entrance, the crowd of nursemaids and house servants came hurrying from the hallway to Demeter's right while Metaneira's daughters rushed down the stairs to Demeter's left. They halted in their headlong dash and threw their hands up to their eyes. Some even screamed in fear. Demeter didn't pause, offered not a word of reassurance as she pushed through the doors of Keleus's palace and into the courtyard beyond. Once there she took on her mortal form. She wanted no frightened mortals obstructing her path when she took to the streets of Eleusis.

"Lady!"

Demeter turned. Iambe hitched toward her across the shadowy courtyard.

"Iambe, what do you here?"

"I bring you glad tidings, Lady."

"What tidings?"

"I've found one I believe will serve as your emissary." Iambe puffed as she halted in front of Demeter.

"Who? Where is he?"

A man stepped out of the shadows on the edge of the courtyard and walked toward Demeter. He came to a stop in front of her. "Greetings, Lady. I'm Orpheus of Pimpleia."

Demeter surveyed the man. The muscles on his gaunt frame were thin and ropy, his skin stretched taut over them. Dark circles pooled below his eyes and his hair hung lank and greasy on either side of his face. He looked barely able to support the weight of the lyre he held in his hands.

Demeter turned to walk away. "He won't suit, Iambe."

A trill of music quivered in the still night air. Demeter's breath caught and she stopped. Indeed, she couldn't have continued moving even had she put all her force, strength, and intent into making herself do so.

Another chord rent the silence. Tears flooded Demeter's eyes and she could do nothing to prevent them.

"I ask only that you give me the opportunity to prove myself," Orpheus said as his music continued to invade Demeter's ears, mind, and heart.

The music ceased. Demeter turned back. It seemed Iambe had been similarly affected. The little woman wiped at her eyes with the back of one hand.

Demeter strode forward and plucked the lyre out of the man's hands. She drew her fingers across the strings, keeping her eyes on Iambe, who dried her hand on her tunic.

"The gift isn't in the instrument, Lady. It's within me." Orpheus reached for the lyre.

Demeter relinquished the instrument, studying Orpheus again. "Pimpleia is a fair distance from here. Near Olympus, if I recall rightly. What do you in Eleusis?"

"An old woman accosted me in the streets of my town and instructed me to seek you out here."

"Did this crone give you her name?"

"She called herself Doso."

"How is that pos—" Iambe began.

Demeter waved the woman into silence. "I would say you lie, Orpheus of Pimpleia, but you could have no way of knowing my relationship to the hag that sent you here. Did she give you a message for me?"

"Only that she believed I could aid you in your aims and you would help me in mine."

Was this somehow another ploy to turn Persephone's heart from Demeter to Hekate? Demeter narrowed her eyes. "And what are your aims?"

Orpheus gestured to Iambe. "Your woman tells me you seek someone to brave the Underworld. Is that true?"

Demeter nodded. The man had ducked her question, but she would ferret out his reasons soon enough.

"She also tells me you're the Goddess Demeter. Is that also true?"

Demeter turned startled eyes on Iambe.

Iambe blinked, shifted, and plucked at the skin on the back of her hand. "I followed you, Lady, the days you went to your temple."

Lips thin with displeasure, Demeter inclined her head. "It's true."

"Can you help me get to the Underworld?" Orpheus asked.

Demeter reached out and twanged one string of the lyre in his hands. "Does your song affect all who hear it the way it affected me?"

"It does. I can make rocks dance should you wish."

"Can you make a three headed dog lie down and be still? Can you make the Lord of the Underworld relinquish his most prized possession?"

"I believe I can."

Demeter leaned forward, bringing her face close to his. "Can you bathe in fire without quailing?"

Orpheus met her stare. "Is it necessary I do so to reach the Underworld?"

"It is."

"Then I can. I will."

Demeter moved back. It boded well that he hadn't shown the slightest hesitation before answering her. "Then I can help you reach the Underworld. Better, I can make you impervious to the rules that govern that realm. You shall be able to move freely through it unimpeded by any of its denizens or laws."

"When can we begin?" Orpheus asked.

Demeter looked from the mortal man's fingers, tapping at the strings of his lyre, to the pits of his sunken eyes which burned with black fire.

"Why so eager, Orpheus of Pimpleia? Most mortals would shrink before such a task."

"I too seek to regain something from the Lord of the Underworld."

Demeter whipped out a hand, grasped the hair at the back of the man's head, and forced his face close to hers. "My daughter's freedom first. After she is returned to me, I care not what you do, but if you come back to the Upper World without Persephone, I'll fill your days with such torment you'll beg the Gods for the mercy of death and won't receive it."

Orpheus's expression changed not a whit. He simply said, "I understand, Lady."

Demeter released him and stepped back, a smile turning one corner of her mouth. "I believe you shall suit after all."

"I will. And I ask once more, when may we begin?"

Demeter consulted the power within her. If Metaneira's command went out on the morrow, Demeter should accumulate enough within a short amount of time to work the rite. "We'll begin in three days, and it will take as long to perform the rite on you."

"Lady," Iambe ventured. "He seems to be much—" Iambe made a gesture that encompassed Orpheus's body "—depleted. Would it not be wise to give him a greater amount of time to rest and prepare himself?"

Demeter rounded on the woman. "Nine days and nine nights I searched for my daughter. I took no rest, nor sustenance in all that time.

What I ask of him is nothing in comparison."

"I need no rest, Lady. I would begin now if we could," Orpheus said.

Demeter looked back at him. "That's not possible, but you may walk with me to my temple, and I'll tell you what will be required of you."

Demeter strode toward the street. Orpheus fell in on her left, Iambe on her right.

Demeter waved Iambe away. "Go home, Iambe. Return to your own kind. What I go to do is no task for you."

"I have no kind, Lady, save you. I go with you to gladden and serve you as best I can."

Demeter's heart gave a queer little lurch, but she only said, "As you wish, but know this. If you go with me now, you become my servant for good or ill."

Iambe's usually lively face turned somber. "Goddess, we are outcasts, the both of us. You would only be here if you didn't belong with those on Olympus. My kind long ago turned away from me because of my infirmity, my only value to amuse them with my mangled body. Your merriment was never at my expense. You laughed not at my jests and tricks, not at my disfigurement, but only when I behaved as any human would, reacting to the taste of a bitter draught. I ached for you in your grief when first I saw you, but I loved you when you didn't see my form as a source of amusement. I vowed to serve you when you accepted my offer of friendship. I stay with you, Goddess, no matter where you go or what you do." Iambe paused, touched the back of Demeter's hand. "Why didn't you tell me about your daughter, Lady?"

"It wasn't a necessity that you know."

"And it isn't a necessity I sorrow for your loss, but I do."

Demeter looked down at the tips of Iambe's fingers which rested against the wrinkled, age-spotted terrain of her skin. How odd this little mortal was with her sympathy, her attempts at comfort and yet this slight touch eased something inside Demeter. She raised her eyes to Iambe's face. "If you're to serve me, I can't have you blinded by my Godlight when I take on my Immortal body."

Demeter put a forefinger in the center of the Iambe's forehead. For a moment the skin there glowed. Iambe gasped. Demeter lowered her hand.

Iambe, mouth slightly open, put her own finger where Demeter had touched her. "Thank you, Lady."

"Come." Demeter began to walk away. "We go to my temple. There's much we must accomplish over the coming days."

20

PERSEPHONE

Stopping outside the closed door to Hades's megaron, Persephone swallowed, dried her damp hands on her tunic, and knocked.

She heard nothing for a time, then came some rustling, a thud, and a muffled curse.

"Hades?"

"Enter."

Persephone pushed the door open and took a hesitant step inside. Hades stood on the far side of the hearth, gripping the back of the chair next to him so tightly his knuckles were white with effort. Lank black hair clung to his wan cheeks and his tunic was rumpled and darkened with sweat at the chest and underarms.

"You're still unwell," Persephone said. "I apologize. I'll go."

Hades held up a hand. "No. Stay. Please, stay. How fares Nadira?"

Persephone took a hesitant step toward him. "She's well now, though she was overawed by the palace and in fear of me at first. She lost some of her caution, due mostly, I believe, to the bathing room. She spends at least a portion everyday reveling in the warm water. In Henna, our ablutions were conducted in an icy stream."

"I felt much the same when I discovered that pool. I could do with a visit there now, though my belly tells me food should be my first concern."

"You could join Nadira and me for the evening meal," Persephone said.

"Would that please you?" Hades asked.

"It would," Persephone said. There was no lie in her words. Nadira's silence had been a heavy and strange burden to bear these last days, and Persephone had missed Hades's presence.

A smile touched Hades's lips. He let go of the chair and straightened. His face spasmed, and he hunched.

Hurrying forward, Persephone reached for him. Then, recalling the last time she and Hades touched, the ardor between them as they rode Akheron back to the palace, she stopped. Heat rose in her face and sunk low in her belly.

Hades watched her hands as they fell back to her sides. Then he returned his gaze to her face, but she couldn't read what was in his eyes. "I imagine you and Nadira have had enough of being indoors. Would you like to show her Elysium?"

"May I? You said Cerberus—"

"I'd be with you."

"Of course, but are you certain you're—"

"I'm well. Can you ready some food for us to take out of doors while I cleanse myself and put on fresh clothes?"

"I can."

Haltingly, he moved toward the door to his bedchamber.

"I could aid you should you need it," she offered.

"Go."

Persephone blinked, startled by the harshness in his voice. Then she turned and moved from the bedchamber. A low groan followed her into the hallway. She paused, but the vehemence with which he commanded her to depart had been unequivocal. He didn't want her aid. She walked away but not without many doubtful glances over her shoulder.

As she descended the stairs, she came upon Nadira studying the frescoes on the walls in the entryway. Persephone called her name.

The woman jumped and spun toward Persephone. Persephone could scarcely fault her for her fear. Nadira had been in the Underworld only six days. Persephone had been resident here for some months and was still neither fully at ease with this place nor with the company she kept here.

"Would you like to dine out of doors today?" Persephone asked.

Nadira smiled and nodded eagerly.

As though in answer to her enthusiasm, a howl rippled through the air: Cerberus, crying out his need to reclaim the one he'd lost.

Nadira's smile turned fixed and rigid as she glanced toward the doors.

"Hades will accompany us. He'll ensure no harm comes to you," Persephone said, walking to Nadira and taking her hand. "Now come. We need to prepare our repast."

Persephone climbed the stairs to her chambers, Nadira at her heels. It was a relief that the ordeal of the past handful of days was at an end. It had been nearly unbearable, enclosed with Nadira in the palace while Cerberus prowled without, howling his discontent all day and through the dark of the Underworld night. It took all Persephone's courage to force herself from the palace each day to free the horses from their stable. Though Cerberus didn't threaten her with bite or bark, he stalked behind her in Elysium, his six eyes following her every movement with unsettling intent. Persephone didn't dare leave the horses even for a few moments to check on her plants' progress in the folly.

Cerberus's vigil also forced Persephone to put aside all thought of fleeing from the Underworld with Nadira and Lethe. Cerberus wouldn't allow them to get ten paces beyond the palace gates. Almost, she was glad of the beast's presence. It freed her from wondering if there were other reasons why she didn't take the opportunity for escape that Hades's infirmity provided her.

Persephone moved to the table in her megaron and collected the bread and cheese left from their noon meal. Nadira took grapes, olives, and figs from a basket and brought them to the table.

Persephone went into her bedchamber to find a bit of cloth in which to tie up the food. She returned to her megaron and started when she saw Hades standing in the doorway, pale, silent, eyes glittering in the dimness. Nadira stood frozen in the middle of the room, eyes wide with terror.

Persephone hurried to the woman. "You needn't fear him. He won't harm you."

Nadira flicked a glance at Persephone then returned her terrified attention to Hades.

Persephone wanted to tell Nadira how Hades, at great personal cost, had restored her to life, but the woman didn't seem to know she'd been dead, seemed to fully believe she'd merely been ill and was in this place only until her convalescence was over. Persephone didn't want to give Nadira more reason to be afraid, but it was wrong that the Sicani woman feared Hades when she owed him so much. The only thing Persephone could do to right that wrong, however, was repeat with all the certainty she felt, "He won't harm you."

"It is as Persephone says. You're safe here, but I'll keep my distance if that makes you feel easier," Hades said.

Nadira nodded vigorously.

"Very well. Shall we repair to Elysium?" Hades asked.

Persephone hurried to the table and packed the food into the cloth she'd brought from her bedchamber. "Please."

Hades turned and left the megaron. Persephone gave Nadira a re-assuring smile and the woman fell into step with Persephone as she followed Hades.

They exited the palace and were halfway across the courtyard to the stable doors when a barrage of blows shook the palace gates. Snarls, whines, and growls reached Persephone's ears. She halted and Nadira did the same.

Hades, however, changed direction, walking toward the courtyard entrance as he called over his shoulder, "Stay here until I say you may do otherwise."

Hades lifted the bar from across the gate. One side sprung open and a snapping, snarling head entered the breach. Persephone gasped. Nadira clutched at Persephone's hand and drew closer to her.

Hades shoved the head out then followed it, yanking the wooden slab firmly closed behind him. The crack of Hades's whip shattered the air. The sound was followed by a short yip. There was silence for a time then a high keening whine, a sound Phlox often made when asking for another honey cake, though Cerberus begged for something much more terrible than that flavorsome delicacy. The whip cracked once again and the whining ceased.

The gate swung open.

Persephone stepped in front of Nadira, tensing for an attack, but only Hades came through. He placed the bar back in its metal brackets, turned to Persephone and said, "He'll not harm Nadira now and a day more should see her fully recovered and ready to return home. Cerberus will no longer pose a danger to her then."

Despite Hades's reassurance, Persephone still kept a tight grip on Nadira's hand as she and the Sicani woman half ran to the stable doors.

Persephone wrestled one open and they hurried inside. Hades followed, head down, shoulders drawn up. Persephone cursed his slowness, for she couldn't close and bar the doors as she longed to do. Nadira darted deeper into the stables.

Hades finally entered. Persephone closed the doors almost on his heels. He gave her a tired, humorless smile and moved to free Styx from his stall. Passing off the bundle of food to Nadira, Persephone released Lethe then Akheron. She left Phlegethon for Hades. The horse reared and squealed, kicked out his heels, particularly restless because Persephone hadn't dared let him run in Elysium during Hades's illness though she had brought the horse armfuls of fresh grass and filled his trough with water every day.

Persephone herded Nadira, Akheron, Styx, and Lethe out of the stable. While the horses ambled into the meadow, Nadira stopped, blinking, as if stunned, as Persephone had been at her first sight of Elysium.

Hades came out with Phlegethon on a lead. The pair walked past Persephone and Nadira. A good distance out, Hades halted the horse. Phlegethon resisted, jerking his head up, snorting and dancing in an effort to break Hades's hold on his tether. It was apparent the animal wanted to be let loose to run and just as apparent Hades had no intention of allowing that. From his belt swung a rope that he'd already fashioned into hobbles, though how he was going to get them on the agitated creature, Persephone didn't know. Perhaps if she held Phlegethon's lead, Hades could calm the horse enough that he would allow himself to be hobbled. But Phlegethon frightened her, and she hadn't Hades's strength or skill in dealing with the tempestuous beast. Likely, if she involved herself, she would only make matters worse.

Shame and defeat pricked at Persephone with twin needles. She looked away from Hades's and Phlegethon's tussle and caught sight of the folly.

The weight on her heart eased some. While she couldn't command Phlegethon, she had succeeded in bringing Upper World plants to life here in this land below, a feat even Hermes deemed impossible. And now she had someone to share that achievement with. Perhaps, Nadira, upon her return to Henna, would speak of it to the Sicani and they would know, at long last, that Persephone didn't herald death and despair.

Persephone took Nadira by the hand and tugged her toward the folly. She pulled open the door. In her enthusiasm, she forgot to warn Nadira to narrow her eyes against the light or to do so herself. The mortal woman's mouth opened in a silent cry while Persephone put up a shielding hand and waited for her vision to adjust. Her skin needed no such transition, however. The warmth and brightness were immediately welcome to her chilled flesh.

After her eyes accustomed themselves, Persephone dropped her hand and stepped inside the hut. She gasped. Greenery abounded in every trough and pot. There were no blooms yet, but from the shape of the leaves it was easy to recognize every plant here as some kind of flower. When they did blossom, the display would be exquisite, just the thing to lift the somber mood and heavy heart of the lord of the Underworld.

Nadira stepped into the room, gestured about, and looked at Persephone with a question in her eyes.

Persephone put a hand to her chest. "I grew them. I did this."

"Indeed, you did."

Persephone spun. Hades stood in the doorway, gaze roaming around the folly. His face was as expressionless as his voice as he took in the profuse growth.

Persephone's stomach churned and her palms went damp with sweat. She'd done something wrong. Or perhaps he was displeased because she succeeded where he had failed.

She stepped toward him, an apology trembling on her lips. Though begging pardon had never mitigated any punishment Demeter chose to mete out, Hades might prove to be different in that regard, as he had in so many other ways.

Before she could speak, he murmured, "This is extraordinary." Then his gaze stopped its circuit of the room, settled on her face and his eyes sheened with sudden tears. "Extraordinary."

Persephone's breath gusted from her in a relieved gasp. "You're not angry?"

Hades swiped a hand across his eyes, gave a little chuckle. "Angry? What cause have I to be angry?" He opened his arms as though he meant to embrace the room. "This is the most marvelous ..." His gaze dropped to her face. "Words fail me, Persephone, but no, I'm not angry, simply in awe."

A God. In awe. Of a thing she'd accomplished. Something in Persephone's chest kindled, swelled, and burned away all her uncertainty. She'd done this all on her own and no amount of angry words or hard hands could steal that knowledge from her. It belonged to her and always would.

Persephone reached up, putting a hand to Hades's cheek. "Thank you."

Hades closed his eyes, then turned his face and pressed a kiss to Persephone's palm. Something as quick and fearsome as lightning shot down her arm. Persephone took in a trembling breath but didn't pull away.

Hades looked back at her, drew her hand away from his cheek, held it between both of his. "I'm the one with all the cause to be grateful."

A soft touch on Persephone's shoulder startled her. She turned. Nadira lifted the pouch containing the food, pointed to it, and raised her eyebrows.

Persephone chuckled. "Yes, we can eat." She looked back at Hades. "I know you're famished."

Hades inclined his head in agreement, then stepped back out of the doorway. Persephone's fingers slid slowly, reluctantly from his as she followed Nadira out of the folly and into Elysium's grasses.

Nadira sat and undid the cloth bundle. Persephone lowered herself so the food sat between them and Hades took a seat at Persephone's side. Amid many darted glances at him, Nadira parceled out the food. While Hades professed to be hungry, he ate with very little appetite. After only a few bites of this and that, he rose and returned to the stable.

Heart pounding, Persephone looked about for Cerberus but the dog was nowhere to be seen. The creature, it seemed, remained obedient to Hades's command.

When Hades exited the stable, he held the bow in one hand and the quiver of arrows in the other. As he walked toward Persephone, he called, "It's been some time since we've done this. I thought you might like to see how much of your lesson you recall."

Persephone had forgotten very little of that lesson, indeed had thought of it overly much in the time since; Hades's hands on her, her buttocks nestled firmly in the cradle of his hips as he showed her the proper way to hold a bow, the catch in his throat when she shifted against him. A flush of heat prickled over her head to toe.

To hide her discomfiture, Persephone turned to Nadira, "Would you care to shoot with us?"

Nadira greeted the suggestion with all the affront of a proper Sicani woman, waving her hands in an emphatic denial.

Persephone rose on legs that trembled ever so slightly and made her way to Hades's side. She couldn't meet his eyes as she took the quiver from him and slung it over her back. When she lifted her head from adjusting the strap between her breasts he quickly looked away as though her gaze would scorch him should it brush his. He handed her the bow without a word then took a step back, making it apparent she would be shooting without his assistance.

Turning so Nadira was at her back, Persephone reached into the quiver and pulled an arrow free. She nocked it, lifted the bow, sighted down the shaft at an asphodel, and let go. With a hiss the arrow excised the top of the blossom. Persephone gave a triumphant laugh.

"May I try?" Hades extended a hand, no sign of his earlier unease.

Persephone relinquished the bow. Hades plucked an arrow from the quiver and in one quick motion nocked, lifted, aimed, shot, yet no flower dropped its laden head. Persephone narrowed her eyes, leaned forward.

"You needn't strain so. I missed," Hades said, a laugh in his voice as he returned the bow to her.

Joining her laughter to Hades's, Persephone selected another arrow. "I never thought to best a man in archery, to say nothing of a God."

Persephone lifted the bow, aimed. In the moment she let fly, something prickled at the back of her knee. Her shot went wild.

She turned to see Hades looking over Elysium, his face a study of concentration. In one hand he held an arrow on which the fletching was slightly askew.

Hades turned his head, met her eyes. "It seems your skill has deserted you, Lady."

"Very well, a contest then to settle who is the better archer."

Hades inclined his head. "What prize to the winner?"

Hades would never grant the one thing Persephone wanted most from him, no matter if she bested him once or a thousand times and asking him to free her would only ruin this lighthearted moment. She waved her hand. "A garland of flowers to wear in my hair."

"You shall have it."

"And what shall your prize be?"

Hades's eyes swept Persephone's face and body. A strange sensation quivered over her in the wake of his perusal making goosebumps erupt from her skin and sweat prickle on her upper lip.

He looked away from her, eyes taking in Elysium once again. "It's been many years since I've had flowers in my hair. Like you, I shall accept a garland as my prize." He looked back at Persephone. "Shall we begin?"

Before giving her assent, Persephone turned to see how Nadira fared. The woman was on her feet now, gathering a bouquet of Elysium's strange blooms.

Persephone turned back to Hades, and offered the bow. He waved it away, gestured for her to go first. A smile on her face, heart thumping at the challenge before her, Persephone reached for an arrow.

In what seemed to be a matter of moments the quiver was empty, arrows scattered hither and yon. For every hit of Persephone's, Hades had an equal number of missed shots.

Persephone cocked a smile at him. "I'll have my garland now."

"And you'll get it. Though it may take me some time to learn the ways of flower weaving. Will you teach me?"

"I'd be pleased to." Persephone bent her neck in a little mocking bow and some strands of hair wafted forward over her face.

Hades lifted his hand, hesitated.

Persephone held his gaze, held her breath.

He brushed the hair back then trailed his fingers down her cheek, the touch warming her like a ray of Helios's light.

Smiling down at her, he said, "I imagine the last week shut up in the palace has made you restive. Shall we walk while I gather your flowers?"

It took a moment for Persephone to regain enough composure and breath to say, "Will Nadira be . . ."

"Cerberus won't dare disturb her so long as I'm near."

Persephone fell into step with him and they walked, keeping on a parallel with the palace, silence holding them close in its friendly folds. The backs of their fingers brushed once, twice. The third time, Persephone slid her hand into Hades's. She glanced at him. He kept his eyes straight ahead, but gave her palm a gentle squeeze.

Lethe grazed his way towards them and soon fell into step with Persephone, though he kept his nose in the grass as if he were utterly unaware of her presence.

After a time, Hades said, "I wish to speak to you of the act of physical love."

Persephone turned questioning eyes on him. The knob in the front of his neck bobbed once, then twice. His chest expanded with the size of the breath he drew in.

Keeping his eyes on the horizon he began to speak. "I lived the first part of my life in darkness, Persephone. I was surrounded by it, inundated with it. When I was released from Kronos's stomach, I was pressed immediately into a battle I knew not how to fight, but fight I did, and we won. Then, after a brief interlude, I came here and spent the next nine years in darkness of a different kind. Though I'm years older than you, I've walked in the world scarcely longer than you have."

He cleared his throat once, then again. "I've known only two women in my life and that was scarcely a comprehensive lesson in how women think, feel, and behave. They each, however, in their own way, educated me in the pleasure lovers can give one another when they share their bodies. The last of these experiences was some years ago. In the time since I haven't ... I ... what I mean to say is, the first night we were together in my realm, I was as a starving man before a feast. I took more than you were willing or even ready to give. In doing so, I hurt you and made you afraid of me."

Persephone stopped walking and yanked her hand out of his grasp. Through thin bloodless lips she said, "I don't wish to speak of what occurred between us that night."

Hades lifted his hands, palms up, beseeching. "You needn't say anything, but I beg you to allow me to say my piece. If I don't, I worry it will forever remain between us."

Though Persephone nodded her permission for him to continue, she wrapped one arm around her own waist and placed her other hand on Lethe's neck, drawing close to the big horse and farther away from Hades. The trembling in her limbs and belly eased some.

Hades began to walk again as he spoke. "Before I brought you here, I believed I could turn your heart to me with proof of my love. I'm not, as some men are, easy with words. I knew it was only by my actions I could show you how much I cared for you, so I adored you. I painted the walls in your chambers with new and different images from what I put there previously. I know the blooms in Elysium can't compare with those flowers that flourish under Helios's light. I hoped my frescoes would return to you some of that lost beauty. When I went to Olympus to ask Zeus for permission to wed you, I plundered his palace for any finery I thought would delight you: ostrich egg cups painted with the daintiest of flowers, carved ivory combs, pots of sweet-smelling ointments, jewelry wrought by the finest of artisans. I collected from the Goddesses the most beautiful of their robes for your use, but still I knew my palace was a chill, grim place. Not one a maid would care for. Then I recalled Hekate telling me of her bed of fleece and blankets on the floor of your hut in Henna where, when you were distraught or afraid in the night, you would go to her for comfort. I fashioned such a nest in your bedchamber here and meant for you to rest in my arms the way you did in hers, hoping it would make you feel as though there were things familiar and loved here in the Underworld. I know now it wasn't enough, could never be enough to make you care for an existence in this place." He paused and then said, "I still hope, however, that my love will make up all the rest."

He lapsed into silence and Persephone glanced at him.

He turned his eyes to meet hers and she looked away.

Hades continued. "When I came to your sleeping chamber your first night here, I meant only to calm and comfort you in the way Hekate told me she did. I was caught unawares by how much I wanted you. I allowed myself to be overcome and selfishly chased the satisfaction of my own desires, making me heedless, for a time, to your pleas for me to stop. When the fear in your voice finally penetrated my haze, I realized how deeply I hurt and frightened you. I abhorred myself, have abhorred myself every day since. I long to make reparation. If I could, I ..."

At his silence, Persephone looked at him once more. Hades dragged his hand over his lower face, swiping at his lips and his beard again and again in obvious agitation. Finally, dropping his hand, he met her eyes. "I can't tell you how deeply I regret that night. If it were possible, I would go back and do it all differently."

Clutching at Lethe's mane, Persephone said, "You stole me away from my home. You used your hands to force me to do your will. You took from me the sanctuary of my own body, the only thing I had left to me in this place. I've spent so much of my time here in fear that you'll force yourself on me again, hurt me more than you did the first time."

"I won't. I vow it. By the River Styx, I vow it.

Persephone shook her head. "How am I to trust that? You took me captive. You deny all my requests for freedom and make it impossible for me to escape. You force your will on me in every other thing. How can I know you won't make me accept your attentions again?"

He scraped his hand over his lips, down his beard again. This time when he lowered his hand, it hit his thigh with a defeated sounding thump. "You can't. Though I hope these past months of being careful and considerate in the ways I touch you has inspired some belief that you can trust my vow."

Persephone looked away from him, her eyes picking out the hazy ribbon of the River Lethe on the horizon. There were so many replies, too many replies she could make: that she knew how alike they were, that she saw the kindness in him, that she longed to allay his loneliness, that her body continually betrayed her in its lust for him, but, despite all that, still, still, she couldn't trust him.

"Is it still your wish to return to home?"

Persephone held herself motionless, kept her eyes on the horizon. Perhaps this was some ruse of his to find out the truth of her feelings. If she told him what she wanted he might rage at her, forbid her from leaving the palace. Or, perhaps, he sincerely wanted her happiness even at the cost of his own. The only way to know was to answer him truthfully. His reaction would, at the very least, clarify how she should feel about him.

"I do."

Hades said nothing for a long moment. She swiveled her gaze to him. He was also staring into the distance, his fist clenching and unclenching at his side. Her stomach plunged and she took a careful step away from him, crowding even closer to Lethe.

Hades drew breath once, twice, turned his head to meet her gaze. "Very well. On the morrow, when Nadira's transformation is complete, I'll convey you both to Nysa. Perhaps being part of her restoration will cause the Sicani to look kindlier on you."

Exultation pulsed through Persephone. With a cry, she flung herself at Hades, wrapped her arms around his neck. His arms came around her waist, and he pulled her close. An awareness of how easily he could overpower her in this moment penetrated her haze of joy. She pulled back from the embrace. He loosened his hold and looked down at her.

Persephone surveyed his face, taking in forehead, cheeks, brows, hair, lips. Her eyes lingered there. He lowered his head. Their breath mingled, heated and humid between them. He didn't press his lips to hers though she found she wanted him to, very much. She made a small sound, one of frustration or need or both. Finally, his mouth found hers, her eyes closing as their lips touched.

His arms were hard as they tightened around her, his body as solid and all-encompassing as the walls of his palace, but this time there was no fear, no thought of escape in her mind. Instead, her hands twined tighter around his neck, fingers tangling in his hair.

Hades abruptly pulled away.

Persephone opened her eyes.

The face that looked down on her was that of the God who'd taken her from her home, cold, hard, impregnable. He stepped back from her, his arms falling from around her waist. "We should return to the palace. You no doubt want to make preparations for your departure."

Persephone reached for him. "Hades, I—" Then she heard the long, baying cry of the beast on the hunt, Cerberus.

21

PERSEPHONE

Persephone spun, screaming Nadira's name.

Akheron and Styx pounded toward Persephone, nostrils flaring, manes flying. They blocked her view of where she'd last seen the Sicani woman. Persephone darted between the horses' big black bodies.

"Persephone, no!" Hades yelled from behind her.

Some distance out, near where Phlegethon plunged and bucked, fighting his hobbles, Nadira fled toward Persephone, hair streaming behind her, mouth open in a silent scream, Cerberus at her heels. The creature almost looked as though he were grinning, his rows of bone-white, knife-sharp teeth revealed by his snarl. The serpents on his back whipped and writhed as their tongues flickered in and out of their mouths, seeking the one they hunted. His muscular legs rapidly ate up the space between him and his prey.

Persephone wouldn't reach Nadira before the beast and even if she did, she wasn't strong enough to fend him off. Remembering the bow and quiver of arrows slung on her back, Persephone stopped, pulled the bow over her head, then fumbled at the quiver, but it was empty. She and Hades had left the arrows scattered in Elysium's grasses. There was nothing she could do to aid Nadira.

Hades's footsteps thudded behind her and a small glimmer of hope pierced her terror and hopelessness.

Hades's hand clamped on her arm and he swung her around to face him. "No, Persephone. It's too late."

A growling bark filled her ears. Persephone craned her head around. Cerberus leaped and bore Nadira to the ground, front paws on the woman's back, one mouth clamped on her nape, the others on her arms, ensuring her immobility as the serpents struck her again and again. Though Nadira writhed and fought, her struggles were conducted in horrifying silence.

Persephone looked back at Hades. Surely, he would intervene, but he made no move, didn't even call Cerberus's name. And he held Persephone in a bruising grip so she could do nothing to help.

"Bring him to heel," Persephone cried.

"Be silent," Hades commanded.

"Bring him to heel. You must."

"When he's caught in the madness of the hunt, he obeys none, not even me. Now be silent if you don't wish to be his next victim."

Persephone looked back over her shoulder, helpless, horrified. Nadira's body jerked and twitched under Cerberus's bulk and blood spurted from every wound Cerberus inflicted. Nadira lifted her head. Pink foam lined the woman's lips. For one sickening instant her eyes settled on Persephone. The plea in them was unbearable.

Persephone turned away, turned to Hades. Sweat boiled from his pores. His skin was waxy, white, his jaw clenched, lips clamped.

Persephone struggled against his grip. "Let me go. Let me aid her if you won't."

Hades hissed from between his teeth, "Despite your months here, you've learned little of my realm. Are you a fool that you don't see this is how it must be? Cerberus has caught his quarry. There's nothing you or

I can do to alter that. If you haven't the stomach to look on it close your eyes until it's finished."

His words throbbing in her ears, Persephone rained blows on him, bucked and twisted. She wriggled from his grasp, darted away. He caught her, dragged her back. She screamed out her fury and helplessness, arching away from him, clawing at his hands.

"It's finished, Persephone!" Hades roared.

When she continued to struggle, he shook her until her head whipped back and forth on her neck. She bit her tongue and the pain brought her back to herself. She went still.

"It's finished." Hades panted, hands tight on her upper arms, eyes boring into hers.

Persephone swallowed the blood oozing from her bitten tongue, nodded her understanding. Hades released her. Persephone whirled and ran, seeking a haven as she had in Henna when her mother's words cut too deep.

Hades pursued as Persephone sped to the place she'd last seen Lethe. The big horse stood, eyes wide and white-ringed, ears swiveling madly, but still there.

With an ease that in different circumstances would have surprised her, Persephone grasped Lethe's mane and flung her leg up and over his back. Hades's fingers skittered over her ankle. She kicked out. With a burst of pain her heel connected with something solid and Hades's hand fell away.

Persephone bent low to Lethe's neck, hissed 'tcha' in his ear and squeezed his sides with all the strength in her legs.

With a surprised snort, Lethe lunged forward. Then, with a fury and speed that snatched Persephone's breath and dried the tears on her cheeks as fast as they fell, Lethe hurled them away from Hades, past Cerberus who crouched, snarling over Nadira's slack and motionless body.

Hades whistled, calling Lethe. Persephone flexed the muscles in her legs, preparing for the horse to turn and hurtle back to his master, but he didn't. He continued galloping without so much as a twitch of his ears in Hades's direction.

"Oh, my Great Heart. Oh, my Lethe. Thank you," Persephone murmured, bending low over his neck.

Even with Lethe's willingness to bear her where she wanted, she wasn't free yet. The other horses wouldn't share Lethe's unwillingness to answer Hades's summons though it would take them some time to return from wherever they'd fled when Cerberus attacked. Then, she recalled Phlegethon, hobbled and near at hand. In but moments, Hades would be mounted and in pursuit. She urged Lethe to greater speed.

As Lethe hurtled around the palace and down the road toward the Temple of Judgment it seemed to Persephone that the rhythm of his hooves pounded out Nadira's name over and again. Under the pain of that poor woman's second death, one for which Persephone was almost as responsible as she had been for the first, pulsed the agony of Hades's betrayal. He was just as Demeter. Beneath all his patience and praise, he too thought her simple, foolish, weak. And, just like Demeter, cruelty had come fast on the heels of his kindness.

When Lethe reached the Temple of Judgment, Persephone shouted with all of her might. The shades that amassed there scattered before Lethe's flashing hooves, calling out in anger and fear as she pounded past.

At the juncture of roads, Persephone urged Lethe to turn toward the River Styx. At that moment, Cerberus's call rent the air again, raising all the hair on her neck and arms. Persephone dug her heels into Lethe's side and squeezed with her thighs. "If you love me, Lethe, run. Go!"

Lethe swung left and loped up the small rise there with hardly a break in his stride. Then they were galloping through the Vale of Mourning and rushing onward into the heart of the asphodel meadow.

When they reached the part of the asphodel meadow where the shades clustered thickest, darkness fell over the Underworld between one blink of Persephone's eyes and the next.

Snorting, Lethe bounced to an abrupt halt. Persephone's buttocks rose from his back and her face slammed into his neck. She settled back into her seat with a muffled 'oomph' of pain then looked wildly about her, envisioning Cerberus bearing down on her from behind.

Lethe reared and danced on his hocks, shaking his head and neighing. He was only moments away from turning and bolting for the safety of his stall. Persephone slid forward on his back, searched with her fingers until she found his ears and, scratching and fondling them at the roots, began to murmur the soothing nonsenses Hades used to calm his mounts.

In pretending to be unafraid for the horse, Persephone found a measure of true calm welling within her. Her breath became less ragged. Her panicked thoughts slowed in their tumultuous circling. She continued to soothe the horse as she looked about her, trying to lay out some semblance of a plan.

She had fled in a panic and took this road because it was familiar and she knew an exit from this world lay at the end of it, no matter that she couldn't reach it. Now she was committed to this route for if she turned and went another way, she would surely meet Hades and Cerberus as they pursued her. Truly though, the only seemingly insurmountable obstacle to escaping this way was Styx. Charon wouldn't allow her on the ferry without Hades at her side and even a single drop of the river's water would cause her pain and plunge her into insensibility. Though she didn't relish the thought of the agony, should she fail in her escape attempt, nine years of unconsciousness might be a welcome respite from all she suffered in this place. Even still, she wouldn't attempt to cross on her own. She could ride Lethe into the river but she wasn't sure if his endurance in water matched that of his on land. She needed to find a narrow crossing point.

With both she and Lethe in a calmer state, Persephone urged her mount forward and he set off in a distance devouring canter. When they reached Styx's bank, Persephone slowed Lethe to a walk. There was a strange, floating ball of pale blue light far out on the river. Squinting, she made out the silhouette of a man with a pole in his hand. The illumination was some sort of lamp on the ferry.

They couldn't cross here, lest Charon see and detain them. Persephone urged Lethe to turn parallel to the river. Then, as Cerberus bayed again, Persephone asked the horse for more speed. He obliged and, as he loped along, Persephone peered at the river.

She spotted a black hulk far out in the water and stopped Lethe so she could further study it. Though she couldn't make out any details, it appeared to be an island. Its distance from the shore they stood on didn't seem too far. Lethe could surely swim it. Once on the island, he could rest before completing the crossing to the opposite bank.

Her heart lifted, but plunged once again when Hades called her name from much too close by. She rode Lethe a short distance upstream from the island. The current looked sluggish but that didn't necessarily mean it was so. She had no way to judge if it would take them to their destination or sweep them past it. The only way to find out was to make the experiment. She kneed Lethe forward to the bank of the river. He balked a bit, but then joggled down the slight slope, easing into the black water.

The cold of it caught Persephone by surprise. She lost her grip on Lethe's back. The current swept her away from him and only her hands in his mane kept her from being lost to Styx's treacherous depths. Rather than trying to remount in the water, it would likely submerge both she and Lethe, Persephone tightened her grip on his mane and floated alongside the horse, kicking her legs in rhythm with the powerful strokes of his. Her neck instantly ached with the effort of holding her head high and keeping her mouth tightly closed against the splashing wavelets.

She whimpered in relief when the bulk of the island loomed in front of them. Before Lethe could climb fully from the water, she swung her leg over his back.

Lethe lunged up the low bank of the island and stopped. The muddy stretch of a marsh pockmarked with gnarled, dead trees and low grassy hummocks lay before them. Lethe flung his head up, snorted, and backed until his rear hooves slid down the bank and back into the river.

"Charon!" Hades bellowed from the riverbank.

Persephone had only moments before Hades learned she hadn't attempted to board the ferry. Then he would search the riverbank. She was sure Cerberus, with his three noses, would have no trouble scenting them out and showing Hades exactly where she and Lethe had crossed.

"Lethe, please, go. You must," she sobbed and kneed him forward once more.

This time the horse went, though slowly, making his way delicately from hummock to hummock as if the mud were hot to the touch.

"Persephone!"

Her heart twisted at the despair in Hades's cry, but she couldn't allow herself to be lured back by his remorse. Should she return to him, he would only hurt her again.

Lethe came to an abrupt halt, his entire body quivering.

"Lethe, go," Persephone cried and dug her heels into his ribs as hard as she could.

He squealed, gave an awkward hop forward and landed in an expanse of mud.

"Lethe? Persephone?" Hades was much closer now, close enough that he'd heard Lethe.

The heave of Lethe's body underneath Persephone drew her attention back to the big horse. Under her legs, his ribs expanded and contracted as he labored to breathe. His head lunged back then forward and down with every step and the time between stretched longer and longer.

She leaned forward to whisper encouragement in his ear and stopped mid-motion, eyes wide. He was sunk to the knee in mud. His muscles visibly shook as he struggled to take a step. Finally, with a sucking sound that made her think of Nadira's mouth fastened on Hades's bleeding arm, Lethe's leg came free. It trembled as he raised it and placed it into the mud only slightly in front of where he'd extracted it.

Persephone turned and looked at his hindquarters. They too were trembling with effort, but he failed with his back legs where he had succeeded with his front and they sunk ever deeper into the ooze around them. The horse groaned and his effortful shaking ceased.

"Lethe. Oh, Lethe," Persephone pressed her face into his mane. "My Great Heart. Don't give up."

Lethe neighed shrilly and tossed his head.

Persephone straightened, looked around, and launched herself toward the closest hummock of grass. Her upper body landed on it, but her legs splashed into the mud. It's cold caress immediately dragged at her calves and thighs. Struggling with a determination borne of desperation, she dug her fingers into the solid earth of the hummock, clutched great handfuls of the dead grass and hauled herself up until she was free of the mire.

Cold, mud-covered, and shivering, she turned to Lethe. The red of his distended nostrils and the whites of his rolling eyes stood out starkly against the dark but his black coat blended with the night making it appear that the Underworld was already consuming him.

"Come, Lethe. Come on. Come to me." Her words were more plea than command. "It's only your weight you have to lift now. Come. You must. You must. I can't lose you too."

Lethe flung his head back, then lowered it as though lunging up a steep slope. His body quivered with effort.

"Yes, Lethe. That's it. Come on. Come on now."

He tried. He tried so very hard to do as she asked, but all his struggle only sunk him deeper in the mire. When the sludge reached the top of his legs, he gave a deep groan and gave up the fight.

22

PERSEPHONE

White-blue light bathed one side of Persephone's body. Momentarily blinded, she turned toward it and screamed Hades's name, the force of her cry coating her tongue with the metal tang of blood. When her eyes adjusted to the light, Hades was wading through the treacherous mud toward her.

"Persephone," he cried, gathering her into his arms the moment he reached her. "Are you well? Did you drink of Styx's water?"

"Lethe!" she screamed, fighting his hold, her entire body straining toward the big horse.

Hades turned. With a guttural cry of pain, he released her.

Lethe was now chest deep in the sucking ooze.

"Charon!" Hades bellowed. "I'll flay your hide, man, if you don't obey me now. Bring Phlegethon and the rope from the ferry. And keep to the grass."

Hades slipped into the mud and splashed, arms swinging, legs lifting high to Lethe's side. His presence seemed to give Lethe renewed strength for the horse began, once again, to battle the mire that bound him.

Hades put his hands on either side of Lethe's face, pressed his forehead to the horse's and murmured his litany of soothing sounds. Persephone turned away from the sight, grief and guilt clawing at her.

"I come, Hades," Charon called.

Persephone raised her head. Charon approached, leading Phlegethon, as they both carefully picked their way from hummock to hummock. When the pair reached a fair-sized piece of solid dirt and grass some way in front of Lethe, Hades called to them to stop.

"Hold to one end and toss me the rest of the rope," Hades instructed Charon.

Charon did as Hades asked. Hades caught the rope, circled it behind Lethe's forelegs, and tied it fast at the base of the horse's mane. Using the line, he hauled himself from the mud onto the bank next to Charon. He pulled his whip from around his torso, circled Phlegethon's neck with it, and tied it there, making a kind of improvised yoke. On one side of it, he tied off a length of line, passed what remained of the rope across Phlegethon's chest and secured it on the other side of the whip, forming a harness. Then he moved well behind Phlegethon's hindquarters, gripped the line and leaned back.

Phlegethon took two stumbling steps backward then, squealing, struck out with his rear hooves, but the harness held. Hades returned to Phlegethon's head and soothed him.

Turning away from the big horse to look at Persephone, Hades said, "I need you to ride Phlegethon. When I say you must, urge him forward while Charon and I push at Lethe's hindquarters."

Persephone looked from Hades to Phlegethon then back. Hades had told her this was a horse that would trample Zeus himself. She couldn't command the beast. Yet, Lethe's life depended on her ability to do so, just as Nadira's had depended on Persephone's ability to face down her mother. Persephone had failed Nadira, but she was no longer the girl she'd been on that day, the day Hades had taken her from the Upper World. She'd learned to ride, to shoot, to bring life in a place meant only

251

to contain the dead. She had to take on this challenge too, for Lethe's sake. And she had to prove equal to it.

Persephone drew in a deep steadying breath, then fixed her gaze on her goal and made her way from hummock to hummock until she was at Hades's side.

Her feet had hardly settled on the ground from her last leap before Hades caught her about the waist and flung her atop Phlegethon. The big horse reared, but Persephone expected this and by tightening the muscles in her thighs, made strong by so many hours on Lethe's back, leaning forward, and clinging to the whip that encircled his neck was she able to keep her seat. Once Phlegethon dropped to all fours, still snorting and dancing beneath her, Persephone shifted to settle herself more firmly. Then, she turned her upper body and watched as Hades and Charon, holding onto the rope, waded into the mud.

The moment they entered the ooze, Lethe began to struggle again, snorting, neighing, and tossing his head while Hades pleaded with him to calm. The light from the ferry cast its eerie glow over the entire scene. Their lean black shadows twitched, jerked, and writhed in its bobbing illumination, lending Lethe's movement a frenetic, disjointed quality as though he were already in his death throes. Panic rising, climbing ever higher, muddying her thoughts, making her limbs quake, Persephone turned from the sight. She must stay clear-headed and agile for what was to come.

"Now!" Hades shouted.

As though she were once again urging her mount to run as he never had before, Persephone leaned low over Phlegethon's neck, dug her heels into his ribs and clenched her legs to his body with all the strength she possessed. Phlegethon came up onto his hind legs, but only for a moment before lunging forward, his muscles quivering immediately with the strain of what he attempted. Behind Persephone, Charon and Hades grunted and cursed. The leather of the whip added its creaking protest to the cacophony of effort.

Lethe let out a squeal of pain and Hades bellowed, "Cease."

Persephone sunk her weight downward, bringing Phlegethon to a halt. Blowing hard, he came to a standstill, gave a half snort-half whinny and shook his mane.

Persephone turned. An empty space opened in her chest. Lethe had, if anything, sunk deeper into the muck. Hades was at his side, peering down at the rope around Lethe's body.

"Cutting into his flesh," he muttered then raised his head, met her eyes.

She blinked away, trying to shield herself from the hopelessness in their depths. Then, shaking her head wildly to dislodge the despair that attempted to roost there, she turned to Hades and called, "Again."

Hades gave a terse nod and took his place at Lethe's hindquarters once more.

"Now," he called and again Persephone urged Phlegethon forward, his front hooves tapping at the ground, struggling for purchase as the muscles in his hind legs bunched and strained against the great weight behind him. Lethe let out another squeal of pain, but Hades didn't give the order to cease, so Persephone squeezed Phlegethon harder with her legs and yelled encouragements and curses as he pawed at the ground, grunted and trembled with effort.

They strove and struggled and pushed into a void that seemed to have no beginning and no end. Then, with a dull snap, the knot on the whip gave.

Phlegethon lunged at the sudden release of the weight behind him and went to his knees. Persephone lurched forward just as the handle of the whip flew up, striking her hard on the cheekbone. She gasped at the pain that sparkled through her face and up into her temple then called to Hades that the whip had come undone.

"Enough, Charon," Hades said.

Persephone dropped from Phlegethon's back and walked to the horse's hindquarters. Lethe was still as firmly mired as before, but she refused to let herself despair. Hades would find some way to get him free. He wouldn't give up as easily on Lethe as he had Nadira.

She took a step forward and her toes bumped something. Looking down, she saw the rope lying on the ground. She picked it up and held the line taut so Hades and Charon could use it to reach the grassy stretch where she stood. However, when Hades reached Lethe's head he stopped. Only Charon continued to slog forward through the mud.

"Hades?" Persephone called.

He looked at her.

"What must we do now?"

Hades's gaze faltered down from hers. He tugged something free from his belt, raised his hand. The light from the ferry twitched, glittering along the length of the blade Hades now held.

"No!" Persephone shouted, darting forward, but the mud immediately impeded her.

Hades pressed his forehead to Lethe's, reached up to fondle the horse's ears with the hand not holding the knife. For a moment, Persephone thought she had misread his intentions.

Then, Lethe shrieked.

"No!" Persephone screamed again, lifting her hands as if warding off a blow.

The red black of Lethe's blood pumped from the slash in his neck. It mingled with the mud at his chest as his head slumped sideways into the muck, his warm brown eye already flat and opaque in the eternal shade of death. Hades moved away from Lethe, his face empty of emotion.

"No," Persephone repeated. Her denial held no power. Lethe was dead and no word or deed could change that. All the affection Lethe held, all the comfort he had given her here in the Underworld, just as Phlox had provided her in the Upper, was at an end, but this was worse, so much worse than Persephone's loss of Phlox. She left the old dog fox voluntarily so he might live out the rest of his days in comfort. Lethe had been ripped from life before her very eyes after an agonizing struggle. She would never be able to erase the memory of Hades delivering Lethe's death blow. Hades would surely be haunted by it as well. She had condemned them both to that, condemned them both to a future bereft of Lethe's love in this place that already held so little.

"Get out of the mud," Hades said, his voice thick and harsh as he wiped his blade on his tunic and returned it to its sheath.

"Hades." She moved toward him, reached for him. "I – I – forgive me. I ..."

"Get out of the mud," he repeated.

A hand closed over her waist and another over her arm. They tugged at her, dragging her from the mire. She twisted and writhed, wanting to go to Hades, to Lethe, though there was nothing she could do for either of them.

"Be still!" Charon bellowed as he hauled her onto the hummock and the malicious spark in his eye convinced Persephone to stop struggling.

Charon placed her on her feet on the grass and released her. Her own arms tight about her waist, she shuddered and shed silent tears as Hades pulled the rope from around Lethe's lifeless body.

Once that was accomplished, Charon gripped the other end of the rope and together the men strove to bring Hades to the bank.

"Hades, I ...." Persephone began again as he clambered, panting and dripping gobbets of mud, onto the grass.

Hades walked past her without so much as a glance. He went to Phlegethon and thoroughly examined him. Seemingly satisfied that this horse, at least, had taken no harm, Hades turned to Charon and said, "We'll have need of the ferry to get us back across."

Charon nodded and moved away. Hades, leading Phlegethon, followed Charon. Persephone cast a long look at Lethe's body, which had now nearly been claimed by the mud. She released one racking sob then turned and followed men and horse to the ferry. Once on board, she sank, exhausted, empty of tears, into a heap on the deck.

The ride across the river was eerily silent. Even the sound of Charon's pole leaving and reentering Styx's water seemed muted. Perhaps because it was blotted out by the sound of Lethe's death shriek, the memory of which still rang in Persephone's ears.

After a time, there was a hollow *thunk*. The boards beneath Persephone trembled. They had reached the bank. She remained where she was, listening to the thump of Phlegethon's hooves as he plodded off the ferry. Hades and Charon muttered to one another. Then hands were again lifting her, dragging her upright.

She looked up through swollen eyes to see Charon's face. Then Charon shifted her farther up in his arms and familiar hands, Hades's hands, grabbed her as both men struggled to seat her on Phlegethon's back in front of Hades.

She allowed them to manhandle her, too exhausted and numb with grief to protest. Once on Phlegethon's back, she slumped forward over the arm Hades circled about her waist. Phlegethon moved under her and then they were riding into asphodel meadow.

They were nearly to the Vale of Mourning when a thought came to

Persephone and she straightened. "Lethe was half Immortal. Surely, he'll revive. We must go back."

Hades shifted behind her, but made no response. She craned her head over her shoulder and twisted her upper body so she could see his face. "Did you not hear me?"

Hades looked beyond her, his voice flat as he said, "The River Styx is anathema to all living things. Even Immortals must pass nine years in a stupor to recover from an encounter with its waters. A mere half-mortal beast couldn't survive it. Lethe is dead. No part of him remains."

In the grip of a sudden, fully ripe, red rage, Persephone shrieked, "Why didn't you do more to free him? Why didn't you do more to stop Cerberus from killing Nadira? You're a God. You could have saved them both, else what good is your power?"

"My power?" Hades's voice trembled with barely controlled fury. "I have only as much power as those who worship at my one shrine afford me and it has not many visitors, Persephone, for I cannot grant the one boon they beg of me. Who asks of a God that never answers? Who sacrifices to a God that only takes and never gives? Even the offerings that come to my realm, the food and wine from the graves, the blood poured into the ground, aren't meant for me, but for the inhabitants of this realm to make their tenure here easier to endure. The only grace I can give my subjects is that of forgetting so they aren't tortured by remembrances of a life they can no longer have. That's my mercy, the comfort of oblivion. Is it any wonder I'm the most hated, most feared, least venerated God?"

He paused, dragged a hand over his mouth, down his beard. When he continued, the rage in his voice had lessened, but wasn't gone. "I have no power save the little accorded me by virtue of my Immortal birth. Nearly everything I do must be achieved by the sweat of my brow. Unlike those on Olympus, my life has been one of toil, agony, and unease, and this day you have taken from me one of the few graces I possessed."

He grabbed her chin between his thumb and forefinger, turning her farther, forcing her to meet his eyes. "Do you think I delighted in Nadira's destruction? Do you not think if I could have saved her from a second death I would? Do you not think if I could, I would have done more than simply spare Lethe the agony of suffocation?"

Persephone wrenched free from his grasp and slunk forward on Phlegethon's neck, heart pounding, stomach churning in fear of the seething God at her back.

Hades gave a grunt of negation and pulled her snug against him.

He was using his hands to force her, just as he had when she first came to the Underworld. All his promises and fine words in Elysium meant nothing in the grip of this fury. He would exact the price of the great wrong she'd done him from her flesh, just as Demeter would have.

This was the true Hades: monstrous, savage, terrifying.

23

PERSEPHONE

Abhorrence and dread weighed heavily on Persephone as she and Hades drew near to the palace. Just as the first time she'd approached this building, she was captive to Hades's hands, captive to his desires.

Hades halted Phlegethon outside the courtyard wall and dismounted. He kept a tight hold on Phlegethon's lead as he pushed the gate open. He needn't have. Escape from Hades, from this realm either on horseback or on foot wasn't possible. That much was now abundantly clear. At least for now Persephone was free from his grasp, though she was too worn to feel anything but palely grateful for that small mercy. She sat quietly on Phlegethon while Hades led the horse across the courtyard and into the stable.

Akheron and Styx, returned from their mad dash in Elysium, milled about in the aisle between stalls. They whinnied in joyous greeting. The dumb beasts had no comprehension of Lethe's death, likely never would. Persephone and Hades would be the only ones to remember him. She should have thought to take a token, a bit of his mane or tail, something to signify that he had lived and been loved.

Hades drew Phlegethon to a halt. The top of Persephone's tunic moved with the force of her heartbeat and her belly quaked. Now Hades would pull her from Phlegethon's back, drag her to the palace, and punish her in whatever way he saw fit. The retribution for Lethe's loss was sure to be terrible. It would make the justice Demeter doled out seem like a mercy.

Muscles taut with horrible anticipation, Persephone bunched her fists, but Hades moved away from her. He walked to Akheron's stall and pulled the rails from the opening to admit the horse. He did the same for Styx.

Then he came to her. "Get down."

She shook her head.

"I need to remove the mud from Phlegethon, and I can't do that with you astride him. Get down."

Persephone swung her leg over the horse, dismounting so Phlegethon's body was between her and Hades. Phlegethon would provide a bit of an obstacle when Hades came for her.

Without so much as glancing at her, Hades began to sweep his hands down Phlegethon's neck, knocking away the worst of the dried muck there.

Persephone's muscles remained taut but Hades only continued his meticulous care of his horse. She turned to walk from the stables. He didn't pursue her, didn't so much as call her name.

Her thoughts whirled as she walked to the palace doors. Was this part of Hades's punishment? To let her steep in terror and uncertainty? He could do so for days, weeks, if he chose and she would have no choice but to bear it. Already he was proving crueler than Demeter. Her castigation had always at least been swift.

Shedding mud with every step, Persephone entered the palace, went up the stairs, and down the long hall to her bedchamber. Once inside, she crossed to the pile of fleece and blankets on the floor and curled herself into it. Hades would come for her eventually. She would make it easy for him to find her, the sooner to have all of this over and done with.

Sometime later, the bang of the heavy palace door carried into her bedchamber. Persephone jerked and gave a muffled cry. Shortly after, the sound of Hades's footsteps, heavy, measured, inexorable, reached her ears. She curled more tightly in on herself.

When he entered her bedchamber the sound of his movements changed, their echoes somewhat absorbed by the smaller space. The blankets beneath Persephone shifted as he lowered himself onto them. A single harsh gasp of terror escaped her.

Hades's legs curled behind hers. He passed one arm over her shoulder and across her chest, and loosely grasped her other shoulder.

Though Persephone held herself utterly still, panic shrieked, battered, clawed at the inside of her skull. It would take her in its grip the instant he threatened violence, but he too held himself motionless. Time passed in a slow ooze of sweat that ran between her breasts, onto her ribcage, and soaked into the cloth of her tunic. The area of dampness grew ever larger, but Hades didn't move.

Finally, Persephone gulped in air, not sure how long she'd gone without. Behind her, Hades expelled his breath in a moist, warm wave that moved over her ear and cheek. The hair on the nape of her neck pressed tight as he bowed his head into it. A moment later, he released a series of body-shaking sobs.

The sound was pure anguish, sheer loss, the pain of years breaking through a dam that had held it in place for far too long. It was the heart's cry of a young boy left by his mother to languish in darkness, of a youth forced to fight before he learned to love, of a young man plunged into darkness again before he had a chance to accustom himself to a life in the light, of a God who had no choice but to deal death to one he loved. There was no anger here. Only agony.

Persephone turned to Hades, pressed his face to her breast. His arms went around her waist, bruising in their force as he pulled her closer. She bit her lip on the cry of pain that struggled for release and held him as he shook and sobbed.

Free of the fear of punishment, her own sorrow welled again and tears slid down her face. "Forgive me, Hades. I didn't mean to cause him harm. I loved him as you did. Please, forgive me."

Hades lifted his head, choked out, "The terrible harvest of this day is as much my doing as yours. I had no right to rage at you. In my pride, I forgot Cerberus is governed not by me, but by the laws of this land. I should have kept Nadira within these walls until she was fully mortal and then seen you both safe to the Upper World. I was a fool today, Persephone, and it cost us both dearly. I give you my forgiveness only if you favor me with yours."

Never, after any of the unkind words Demeter hurled at Persephone or blows she rained down, had she ever admitted fault or asked for forgiveness. The error was always all Persephone's, her pain a just consequence for her actions. Persephone had harmed Hades more deeply than any offense she ever perpetrated against her mother, yet, he was claiming his contribution to the ills of this day, begging her forgiveness for them and giving her his. It wouldn't free either she or Hades from their suffering, but at least they could mourn, and perhaps, given time, heal together.

"I do. I do forgive you." She pressed her brow to Hades, closed her eyes, and let sorrow have its way with her until it eventually gave way to exhaustion and she slept.

When she woke, she was alone among the blankets and fleece. She rolled to look for Hades and winced at the million darts of pain that stabbed the various parts of her body. Gingerly, she pulled herself into a sitting position. Most of her was still coated with dried mud, including her tunic.

She rose to her feet and reached for the hem. Dirt flaked from her as she peeled the garment away from her body. After she was free of it, she discovered the tunic had two large tears in it and a long streak of Lethe's blood on the back. It must have transferred from Hades to her on their long miserable ride back to the palace.

Shuddering, turning her thoughts away from the nightmarish images the dull brown stripe called up, she stood, carried the garment to the hearth and dropped it in. It landed with a whump and a hiss. Flames licked at the faded embroidery of the lilies around the hem, her mother's handiwork.

Crying out, Persephone reached for the garment, then drew back. She could rescue the tunic but she was sure to get burned in the attempt. Hadn't that always been the way of things, reaching out for her mother's love, only to be singed time and again? Perhaps it was time to stop grasping after something that only ever caused her pain.

Persephone watched until the lilies were completely black, then turned away from the hearth. Small explosions of pain accompanied every movement. The warm water in the bathing pool would soothe the aches in her body. Perhaps it would prove beneficial to the ache in her heart as well. She walked as quickly as she could manage to the bathing room.

As soon as she entered, she saw Hades, bared to the waist, his lower body obscured by the pool, scrubbing mud from his face and neck. His eyes fell on her, and he slowly lowered his hands.

Persephone hesitated for only a brief moment, scarcely enough to break her stride before descending the steps to join him in the warm water. He took her hand as she reached the bottom stair and pulled her to him. She raised her face to his. He put his palms on either side of her face, his thumbs aligning with her jawbone, his fingertips resting lightly on her cheekbones and his mouth came down on hers.

She parted her lips and he delicately traced his tongue along their inner curve. His fingers trailed down her face, her neck, swept along the line of her collarbone then drifted to her breast. Cupping it, he stroked his thumb over her nipple. Stomach fluttering, legs shaking, she pulled away from the touch, from the kiss. She wasn't ready do what he so obviously desired.

She had to tell him how she felt, but it would be so much easier if he wasn't still cradling her face in one hand. "I don't ... I ... this frightens me. Please I can't ... I can't do this."

She waited for her fear to erase the slight smile on his lips, for sadness to darken the clear gray of his eyes, but his expression didn't change. He circled around behind her and lifted the weight of her hair in both hands. The trembling in her belly and legs increased. What did he intend with this?

"Sit. Please," Hades said.

Persephone did as he asked, sinking down onto one of the steps that led into the pool. He eased her head back until her hair was fully submerged, then moved to the side of the stairs, his careful pulling and plucking telling her he was removing the mud from her hair as carefully as he had taken it off of Phlegethon.

His brow was lightly furrowed, his gaze intent as he focused on his task. After a time, he ceased working at the strands, instructed her to lift her head and began to pull his fingers gently through the tangled mass. When he completed that task, he cupped water in his hands and poured it over her neck, shoulders, and chest. Then he turned his attention to her face. He trickled water over her brow, carefully examined the bruise on her cheek where the whip had struck her.

His tender cleansing of her body had not only banished Persephone's fear but had aroused her in much the same way her dreams of him did. His closeness now was an exquisite temptation, one she had no wish any more to resist.

Persephone rose to her feet, pressed her lips to his. He put his arms around her, holding him to her, then kissed his way down her neck, lightly flicking his tongue into the hollow of her throat. Persephone gasped.

Hades lifted his head, murmured, "If what I do isn't pleasing you need only tell me to stop and I will."

In response, Persephone raised one hand from the water and slipped it around the back of Hades's neck. She pulled him to her, opening her lips, once again welcoming his tongue in her mouth. With her other hand, she guided his palm upward and placed it on her breast. As his fingers moved over the tender skin, a low moan escaped her.

Hades's mouth left hers. She opened her eyes as he moved to her side. He slid one hand around her back, bent slightly, and put the other behind her knees. He lifted her in a sucking splash of water, carried her from the pool, and then from the bathing room.

As he stepped into the hall, his feet slid on the plaster. The squeak of wet skin, and the flex of the muscles in his midsection which pressed against her side told Persephone he was struggling to maintain his balance. She too tensed in anticipation of the fall. He went down, grunting as he landed, Persephone splayed across his legs. Even with his resistance to physical hurts such a fall had to have pained him.

"Are you well? You aren't hurt?" He gasped, his voice revealing that he was.

Persephone tried to hold back the laugh building in her throat, but she, like Hades's before her when trying to maintain his balance, struggled in vain. The grimace on Hades's face was too much. She began to laugh, great gulping whoops of merriment that echoed around them in the hall.

After a moment, Hades's stomach began to tremble where it pressed against her arm and soon, he guffawed along with her.

When Persephone's abdominal muscles could bear no more, her laughter trailed off into a few scattered, gleeful chortles. Still chuckling, she rolled away from Hades to get to her feet. As she came to her knees, Hades put his hands on either side of her face, pushed the wet hair back from her cheeks with his thumbs and looked into her eyes. "You are my light and my life, Persephone."

His light. Her eyes filled with quick tears. They weren't tears of sadness but he had no way of knowing that, no way of knowing the deep wound his words had salved. She would tell him one day, but not now. Instead, she hid the telltale moisture from him by pressing a kiss to his lips then clambering to her feet. Once she was upright and her emotions in check, she extended a hand and helped Hades to his feet. Then they walked hand clasped to her bedchamber.

Halting on the threshold there, Persephone let her hand slide from Hades's as he strode inside. He shook the mud from the blankets and fleece on the floor, turning and rearranging them so their clean sides faced up. His movements were all lithe grace, the flex and flow of his muscles stealing her breath, but observing him didn't bring only pleasure. Hades was in her sleeping chamber. They were both naked. She knew what would follow.

After arranging the nest to his apparent satisfaction, Hades beckoned to Persephone. She commanded her feet to carry her forward but they didn't move.

"Again, if what I do frightens or hurts you simply tell me to stop. You need have no fear of me. I mean to go gently with you, to make this as pleasing for you as I'm able." Hades lowered himself into the midst of the nest of bedding, his hold on her now consisting only of the hope in his gray eyes.

Taking a deep breath, Persephone walked into the room and sank down to join him.

He immediately gathered her to him and she tilted her head back to meet his mouth with her own. His tongue moved against hers, delving deeper, then deeper still. His hand found her breast once again. She moaned and her eyes drifted closed. Still kissing and caressing her, he lay her back among the blankets.

His lips left hers. He followed the line of her neck with the tip of his tongue, dragged it lower, circled her nipple with it. She gasped, opened her eyes, came partially upright.

He stopped immediately, looked up, his eyes searching hers. Her pulse pounded in her wrists, her throat, but very little of that was fear. She offered him a smile of reassurance and lay back down. Still holding her gaze, he took her breast in his mouth. Eyelids fluttering closed, she moaned. His fingers slid between her legs then, moving against slick, heated flesh. He touched her there until she writhed, panted 'please,' but what she begged for she didn't know.

He drew back from her, pressed a series of kisses into the valley below her ribs down to her navel and then lower still. His tongue took the place of his fingers, entering her innermost part. She arched, a cry escaping her. As before, he stopped what he was doing, met her eyes, a question in his.

In response, she opened her legs wider.

He smiled, then lowered his head. His lips closed on the small nub just below the mound of her womanhood.

Persephone moaned, curled her fingers into his hair, and pressed down, deepening the contact. He continued to suckle there, and the sensation was so overwhelming nothing else existed except that sublime pleasure. Her hips, of their own volition, lifted and dropped to match the rhythm of his mouth. Her breath came faster, almost in a pant. Sweat sprang from her pores.

A sensation like nothing she had ever felt before built within her. She had to end it, release it, or be obliterated by it. She could ask Hades to cease and he would. She had no doubt of that but oblivion seemed preferable to the removal of his hands and mouth from her body. No, she would ride this tide of feeling, see what wondrous or terrible thing awaited at its conclusion.

When her pleasure reached the peak of its exquisite crescendo, Persephone cried out, tightened her grip on Hades's hair and surged toward him, writhing and releasing a series of small panting cries as his tongue and lips continued to move against her.

Her cries changed to gasps as the feeling ebbed. The tension left her body. She dropped back, settling deeper into the blankets. Hades's mouth left her but only for a moment. He planted a kiss on her lower abdomen then retraced the trail of kisses he'd left on her body earlier until he lay beside her.

She rolled to look at him. He smoothed the hair back from her sweat-damp face and kissed her lips.

When he pulled back, she asked, "Is that how physical love is supposed to be?"

"Was it pleasing?"

A flush climbed up her chest, neck and into her face, but she held his eyes as she responded, "Very."

"Then yes." He kissed her again.

"Do you ... Did you ... was it pleasing to you as well?"

"I enjoyed satisfying you."

"And you received satisfaction, also?"

He drew a fingertip down her chest, between her breasts. "Touching you and tasting you was very gratifying."

"But did you . . . I felt something I've never felt before, pleasure so overwhelming I lost myself completely in it. Did you . . . experience that?"

"I didn't, but—"

"Am I at fault for—"

Hades silenced her with another kiss. "There's no fault in you, Persephone. I didn't receive the stimulation needed to reach my satisfaction, but that was by my own design. Your pleasure in this is paramount, not mine."

"I know very little of what men need in the marriage bed, but if you'd guide me, I would gladly ...." She knew so little of these matters she didn't have the necessary words to conclude the sentence.

He studied her face for a moment, kissed her again, then pulled her closer. Something rigid, yet as soft as Lethe's muzzle, pressed into her lower belly.

He took one of her hands, placed it on him. "Hold me here, against you."

He gripped her lower back, drew her closer still. The part that made him a man pulsed twice quickly against her hand and stomach. His eyes fluttered closed and he moaned. Heat flared through Persephone once again.

Hades began to slide up and down, rubbing himself against her. Sudden sweat glistened on his brow. Her breath sped up to match his and she tightened her hold on him.

He panted. "Gods, I want to enter you."

"As your tongue did?" she asked.

Eyes still closed, he nodded.

"You may, if you wish."

He stopped moving, opened his eyes. "I don't want to hurt you."

"Is it ... will it be painful?"

"When a maid takes her first lover it can be."

Persephone looked down, her heart thudding with anxiety now rather than arousal. "It would bring you pleasure?"

"And you also, I hope, once the pain passes, but you needn't—"

She raised her eyes to his face. "If I tell you to stop, will you?"

"You'll have no need to tell me. You may move away anytime you wish." He took her hand from him, kissed it, released it, then rolled to his back. "I'm at your mercy, Lady."

Persephone rose onto her knees and looked down on him, eyes sweeping the muscled length of his chest and belly. He shifted position slightly and his man part wobbled. She laughed.

He looked down at himself, then grinned up at her. "Desire makes us all ridiculous, men and Gods alike."

She looked him over again then drew a deep breath. Still on her knees, she brought one leg over his hips to straddle him as she would a horse. "I'm not sure how ...."

Hades moved a hand between her legs, slid two fingers inside her.

She gasped.

"Guide me here, but go slowly, carefully."

She nodded. He pulled his fingers out. All the anxiousness she felt was reflected in his face but she'd done so many things in this land below of which she hadn't thought herself capable. He didn't need to worry for her. She didn't need to worry for herself.

Persephone looked down and took him in a tentative grip. He groaned. She glanced at him to be sure she hadn't hurt him. The bliss on his face, his closed eyes were answer enough.

She positioned herself a bit better, then held him in place as she eased down. As he entered her, they gasped in unison. She slid her legs farther apart, muscles clenched against anticipated pain. And there it was, raw and harsh, like a slash from a dull blade. Persephone gave a small cry.

Hades eyes flew open. "Persephone ...."

She took a few breaths and the pain subsided. She lowered herself farther. He slid fully inside her. She cried out again, this time with pleasure.

He made a guttural sound, grasped the top of her hips, and arched. She pushed against him, pleasure washing through her as he delved deeper. His fingers dug into her skin, pulling her forward, then pushing her back. At his urging, she began to move faster. Hades moaned her name and thrust himself upward and deep into her again.

As she continued to move, the feeling from before mounted in her again. Hades shifted one of his hands from her hip, slid a finger between her legs and found the nub that he'd suckled before. He touched her there, matching the frantic speed of her hips. Again, she reached that superb pitch of ecstasy but this time Hades climbed the peak with her. He called her name again and again as they rocked together.

After a time, the feeling within her again subsided, though this time she gasped and trembled in its wake. Silver-starred blackness danced at the edge of her vision. She leaned forward until her breasts rested against Hades's chest and her forehead touched his shoulder. His skin was sweat slick and his panting breath stirred her hair. When her vision cleared and her trembling eased, she raised herself again.

Hades smiled up at her. He lifted a hand, trailed a finger down her arm. "So lovely."

She bent again, a smile glimmering over her face and pressed a kiss to Hades's mouth; a hard smack that ended with a satisfying sound. Laughing, he put his arms around her and rolled to the side, so they lay nose to nose, flank to flank. He soothed his hand over her hair, down her neck and arm until she drifted off, his soft murmuring of 'Shh. All's well' the last thing she heard before she slept.

24

DEMETER

Head bowed against the driving rain, Orpheus at her side, Demeter walked the road that led out of Eleusis to the East. Would that she had her Sicani tunic and shawl. They were much better suited to this weather than the laced bodice and flounced, begemmed skirt, that soaked as they were, clung like cold, clammy fingers to her body. She couldn't afford the distraction of her discomfort. Every time she lost her focus, the plant life within her surged, striving for release so it could bury itself in the wet ground. The battle was constant and exhausting and all this rain only exacerbated the situation.

Hands clapped to her churning guts, she muttered, "He thinks to bring life from Gaia's flesh by drenching it with rain, when all he accomplishes is to wash away the soil that nourishes plants best. Dolt. Though at least it damps the smell of rot from the Rarian fields."

"Lady?" Orpheus enquired, the rain seeming not to bother him one whit.

Demeter dashed the water from her eyes and snapped, "The words I spoke were not for you."

Orpheus shrugged, shifted his pack, and plodded on.

Demeter, however, paused and looked about her.

"Here," she called to Orpheus, then turned from the road and set off through the dead and dripping undergrowth. Eventually, they reached the mouth of a cave tucked inside a small hill.

"This is the entrance?" Orpheus asked.

"One of them."

Orpheus wiped water from his face, shifted his pack once more, and strode toward the dark hollow.

Demeter grabbed his upper arm, arresting his movement. "I've allotted you three days to accomplish what you must. Track the time well, Orpheus, for if you do not return to me on this spot with Persephone at your side, I shall know you've failed me and I won't rest until your existence is a misery."

Orpheus inclined his head. "As you said, Goddess."

Demeter released him. Orpheus turned from her and picked his way past the boulders in front of the cave. Demeter watched him until the darkness swallowed him up. His taciturn nature was irritating beyond all measure. No matter the threat, he refused to be perturbed. She would feel much surer of him and his success in the task she set him if he showed he was at least a little afraid of her.

She turned to make her way back to the road and a gust of wind drove rain into her face. She hurriedly stepped onto the God Road where the deluge couldn't follow her. When she stepped off it again outside her temple, the rain still misted down but not with the same force as it had outside the cave.

In front of Demeter's hovel of a temple, a knot of men huddled around Iambe. As the woman pressed bread and fruit into their hands, they appeared furtive and guilty. A smile turned Demeter's lips.

"Iambe," Demeter called.

The mortal woman flinched and a variety of foods tumbled from her arms. Most of the men gathered around her quickly dispersed, save one who first went to his knees to gather up the food Iambe had dropped.

"Lady." Iambe limped toward Demeter. "Forgive me, I—"

Demeter waved a hand. "It suits my purpose that you keep those who build my temple healthy and hale."

"Thank you, Lady. I know they too are grateful for your mercy."

"And so they should be. I feed them from my own stores."

Watching the men as they returned to their work, Iambe said, "What of those in the palace, Lady?"

"What of them?" Demeter scanned the land at the base of the rise on which her temple sat. The mortals had made progress on clearing it, but no building had yet begun. It would be a long time before she and Iambe could make their home there. For now, they had no choice but to continue to reside in her current place of worship, inadequate as it was.

"Metaneira, Keleus, their daughters, and Demophon will surely perish if we don't share our bounty with them. Won't you take mercy on them as they did on you when you were in need?"

Demeter let her eyes roam over the building site a moment longer before she answered. "Very well. Give them only what you must and no more."

"Thank you, La—"

"Be about your work."

Iambe bobbed her head and turned to the temple doors.

"Iambe," Demeter called.

The woman turned back.

"When you've finished dispensing my mercy, I need you to travel to Orchomenos and Mycenae. You know your duties. Praise my name and tell the peoples of those cities they must worship me to entice me to lift the famine from their lands."

Iambe looked at the men laboring on Demeter's temple then looked back at Demeter. "Is Orpheus away to the Underworld?"

"He is."

"We may look for your daughter's return soon then?"

"That's my hope."

"And mine also, Lady. Then we may see an end to this famine."

"Are you growing weary of your duties, Iambe?" Demeter asked, her voice as sharp edged as a knife.

Iambe shook her head, matching Demeter stare for stare. "I said I would serve you in all things, Lady and so I shall. I . . ." Iambe shook her head again, but this time her eyes dropped from Demeter's face. "Only I wish the effects of your famine weren't so dire."

"It would be best if you inure yourself to the effects of my famine, as it's likely to continue for some time."

"How long a time?"

"I know not," Demeter snapped. "What does it matter? You have your duties. Go to them."

"As you say, Lady. I'll fetch my pack and be off." Iambe turned again to the temple and limped inside.

Demeter followed at a more circumspect pace, though she was eager to get out of the wet and the cold.

When she entered, she nearly toppled Iambe who squatted in front of the piles of foodstuffs filling her pack.

Iambe tossed a few more figs in her bag and rose. "I go now, Lady."

"Be off then." Demeter moved around the woman. A moment later, the temple door banged shut.

As Demeter walked toward her throne, she surveyed the piles of offerings heaped high on the altar, and stacked against the walls. All this she held back from Zeus. He would never have even the smallest portion of it. The accumulation of months' worth of offerings also guaranteed that, even with Iambe's plundering of it, Demeter had food enough here to withstand a long famine. When the peoples of the neighboring cities added their worship to those of the Eleusinians, Demeter would add not only to her store of foodstuffs, but also, and more importantly, to her reservoirs of power. Her skin tingled in anticipation.

"When do you mean to cease this madness, Demeter?"

Demeter startled at the unexpected voice. It came from the small antechamber at the rear of the temple where she and Iambe slept. Had some thief dared to penetrate her safehold here? Demeter hurried into the room. Hekate sat at the table there, hands folded on its top.

Demeter stopped. "What do you here, Hekate?"

"Do you think she would approve, our *kore*, with her tender heart and warm ways, of the harm you perpetrate to gain her freedom?" the older woman asked, her dark eyes as cold and reflective as black marble.

Demeter's only response was to lift her chin and allow her gaze to go distant and frosty.

Hekate sighed. "Sit, Sister, that we may speak."

"I won't."

"Stand then and be in discomfort, I care not."

Demeter lowered herself to the chair across from Hekate.

"Have you completed your rite, Demeter?"

"I have."

"Have you sent Orpheus to the Underworld to collect Persephone?"

"I have."

"Then what further need do you have for this famine? What's your intent in continuing it?"

Demeter folded her arms over her breast. "You know my intent. I must ensure Persephone's freedom so I may tell her of the ways you sought to turn me from her. She must know I love her, that I always loved her, but that for you, I would have been kinder to her."

Hekate leaned forward. "When I left you and Persephone, I meant to draw you together. Your famine will only widen the chasm between you. You must restore life to Gaia's flesh."

Demeter unfolded her arms and bent over the table until her eyes were on a level with Hekate's. "Why would I heed your counsel? It's you who tainted my love for her, the flapping of your tongue that resulted in her abduction. I will not cease the famine."

Hekate settled back in her seat, shaking her head. "Then you make waste of all I meant to do when I gave Persephone up. She won't, she can't, love you when she sees the wrong you've committed here. Her heart will turn from you forever. The two of you will be separated for eternity."

Demeter straightened, looked away from the older Goddess. "Are we not separated for eternity if she remains in the Underworld?"

"Separated in body, Demeter, but not in spirit, for she loves you and you love her. Can you not make that enough? Will you never learn to make what you have enough? End the famine. Wait upon Orpheus's success. Should he fail, leave her below and be satisfied in the knowledge of her love."

Demeter rose and swept all the food from the tabletop with a swing of her arm. "That would please you, wouldn't it? That she remain forever in ignorance of your treachery, believing of the two of us, you loved her best? Once she sees the lengths I went to for her, she'll never doubt the magnitude of my devotion."

Hekate remained seated, impassive in the face of Demeter's rage. "You recreated an entire rite to ensure her return and sent an emissary to Hades to gain her freedom. Let that be proof enough."

"No. I must tell her myself."

"When Orpheus has returned her to the Upper World then will you cease this famine?"

"My choices are my own, Hekate. You need have no concern for them."

Hekate shook her head again, the corners of her mouth turning down. "Are you truly such a fool that you believe those words? Can you not see the threat this famine poses to we Immortals? You ignore the humans' pleas for this famine to cease. You make it impossible for Zeus to answer. If this deprivation continues unabated, mortals will turn to other Gods seeking one who can ease their suffering. Should that occur, Zeus will fall and we will all tumble with him."

Demeter snaked a hand out and seized Hekate's forearm. "You care nothing for me, nothing for my desires, nothing for Persephone. With all your fine words about doing good for mortals, answering supplicants' prayers, truly at the root of it all is your wish to remain in power."

Hekate extracted her arm from Demeter's grip, her eyes snapping. "You overstep yourself, Sister. I do wish to retain my power, but not for the reasons you suppose. I'm an ancient Goddess, brought into being when the Titans ruled. I've seen the bloody consequences of the shift from one Godhead to another. I don't relish another such contest, and I can't look lightly on all the mortals who will surely perish in the struggle. But more than that I fear Zeus's fall, for he is a pleasure seeking, idle, and neglectful God. As such, he's too lazy to do away with any but those who draw away large numbers of mortals to their shrines. But I, because I have not many worshippers, am allowed to go about largely unmolested helping mortals wherever I may. What I fear, Demeter, is the rise of a jealous God, one who cannot tolerate my continued veneration and feels he must reign supreme. One who insists on warfare and bloodshed to ensure his worship dominates the whole of the world. One who will take from me my power and cease my ministrations so mortals, with no one to ease their way, will spiral ever downward into destruction and despair."

Demeter's eyes roamed over the old Goddess's face. "Why this obsession with mortals, Hekate? Why do they mean so much to you?"

Hekate, a fervent flame kindling in her eyes, said, "Can you not see, Demeter? Against all odds they've persevered and borne up under the Gods' neglect and ire. Their existence is mindless toil, heart-wrenching loss, physical pain, and so tenuous that something as small as the bite of an insect may end it. They live by slurping from the dregs of our cups. Rather than letting the dreariness of their existence turn them bitter and impervious to higher emotions, they, for the most part, display astonishing resiliency, strength, compassion, mercy, and kindness to one another, forging bonds of love so strong even the Gods can't sever them. You see nothing extraordinary, nothing worth admiring in that?"

Demeter looked away from the older Goddess. She could feel Hekate's eyes on her but refused to meet them.

After a moment of silence, Hekate asked, "Do you recall the words Hera spoke when she tricked you into drinking the wine and eating the bread in the final step of the rite to take your Immortality?"

Still not looking at her, Demeter flapped a hand at Hekate, "Be gone, crone. I haven't the time nor the inclination to recall those times now."

As though Demeter hadn't spoken, Hekate said, "She told you to eat and drink and then she would lift the bonds her husband had placed on you so you could change."

Demeter finally looked at Hekate. "So she did. What does that matter?"

"What did you believe she meant, Demeter?"

Her rage rising again, Demeter responded, "I thought she meant to release me from the constraints Zeus placed on me so I could take on my

Goddess form. I hoped to labor without pain and so did as she asked. She deceived me. I was a fool. Is that what you desired me to say?"

"Not at all," Hekate said mildly. "Though I do believe you're wrong in your estimation of our sister. I think Hera hoped to make you both stronger and wiser than she, to spare you the madness Zeus's actions drove her to."

Demeter scoffed. "To accomplish that she turned me into a mortal?"

"Perhaps she knows mortals are better instructors of most virtues than any on Olympus." Hekate took hold of Demeter's hand. "Don't lay waste to all Hera meant to accomplish. Let those years among the Sicani serve some purpose now. Harken back to your time as a human. Use it to find some compassion in your heart for those who were once your fellows. End this famine."

Demeter yanked her hand from Hekate's. "I was never as they. Never! I'll do what I must to ensure Persephone's return even if it slays a thou-sand-thousand mortals, even if it lays waste to all the land of the Achaean people, even if it topples Zeus from Olympus."

Hekate sat back and surveyed Demeter, eyes hard, mouth set. "At last, the truth. That's the result you seek. Not Persephone's freedom. Tell me, Sister, how do you mean to justify the continuation of the famine when Orpheus returns with our *kore*? Do you think any explanation you give her will make her condone the deaths you perpetrate after she's restored to you?"

Demeter pointed to the door. "Go, Hekate. Your words weary me, and I have much yet to do."

"As do I."

"What do you seek to accomplish?" Demeter asked, voice sharp with suspicion.

Hekate rose, passed Demeter, and walked to the door.

Demeter followed after her. "Hekate?"

The crone stepped from the antechamber. By the time Demeter reached the main room of her temple, Hekate had departed on the God Roads.

Belly roiling with apprehension, Demeter turned to look in the direction of Olympus.

25

PERSEPHONE

Persephone looked around her room through eyes still bleary with sleep. Her gaze settled on the mussed pile of blankets where Nadira had slept the last few nights, but no dark head peeped above their edge. No hand or foot extruded from their folds.

Remembrance settled its aching weight in Persephone's chest. She made a small miserable sound.

Hades's arms came around her from behind, his bare flesh enclosing her in warmth. Persephone turned in his embrace and crushed her lips to his. She didn't want comfort. She wanted to forget, wanted Hades to blot out the memories, at least for a time, with his hands and tongue and teeth.

Hades obliged.

Sometime later, panting, sated, still throbbing with sensation that was part pleasure, part pain, Persephone settled back onto the blankets. Hades rolled to his side and smiled at her, a grave smile that didn't quite reach his eyes. He also still mourned.

She closed her eyes on the knowledge. A moment later, Hades's hand settled in the valley of her ribs just below her breasts. He dragged it the length of her torso, then ran his fingers over her hand and up her arm to her shoulder.

She kept her eyes closed, focusing only on the sensation of his broad, calloused palms stroking her body, letting it drive all other considerations from her mind.

His hand passed over her hair. He whispered her name. Sucking in a breath, Persephone's eyes flew open. Hades paused mid stroke.

Persephone sat up. "It was you in the cavern, that day in Nysa."

"It was," Hades admitted, not quite meeting her gaze.

"But how could I not see you?" Persephone asked.

He kept his eyes down, focusing on his hand as he traced small spirals on her belly. "In the battle with the Titans, I was granted a gift called the Helm of Darkness; a truly hideous thing made of dog skin with wings on either side. It renders me invisible to all, Gods and mortals alike."

At last, he raised his eyes to hers. "I wore it when I went to the Upper World, curious to see the girl of whom I'd heard so much from Hekate."

Cocking a smile at him, Persephone asked, "And what did you think of me?"

"That the Fates crafted you for me." He lifted a length of her hair and watched it slide through his fingers. "With your hair as vivid and shining as the light of Helios when he descends in the sky; with your eyes as green as Gaia's fields on their most bounteous day; with your ankles as slender and supple as the branch of a willow tree, all things I long for, yet see but little. And more which I learned from Hekate: that you were another such as myself, a part of two worlds, yet belonging to neither, loving those who could never give you the love you longed for in return, and alone, though crowded on every side by those who made up your existence."

His assessment of their shared circumstances echoed so closely the conclusion Persephone had come to those months ago when she'd tried to flee across Elysium and she told him as much. Then she asked, "If you truly believed I was made for you, why then didn't you show yourself? Surely if the Fates crafted me for you, then they crafted you for me. Did you think I wouldn't recognize that?"

"I meant to. The moment I saw you in the cavern I meant to reveal myself and my intention to win your love."

"Why didn't you?"

Hades rolled to his back. Eyes focused on some point above him, he drew in a breath, then released it slowly. "Though I know I'm not a horror, at times the certainty that I am overwhelms me. I was responsible for the death of my first love, and the only other woman who claimed to want me truly desired the access to Olympus that her connection with me gave her. Those in the Upper World believe me so terrifying they dare not speak my name. Even my brother and sister Gods avoid me for they find me unsettling. With all these proofs of my monstrosity, I often wondered if I could ever be pleasing in any way to anyone ever again. That's the question that visited me and stayed my hand when I reached for the Helm." Hades turned his head to look at her. "Are you angry?"

Persephone had many questions about his previous lovers but now wasn't the time to ask them. In this moment, she needed most to reassure Hades. "How can I be angry when I likely would have done the same? That day in Nysa when I met the Goddesses, the day you took me, I would have hidden myself away and observed them from afar had I been given the choice. So deeply did I believe what the Sicani said about me, I expected the Goddesses to also reject me as abhorrent. I was stunned to speechlessness when they didn't."

Hades pulled Persephone back down. She curled herself against him and put her head on his chest.

His arm came around her and he pressed a kiss to her forehead. "It makes me ache to know you believed yourself loathsome."

There was no reply Persephone could think to make to this, no words to capture the way his simple statement made her chest burn and her eyes well with tears of gratitude that she need never think that about herself again.

"It wasn't my intent to take you that day, the day you met the Goddesses." Hades slid a thumb down her upper arm, then back up. "It wasn't my intent to take you at all. I meant only to visit you in Henna, let you accustom yourself to my presence, and woo and win you over time. Then the Goddesses appeared. When I heard your conversation and realized you meant to build a life around them, I knew I had to spirit you away."

Persephone craned her head back to look into Hades's face. "Why? Could you not have wooed and won me while I waited upon their visits?"

Hades splayed his hand above her left breast. "The Goddesses have no care for those whose hearts they hold. They would have rent yours between them and thought nothing of the destruction. After all the hurts you'd already suffered, I couldn't leave you in their uncaring hands."

Persephone drew away from him. "They didn't seem cruel."

"Olympus's creatures aren't cruel, but neither are they kind. They think only of what brings the most pleasure in the moment. They care not who they injure or destroy in the taking of that pleasure. In time, the Goddesses' fancy would have drawn them away from Nysa, from you. They would have left that place and never returned, giving no more thought to leaving you desolate than you give to the pain of an ant you happen to trod on."

Persephone fingered a strand of her hair. "But they touched me in kindness."

"They drew you into their circle because you were a novelty and it gratified them to do so."

Persephone looked away from Hades, eyes drawn to the fresco of the circle of maidens in the meadow, the green-eyed fire-haired one, distant from them and alone. She had never had a place among them, would never have a place among them.

Hades lightly touched her cheek, turning her attention back to him. "Rather than abducting you and ... and forcing my attentions on you so that your terror of me overthrew all other emotion, do you believe had I revealed myself to you in Nysa you would have recognized me as one created for you by the Fates?"

Persephone surveyed Hades. Did she love him now because the Fates crafted him for her? Or did she believe the Fates crafted him for her because she had come to love him? It was a mystery to which she would never have the answer and it mattered not to her, though the answer likely mattered greatly to him. She put a hand to his cheek, smiled. "I would."

Hades drew her close. As his lips met hers, his belly roared. Mouth widening into a grin, he placed a hand to his stomach. "Alas, my gut hasn't the sensibility to know when to keep silent. Shall we eat?"

Her laughter mingling with his, Persephone stood up and extended a hand to Hades. He took it and got to his feet.

Standing made her aware her body was still bruised and sore from all she had demanded of it the previous day. She lifted her arms to stretch the stiffness from it. At the motion, Hades's gaze fastened on her.

Somehow, the intimacy of the fleece and cushions had made her nakedness seem natural and unimportant. Now out of the bed, whatever spell it cast was broken. Flushing, Persephone put an arm across her breasts, turned away. Realizing the movement only presented him with her bare buttocks, she turned back, snatched up a blanket from the pile of them on the floor, and wrapped it around herself.

To the accompaniment of Hades's laughter, she looked about for her tunic. An image of leaping flames and one curled, blackened lily appeared in her mind. A stab of pain went through her and she went still.

Hades rose, moved to the other side of the room, opened a chest—thankfully, not one of the ones she had plundered for material to make the drape which now hung in the folly—and turned to her. "There is clothing here."

Persephone hesitated, took in Hades's wide unblinking eyes and white knuckled fist clenched on the chest lid. She crossed the room, put a hand to his cheek, then bent and began sorting through the chest. She pulled out an indigo skirt encircled by rings of material its whole length. Gems and golden discs were sewn to each flounce. Persephone set it aside as it was too fine. Next, she pulled out a bodice with lacing running the full length of the back. The lacing in front went up only a quarter of the way. The rest of the bodice was open, cut to show the wearer's breasts. This too she had seen on the Goddesses, but underneath the bare front some of them had worn shirts of smooth, fine-woven cloth.

Persephone dug through the chest seeking such a garment, but reached the bottom without finding one. She did, however, happen upon a tunic. Its original color had faded to gray, and it was somewhat worn. She pulled it out and drew it over her head. Though it fell past her knees and the neck opening slid to one side, baring her shoulder, she deemed it more suitable than the clothing heaped in piles around her. Turning to one of those piles, Persephone selected a length of cloth from it and tied it around her waist. The rest of the clothing she bundled back into the chest and closed it.

"The Goddesses made an unnecessary sacrifice in giving me the clothing in that chest. It seems my castoffs are more to your liking," Hades said as Persephone got to her feet.

Persephone tugged at the tunic. "It suits me better than such finery."

"Rather you suit it, as you would anything you chose to wear."

This pretty compliment made the corners of Persephone's mouth dimple, as Hades moved to another chest, took from it a tunic similar to the one she had selected and clothed himself in it. Then he took her hand and led her into her megaron.

A male shade placed a final dish on the table as Hades escorted Persephone to her chair. Taking her seat, Persephone watched the shade. What sort of man had he been? Had he left any behind to mourn him? Why was the thing that remained with him even beyond death the skill of serving food?

Persephone watched the shade until he departed the room. Then she looked at Hades. "There's truly nothing that can be done to better the plight of our subjects?"

Hades's gaze flew to her face and stayed there for moment before he returned to his food. "There isn't and I beg you not to ask again."

It was only then Persephone noticed Hades still looked pale. His hands as they worked at the food on his plate trembled slightly and sweat beaded his brow.

She reached across the table and caught his hand. "Are you well?"

A smile like the opening of a flower to Helios's rays broke across his face. "It's an impossibility I be anything but."

Persephone returned his smile but continued to study him for a moment longer before turning her attention to her plate.

Though her stomach begged almost as loudly as Hades's for nourishment, she poked and prodded at the withered pears, the wizened grapes, the stale bread on her plate. It had been some time since Hermes' last visit and Upper World food seemed not to keep well in this land below.

Persephone's gaze wandered to Hades's plate. Olives and dates mounded on one side. Figs bursting with ripeness rocked on their plump bottoms. Pork, succulent in its rind of crackling fat, dripped its juices down Hades's arm as he brought it to his mouth. To the left of his plate sat a brilliant pink pomegranate. Saliva wetted Persephone's mouth.

Hades's hand closed over the pomegranate. Persephone returned her attention to her own plate and picked up one of the pears. She heard the wet rending of fruit flesh. Half of the pomegranate took the pear's place.

Persephone looked up. Hades, gaze firmly fixed on his plate, toyed with an olive. She looked back down at the pomegranate. She raised her hand, lowered it, raised it once more. Battling down her gorge, she plucked a few seeds from the rind.

Hades drew in an audible breath. Persephone's heart thudded, shaking her chest, her head. Her very teeth vibrated with it. She tightened trembling fingers on the seeds and lifted her eyes. Hades's gaze was fixed on her as he mashed the olive into a pulpy mass.

Persephone lifted her hand slightly. Her stomach heaved. She raised her hand farther. Hades made an inarticulate sound.

Persephone brought the seeds to her mouth, tears pooling in her eyes. She took a deep breath. If only the roiling in her stomach would cease. She opened her lips. Hades leaned forward.

A loud hollow boom rent the silence. Persephone jerked and lowered her hand. Hades turned his head toward the door of her megaron.

The noise came again, followed by what sounded like muffled shouting.

She looked at Hades. "What is that?"

Hades got to his feet, crossed to the door of her megaron and stood there, head cocked, brows drawn down. The thudding came again, fell into a rhythm. Hades went through the door and she could hear the slap of his feet as he walked down the hallway.

Persephone rose and followed. She'd traversed half the length of the corridor when she looked down and realized she still held the pomegranate seeds in her hand. She tucked them in her belt and hurried to catch Hades up, taking his hand in hers when she reached him.

"Is it Hermes?"

Hades shook his head. "Hermes enters and leaves as he pleases. He has no need to batter at our door."

"A shade then?"

"Aecus wouldn't allow any, save those he sends to Elysium, to penetrate so far into our realm and a shade would have no reason to stop at my palace."

A quick flash of Demeter's face appeared in Persephone's mind. Her hand spasmed on Hades's.

He looked down and quirked a brow at her.

"Perhaps a mortal?" she asked.

"None can reach us here. Cerberus ensures that."

As they descended the stairs the shouting grew louder, more articulate, but Persephone still couldn't make out the words.

At the bottom of the stairs, Hades halted. "Stay here."

Hades was still pale, his eyes pouched in bruised flesh, sweat darkening the top of his tunic. Demeter's cruelty could be waiting for him on the other side of that door. Persephone knew he had heard much about it from Hekate but that didn't mean he was prepared to face it, especially in his current state.

"Do you have strength enough to withstand whatever lies without?" Persephone asked.

"The only thing I lack strength to withstand is your loss. Stay here. I beg you."

Persephone shook her head and tightened her grasp on his hand. "I will neither leave you alone nor allow myself to be separated from you. We'll face whomever or whatever it is together."

Hades's gaze traveled over her face. He nodded then moved toward the door. The blows thudding against it were much like those Cerberus had rained against the palace gates when he sought to reclaim Nadira. Persephone shuddered at the association.

When they reached the entrance, Hades hesitated before grasping the handle of the nearest door and pulling it open. On the other side a man stood, fisted hand upraised, eyes large and dark in a too-thin, too-pale face. He looked mortal but seemed to have no trouble gazing directly at Hades, a feat which, according to the Goddesses, would drive any without Immortal blood mad.

The man dropped his hand and swallowed. His throat made a dry click, audible in the heavy silence. He drew in a breath, drew himself straight. "I am Orpheus of Pimpleia, and I come to barter with the Lord of the Underworld."

26

PERSEPHONE

Hades took a step forward, his gaze roving over the palace courtyard at Orpheus's back. Then he put his fingers to his lips. He meant to summon Cerberus.

Persephone put a hand on his arm. "Wait."

Fingers still at his mouth, Hades looked at her.

"Let him speak."

Hades lowered his hand. "There's no need. I can tell you all he means to say. He wants me to restore his lost one to him. There has never been such love, such devotion in all the time of man and it would be cruel to deny one who has traveled so far and withstood so much." Hades shook his head. "I can't give him what he wants."

"But you can," Persephone murmured.

Hades gave her a long, measured look. Persephone dropped her eyes.

"I must call Cerberus. There's no purpose in prolonging this mortal's agony," Hades said.

Still looking down, Persephone nodded. Instead of the sharp sound of Hades's whistle, however, a pure note shivered into the silence of the Underworld, then another. At the third note, a nameless longing swelled and burned in Persephone's breast. She tried to raise her eyes to look for the source of the sound, but was unable to make even the slight motion necessary to do so.

"I didn't come to beg, but to barter, as I said," Orpheus stated. "I entered here undetected and unimpeded by any who live in this place including the three-headed dog that guards your kingdom. I need not have come to your door and made you aware of my presence in your realm. I could have slipped within your walls and bore your lady away with me, using my song to prevent you and your beast from pursuing when you realized she was gone."

A spasm passed over Persephone's body as she struggled to lift her eyes, to cry out her outrage at Orpheus's words.

Orpheus's tune changed. "This is a summoning song, one which will draw your lady away with me to the Upper World."

Persephone stepped forward once, then again. She bent all her effort, all her strength into breaking the bonds of the music. Her head began to ache with the force of her pounding blood. Her fingers twitched once and that was the only result of all her exertion. Hades's feet shuffled through the dirt at her side. From his effortful grunting and gasping, it seemed he too sought to free himself, but she was unable to look at him to be sure.

The song changed once more and Persephone stopped. Her whole body seemed composed of some dense matter too weighty to move.

"Now perhaps you'll listen to my terms." At these words, Orpheus's music quieted, and Persephone was at last able to raise her eyes, but such a small motion as turning her head was still beyond her capacity.

Her gaze immediately went to the stringed instrument Orpheus held. He braced the bottom of it with one hand, fingers holding the strings steady. The other hand moved a small, rounded chip of some white material over the upper part of the strings; such a simple thing and yet it bound her and Hades wholly.

"I don't wish to deprive you of your lady," Orpheus continued. "I seek only to obtain my own, my wife, my Eurydice."

For a moment Orpheus's fingers faltered. Hades lifted a hand slowly, as though the air were constructed of Styx's lethal ooze. The melody steadied and Hades's arm fell back to his side.

"I heard that you, my lord, have the ability to restore a shade to life. Here is my bargain. If you'll use your power to return Eurydice to me, I'll leave you your love." Orpheus's song softened. "You may speak and tell me if these terms are agreeable."

"Cease your playing," Hades said and his voice echoed strangely, sounded deeper, somehow larger.

Orpheus's lips curled in a lopsided smile. "Your Godvoice will exact no obedience from me, my lord. Though my father is mortal, my mother is the muse, Calliope. No God save Zeus can command anything of another with even a drop of Immortal blood. Surely you don't believe a mere man's song could bind you and your lady?"

After a moment of silence, Hades's words emerged slowly, effortfully. "I see I have no choice but to agree to your terms. However, I add one of my own; you must give me your lyre after I restore your wife to mortality."

"I can just as easily bind you with my voice," Orpheus said.

"I have no doubt of that, but when singing you must pause for breath. Your fingers require no such rest."

"You speak true, which is why I'll retain my instrument. It's my only surety Eurydice and I can safely traverse your realm to reach the Upper World."

"No harm has yet come to you here. You yourself said nothing in this land can impede you," Hades said.

"It's not for my welfare I fear, but my wife's."

"Her welfare is of no concern of yours so long as she remains a shade and I won't restore your wife to mortality unless you agree to surrender your instrument to me."

Orpheus moved back. "I won't give up my lyre."

"Then we're at an impasse."

"On the contrary. If you won't give me my wife then I shall deprive you of yours."

"What do you want with me?" Persephone burst out.

Orpheus turned his gaze on Persephone. "I? I want nothing with you, Lady. It's your mother who desires you. It was she who sent me to reclaim you from your lord and return you to her."

The breath left Persephone's body in a harsh gasp. "My mother?"

"She desires your return above all else."

Persephone tried to shake her head but managed only the slightest motion. "You're mistaken. You must be mistaken. My mother is Demeter of Henna."

"Nay, Lady, she is Demeter, Goddess of Eleusis."

"She was mortal when I saw her last. A Goddess once, but no more."

"I assure you she's an Olympian. She worked the rite on me that allows me to move through this land unruled by its governances and untouched by its denizens."

Persephone tried to turn her head to look at Hades but could move only far enough to see him from the corner of her eye. "Hades, is this possible? Can she have been restored to her former state as an Immortal?"

"If Zeus willed it, then, yes."

"Would Zeus have gone to her in Henna, perhaps, to comfort her after my abduction?"

"That isn't in his nature."

"She traveled to him on Olympus then?"

"I have no way of knowing, Persephone."

Persephone returned her gaze to Orpheus. "Do you know? Did she go to Olympus?"

"I know not, Lady. Only that she's a Goddess who wields her power ruthlessly and that she bade me take you to her in her temple at Eleusis." His gaze shifted to Hades. "Which, if your lord denies me, I shall do."

It was as Persephone feared on the day she met the Goddesses. Her mother had given no thought to Persephone's welfare or whereabouts when she disappeared. Freed of the burden of the daughter she never wanted, Demeter had dashed to Olympus and been reinstated there, while here in this Underworld Persephone longed only to be reunited with her mother.

"What answer do I give this Orpheus, Persephone?" Hades's quiet question blended with the soft strains of Orpheus's song so Persephone only just heard him.

Persephone twitched her fingers against the hem of her tunic, but there were no silken threads of embroidery there to prove Demeter's love, only the worn wool of Hades's castoff. Persephone swallowed once, then again. Orpheus's eyes were avid on her face.

"Can you find she whom he seeks among all the shades in our kingdom?" Persephone asked Hades in a voice that trembled though she strove to keep it steady.

"I can," Hades said.

"I ask that you do so then."

Orpheus's music spiraled higher, sweeter, wild with jubilation. The sound lanced Persephone's heart.

At her side, Hades's murmured. "You're certain?"

"Yes."

Hades's breath caught and his voice emerged thick and clotted with emotion. "And so, you'll stay with me and be forever my light."

Struggling to breathe through the ache in her chest, the tightness in her throat, Persephone willed her tears away. Her mother didn't love her. She had no reason to return to Henna. She couldn't conceive of never seeing the Upper World again, of living forever in this horror of a land, but perhaps as he hoped, Hades's love would make up for all his realm lacked. She opened her lips, and said, "Yes."

"Very well, Orpheus," Hades said. "I accept your terms, but you must unshackle me from your song if I'm to restore your wife to you."

Orpheus's song softened until it had no more volume than a breath of breeze on a warm day.

Persephone turned to look at Hades. He reached out and cupped her face with one hand.

Persephone murmured, "Is all he said true? Can my mother have performed a rite to free him from the governances of the Underworld?"

Hades stroked her cheek with the ball of his thumb. "I think it's likely so for Cerberus neither raised the alarm, nor prevented Orpheus from penetrating our realm,."

Persephone closed her eyes, pressed her cheek deeper into his hand. "Why did she do this? She doesn't love me. She went first to Olympus to gain her power before seeking me."

"I have no way of knowing, Persephone, but I'm sorry for your pain," Hades said and then his hand fell away, depriving Persephone of the comfort of his touch.

Persephone opened her eyes.

"Come, Orpheus," Hades said. "And we shall find your lady."

Orpheus moved back from the doorway. "Lead on. I'll follow."

Hades curled his hand around Persephone's and stepped forward. As they passed Orpheus, Persephone darted a glance at his lyre, then up at his face. As though guessing her intent, he moved well out of her reach and the volume of his song increased a bit. It was suddenly all Persephone could do to place one foot in front of the other.

Persephone and Hades proceeded across the palace courtyard and through the open gates, Orpheus at their heels, his song dictating their steps.

Hades crossed the road in front of the palace and waded into the asphodels on the other side.

"Could we not find her more quickly if we used the horses?" Persephone asked. Anything to hasten the end of this ordeal.

"There's no need. She'll be drawn here by the feelings she shares with Orpheus. That's how Nadira found you in the asphodel meadow. You both longed for the same home. It's those desires that give the lodestone its power over my subjects. Like calls to like." Hades jerked his head in Orpheus's direction. "His woman has undoubtedly been on her way to him since the moment he entered our realm."

Among the asphodels the shades swayed to the pull of the lodestone. Their repetitive motions made it a simple thing for Persephone to pick out the one who moved with purpose. The shade drew close, a short, bird-boned woman with a halo of curly dark hair.

Orpheus drew up alongside Persephone. The aching sweetness of his song wrenched tears from Persephone's eyes.

Orpheus took another step forward, his song all for Eurydice now.

The shade stopped walking, cocked her head.

Orpheus stumbled toward her.

She came forward again, her hands working with a shuttle of air and threads of nothingness. Her eyes were a vast well of emptiness.

"Eurydice," Orpheus cried, the melody of his heartache making Persephone breathless with pain. Hades made a guttural sound and his hand clenched on Persephone's.

"Restore her. Now," Orpheus commanded rounding on Hades, his notes twanging with discord.

Persephone's skin twitched in answer.

Hades fumbled at his belt, took the knife from it and slashed at his forearm. Persephone winced, made a little sound of protest. Hades stowed the knife, gave Persephone a smile that didn't reassure her as she knew he meant it to. Then he moved toward the shade, pressed a hand to her forehead and she slumped, empty eyes slipping closed.

Hades caught her before she hit the ground and held her in his arms with all the tenderness of a father with his newborn babe.

"Turn away," Hades instructed Orpheus.

"Why?"

"What I do here isn't for your eyes. You mustn't look on your beloved's face until her transformation from shade to mortal is complete. Should you see even a glimpse of her face in the next seven days she'll revert to how you see her now, and I'll be unable to restore her to mortality again, no matter that you threaten me with the theft of my wife."

"I looked upon Nadira," Persephone said, a question in her words.

"You're fully Immortal. He isn't." Hades looked back at Orpheus. "Do as I say."

Still Orpheus hesitated.

"I'm in your thrall, man. I can do no harm to you or your lady without risking Persephone. Turn away."

Orpheus looked long at Eurydice as the notes he played took on a plaintive tone. At last, he did as Hades commanded.

Hades turned his attention to the shade in his arms then tilted her head, and pushed at her chin until her mouth fell open. He pressed the slash in his forearm to her pale lips. Eurydice fastened on Hades's arm and all was as it had been with Nadira: the grotesque slurping, the flush of life returning to the gray white skin, the gleam to the hair, the spark to the eyes.

Eurydice struggled up in Hades's arms. Her lips moved, forming her lover's name, but she made no sound. Then she reached for Orpheus, her heart-shaped face soft with longing.

Hades grasped her hands, and drew them down. "He may not look upon your face nor feel your touch until seven days have passed. You will do him grievous harm should you disobey. Do you understand?"

Eurydice's eyes widened and her mouth seemed almost to swell with questions, but she couldn't ask a single one. Finally, she nodded.

Hades released Eurydice, his face already drawn in pain as her transformation commenced.

In the distance, Cerberus bayed.

27

PERSEPHONE

"Your wife has been restored. Release us from your song," Hades said.

Orpheus's music swelled in volume. "Should I return to the Upper World without her daughter, Demeter will make my life a misery and Eurydice's as well. I must return with both my lady and yours, my lord. I beg your forgiveness for my perfidy, but surely you see I have no choice."

Something like a growl issued from Hades's mouth but Persephone felt none of the rage evident in the sound. Terror cloaked her instead. There was no telling what Demeter would do to punish Hades once she had him in her grasp and Persephone would be forced, once again, to share a home and a hearth with her mother. It was unthinkable and also, seemingly, inescapable all due to this sickly looking half mortal man.

Orpheus began to speak again, his words cutting into Persephone's thoughts. "Eurydice, I know you may not speak, my love, but be assured my heart is full, and I number the moments until I can look on your face and feel your sweet hand in mine once more."

Eurydice took a few steps forward, lifted a hand. She looked at Hades. He shook his head. Tears glittered in Eurydice's eyes, but she made no further attempt to touch her lover.

Persephone turned her head toward Hades. At her look, he reached for her, cocooning her cold, trembling hand in the warmth of his own.

Persephone's eyes were drawn to Orpheus. He had wronged her and Hades greatly in this, and yet, she would do the same as he, if necessary, to reclaim her love from death's grasp.

Orpheus turned toward the palace, his tune metamorphosing again. At the change in his song, Persephone plodded along in his wake, Hades and Eurydice on either side.

Cerberus's cry rent the air once more as they neared the road. Eurydice started and turned to look over her shoulder.

In her thoughts, Persephone chivvied the beast on, seeing in him her and Hades's only hope of salvation.

Orpheus moved onto the road. Hades, Persephone, and Eurydice stepped from the asphodels behind him. In perfect sync, they moved toward the lodestone.

Cerberus howled. Eurydice turned to look over her shoulder and seemed to want to hurry her steps but she too was entangled in the mesh of Orpheus's summoning song and could go only at the speed he dictated.

Persephone looked at Orpheus. Surely, he would quicken their pace at the sound of pursuit, but, no, he strode along, outwardly indifferent to Cerberus's cries and their decreasing distance.

Hades's hand tightened on Persephone's. She turned. His lips were peeled back from his teeth in a rictus of pain. Sweat poured down his face, plastering his hair to forehead and cheeks. Eurydice's transformation seemed to be taking its toll both faster and in greater magnitude than Nadira's had. He'd looked unwell all day, and this seemed to be a further manifestation of some ailment.

A confrontation with Demeter awaited them at the end of this forced journey. She could and likely would take great delight in punishing Hades for taking Persephone captive. Hades was in no fit state to defend himself against Demeter's ire, and, as had been proven time and again, Persephone hadn't the capacity to defy her mother.

A chill sweat broke from Persephone's pores. She strained against the bonds of the song again, tried to bring her body back under her own control. The effort left her gasping, her muscles cramping, and still she trudged along in rhythm with Orpheus's tune. At her side, Hades grunted in pain with every step.

Cerberus hadn't caught them by the time they rounded the lodestone, but the volume of his baying told Persephone he would be on them soon.

Persephone held to this hope for it was her last. The thud of his paws behind her made her heart surge with hope. She turned to look over her shoulder and Eurydice did the same. As the beast churned toward them, his serpent's mane upright and writhing, the mortal woman, like Nadira had before her at the sight of the creature, opened her mouth in a soundless scream, but because of her lover's melody she was unable to run.

Cerberus took three more distance devouring strides, then stumbled, fell, rolled to his feet, and shook all three of his heads. He stood for a moment, ears cocked. Then his tongues lolled out and he began to trot toward them, tail lashing his haunches as he came.

Persephone shook her head as though the violent motion could clear the sight from her eyes. "No. No."

Hades's hand contracted on Persephone's once more. She turned her gaze on his face. He was suffused with color, the lines of pain, though not gone, much less deep and carven.

"What—" She began just as Orpheus cried out and doubled over, his song ceasing.

Persephone darted forward but not quickly enough. The man straightened, picking up his tune, but his playing lacked its former crystalline quality. It was, however, enough to bind Persephone, Hades, and Eurydice once more to their plodding pace. Behind her Persephone could hear Cerberus's panting as he too joined in their march.

A moment later, Orpheus ground out, "What sort of curse have you worked on me? I'm in agony."

Persephone turned questioning eyes to Hades but his gaze was fastened on the back of Orpheus's head.

Persephone looked to see if Orpheus's affliction also affected Eurydice, but the woman was no longer at Persephone's side. Glancing around, she found Eurydice, legs still moving to Orpheus's rhythm but making no forward progress at all. The mortal woman's arms were upheld, hands straining toward Orpheus.

"Your lady obeys your summons no longer," she called to Orpheus.

The man turned then charged past Persephone to go to his wife. As he passed her, Persephone snatched the lyre from his hands. Orpheus stumbled, then righted himself and lunged toward Persephone. Persephone darted out of his reach, lifted the lyre high, and dashed it against a large stone. The wood of its frame shattered and the strings still attached to the wood writhed as they flew through the air but the turtle shell that was the instrument's base remained intact. Persephone slammed it onto the rock. It cracked into two pieces and Persephone flung them from her. She spun to Hades. He was stooped in a half crouch, arms held away from his body, fingers fluttering as though preparing for an attack.

Persephone followed the direction of his gaze. His intended opponent wasn't, as she expected, Orpheus, but Cerberus.

The beast's three heads were lowered, low growls issuing from all of his mouths as the serpents on his neck writhed and hissed. Then Cerberus's haunches bunched and, mouths wide, baring wicked white teeth, he leaped at Hades. Persephone cried out, ran towards Hades, tripped, and fell. Cerberus's forepaws landed on Hades's chest, bearing him to the ground.

"Hades!" Persephone screamed as he disappeared beneath Cerberus's great hairy body. Her fingers scrabbled in the dirt, and bashed into the stone she had used to break the lyre. She frantically dug around its base until it came free. Then, with the rock gripped in both hands, she clambered to her feet and sprinted toward the melee.

All was chaos, flying dust above, flattened grass, churned blood-colored dirt below. Inhuman snarls, grunts, and groans filled the air in a gross harmony of effort and fury.

Persephone hammered the rock down on any part of Cerberus she could see, but her blows had little effect. She backed up a bit, raised the stone high over her head, and waited.

Cerberus surged upward, his central head presenting a clear target, precisely the opportunity she'd hoped for.

Hades shouted, "No!"

His arm came up as Persephone brought the rock down. Her blow impacted Hades's forearm with a hideously solid thud. Hades grunted.

Crying out, Persephone released the boulder; it glanced off Cerberus's head but without the force necessary to injure him. Cerberus yelped.

Persephone stepped forward, put out a hand. "Hades, are you—"

Before she could say more Cerberus slewed to one side. Hades fully emerged from beneath the creature's body, teeth clenched together in a grimace, both hands clamped around the spot where Cerberus's three necks merged. Hades rolled the beast onto its back, never loosening his white-knuckled grip on the animal's throat while he stared into its central set of eyes.

After a moment, Cerberus stopped struggling. His gaze slid away from Hades. The furry ridges above his eyes twitched and a whine quested from his throat. Hades loosened his grip. The beast's central tongue rolled out from a foam and blood-flecked mouth and swept over Hades's cheek. A harsh sound, almost a sob, broke from Hades. He sank back onto his heels, completely releasing the creature.

Cerberus immediately got to his feet. He took a few unsteady steps and shook himself. Then he stilled, his eyes once again lit with malevolence. A few of the serpents rose on his neck, forked tongues flickering from their mouths, their eyes as cold and glittering as gold and all fixed on the same thing.

Persephone turned to follow the direction of the beast's gaze. Orpheus knelt in the grass, Eurydice clutched in his arms. The mortal woman's body seized and bucked, and blood, Hades's blood, ran from her nose, both sides of her mouth, and one ear.

Cerberus gave one guttural bark. Orpheus lifted his head, saw Cerberus, and reached for the lyre that was no longer there.

Cerberus bounded toward the pair, seized one of Eurydice's legs, and dragged her from Orpheus's arms. The serpents on the beast's neck buried their fangs into Eurydice's feet and ankles. The woman went still.

Weeping, cursing, Orpheus grabbed Eurydice's arms.

"Orpheus," Hades called. "Your lady is lost. Let Cerberus bear her back to the asphodels where she belongs, or he'll turn his attack on you."

Hades made no move to enforce his order but remained on his knees. Blood and dirt streaked his face and bare torso. He cradled his left arm, the one Persephone had inadvertently struck, across his midsection. As if he felt Persephone looking at him, he rolled his eyes towards her, and her chest hollowed out at the bleakness in his gaze.

Orpheus's only response was to climb to his feet and redouble his efforts to reclaim Eurydice from Cerberus. The dog dragged them both toward the asphodels.

"Let her go, man," Hades said, struggling to rise. Once on his feet, he staggered. Persephone hurried forward to help him. He halted her with a brusque gesture.

Hades lurched toward Orpheus, exhorting him to release his lady. Sputtering denials and curses, Orpheus hung onto the woman's slack form.

Eurydice convulsed suddenly. Orpheus looked down, spoke her name. Eurydice wrenched one hand free of Orpheus's grip, buried her fingernails in his cheek, and drew them down, opening five gashes in Orpheus's flesh. She heaved upward, tongue flicking out to catch the blood that welled in the wounds.

Orpheus drew back from her, heartbreak and horror mingling on his face. This would have been Persephone's experience with Nadira if Hades hadn't intervened.

"That isn't Eurydice," Hades said, nearing the trio. "Surely you must see that. Relinquish her shade to the world where it belongs."

"No." Crooning a soft song, Orpheus tried in vain to draw the shade into his embrace. She tore at him, using teeth and nails with horrifying silence and intent.

Weeping and bloodied, Orpheus finally let go of Eurydice and Cerberus pulled the vacant-eyed woman toward the asphodels.

Orpheus covered his face with his hands and sank to his knees.

"Hades?" Persephone called. "What do you intend to do with him?"

Hades considered the man for a moment. "Nothing. No punishment I mete out could compare with his present agony. Moreover, he has your mother still to face when he reaches the Upper World."

Hades turned away from the grieving man and began to walk toward Persephone, weaving on his feet. His tunic was streaked with dirt and wet with sweat from neck to waist. The wounds opened in his struggle with Cerberus still welled with blood and he cradled the arm she had struck with the rock as though it still pained him greatly. All were hurts his Godbody should have healed moments after they were inflicted. Her former unease over his physical well-being returned, and she hurried forward to meet him.

When she reached him, she drew his uninjured arm over her shoulder. His lack of protest at her aid increased her concern. They went a few steps. Hades groaned and lurched forward, his arm sliding free of her grasp as he fell face down in the grass.

Persephone dropped to her knees next to him. "Hades? Hades?"

She rolled him to his back. The whites of his eyes showed under partially closed lids and no breath moved between his lips, but he couldn't die. That was an impossibility. Wasn't it?

Footsteps sounded behind Persephone and Orpheus said, "Lady, I—"

Surging to her feet, Persephone rounded on the man. "Go! Go from this place or I vow to find some way to take the price of this day out of your flesh. I'm not nearly so merciful as my husband."

Orpheus fled.

Persephone turned back to Hades, knelt again at his side. His eyes fluttered open. He moaned. His eyes closed again. But he lived. He lived.

"Hades, how can I help you? What must I do?" Persephone heaved his upper body onto her lap and turned his face to hers.

His head lolled from her supporting hand, spittle from his open mouth pattering onto her tunic.

"Hades." She bent, pressing kisses to his lips, his forehead, his cheeks. "Hades, please, wake. Please tell me what ails you."

His only response was a low moan. Persephone looked over the empty expanse of waving grasses. The utter silence of the Underworld coalesced as a roar in her ears. There was no help to be had here. It was up to her alone to decide what must be done and then to see it through.

Drawing her legs under her so that she squatted before him, Persephone grasped Hades's arms and pulled him forward and up until his upper body dangled down against her back, his pelvis resting on her shoulder. Panting, wet with sweat, she heaved, struggling to rise. Her legs trembled and then betrayed her. She collapsed back to the ground, Hades's weight pinning her there.

"No. No!" She wriggled from under him, then worked to get him over her shoulder once more.

Still trembling from her previous attempt, Persephone closed her eyes, and tensed her legs, focusing all her force, all her will into her shaking muscles, demanding that her body give her more. A flush of heat swept over her and her skin felt swollen and tight as though there were something within that could no longer bear the confines of her body. The darkness behind her closed lids flared red in a flash of light. Strength coursed through her. Impossibly, she began to rise.

Opening her eyes, she bore Hades upward. A strange illumination eddied around her. Perhaps this was what Hades meant when he spoke of her Godbody but she had neither the time nor inclination to puzzle it out now. She was only grateful the transformation gave her the means with which to convey Hades inside.

She lurched around the lodestone, down the road to the gates, through the courtyard, into the palace and up the stairs. Staggering, she pushed open the door to Hades's bedchamber, made her way to his bed, and eased him down onto it. He twitched and groaned.

Persephone bent over him. "Hades? I know not what aid I can give you or if there's any cure to be had for your ailment. Please tell me what I must do." She gripped his tunic and shook him. "Tell me."

He made no response. Indeed, he was so still Persephone pressed her ear to his chest to assure herself that the heart within still beat.

"He can't die," she muttered as tears dripped off her face and soaked into his tunic.

Leaving her head on his chest, wrapping one arm about his torso, Persephone drew her legs onto the bed.

"Please," she murmured, not sure of whom she begged. "Please."

28

DEMETER

As the last slivers of Helios's light left the world, Demeter paced before the mouth of the cave. She stopped and peered once more into its darkness, but there were no answers to be found in its dumb gaping. It couldn't tell her whether Orpheus had betrayed her or merely failed in his task and was now a prisoner alongside Persephone in that land below. She clenched her jaw and her hands. If he walked in the world, Demeter would find him and make good her vow to curse him with misery, but not yet, not until Persephone's freedom was a surety.

Demeter turned away from the cavern, looked toward Olympus. Anticipation fluttered in her belly and she fought back a smile. Drawing breath, she steadied herself and called forth her Godbody. Then, mouth set, eyes narrowed, she lifted a foot and placed it on the God Road. Only moments later she was tumbled from her path when it came to an abrupt end before Zeus's walls.

Cursing, she picked herself up, dusted off the flounces of her skirt, straightened her bodice, and smoothed her hair. Then, squaring her shoulders and lifting her chin, she walked across the courtyard to Zeus's palace. In his megaron, every God and Goddess of Olympus who dwelt there, including a restored Hephaistos, feasted in raucous celebration.

Demeter entered the big room. Her gaze went to Zeus and Hera where they sat on their thrones. Zeus pretended at watching a group of nymphs and satyrs who danced to music provided by Pan on his pipes, but his eyes were glazed and the fingers of one hand drummed on his thigh. Next to him, Hera beamed down at a swaddled bundle in her arms. Rage burned hot and sudden, scorching away Demeter's keen expectation.

Pushing her way through the roistering Immortals, Demeter called, "Zeus."

Hera lifted her head. Gone were the suppurating sores, the ravening eyes, but Hera's Godlight still had that same muddied look. Likely Hera's madness was held at bay solely by the tiny bundle in her arms.

Hera found Demeter in the crowd and her smile widened. She extended one hand toward Demeter. "Welcome, Sister. I hoped you would come to celebrate with us the birth of our babe, our Ares. He's as perfect a boy as any father could wish. Come look upon him."

In response to Hera's words, the crowd shuffled back, clearing a path to the dais, but their boisterousness continued nearly unabated.

Demeter wanted to cry out, 'I could destroy you all. But a few more months of my famine would see every one of you brought as low as I was the last time I was in this place.' Instead, she strode forward as though unaware of their riotous presence. "I heard nothing of his birth and I don't come to wish him or you well. My business is with your husband."

At her words, the flock of Immortals to either side of her quieted, stilled, their laughter and chatter replaced with rustlings and whispers.

Zeus shifted in his chair, the blue of his eyes deepening with interest. "What business have we, Demeter? Has my rain worked its miracle? Have you come to confess your wrongs and render to me the portion of your offerings that is rightfully mine?"

His eyes raked Demeter's body as she mounted the dais and her hand twitched with the sudden urge to strike him. "Your rain has done nothing but strip Gaia's flesh more even than my famine and I shall never again give to you any part of that which my supplicants sacrifice to me. I come to speak with you of Persephone. She is yet in Hades's clutches. If you do not return her to me—"

Zeus cut across her words. "I thought all was settled, yet you come again to bother me with this, Demeter?"

"I'll have my daughter freed. If you don't submit to me your throne is—"

"And you won't cease this," Zeus made a circular motion in the air with one hand, "famine until she's released from the Underworld?"

Demeter blinked, shifted. "I won't."

Hera leaned toward Zeus and murmured something in his ear.

Plucking at his beard, he looked at someone behind Demeter and called, "Hermes, go to Hades and tell him I command Persephone's return to the Upper World. She must remain in this realm with her mother. If Hades refuses, remind him I have the power to force his obedience. Take my daughter to Demeter in her temple at Eleusis." Zeus's gaze shifted to Demeter's face. "And collect from the temple that part of Demeter's offerings due me. Should she defy you, she'll suffer the consequences."

Demeter's eyes faltered from Zeus's. Her insides as cold and empty as they were after Hera robbed her of her Godhood, she turned and watched Hermes flit from the palace on his winged sandals.

Zeus's hand closed on Demeter's shoulder and he pulled her back around to face him. "Stay with us a while, Loveliest. It will take some time for Hermes to travel to the Underworld and some time more for our daughter to reach Eleusis. It's been a long while since I've enjoyed your company."

Demeter jerked free of his hand. His bottom lip jutted, a storm of

petulance gathering in his eyes. The urge to strike him was nearly unbearable, but she wouldn't lose control of her emotions before him
again.

"I take my leave of you." Demeter stepped down off the dais, began
to walk toward the door. Behind her, Hera said, "I trust this will satisfy
Hekate."

Zeus rumbled laughter, all ease and pleasantness again, as though
Demeter's denial of his request caused no more disturbance than a
thrown stone in a pond. "Where has the old woman taken herself off
to? Ah. well, it's over now and she has no more reason to carp on about
the danger this famine presented to our power. Surely if it threatened
us so mightily, we would have noticed some change. Yet had Hekate
not informed us of it we wouldn't have known anything untoward was
occurring."

Heat flamed in Demeter's face. She wouldn't give them the satisfaction of tucking her head to her chest and scurrying through the crowded
room, though that's what she longed to do. Instead, she drew herself up,
lifted her chin, and met every eye with a cold, distant gaze, even looking
away as though she didn't know him when Hephaistos beckoned to her.

When she reached the concealing shadows in the corridor outside
Zeus's megaron Demeter turned and looked back. Hera and Zeus's heads
were bowed, her dark hair mingling with the golden hues of his as they
looked down into their babe's face. A small fist waved up at them from
within the swaddling cloth. Choking back a cry, Demeter turned and
fled. Never again would she trod Olympus's soil.

29

PERSEPHONE

Persephone stood in the corridor outside Hades's chambers, her back pressed against the door, bracing the stout wooden bar she'd wedged in place to hold it closed. The door shuddered with the blows Hades rained on it from within. Biting her bottom lip, she held back the words of reassurance she longed to say to him. She had learned from his previous bouts of madness over the past two days that any sound she made would incite him into further frenzy.

The door shook with another blow but this one was less forceful than its predecessor. Three more strikes impacted the wood, each with diminishing ferocity and strength. This fit, too, was ebbing.

When at last all was silent within, Persephone waited the space of ten breaths, then peeled away from the door. She moved the wooden bar aside. Easing the door, which was beginning to splinter, open, she peered into the room. Hades lay curled on the floor, eyes clenched shut. Sweat drenched his body and he shook as though taken with an ague. His eyes fluttered open and settled on Persephone's face. Putting out a hand, he slurred something incomprehensible. Persephone hurried forward, crouched, slung his arm over her shoulder, and together they staggered upright. Chest pumping like a bellows, Hades slumped against her as they shuffled into his bedchamber.

Persephone eased him onto his bed. He looked up and touched her face. He tried again to speak but Persephone hushed him with a hand to his lips. His frustration at his inability to communicate might provoke him into a frenzy again and she couldn't bear to witness another so soon.

Under her touch he subsided, but continued to gaze at her, tears streaking from the outer corners of his eyes and soaking the cushion under his head. Persephone lowered herself next to him. She stroked the hair back from his brow and murmured soothing words until he moved from troubled consciousness into disturbed sleep.

When she was sure he slept, she rose and began to put the chamber as much to rights as possible, though there was not, after three days of his rages, much left to salvage. Even the frescoes on his wall had suffered under his maddened blows.

After she finished straightening the room, Persephone returned once more to Hades's side. Even in slumber he tossed and moaned. The abrasions and cuts he inflicted on himself in his fits oozed blood. Bruises spread over the bared flesh of his arms and face.

Persephone knew the recipe for several tinctures that would soothe these smaller hurts and speed their healing but, even if she could find the ingredients in the Underworld, she dared not leave Hades to make the attempt. She had left his side only once to release the horses in Elysium. When she returned to the palace it was to find Hades rampaging through it, screaming curses, trying to shatter himself against the stone walls, floors, and furniture. Since then, she didn't dare absent herself for there was no predicting when a fit might take him. Closing him up in his chambers was the only way she had of mitigating the damage he did to himself in his maddened state.

Pressing her lips to his furrowed, sweat-dampened brow she murmured, "I know not how to heal you."

Hades groaned and turned away from her touch. She lowered her head onto his chest too full of despair even to weep. Her eyelids grew heavy, slipped closed then flew open when she thought she heard someone calling her name. She sat up, listening closely, sudden hope siphoning away her misery and exhaustion. The call came again, unmistakable this time.

Persephone leapt from the bed, dashed to the door of Hades's chambers then through it and down the hall, all the while shouting Hermes's name. As the God turned the corner at the top of the step, Persephone nearly collided with him. Not bothering with apologies or explanations, she clutched his hand and ran back the way she came, dragging Hermes behind her. He made indignant protest, but she hardly heard and she didn't ease her grip on him until they both fetched to a halt next to Hades's bed.

"What ails him? What can be done to correct it? You must know. Tell me."

Nose wrinkled and lips pursed, Hermes stepped back. "He's foul."

Persephone turned to Hermes and slapped him with all the force she could muster. "How can you be so unfeeling?"

Hermes grabbed Persephone's wrist and yanked her to him. "You'll answer for that. And as your lord is in no fit state to protect you, I know just how you shall answer."

Persephone reached between Hermes's legs with her free hand and grasped what dangled there. She squeezed and jerked upward. Hermes screamed. He let go of her wrist to slap ineffectually at her arm as he shrieked over and again.

"Enough, Kore. Any more and you'll unman him completely. While that wouldn't be a great loss, I don't think your father would be best pleased to have his messenger maimed in such a way."

The voice was one Persephone had never heard before, but something in it seemed familiar. Persephone released Hermes. He groaned and stumbled to the wall, where he leaned gasping. This gave Persephone an unobstructed view of the speaker. An older woman, bent nearly double, a shawl obscuring most of her face stood in the doorway.

Persephone took a step forward, tried to peer under the cloth. "Who?"

The older woman straightened, fully revealing herself. "Doso that was. Hekate that is. Greetings, my Kore. Oh, how I've missed you."

Persephone flung herself at Hekate. The woman's arms, with their customary wiry strength, closed around Persephone, enveloping her in lavender-scented wool.

After only a moment, however, Persephone pushed out of Hekate's embrace. Taking the woman's gnarled hand, she tugged her to Hades's bedside. "You have more knowledge of sickness and healing than I. What can be done for him?"

Hekate surveyed Hades, her lined face sagging. "No salve or tincture or draught will cure what ails him. He's worse even than I feared."

"What do you mean? You knew of his illness before you came?"

"It's why I bade Hermes bring me here."

At this, Persephone recalled the pitiless messenger God. She glanced around. Hermes, his face still twisted with anger and pain, had moved to lean against the doorframe of Hades's bedchamber.

Hekate made a shooing motion at him. "Go glut yourself with the food you brought for Persephone, Hermes. We have no further use for you just now."

"You know I must—"

Hekate interrupted. "I know what you must do. I'll call you when the time is right. Now go."

With mutterings and a baleful glance or two over his shoulder, Hermes quit the room.

"How did you know of Hades's illness?" Persephone asked the moment he was gone.

"I sought out Orpheus on his return to the Upper World. He told me of Hades's collapse."

"That man," Persephone spat. "It was his visit that precipitated Hades's ailment and brought him to this."

"Nay, Persephone, the fault is not Orpheus's. He was but a piece played by another's hand, in a game much too large for him to comprehend. Though I'm sorry his visit caused you such pain. I thought only of freeing you when I sent him to your mother."

Keeping her face averted from Hekate, Persephone said, "I don't wish to speak of my mother."

A sound like wind rustling dried leaves came from Hekate.

It took a moment for Persephone to realize the woman was laughing. "You find humor in that?"

"Only that your sentiment nearly echoes one your mother expressed to me some months ago about her mother. And as your mother before you, I fear we must speak of the one you desire not to."

"I won't speak of anything at all unless it is some way to ease my husband."

"Husband? Ah then, it's as Orpheus said. You're here because you wish to be." Tears welling in her eyes, Hekate put a palm to Persephone's cheek. "That eases me, Kore. For I fear it was my maunderings that inspired Hades to remove you to his realm. I wouldn't have spoken of you to him had I known."

"Hush. Your error in speaking to him of me was my salvation."

Hekate patted Persephone's cheek. "Though it complicates my task a great deal, it gladdens me that you've found solace in one another."

Persephone turned away from Hekate to touch Hades's chest. "No solace now. Not until he's healed."

"Alas, Persephone, his healing lies not within my power, but your mother's."

Persephone gave Hekate a sharp look. "What has she to do with this?"

"To explain that to you was partially my purpose in coming here, but it may take some time."

"I must bathe Hades and change his clothing. Can you tell me while I do?"

Hekate nodded.

"I'll fetch the necessary supplies and return in a moment."

"No need." Hekate closed her eyes. Her brows drew down and her lips puffed out with effort. There was a soundless concussion of air and an ewer of water, a basin, a small pile of cloths, and a vial of oil appeared next to Persephone's feet.

"I don't usually waste my power on such trivialities. However, there is some urgency in what I came here to accomplish and even one lost moment is too many," Hekate said.

Persephone couldn't look away from the items on the floor. "You simply conjured them out of nothing?"

The same dry crackle of laughter emerged from Hekate. "None is that powerful, Kore. No, I only removed them from the place they were and brought them here."

"I thank you." Persephone stooped, filled the basin from the ewer, wetted one of the cloths and put it to use on Hades's face.

Hekate reached for another cloth, dipped it in the water, and moved to Hades's other side. "What did Hades tell you of his coming to the Underworld?"

Persephone paused in her washing, stroked her fingers over the arch of

Hades's brows, trying to soothe away the deep line between them. "Very little. Only that he was tumbled into the Styx by the shades on its bank and that he spent the nine years following that in unconsciousness."

"I thought as much," Hekate murmured, then, "Would it surprise you to know that after he lapsed into insensibility, I packed him about with fleece, poured warm broth down his throat, and watched over him in his slumber?"

Persephone looked up from wiping the crust of sweat off Hades's neck. "Why were you in the Underworld?"

"I came here to wait while the new pantheon of Gods settled themselves. I wanted to see if Zeus would tolerate my worship or if he would wrest my followers from me and so take my power. As I had few worshippers, I was no threat to his supremacy and Zeus let me be. Once I was sure I wouldn't be struck down, I made my way to Olympus and told Zeus of the young God slumbering on the banks of the River Styx. I believed Zeus would come collect him and take the God to his proper place. I was sure he didn't belong in this dreary land. Indeed, to my eyes, he looked built for joy and youthful pursuits and pleasure."

Hades was indeed built for pleasure. The thought caused a hot rush of blood to creep up Persephone's neck and into her face. To divert Hekate's attention from her discomfiture, Persephone asked, "I know Zeus didn't collect him. Did he at least send another to look after his welfare?"

Hekate shook her head. "When it became clear Zeus meant to do nothing for his brother, I returned to the Underworld and continued caring for Hades. As the ninth year waned, he showed signs of rousing. I hastened to Olympus and told them of his return to consciousness. With me as a guide, Helios came to the Underworld to deliver to Hades his chariot and four steeds."

Persephone began to tug Hades's tunic up. Hekate moved to help her and together they removed the soiled garment.

Persephone dipped her cloth in the basin again then moved it over Hades's chest. As the dark curling hair caught at her fingertips and on the base of her palm, the memory of the touches— needful and sweet, hungry and hesitant—they had shared opened an aching rent in her chest. She gripped the rag, breathed the pain down.

Resuming her task, her voice only a little tremulous, Persephone said, "Hades told me he didn't realize he'd been unconscious for nine years until Helios told him it was so."

Hekate reached into one of the pouches that hung from her belt, pulled out a small container, and opened it.

Persephone recognized it immediately from its sharp scent: wound-wort compounded with lard.

Hekate dipped her finger inside, brought it out laden with the ointment and applied it to the lacerations on Hades's face. "I thought as much. I hung back during their reunion, but I could hear Hades asking again and again if Helios were the only one of the Gods to journey to the Underworld to see how he fared in all that time."

Hekate looked up from her work. "Say what you will of your mother, Persephone. She never deserted you in this Underworld the way Hades was forsaken by those who had most cause to love him."

Persephone continued bathing Hades, wiping at his belly, but her lips thinned at the mention of her mother.

Hekate continued. "I expected Hades to return to Olympus with Helios, never again to show his face in this place. Instead, he immediately set out to gather enough wood with which to construct a raft; a difficult task indeed in this mostly barren land. After the raft was complete, he poled it across the river. I couldn't imagine what he was about, for the shades there had bested him once already. He didn't land on that shore though. He held the raft in a small eddy some way away and conversed with the shades. After a time, a contingent of them came forward bearing the remains of what appeared to be a young woman. Hades cried out and went to his knees at the sight. After he recovered himself somewhat, he moved the raft forward, collected the woman's remains and took the group of shades who had brought her to him onto his raft. When he reached this shore again his deep grief at the young woman's death was evident."

Unable to contain her curiosity any longer, Persephone looked up from cleaning Hades's thighs and blurted, "Who was she? What was she to him? And why, if her death saddened him so, didn't he use his power to return her to life?"

"I believe she was an Okeanid nymph called Leuke. From stories I've overheard on Olympus it seems she and Hades formed an attachment during the war with the Titans and she came with him to this realm intending to help him rule here. I don't know if it was the shades on Styx's bank who killed her or if she, like Hades, was pushed into the river and its waters spelled her demise. It was apparent Hades felt her death keenly and blamed himself for it, but he was unable to return her to life because he can't regenerate a shade within a body, only a body around a shade."

Persephone put a hand to Hades's cheek, and gazed down at his gaunt face. "He was so brusque with me when we first emerged from the cavern on Styx's bank, I thought then he hated me and intended to do me some violence. I see now he was likely terrified I would share Leuke's fate and that's why he behaved as he did."

"You couldn't come to the same end as Leuke for you're an Olympian. She was only a nymph, but I'm sure Hades wanted to spare you the terror of being attacked by the shades as well as the agony and unconsciousness that comes from drinking Styx's water, and spare himself the guilt for subjecting you to those things."

"What did he do with Leuke's body? Did he return her to the Upper World?"

Hekate shook her head. "He placed her in his chariot and then spent days shuttling as many shades as had the toll across the river. It was only when he completed that task Hades harnessed his horses to his chariot and ventured deeper into his realm.

I followed along at a distance, fearful of what would happen to this strange young God when he encountered Cerberus though it took nearly the whole day for Cerberus to seek him out. I believe the beast had become accustomed to Hades's scent in the nine years Hades lay unconscious and the creature didn't realize he was up and about. Hades had time to travel to Elysium and bury Leuke there. If you're curious to see her grave, it's easily found. A white poplar grew from her body and marks the spot even today.

Persephone had seen that tree. Hades had told her it was farewell gift from a dear friend but there was so much more to the story, more he would likely never share with her because, like his time in his father's stomach, it was an experience too painful to recall. At least now she knew a bit about one of the two women who had preceded her in Hades's affections.

Persephone picked up one of Hades's hands and dabbed at the blood on his swollen abraded knuckles as Hekate continued. "That tree also commemorates the spot of Hades's first battle with Cerberus for that's where the beast found him. It was a fearsome fight with much blood shed by both parties. Had it not been for the charioteer's whip Helios gave Hades I don't think he would have prevailed, but he did. And in doing so he truly became ruler of this realm."

"What do you mean?" Persephone looked up from her work on Hades's hand. .

"To bring Cerberus to heel is to take on the mantle of stewardship for this land."

"It is?" Persephone asked, paused then said, "After Cerberus was subdued by Orpheus's song, Hades looked as though a yoke had been removed from his neck." She paused again. "And so it had. But why did he take it back? Why did he battle Cerberus once more?" She drew in a sharp breath. "Hades deflected my blow to Cerberus's head. But for that I ..." She motioned at Hekate. "Go on, please."

Hekate lifted Hades's other hand, tutting at its bruised and battered state. As she treated it with the woundwort she continued, "I felt great pity for Hades. I couldn't imagine what it would be to be chained to this realm, and to take on the agonies of its various inhabitants."

Persephone let out a small gasp. "Hades feels that which his subjects feel?"

"He does. Chaos made it so to inspire any who rule here to be conscientious in their stewardship." She added in a tart voice, "It's a pity Zeus didn't draw the black stone. Time ruling a realm such as this might somewhat temper his pleasure-seeking ways."

Persephone hardly heard Hekate for she was recalling Hades's words when he saw the increase of shades on Styx's banks, and the agony on his face as Nadira and Eurydice were ravaged by Cerberus. "I should have realized."

Hekate gently lowered Hades's hand, patted it then met Persephone's eyes. "And so we are at the crux of the matter, Kore. This ailment your husband suffers from is no more and no less than the combined agonies of all the shades on Styx's bank."

Persephone shook her head. "I think you're mistaken, Hekate. There have been shades on Styx's bank since I first arrived here. It's only over the course of ..." Persephone cast her mind back. The first signs of Hades's weakness had manifested after he restored Nadira.

She continued. "He's been sickening for some time, but Hades told me when he first arrived here all the souls of all the world's dead clustered on Styx's bank. He bore up under their distress then. Surely those that are there now don't outnumber that quantity."

"Hades shuttled a large portion of their number across Styx prior to besting Cerberus. Most of the shades that he was unable to ferry over then had been there for many years and their distress had been tempered by time. It wasn't so immediate as the despair and confusion of those that arrive there daily now, though this isn't the first time Hades has been affected so. I've seen it happen in times of plague or war, whenever there's an abrupt and sizeable increase in those arriving in the Underworld. I will say, however, I've never seen him so laid so low as this."

"He attempted to restore two shades to their mortal form only a matter of days apart. I believe that weakened him a great deal."

"I know he gave Eurydice her life, but who was the other?" Hekate asked.

"This isn't a time to answer that question, but I will one day when there are less pressing matters at hand." Persephone stroked the hair back from Hades's brow. "What I must know now, is can we sever his tie to this realm?"

"We can, but Hades wouldn't thank us for that."

Persephone looked up. "Not thank us for saving him from an eternity of this agony?"

"May I return to my tale?"

Persephone cut her hand across the air. "No, I have no wish to hear more of it. I know now what must be done to spare him. I only need the method by which it can be accomplished."

"Don't act in haste in this, Kore."

"In what other way can I act? You see his pain. You said yourself there isn't much time."

"There are things you must understand and only in listening to me can you hope to gain that understanding. There is time, at least, for that." Hekate reached over Hades's body and touched Persephone's cheek. "Trust me. Please."

30

PERSEPHONE

Persephone surveyed Hekate's face. The older woman had always acted out of love for Persephone. There was no reason to question her motives or reasoning now. "Very well. Continue."

Hekate took up the tale. "Once Hades had beaten Cerberus, it didn't take him long to discover the terrible pull of the lodestone or that the only way to escape it was on horseback or riding in his chariot. I imagine you felt the draw of that rock in your time here?"

"I have. It's . . . terrible," Persephone said as she carefully washed Hades's lower legs.

Hekate continued. "I heard, though I did not see, the mad dash Hades made for the Upper World that day. By the time I reached the road to see what caused such a tremendous noise, he was already on the ferry with his chariot and horses, poling his way across. I left the Underworld then to lift the burden of Hera's persecution as much as I could from poor Alkmene and her babe, Herakles. I had not the time to wonder what happened to Hades but was surprised when I returned to the Underworld to find him here."

Hekate handed Persephone a cloth with which to dry Hades. As their eyes met, Persephone asked, "Did he make his way to Olympus? And if he did, why didn't he stay there?"

"Because he was still the ruler of this realm. So long as he's Cerberus's master he can't bear to be out of this land for too long."

Hekate's words slayed a hope Persephone didn't even know she had. "If I'm to be Hades's wife, I must make my residence in this place?"

Hekate gave a single solemn nod.

Persephone closed her eyes for a moment. Then, opening them, she asked, "What was Hades doing when you returned to the Underworld?"

"Seeking out the mysteries of his kingdom by speaking to the Titans in Tartarus and ferreting out the few older Gods like me and his mother who had escaped Zeus's wrath. None knew a great deal about the Underworld, but by putting their bits of information together Hades was able to come to an understanding of his realm. After that, he traveled to the Upper World, sought out the few men and women among the Achaeans who would consent to serve him, instructed them in proper burial rites, and exhorted them to spread the word among mortals so no shade would be abandoned on Styx's banks. Upon his return to the Underworld, Hades judged the souls he'd already brought across the River Styx and sent them to whatever eternity they earned. Those who retained their building skills, he put to work on his palace and the Temple of Judgment. At the time of Aecus's death, Hades placed him on the throne there. After that, Hades's sole occupation was conveying shades across Styx which he did until Charon took up those duties."

Persephone crossed to the other side of the bed, fetched the oil Hekate had conjured, and poured a little into her hands. "Why did Hades not simply use one of the shades to work the ferry?"

"I believe the duty filled his days and made them pass more quickly."

Persephone settled herself next to Hades's head and spread the oil over one of his shoulders. "Why then did Hades make Charon Immortal?"

Hekate dropped down on the bed by Hades's feet. She remained silent for so long Persephone thought the old Goddess had slipped into sleep. "Hekate?"

"Patience." Hekate huddled into her shawl and drew her arms tight around herself as though she felt chilled. "Hades's original intent wasn't for Charon to be the ferryman."

"What purpose was he to serve then?"

"In seeking knowledge of the Underworld, Hades became friends with a river God here by the name of Kokytos. Kokytos had a daughter named Minthe with whom Hades formed an attachment."

Here then was the mystery of the second woman solved. Hades had taken another nymph as a lover. Something must have gone very much awry between them long ago, however, for Hades had said Kokytos ended their friendship and Hades also stated he hadn't been with a woman in many years. A seed of satisfaction sprouted in Persephone's chest. Leuke and Minthe had held his regard for a time, but no other woman could or would ever mean as much to Hades as she.

Persephone shook herself free of her thoughts, concentrating once again on Hekate as the old woman continued speaking. "Minthe was ... discontented with her lot. She hated living in the Underworld and longed to dwell among the Olympians. She believed a connection to Hades would provide her with the status to become part of that elite group. However, Hades was much too scrupulous to leave off his duties to live with her there. She told Hades that if another subdued Cerberus, Hades could make that person caretaker to this realm and Hades would be free rule it from afar. Hades refused to force some hapless mortal to the task and he and Minthe had many bitter arguments about it. When Charon ate the food of the dead, though he was a living being, Hades saw in him a way to free himself from his duties here and make Minthe happy. Hades went immediately to the Upper World to collect Charon and conveyed him to Zeus's palace so Zeus could make Charon Immortal.

"Hades waited in the Underworld while the rite was performed. In that time, he was a different man, smiling, laughing, at ease in a way I'd never seen him. He and Minthe, for the first time, seemed truly content with one another. When Hades left to collect Charon, it was apparent he had already shaken the burden of the Underworld from his shoulders. I watched him go with trepidation for it is seldom so easy to escape one's fate." Hekate put out a hand. "Give me the oil. I need a task while I tell this next."

Persephone passed the vial to Hekate. The old Goddess poured a small amount of oil on the leg farthest from her and began to work it into Hades's skin. "I heard Hades return with Charon and hurried to the palace to wait their arrival. Hades called for Cerberus. Then all was silent for a very long time. So long I thought Charon had failed in his task. Then, I heard a cry of such great joy I thought my heart would break, and I knew the Underworld had gained a new guardian."

"Why then is Charon not warden of this place?" Persephone asked.

"I'm coming to that." When Hekate poured oil onto Hades's other leg, her hand shook so that it spattered onto the bed. "They came to the palace. Hades made me known to Charon and asked me to advise and aid him in his new role. I agreed. Then, though it was getting onto dark, Hades and Minthe boarded Hades's chariot and set out for Olympus. Charon bid me stay at the palace and retired to his bed. I was leery of the new ruler, however. There seemed a darkness about him in spite of the sheen of Immortality that overlayed his skin. It frightened me and I crept off to my cave to sleep instead. During the night I heard Charon calling for Cerberus. I have no way of knowing, but I believe he intended to command the beast's serpents to bite me and put the water of the River Styx in my veins. I kept my peace and kept to my cave, wondering why

Charon wanted me insensible for nine years."

Hekate lowered her head and the light caught the angled bones in the older Goddess's face, leaving her eye sockets and the hollows of her cheeks in pools of blackness. Persephone reclaimed the oil from where Hekate had placed it and began to anoint Hades's chest, keeping her eyes down. Hades's battered body was preferable to Hekate's haunted visage.

Voice shaking, the old woman continued, "The next day, Charon went to the ferry as Hades had instructed. I followed, taking care not to be seen. When he reached Styx, rather than shuttle the shades, Charon merely sat on the bank and watched them. They called out for him to take them across. They begged. They wept. They tore at their hair and skin and flung themselves to the ground, rolling in paroxysms of grief and still he did nothing."

Persephone raised horror filled eyes to Hekate's face, too stunned to speak.

Abandoning her work on Hades's legs, Hekate pulled her shawl more tightly about her. "I couldn't understand it, for the agony the shades feel he felt also, but he seemed to take some sort of malformed satisfaction from their pain and his own. The next day he traveled to the River Lethe where those sentenced to the asphodel meadow partake of its water if they wish. He commanded Cerberus to bring down any who attempted to drink and again he squatted, watching, like some monstrous, misshapen toad, as the shades were brought to the very depths of despair by his denial of their one mercy. And so, it continued. Day after day he caused greater torment and misery to those who already suffered under the burden of so much."

Hekate's entire body trembled. Persephone left off her ministrations to Hades, drew closer to Hekate, and ran a soothing hand up and down her back, as the older woman had done so often for Persephone when they lived together in Henna and Persephone was in need of comfort.

Seeming to take strength from the contact, Hekate calmed enough to go on. "Charon made his way to Tartarus and found there all the blood and pain and anguish he could ever desire to satiate his dark need. I left him then, intending to go to Hades and tell him all that had befallen those whose plight he had worked so hard to lessen, but I found I couldn't leave. My abhorrence of this place had grown so great the lodestone now held power over me. I hid in the palace, shifting from room to room to stay out of Charon's sight, but always breathing in the scent of the misery and pain on which that grotesque being seemed to thrive. Finally, Hermes came, as I knew he would, and I begged him to bear me away to Olympus."

Hekate went silent again and for the first time since she began this tale, Persephone wished the older woman wouldn't continue, but continue she did. "I found Hades there, flowers in his hair, Minthe curled under his arm, Zeus laughing at his side, naiads and dryads at his feet as he told them some story to brighten their eyes. He says he hasn't a way with words, but our Hades is a storyteller is he not?"

Persephone gave a small laugh that ended in something akin to a sob. "He is."

"I truly didn't recognize him for a moment, such a changed man was he. And then when I did, I could hardly bear to go forward with what I knew I must. I parted that divine company and pulled Hades from its midst, pouring my cup of sorrow into his ear even as they still laughed behind us at the jest he'd only just finished."

Hekate leaned forward and buried her face in Persephone's chest for a moment as though the remembrance were more than she could bear. Persephone put her arms around the woman and rested a cheek on top of her head.

After a time, Hekate shook free of Persephone's embrace, straight-ened, and went on with her tale. "He merely nodded when I finished, went to Minthe, and told her they must return to the Underworld. Minthe tried to dissuade him and Zeus joined in. Neither understood when Hades explained why he had to go back . Finally, in anger, Zeus commanded Hades to be gone then and good riddance to him. Hades put out a hand to Minthe. She spurned it, turned her back on him, and walked away. It was apparent her desertion devastated Hades, yet he didn't hesitate even a moment before going to the stables to fetch his horses and chariot. The naiads and dryads and lovely young Gods and Goddesses all called to him to come back. Hades looked neither to the right nor the left and spoke not a word in response to their inducements to rejoin them. They finally fell silent, struck at last by his quietude and his stern countenance. Yet, as we left Olympus's heights, I heard the silence behind us fill with laughter and chatter as quickly and easily as water closing over a thrown stone, Minthe's ringing out loudest of all."

That then was what had gone awry between them. Minthe had desert-ed Hades at a time when her companionship would have meant so much. And perhaps Kokytos blamed Hades, however unfairly, for the loss of his daughter to Olympus's illustrious company. Minthe's desertion had likely cost Hades one of his few friends in this place, just as Persephone's mad dash for the Upper World had deprived him of Lethe. Yet Hades had forgiven Persephone that great wrong. It was astonishing that he had been subjected to so many heartbreaks and still retained such great capacity for love and Persephone's great blessing that she had discovered it.

Hekate continued, "That ride to the Underworld was a long and silent one. We entered from a cave near Eleusis so the shades on Styx's bank wouldn't raise a furor at our coming and warn Charon. Before we crossed the River Lethe, Hades bade me stay with the horses and told me if he was conquered then I was to return his steeds to Helios's care as fast as I could. He didn't want Charon to claim them for his own and misuse them. I don't know what occurred after Hades left me, only that I heard him summoning Cerberus.

Hekate drew in a deep breath and as she sighed it out, some of the tension eased from her body. "Hades returned after what felt like an eon, though he informed me less than half the day had passed. His clothes were torn, and his torso, arms, and face were streaked with blood. He said nothing to me of his struggle, only mounted the chariot and we returned to the palace from which he and Minthe had departed so joyously only a month before. He told me he intended to make Charon the ferryman so he could keep watch over him and make sure he harmed no one with his malformed desires. Then, for the first time, Hades partook of the food of the dead."

Hekate put one hand on Hades's shin and grasped Persephone's hand with the other. "Do you see now, how this land is as much a part of him as his Godhood? If we sever him from his stewardship of it, he's still bound to this realm. He'll likely take on Cerberus again in order to resume ruling it once his strength has returned. And the pain Charon could inflict in the time of Hades's absence would be enormous."

"What can we do then?" Persephone cried. "He can't die, but to condemn him to an eternity of agony would be a worse fate. I must do something, Hekate."

"Yes, my Kore, you must and you're the only one who can." Hekate removed her hand from Hades's shin, used it to enclose Persephone's hand in both of her own. "It breaks my heart to ask this of you for I know now how deeply you feel for him, but there's no other choice. To save him you must leave him."

"I don't understand."

"The shades that congregate on Styx's bank and bleed their agony into Hades are those belonging to the mortals slaughtered by a famine your mother manufactured in the Upper World. She vows she won't cease it until you're returned to her."

Persephone began to shake her head slowly, then faster. "That cannot be."

"I assure you it is."

"Why?" Persephone's voice broke. She snatched her hand from Hekate's, rose from the bed, paced away from it, spun back to face Hekate. "My mother found my company barely tolerable when we lived together in Henna. After I was abducted, she went straightway to Olympus to have her Godhood restored. If she desired me so much, why then didn't she seek me before going there? Why didn't she come here herself to free me rather than sending Orpheus? Rather than sending you? Rather than slaying thousands of mortals to gain my freedom?"

"Your mother wanted to come when we found out this was the place to which you were taken. I feared reprisal from Hades. It was on my counsel she didn't venture here and it was on my counsel that she sent Orpheus as proxy to free you."

Persephone flung out her arms. "And was it on your counsel that she hied to Olympus to gain back her Godhood before doing anything to obtain my freedom?"

"How did you come to believe that?"

"Orpheus told me she performed some peculiar rite on him to make him impervious to the laws of the Underworld. She couldn't have accomplished all that if she were still mortal."

"Indeed, she's a Goddess once again, but it wasn't a boon she sought. She went to Olympus intending only to secure your freedom. She went on her knees before Zeus to beg for your release. He wouldn't grant that request but did restore her Godhood, though she didn't ask that of him."

"She may not have appealed to him for it, but it seems she has no compunction making full use of it now—full and abominable use."

Hekate rose, walked to Persephone, and grasped her upper arms. "She's still your mother, Kore, and worthy of your pity at least. Perhaps, given time, you can forgive her and learn to love her again."

Shaking her head wildly, Persephone pulled free of Hekate's grip. There weren't adequate worse to express the abhorrence and anger that surged through her each time she thought of what her mother had done. Finally, she spat, "She never was and never will be worthy of my love."

"If you speak of the harshness with which she treated you when we lived together in Henna—"

"Of course, I speak of the harshness which with she treated me in those days." Tears welled in Persephone's eyes, and she flung them away with her fingers.

Hekate's lips turned down, indeed her entire face seemed to slump. "Your mother did a great deal wrong then, but not all of it was her fault."

"What do you mean?" Persephone asked, the solemn expression on Hekate's face calming her ire somewhat.

"Come." Hekate returned to her seat on the bed and gestured Persephone to her side.

After a slight hesitation, Persephone perched next to the old Goddess.

Hekate stroked one hand over Persephone's hair. "I loved you from the moment of your birth. So much that I wanted you for my own." She dropped her hand to her lap and looked down at it. "I took steps to turn your mother's heart from you, to make her long instead for all she lost on Olympus. I hoped she would return there and leave you with me to raise. When I realized what I—"

"Why didn't she?" Persephone cried. "Rather than bringing us all to this, why didn't she give me to one who truly loves me?"

"Kore." Hekate once again took Persephone by her upper arms, gently shook her. "Did you not understand what I said to you? It was my doing that your mother was so unkind to you.. She loved you so much, was so tender with you as a babe. It was the actions I encouraged you to that turned her bitter and unkind. I didn't realize what I was doing and when I did, I left in hopes she would draw close to you again, but it was me who turned her heart from you."

Persephone nodded to show she comprehended Hekate's words but said, "Is it so easy then to turn a heart, Hekate? It seems to me to make such a change within another would be a hard thing indeed were the other's heart not ripe for it. My love for Hades came at great cost to both he and I. I don't regret it, but had I not been left so lonely in my existence in the Upper World perhaps Hades would have found me an impossible conquest. No, the fault of what lies between me and my mother is hers alone. She loathed her mortal existence, and I was the thing that chained her to it."

Hekate retained her grip on Persephone, her voice emphatic. "She loves you. You didn't see her in the days after Hades took you. She searched for nine days and nine nights and returned to your hut in Henna half mad and near to death. Had she known at the time that you dwelt in the Underworld she would have allowed herself to perish if only to ensure she could look upon you once more and tell you how deeply she loves you."

"So deeply that my lover lays in agony because of her actions, so deeply that in my name, she caused the deaths of countless hapless, blameless mortals. Am I to rejoice in that?"

"Be easy in your judgment. Or at least try. Demeter lived in darkness a good part of her existence and, though much of it was her own creation, things twist and go awry when forced to grow without light."

Persephone turned her head to look at Hades, taking in the planes of his face, the architecture of his body, the injuries that marred it all. "In his existence Hades has known little of light. Yet he is not twisted, or dark, or bitter, or unkind." She returned her gaze to Hekate. "It's only under his care that I learned I am not clumsy, or foolish, or weak, or unworthy, or any of the things my mother made me believe I was." Persephone paused, her breath hitching in her chest, and turned so her tears fell on Hades. "He calls me his light, and she means to take me away from him. She would douse the world in darkness to have her way."

Persephone put a hand on Hades's chest, wiping her tears from where they caught in the stiff, silky hairs there. "There's no other way to save him?"

"None. If you refuse to go to her, this famine will continue unabated and the shades on Styx's bank will only multiply."

Persephone looked at Hekate. "Hermes purpose here is to bear me to the Upper World?"

"It is."

"Will my mother allow me to return here?"

Hekate gave a slow, sad shake of her head.

Persephone looked back down at Hades. "Will you stay? Explain all to him when he wakes?"

"I will."

Persephone let her gaze travel over Hades once more. It would take but a moment to press her lips to his, press her body to his, to imprint the feel, the taste of him on her flesh one final time, but such a touch might shatter her resolve and she couldn't risk that. Instead, she embraced Hekate and fled the room, calling for Hermes as she went.

31

DEMETER

"Lady, she'll come. Be calm."

Ignoring Iambe, Demeter spun on her heel to walk the short length of her temple to the front doors once again. When she reached them, a sensation, like a fist wrenching at her guts, made her double over and retch. The plant essence heaved. Drawing on her power, Demeter managed to contain it, but only just. Shaking, sweating, one hand pressed to her belly, she straightened and wiped her mouth.

Through the door of her temple came the sound of a man's laugh followed by a woman's voice which, even muffled as it was by the temple walls, sounded angry. Demeter burst through the doors just as Persephone broke free from Hermes's grip.

"I've born your touch for as long as necessary. Leave me be," Persephone cried.

Hermes advanced on her.

Demeter flung out a hand. Lengths of stinging nettles erupted from the ground at Hermes's feet and twined themselves about his body. He fell to the ground, gibbering and writhing as the vines coiled around him, the skin beneath their green tendrils blistering.

"Mother, stop!"

Demeter looked at Persephone in surprise, but closed her hand in a fist. The vines withered and fell away from Hermes.

Fingers scuttling over his blistered face, Hermes got up. "You dare use your power against me? I'm on an errand set by Zeus himself. In that capacity I'm sacrosanct and none may molest me."

Demeter stalked toward him. "I answer no more to Zeus. Be gone, Hermes. Your purpose here is served."

Face contorted with rage, Hermes strode forward. "I have a further charge to fulfill here, Demeter, as you well know. I must collect—"

Demeter flung open her fist. Hermes exploded from the ground in a fury of beating wings and flapping cape and retreated into the blue of Zeus's heaven.

Smiling, Demeter closed her hand and turned to her daughter, finally able to look her fill. Persephone was pale, the flesh around her eyes swollen and red as though she'd been weeping. Most of her hair had straggled out its plait and she was garbed in a faded, too-large tunic with various stains splotching it from neck to hem, a particularly deep pink one at the belt. However, Persephone's disheveled appearance couldn't disguise the gold eddying over her skin. She had claimed her Godbody. Before Demeter stood a Goddess with strength of her own.

Demeter's smile faltered. She steadied it, moved toward Persephone, then raised her arms, and embraced her daughter. Persephone made a small miserable sound and lifted her hands to Demeter's shoulders. Her head tilted down as though she meant to settle it into the curve of Demeter's neck.

Tears started in Demeter's eyes. "Oh, Kore. Oh, my Kore."

Persephone stiffened, paused in her movement, then raised her head and dropped her arms.

Demeter leaned back in order to see her daughter's face. Persephone's eyes were full of pain and an animal wariness.

"What is it, Kore?"

Persephone's mouth worked, but she made no sound.

Demeter reached to smooth back the hair from Persephone's forehead. Persephone jerked away from her touch and pushed back out of Demeter's embrace.

"Kore?"

"Call me by my right name, Mother."

Demeter stiffened, a sharp retort on her lips. She drew breath, forced it down before saying, "I know there was much unkindness in my behavior toward you when we lived in Henna but I wasn't to blame. Unbeknownst to me, Hekate worked to—"

Persephone backed away. "Hekate told me how she tried to turn my love to her instead of you. And she told me more, Mother. She told me how you schemed and machinated and murdered to ensure my return from the Underworld."

Demeter sucked in a breath, nostrils flaring. "Even still she works to make you hate me. Surely you must see that was her intent in telling you of those things."

"On the contrary. She spent much of her time below exhorting me to find some pity, perhaps even love for you in my heart."

"Pity? I have neither need nor desire for your pity. All I wanted was to show you how much I love you. Surely you can't doubt that after all I've done to free you from Hades." Demeter lifted her arms and stepped once more toward Persephone. "Now come, Ko– Persephone, let us cease this bickering and embrace."

Persephone evaded Demeter's hands. "You believe what you've done is proof of your love? All the abominations you engaged in? All the anguish you've caused?"

"Abominations?" Demeter narrowed her eyes. "I did what was necessary to ensure your freedom. Had Hekate not flapped her tongue to Hades, he would never have abducted you. My abominations, as you call them, wouldn't have been required. If you wish to lay blame for this then put it at the door of the one who is truly responsible. It was Hekate who betrayed you, not me. I only ever sought your freedom."

"If that's truly all you desire then you've accomplished it. There's no need any longer for your famine. End it, Mother."

Demeter raised her eyebrows, her anger, so hot a moment before, now chilling into something hard and implacable. "You've learned to command in your time below, but I'm not one of your subjects."

"Are you truly that proud, that you would force me to beg? Very well. If that's what you need then so be it." Persephone extended her arms, palms up and open to the sky, and bent her head to gaze at the ground. "I beg you to lift your curse from Gaia's flesh and allow life to abound there once more. I only hope the prayer of your daughter carries more weight than those of the mortals who are perishing even now at your hand, more weight than the agony of my lover who suffers in that land below."

Demeter lunged forward, struck Persephone's arms down. "Cease that. You won't beg. Not on behalf of mortals and certainly not on behalf of that man—you dare call him your lover—who stole you from me."

"End this thing, Mother."

Demeter looked into Persephone's jewel-bright, stone-hard eyes and said, "All I did, I did for you."

Persephone's mouth spasmed. She swallowed and blinked but no words of reconciliation tumbled from her trembling lips. Instead, she said, "Why then do I feel more in bondage to you now than ever I did to him?"

Demeter closed her eyes for a moment, then, opening them, turned from Persephone and walked toward her temple.

"Mother."

Persephone's footsteps told Demeter her daughter followed. Demeter didn't turn. Hands closed on Demeter's shoulders and spun her around.

Her grip almost bruising in its force, Persephone said, "You will hear me. You will know the fullness of what you've done. I have strength to match your own now and I will employ it."

Demeter arched an eyebrow. "The strength perhaps, but have you the power?"

Persephone stepped back, lowering her arms. "Strike me as you did Hermes then. For it's the only way you'll silence me."

Demeter's hand twitched. She clamped it back to her side and turned away from Persephone's accusing eyes.

"Have you been to the fields outside the walls of this city, Mother? I have. It was my welcome to Eleusis as Hermes and I overflew it. Bodies are stacked there like cordwood, both human and animal. Carrion birds caw and call and hop about gorging themselves on tongues and eyes and guts. The stench of putrefaction hangs over it in an almost visible pall. The very air shimmers with decay."

Demeter turned, began once more to move toward her temple. "What do I care for this?"

"If you want me to remain here with you, you'll listen."

Demeter stopped but didn't turn back.

"Those that suffer above the ignominy of providing sustenance to the crows and buzzards and insects are tormented worse in that land below. They wait on the banks of Styx, sorrowing eternally for their lost lives, unable to cross for their bodies haven't undergone the necessary rituals of burial and they haven't the proper fare to pay Charon his due. Even had they, what awaits them on the other side of the Styx is no kind eternity, but a wiping of all their memories, an existence in the asphodel meadow, their hands working at meaningless tasks, their minds and eyes vacant, until they fade into nothingness. That's the existence to which you sent them."

Demeter clenched her fists and ground out, "All that is nothing to me. They're mortals."

"As you once were," Persephone nearly shouted, then added more quietly, "As I believed I was."

"We were never as they!" Demeter shrieked, rounding on Persephone. Her daughter didn't flinch, didn't retreat. This lack of reaction to her ire struck Demeter like a blow. She stiffened, stilled.

"You were," Persephone said. "And had you not regained your God-hood, you would have woken from your death to find yourself on the banks of the Styx, but in better care than those mortals who have entrusted themselves to you here. You have none of the conscientiousness that dictates Hades's actions nor any of his compassion. For all else, Mother, I might have, in time, forgiven you, but for the torment you inflict on him even now I can't reconcile myself to you. I ask, once more, cease this famine to ease his pain and mine."

Demeter's mouth worked. She cleared her throat, began to speak, but couldn't force the words past the constriction of her throat. She swallowed, tried again. "If I do, you'll return to him."

Persephone looked down. She drew in breath, once, twice, then raised her eyes once more. "I won't. If you allow Gaia to give her bounty to these mortals so that no more perish, I'll spend my Immortality at your side."

Still, Demeter hesitated. Zeus and Hera's image appeared in her mind as she last saw them, heads bent, cooing over the swaddled bundle in Hera's arms.

"What more do you want, Mother?"

"Come inside, Kore. I must think on this." Demeter turned to her temple.

"There's no more to think on," Persephone called after Demeter, and yet Persephone's feet slapped against the dirt of the temple forecourt as she followed, giving the lie to her words. She would continue this negotiation.

As Demeter approached, Iambe came around the corner of the temple and disappeared inside. Demeter pursed her lips. Had the woman heard all that passed between her and Persephone? Well, if she had, it made no matter. Iambe, unlike Persephone, accepted Demeter just as she was and didn't require bartering or coercion to stay at Demeter's side.

Demeter reached the temple door, pushed it open, and entered. She looked about for Iambe, but there was no sign of the woman. Doubtless, she hid herself in the antechamber.

A gasp came from behind Demeter. She turned. Persephone stood in the open door, her gaze moving over the piles of foodstuffs in their various containers lining the walls, taking in the baskets which held precious stones and items made of gold, silver, electrum and iron; prized things that lost all value when the folk of Eleusis realized metal, no matter how precious, couldn't fill their bellies.

Persephone's green eyes fastened on Demeter's face. They blazed as though Zeus's lightning flickered in their depths. Demeter's stomach contracted into a small, hard knot. Only with great effort of will did she keep herself from shuffling over and spreading her skirts to hide the caches of grain which spilled from the tall jars at her side.

Persephone whirled away from the door and called out. Demeter couldn't think who her daughter was summoning. In a moment, however, the question was answered as a crowd of dust-covered, leather-skinned workmen shuffled up to the temple, eyes cast down to shield their gaze from the blaze of Persephone and Demeter's twin Godlights.

"Who leads you?" Persephone asked.

After a moment of shifting and muttering one man pushed to the front. "I, Lady."

"What's your name?"

"Gorka."

"And who among your men can you most trust to do as he is charged?"

The man pointed to one in the middle of the group. "Alastrom, there."

"Come forward, Alastrom," Persephone beckoned. The men parted to allow him through. When he reached her, Persephone said, "I want both of you to select a ...." She paused, surveyed the men once more, "Score of men each. Alastrom, I desire you and your men to take the food from this temple and distribute it among those in the city who are yet alive."

The man straightened. "I will do so and with thanks, Lady."

Persephone turned to the other man. "Gorka, to you I give a weightier task. Take your men to the fields outside the walls of this city. I charge you, as best you can, to perform funerary rites on the dead that wait there. Take those baskets of precious things." She gestured. "And be sure each body is buried with some small token from them. Can I trust you to do this?"

Tears streaking his cheeks, he said, "I'll go to it with a will, Lady. Though my family have been spared, many of my friends rot in the Rarian Fields." He sniffed, scrubbed at his face. "May I have your name so we may tell all to whom they should offer their gratitude for these mercies?"

"My name?" A sour smile twisted Persephone's lips. "Kore or Persephone. I answer to either."

The men murmured praises and thanks as they moved into Demeter's temple and toward those items needed to accomplish their tasks.

Demeter rushed forward as the first man laid his dirty hands on a basket overflowing with fruit. "Stop. How dare you? My food kept you alive during the famine. Is this insolence my recompense for that generosity?"

"Nay, Lady," a man hefting one of the baskets of precious things replied. "It was our food that kept *you* alive during the famine."

Demeter gave an incoherent cry of rage and surged toward him.

The man stumbled back, the basket tumbling from his hands, as he flung them up to his eyes to protect his sight from Demeter's flaring Godlight.

Persephone stepped in front of him. "Leave him be. He's merely doing as I instructed."

"As *you* instructed. These things aren't yours to dispense. They're mine, and you didn't ask my leave."

"I'm done with asking anything of you, Mother. It's apparent my pleas fall on deaf ears. You don't intend to end the famine so I must do what I can to mitigate its effects." Persephone turned, gestured the cowering man onward. "Go to."

Men closer to the door of the temple were already departing, their hands full of foodstuffs. A tremor rippled through Demeter's Immortal essence. This shouldn't be happening, couldn't be happening, for mortals could cease their worship but couldn't take back what they'd already given. No matter its cause, however, the disturbance in her power wasn't to be borne. She strode forward, exhorting the men to stop.

They ignored her commands and exited the temple. She burst through the doors after them and into the temple forecourt. "No. Bring that back.

Bring it back. I command you!"

Demeter's Godvoice reverberated in the still day. As one, the men halted, turned on their heels, and began to tramp back to the temple.

"No. No." Brushing past Demeter, Persephone hurried forward. "You must do the tasks I charged you with. Go. Go on." She shooed at the men as a farmer's wife at heedless chickens. The men marched toward the temple, oblivious.

"Gorka." Persephone stepped to the man's side, touched his shoulder. The man blinked up at Persephone, then down from her Godlight, nearly dropping the basket he held. He grasped it tighter, gave his head a shake and turned once more toward Eleusis.

Demeter's ire grew as Persephone darted through the group of men, touching them, encouraging them to return to the duties she gave. One by one, the men responded to her. Behind Demeter, more men streamed from the temple burdened with baskets and jars and sacks overflowing with offerings.

As the troop of mortals, her daughter moving with them, neared the edge of the rise and the road that would lead them into Eleusis, Demeter felt a great shift in her power, not unlike one of Poseidon's ground shakings.

Lips peeling back from her teeth in a snarl, Demeter lifted her hands and a bush sprang from the earth. Demeter snapped off a branch as thick as her forearm. Wicked thorns studded its length. She honed the tip to a point with one sweep of her fingers and hurled it at Persephone. A terrible wrenching tore at Demeter's belly. She cried out and snatched at the air to call back the spear, but it was too late.

Persephone turned at Demeter's cry. She brought her arms up, shielding her face, but the branch of thorns passed under them, hitting her chest instead. Persephone's skin bubbled and blistered, but no cries of pain broke from her lips. Instead, the spear sunk into her flesh, fully consumed. Her skin rippled once over the entirety of her body.

Persephone lowered her arms, passed shaking hands down the length of her torso. Then, she looked up at Demeter, her fingers skimming the impacted spot on her chest. "You meant to punish me? As you did Hermes?"

Hands clamped over her mouth, tears welling in her eyes, Demeter shook her head.

Persephone took a step toward Demeter, then gave a murmured exclamation and looked down. Demeter followed the direction of her daughter's gaze. Pale green shoots of grass emerged from the mud with each step Persephone took.

Brows furrowed, lips pursed, Persephone dropped to a crouch and passed a hand over the clump of grass. The blades stretched upward as though desperate for the brush of her fingers.

The same sensation of a fist twisting in her guts came again and Demeter's stomach bulged. Green and gold wisps filtered between the lacings of her bodice. Demeter put a hand over them to prevent their escape, but they flew to Persephone, twined about her fingers, then sunk into the back of her hand. Persephone looked up, scanned Demeter, paused, then touched the barren ground at the side of the grass. As tender shoots erupted from the soil beneath Persephone's hand, Demeter retched.

Thinking back to the golden glow that had suffused her pregnant belly on that long ago day when Hera had taken her Immortality, Demeter said. "Still Hera exacts the price of my treachery. Because she ceded you my power. I can't use it in my defense. Not against you."

Persephone stood, one hand rubbing again at her breastbone. "You did mean, then, to strike me down?"

Tears slid down Demeter's cheeks. She hurried forward, gathered her daughter's stiff, unwieldy body to her. "Oh Kore, forgive me as I forgive you for your theft of my offerings."

Persephone's hands settled on Demeter's shoulders. Though Demeter struggled, Persephone, with gentle, but firm pressure still managed to push Demeter back. "The time for reconciliation is over, Mother. I no longer need you to end the famine. That, it seems, is within my ability."

Persephone moved away. Demeter grasped one of her daughter's hands to stop her. "It is. It is, Kore. But think before you squander it. If we combined our efforts, we could overthrow Zeus, overthrow Hera, have our recompense for those years spent in exile among the Sicani, for your abduction, for my pain at ... at your loss."

Shaking her head, Persephone said, "Nay, Mother. I've no wish for recompense. Despite their loathing of me, I never despised the Sicani. Indeed, I have some treasured memories from the time I thought I was nothing more and nothing less than a mortal maid, and my abduction led me to the greatest joy I've ever known. For your pain, I'm sorry, but it's not mine to avenge. When I've made certain Gaia is bounteous once more, I intend to return to Hades."

Speaking through clenched teeth, Demeter said, "If you do, I'll force your return by the same method."

Persephone tried to extract her hand from Demeter's grasp. "Why? I take no joy in your company. You took but little in mine when we were together in Henna. Let me go."

Demeter reached forward, grasped Persephone's other hand and clutched at both. "I refuse to return to Henna. I can't go back to Olympus. You're all I have now, Kore. You must stay with me."

Persephone tried to pull away, but each time she got one hand free, Demeter grappled on to the other. This continued, until, fingers slick with sweat, Demeter could no longer retain her grip. Panting, face wet with tears or perspiration, Demeter wasn't sure, Persephone broke away and fled, vegetation springing from the earth with her every step.

"You will return to me!" Demeter shrieked after her. "As many famines as I must, as many deaths as I must, more agony than your husband can bear. I will make you return to me." But the green-gold light trailing after Persephone gave the lie to Demeter's words. It might not be possible for her to retain the power necessary to make good her vow.

32

PERSEPHONE

Persephone clamped her hands over her ears to block out Demeter's shrieks and ran, heedless of direction; leaving her mother behind was the only thing that mattered. It wasn't until the echoes of Demeter's screams faded to nothingness that Persephone stopped, slumped against a withered tree, and put her head in her hands.

She'd successfully opposed her mother. Yet, there was no triumph in the victory as there had been the first time Persephone rode Lethe on her own or hit an asphodel with an arrow or discovered the seeds sprouting in the folly. Though certainly not the fool she once believed herself to be, Persephone had still, upon her arrival at Demeter's temple, harbored a fool's hope that somehow, some way, she and her mother could work through the tangled knot of their past, tease out the old pain, make amends and make something new, something better of their relationship. Instead, in attempting to harm Persephone, Demeter revealed the true reason she'd so cruelly driven Persephone from the fields during her childhood. Far from being concerned Persephone would be unable to master the art of cultivating plants, Demeter was instead afraid Persephone would discover the only thing for which she had a true affinity. Persephone had come to see herself as clumsy, insufficiently skilled, and worthless because her mother couldn't bear to share the smallest scrap of her power or even her knowledge of Persephone's heritage. Now that Persephone knew the truth of who she was and of what she was capable, there could be no rest, no reconciliation. This war with Demeter would last for eternity, each forever battling for ascendancy to keep the other from their aims.

Persephone slid down the trunk of the tree, drew her legs up and pressed her forehead to her knees. She waited for tears to come, but, evidently, she had no more to shed over the loss of her relationship with her mother; perhaps because she'd already been grieving it for so many years.

She lifted her head and glanced about. Buildings of some sort were in front and to both sides of her. Her flight must have taken her into the streets of Eleusis.

Persephone stood, straightened her tunic, and looked at the sky. Helios's position would tell her what direction she must go to reach the Rarian fields. Hopefully, she would find Gorka and his men there, laboring at the tasks she set them. As she turned to set out, her gaze snagged on the tree she had leaned against.

Red-brown buds sprouted from its branches. She reached forward, plucked one off, and examined it. Its covering burst open to reveal the pale green of an infant leaf. Persephone looked down. The ground where she had crouched was now furred with shoots of grass. The path she had taken from her mother's temple to the tree also boasted its own covering of green.

It was a tiny rivulet of life in the vast area of blasted earth she had seen when she and Hermes flew over Eleusis on their way to her mother's temple. Her feet would have to tread all of it, her hands touch every tree, every bush, every stalk of maize to undo all the death her mother had delt out. No one could assist her in it. While restoring life to the land, she also had to ensure the mortals do all they could to properly prepare and bury their dead. She passed a hand over her eyes. It was too much for her alone to accomplish, and yet, there was no one else.

Turning down the street most likely to lead her to the fields, Persephone set out. She hadn't gone far when she came upon a group of mortals clustered around one of the men from her mother's temple. He stood on something that allowed him to see and be seen above the heads of the crowd and passed food into their reaching hands as quickly as he could. Persephone drew closer, taking in the enfeebled state of the mortals who surrounded the man. She put a hand to her mouth, tears pooling in her eyes.

The man caught sight of her and quickly shielded himself from her Godlight. He murmured something to those closest to him. The whisper spread through the crowd until it sounded like the low rumble of Hades's horses at a full gallop. In clusters of two or three, the mortals turned, most of them pointing out the greenery abounding at her feet to their companions. One by one, they raised their arms, her name tumbling from their lips as they voiced their gratitude. In but moments, the whole group made obeisance to her, their cries of praise and thanks almost deafening.

A strange sensation passed through Persephone, making her legs quiver and her insides turn molten and malleable, as though they were constructed of melting wax. Persephone clutched at her abdomen. Despite the way she felt internally, her skin was still reassuringly solid. She turned and set off in another direction as quickly as her trembling legs could carry her, escaping the crowd but not the unsettling pliability at her core.

As Persephone traversed the streets, she passed more groups of mortals partaking of the food from her mother's temple. Her Godlight made inconspicuousness impossible and each time she encountered these gatherings the people fell to praising and thanking her, which only magnified the strangeness that coursed through her.

The disturbing feelings soon became a secondary concern, however. They were crowded out by her concern over the number of doors that remained closed despite the furor in the streets. No doubt behind a portion of them languished some of the city's dead, those who had not yet been removed to the Rarian fields. Persephone would have to charge some of the men from the temple with the task of seeking out these concealed corpses.

When the sound of praises from the most recent host of mortals she encountered faded, Persephone slowed, stepped to one of the doors, and called out. When no one answered her inquiry, she pushed against the wood and it swung inward.

Her gaze swept the interior and settled on a low bed near the far wall. A woman lay there, vacant eyes staring into nothingness, her twig bundle arms clasping the tiny body of her babe to her breast. A man slumped on the floor beside the bed, one hand still resting on his wife's hair. Persephone moved to the corpses and knelt near them. She had no desire to break the tenuous hold they kept on each other even in death, but she had to so they could receive the necessary burial rites in order for their shades to cross Styx.

After a moment's consideration, Persephone reached for the babe first, disentangling the folds of its blanket from its mother's hands.

Persephone laid the tiny body on the ground then looked around. A jug of water and small basin sat on the table. She rose, collected the items, and went to her knees once more at the babe's side. A small basket of cloths lay on the floor at the foot of the bed. Persephone pulled one from the top of the pile, immersed it in water, and washed the tiny body.

Using a second cloth, Persephone dried the infant then wiped the wetness from her own cheeks. She looked up from the small corpse and scanned the room once more, but didn't find what she sought. She rose and, with quick movements and an apologetic glance at the deceased, poked through baskets and jars and chests until finally she found a small container of scented oil. After rubbing some onto her hands, she knelt and smoothed it over the small expanse of cold flesh.

When that task was complete, Persephone lifted the blanket which she had laid on the floor next to the infant's body and wrapped the babe. Then she pressed a kiss to his forehead and placed him in a basket.

Her previous search of the house's contents revealed there was nothing of value to be found here, so she closed her eyes, thought of the basket of clinking, glittering things Gorka removed from her mother's temple and tried to summon one as Hekate had summoned basin and ewer in Hades's palace. Persephone opened her eyes, looked at the ground around her, and blew a short, audible puff of air through her nose. She tried the process again and once more was disappointed.

Though there was none to observe her failure, Persephone's belly began its familiar furor and her hands set to trembling. If Hades were here, he would soothe her, perhaps even instruct her, in his patient, kind way, of this trick of the Gods. He would tell her, as he had when she missed her shot, that she was holding too tightly and needed to ease her grip.

Persephone closed her eyes again, but this time instead of concentrating so fiercely on Gorka's basket, she allowed her need to permeate her from the bottom up, like a goblet being filled with wine. She drew deeper into the darkness of her mind. Pale green and gold sparks exploded at the edges of her vision. Something fell through the void. She didn't see it, only sensed its passing.

Persephone's eyes flew open at a sound that could only be the chink of metal hitting metal. She looked down and at her feet lay three small rectangles of bronze. Too stunned by her success to feel anything except a vague disbelief, she reached down, plucked one up, and slipped it between the babe's lips, resting it on his tongue.

Taking up her cloth again, Persephone next turned to the man. Preparing his body was so much like the ablutions she'd performed on Hades before leaving the Underworld that she hurried through it, hands shaking, tears splashing down to mingle with the wash water and oil on his flesh. After she placed the bronze piece in his mouth, she had to take some time to collect herself before moving on to his wife.

As Persephone moved the cloth over the woman, she noted the flaccid skin of the abdomen, the purple weals on her stomach, hips, and thighs, the bloody cloths between the woman's legs. Only days ago, this woman had birthed her child, but her breasts were empty of milk that should have nourished the boy for she had not enough flesh on her bones to sustain even herself.

Placing her fingers on the woman's lids and drawing them down, Persephone hoped the new mother had passed first, that those sightless orbs hadn't been witness to the babe's short and tortuous life.

After slipping the final piece of bronze between the woman's lips and placing the infant back in the woman's arms, Persephone rose and left the house. A tumult of voices reached her as she stepped onto the road. She couldn't bear another phalanx of grateful mortals, not now.

Persephone closed her eyes, retreating once more to that green glowing cavern within herself and called forth her mortal form. A small cry of dismay escaped her as the pained weightiness of her mortal flesh enclosed her Godbody. The dragging fatigue made Persephone long to retreat within the house, curl herself with the corpses, and sleep. Only her knowledge of what they still suffered on Styx's bank turned her feet instead to the small plot of land at the side of the building.

There Persephone found, as she hoped, digging implements. She also found the beginnings of a grave. Taking up the shovel and pick that lay at its side, she slipped into the shallow indentation and set about widening and deepening it. When it was finished to her satisfaction, she hoisted herself out and returned to the house. It took much doing but finally the family rested in the grave all together.

As Persephone heaped dirt back into the hole, she pictured them pushing their way through the throng on Styx's bank, handing their bronze pieces to Charon and riding with him across those dark waters. Perhaps Hades felt some slight ease at their passage. The thought lightened, somewhat, the burden of her fatigue, but it was a short respite.

She looked down on the young family curled together in the bottom of the hole. Once they partook of the River Lethe, they would know each other no longer, not even mother and child, their short time together at an eternal end.

Persephone's shoulders slumped once more with exhaustion. All those slaughtered by her mother's famine would share the same fate and Persephone could do nothing to allay or alter it.

When the grave was filled, though she was weary with an enervation that went beyond the merely physical, Persephone returned to the road. There were too many in Eleusis for her to perform the same services she had for these folk, but she could tap on every door she came to before reaching the Rarian fields. If the occupants were deceased, she would mark the house so Gorka and his men would know there were those within who needed burial rites.

The enormity of the task before her once again overwhelmed Persephone. She turned and looked at the carpet of green stretching out behind her. Almost, it seemed, to beckon her, coaxing her to follow it back through the streets of Eleusis, back to her mother. Demeter would agree with Persephone's estimation that the undertaking was beyond her abilities, beyond her strength, that it was foolish of Persephone to pursue such a course of action. The burden would be removed from Persephone, not, however, to be taken up by another but to be cast aside as tiresome and unnecessary.

Persephone turned to the dusty street before her, passed a hand over her eyes, then trudged forward, her weary step leaving life and growth in its wake.

33

DEMETER

A strange sort of stillness surrounded Demeter as she returned to her temple. If she placed her foot down too hard or turned her head too quickly, it would shatter and she would become once again that shrieking maddened thing that caused Persephone to flee.

Arms crossed over the ceaseless tug in her belly, elbows cupped in hands, she walked through the temple door. Still trying to preserve her brittle shell of calm, she lowered herself into a chair. After she sat, she looked from empty wall to empty floor to empty altar.

A scuffing sound drew Demeter's attention to the antechamber. Iambe limped through the doorway. She stopped when she saw Demeter but said nothing, only blinked her wide brown eyes.

Demeter met the woman's gaze for a moment then said, "She's lost to me, Iambe."

Face twisting in sympathy, Iambe said, "Oh, Lady."

Demeter whimpered and hunched over, hands lifting to cover her face. Sobs welled up and burst from her mouth like blood pouring from a new wound.

A moment later, the warmth and weight of Iambe's hand settled on Demeter's back between her shoulder blades. Still sobbing, Demeter leaned to the side until her head was pillowed on the little woman's breast.

"Hush, Lady, hush," Iambe said, soothing her hand over Demeter's hair.

Nearly choking on tears, mucus, and saliva, Demeter could do nothing but let sorrow have its way with her.

Iambe continued her ministrations until Demeter's tears ebbed. Then, crouching a bit, peering into Demeter's face, Iambe said, "How is she lost to you, Lady? Did her husband reclaim her?"

Demeter swiped a hand over her upper lip then shook her head. "It was as Hekate said. It was all as Hekate said. Persephone saw what I did to free her as an ... an abomination. She loathes me."

"Is there no hope of securing her affections again?"

"If there is, I can't see a way to it. I fear I've severed the last tie of her love because I ... I ...." Demeter couldn't tell Iambe her last unspeakable sin, that she used her power with the intent to strike her daughter down.

"What, Lady? What did you do?"

Demeter straightened, wiped her face again. "It matters not. She's lost to me, Iambe."

Iambe took Demeter's hand. "I heard what your daughter said in the temple forecourt about the suffering of those slain by this famine."

"Do not speak to me—"

"Hold, Lady. Please let me say my piece."

Though she narrowed her lips and raised an eyebrow, Demeter kept silent.

"What if we were to make recompense? Perhaps that would soften your daughter's heart toward you."

"What recompense can be made to the dead? They're beyond anyone's power save Hades's."

"That's true, but what of those left? Surely, we can make some amends to them."

Demeter pulled her hand from Iambe's. "I've given them food from my temple. My daughter is with them even now in their distress. What more can I give?"

"Favor all those who suffered in the famine with the rite you worked on Orpheus. In that way, you may spare them the suffering their loved ones know in the Underworld. Its laws won't rule them. They need have no fear of death or what awaits them in Hades's realm. Surely this is the greatest boon of any you could give. I believe your daughter would see some merit in that and would be inclined to think kindlier of you."

Demeter shook her head. "None would brave the fire. Orpheus was the fourth mortal man on whom I worked the rite. He was the only one with courage enough to bathe in the flame willingly."

"Orpheus wished to be reunited with his loved one who had died. That's why he succeeded. Surely there are more among the Eleusinians who would take on that portion of your rite for the same purpose."

Demeter considered Iambe's words for a time. There was truth in them. There would be many desperate for such a reunion given all those killed by her famine. "Yes, Iambe. Yes. Go into the city. Now. Tell the Eleusinians of my rite. Bid them come to me if they wish to be spared the horrors of the Underworld. Carry the same message to all the cities roundabout just as you did the command to worship me."

Tears dampening her eyes, Iambe took Demeter's hands, and pressed a kiss to the back of both of them. "I knew you too would wish to make recompense for the great wrong we perpetrated. Your daughter will surely see how merciful, how kind you are and love you for it as I do. Thank you, Lady."

Iambe released Demeter and took her leave. Demeter looked once more about her plundered temple and put a hand to her belly, now cavernous. A smile curving her lips, she looked toward the door. Soon enough, droves of mortals would resume their worship and her reservoir of power would once again overflow.

34

PERSEPHONE

Persephone paused in her digging, dragged a forearm across her brow, then gripped the shovel handle again. She winced as some of the blisters on her hand burst. Similar wounds formed over the last four days of almost ceaseless labor had turned her palms and fingers into a mass of oozing, bloody flesh.

Gritting her teeth against the pain and ignoring the protest of her aching back, Persephone bent to her work. From all around her came the *shush* of other digging implements sinking into the dirt, the muffled thump of bodies being laid in the ground, and the thud of earth tossed on top of the corpses. Gorka and his men had followed her orders with a will, excavating these large pits in which the bodies were being interred.

Soon enough, the shades of these newly buried dead would board Charon's ferry, their conveyance to the opposite bank of Styx restoring the balance in the Underworld, restoring the balance in its ruler. Perhaps even now he woke, found his voice, found his strength, found her gone.

Persephone passed the back of her hand across her eyes and blinked several times before her vision cleared enough to allow her to return to her task. She thrust the shovel down into the pile of displaced dirt, meaning to scoop up some to toss into the pit. A hand closed about the handle above hers, arresting her movement.

From behind her came a snort and an impatient stamp of a hoof. Persephone relinquished her grip on the tool and spun. Hades stood there, pale, worn, but undeniably returned to himself. Persephone hurled herself at him.

His arms came around her, but with a careful rigidity and after only a moment he gently pushed her away from him.

"Hades—"

He gestured to the pit behind Persephone. "I came, Lady, to thank you for the great service you do me and my subjects." He drew in a deep breath. "And also, to bid you farewell."

"No!" Persephone reached for him.

Without meeting her eyes, Hades stepped back, evading her and widening the distance between them.

She followed, hands still outstretched. "Don't go. Please. Listen to me. This needn't be farewell." She grabbed his wrists, gripped them tightly, halting his retreat. "I've thought long over the past days and I believe I've found a way we can be together. At least for a time out of each year."

Jaw clenching and unclenching, Hades kept his eyes forward, gazing at some point over her head.

"Hades. Listen to me."

Slowly, almost as if the small movement pained him, Hades bent his neck to look into her face.

Persephone slid her hands down until she clasped his. "I possess the same power my mother does. Despite her hold on it, I brought life to this land and am managing to keep her blight at bay. If I go with you now to the Underworld, she'll destroy all I worked to accomplish here." She reached up to touch Hades's cheek. "And all I worked to accomplish within you as well. I must stay, at least until after the harvest so mortals may gather enough sustenance to carry they and their beasts through a season of want. Once that's accomplished, I can join you below for a time before I must return and restore Gaia's flesh once more."

Hades pulled his hands out of her grasp. "It can't be, Persephone. Zeus himself commanded you to remain in the Upper World. What he decrees both you and I must obey."

"My mother bucks his power. Why must we heed him?"

"Demeter will pay for her insolence. Zeus may seem foolish, desirous only of pleasure, but the true fools are those who underestimate and defy him."

Persephone clutched great handfuls of Hades's tunic, and shook him. "Then be a fool. Don't close yourself off from hope, from me. There must be a way. Please, Hades. All your life you've bowed to Fate's decree, to Zeus's power. Will you let others dictate your actions in this also? Will you let me be lost to you so easily?"

He reached up. Persephone tightened her hold, but he didn't try to disentangle himself, only covered her hands with his, his eyes suddenly alight in a face that reflected her own apprehension and frustration and also a dawning hope.

"The food!" He exclaimed, releasing her to pat at his tunic as though he thought to discover some wayward remnant of bread hidden in its folds. "If you partake of the food Zeus can't force you to remain aboveground, for that's a law both more ancient and powerful than he. He would have to concede your absence from the Upper World at least for a time each year."

Persephone put a hand to her belt and stuck her fingers between the band of cloth and her tunic. She lifted the dark, shriveled things she found there and waved them at Hades. "Here. I still have them. The seeds."

Hades peered at her hand. "Seeds? What seeds?"

"The day Orpheus came to us below, you gave me a pomegranate from the Underworld, do you recall?"

Hades's brows drew down. After a moment, he nodded.

"I tucked these in the belt of my—your—this tunic after we departed my megaron to answer Orpheus's summons. During your malady I took no time to bathe or change for I was afraid to leave your side even for a moment. When I left the Underworld, I brought them with me. But for your words I wouldn't have recalled them."

She put her hand to her mouth but hesitated as her stomach convulsed and her throat closed.

Hades's gripped her wrist. "Hold, Persephone. You must know what you do in eating those."

"I know what I do. I bind myself to you."

"No, not to me, to my realm. You become a creature of the Underworld. Just as the food from the Upper World thrives not in the Under your time here above ground will be a burden to you, Helios's light too bright, the air too close, too hot, the noise and bustle an agony to your ears. Your only relief will be the portion of time you spend below with me."

Forcing a smile through the dismay she felt, she said,. "For my relief, I would spend all if I could below with you."

Hades brushed the hair back from her face. "No falsehoods between us. I know why those seeds found their way not into your mouth but into your belt that day. You couldn't bring yourself to utterly forsake the Upper World."

Persephone scanned the vibrant green of the fields around her, inhaled the scent of rich dark earth and the sharp tang of sap flowing into the trees, the smell of her own skin baked by Helios's warmth. She moved her toes, burrowing them into the dirt. Tears filmed her eyes as she looked at the seeds in her hand. "If I partake of these, I sacrifice my place in the Upper World. And my mother denies me a lasting home in your realm." She paused. "I shall never truly belong anywhere."

She raised her eyes to Hades's. He brushed the tears from her cheeks, but she saw in his face that he had no solution for her and only himself to offer as recompense for her loss.

Keeping her eyes locked on his, she lifted the seeds to her lips. In defiance of the heaving in her belly, she placed them on her tongue, chewed the desiccated things, and swallowed.

With a whoop, Hades put his arms around her waist, lifted her, and spun so Persephone's feet flew out behind her. Arms going tight around his neck, she shrieked in surprise. Then they both began laughing. After another few revolutions, he placed Persephone on her feet. He pressed his lips to hers and she clung to him as though she meant to meld her flesh to his. When he drew away, their mingled tears sparkled on his lips.

He looked beyond her, then back at her face. "I would help complete this labor you've begun."

"Can you stay so long?"

"Hekate is below watching after the welfare of our realm." He glanced up at Helios and then away, his eyes watering. Persephone also looked up. How long before she too shrank and winced at that glorious glow? Would she be able even to bear spending time in the folly growing her little garden when she was in the Underworld? Or would that small comfort be taken from her too? Her decision to eat the seeds had cost her greatly and yet, she had surely gained as much as she'd given up.

Hades stooped to collect her dropped shovel. "I can stay a little time more."

Persephone worked at his side until all that could be seen of the pit was a long rectangle of raised dirt. Persephone bent and put a hand to the mound. In moments, it flushed a pale green. The mortals who hadn't yet seen her do this cried out in wonder and surprise but Persephone scarcely noticed. All her attention was on the dirt-streaked, sweat-damp face of her husband.

His eyes were dark, his mouth grim as his gaze moved over her. "I must go."

Persephone nodded. "I would go with you now if I could."

Hades smoothed his fingers over her brow, trailed them down her cheek. "I'll have what I can of you and be grateful for the gift."

He kissed her once more, holding her so tightly her bones creaked. Then he abruptly released her, strode to his chariot, and climbed in the basket. He clucked and shook the reins. Snorting and tossing their heads, Akheron, Phlegethon, and Styx circled until they faced the road.

Crying out for Hades to wait, Persephone dropped to a crouch and picked a handful of tender green shoots from the ground. Next, she went to a stand of willows and worked to free several of the branches, fresh and limber with sap, from the tree. With a slight caress, she coaxed a budding narcissus to reveal its white petals and plucked one from among its sisters.

She hurried to Hades's side, asked for the knife from his belt, and cut a bit of her hair. She wrapped the strands around grass, branches, and bloom, infused the bundle with a bit of her power, enough, she hoped, to keep it all alive and vibrant until she could join Hades again, and pressed it into his hand. "To keep you until next we meet."

He brought it to his lips. "I thank you, Lady."

He tucked the bundle into the breast of his tunic, surveyed her for a long moment, as though to memorize her down to the last glimmer of gold in her hair, then lifted his whip and cracked it over his steeds' heads. They plunged down the road at a gallop. Persephone watched them go.

She wouldn't let herself weep. There was no reason to mourn. She'd see him again as soon as her work in the Upper World was complete.

35

DEMETER

As Demeter walked through the field, the shorn stalks pricked at her sandaled feet. The mortals, at her instruction, had harvested the grain some months ago and would soon set about gathering the grapes and figs. This lull, while the ground lay fallow and undisturbed was the best time to assess its health. Demeter squatted, picked up a handful of soil, hefted it, then dropped it back to the ground.

"I thought to find you in your temple, Sister, not scrabbling in the dirt like a common laborer."

Still in a squat, Demeter whirled, lost her balance, and fell on her buttocks, landing with a grunt. Heart thudding loudly, she looked up. Hekate stood over her.

Chuckling, the older Goddess extended a hand.

Demeter struck it away and, scowling, got to her feet. "I thought myself rid of you."

"I'm not so easily escaped."

"And yet you are skilled in helping others escape. I heard tell it was you who sent Orpheus off on the Argo and beyond the reach of my retribution."

Hekate said nothing, but her smile broadened and that was answer enough.

Demeter folded her arms. "Have you some further mischief to work, Hekate? If so, you may take yourself off and wreak your havoc on someone else."

Hekate's smile disappeared into the weighty creases of her face. "I only came to tell you our *kore* is gone below."

Demeter's hand dropped to her navel. The insistent tug she felt there during the last few months had been absent when Demeter rose from her bed that morning. Her power now coalesced heavy in her belly and remained there. "I know."

"How do you fare?"

Demeter turned, let her eyes take in the expanse of harvested grain and didn't reply.

Shifting closer to Demeter, Hekate said, "I've heard rumors of—what have the mortals named it—the Eleusinian Mysteries? That rite you created to allow Orpheus to travel through the Underworld ungoverned by its laws."

Demeter didn't take her eyes from the field. "Yes, it's that rite and, yes, that's what they call it. Though few enough have the courage to subject themselves to its rigors. What care you for that?"

Hekate's hand settled on Demeter's forearm. "It's gone some way to reconcile Persephone to you. When she reached there today, she saw for herself those shades who are happy in Elysium because of the Mysteries rather than vacant-eyed and mindless in the asphodel meadow. She bade me come to you bearing words of gratitude."

At this Demeter finally looked at Hekate. "Why did she not come herself?"

Hekate's hand dropped away and the hump on her back reared a bit higher as she lowered her head. "She could not."

"He wouldn't let her, I suppose."

"Nay, it's nothing so simple as that." Hekate drew a deep breath. "Persephone partook of the food of the Underworld. Zeus's decree that she must remain in the Upper World with you made it impossible for her to return to her husband in any other way."

Demeter flinched and pressed a hand to her breast. Persephone had been so desperate to escape her that she'd eaten the food of the dead. Her daughter was truly lost to her.

Turning her face away from Hekate's dark gaze, Demeter closed her eyes for a long moment refusing to let the pain topple her.

"Demeter?" Hekate touched the back of Demeter's hand.

Demeter knocked Hekate's fingers away and opened her eyes on the bristling expanse of shorn grain. "These Eleusinians manage their fields poorly. They give no thought to soil quality or the availability of water. They let grass rise up and choke the grain. They don't know letting the land lie fallow and rest for a time is essential to plentiful harvests."

Demeter stooped, hefted another handful of soil. "If they have none to instruct them, they'll only continue their mismanagement." Demeter paused and let the dirt trickle through her fingers. "I mean to be a teacher to them."

The warm weight of Hekate's hand fell on Demeter's shoulder. "The harvests that result from your instruction will surely put enough in their stores to see them through any time of privation. They'll be—"

Shrugging off Hekate's hand, Demeter rose. "It isn't for mortals' benefit I do this. My daughter bestowed on them her bounty, and they care for it ill. They must be taught how best to nurture the gifts she gives."

"Do you mean then not to bring another famine?"

Demeter looked down, crushed some truncated stalks under her foot. "If I don't, I'll never see her again."

"I'll believe you will, in time," Hekate said her voice soft.

"How long?"

"I know not. It will take the time it takes."

Demeter spun away from Hekate, opened her hands, and then slowly closed them into fists. The golden stubble on the ground around her turned nearly white and rattled in the sudden hot wind that swept over the field.

Demeter turned back to the old Goddess. "Let that be the message you return to Persephone in exchange for the one she sent me."

"Demeter." Hekate shook her head, reproof in her face and voice.

"You've done the duty with which you were charged. Go now, Hekate. I have other business to which I must attend and you keep me from it."

"That's all you wish me to tell her? That you'll kill once more to ensure she returns to you."

Demeter nodded.

Hekate shook her head again, sighed, and turned away.

Demeter shifted her weight from foot to foot, clenched her fists, then flung her fingers wide and took a step after Hekate. "Wait."

The older Goddess turned back.

"Tell Persephone of my plans to teach the Eleusinians how best to care for their crops so they'll have sufficient stock to see them through the months of famine. If she returns to me in a timely manner, far fewer folk will perish." Demeter squatted, pressed a hand to the ground, and a cluster of asphodels sprung up. After plucking them, she wove them into a garland and pressed it into Hekate's hand. "Tell her I vow it by the River Styx. And take this to her as a token of my promise."

Hekate's face wrinkled in a smile. "Gladly, Sister. Gladly. It will make a fitting crown and I'm sure she'll be grateful for the gift."

ACKNOWLEDGEMENTS

I completed the first draft of *Seeds* in 2009 and it made its official debut in February of 2025. As you can probably guess from that timeline this book's journey into the world was anything but smooth. However, there were so many people who helped the book and me along the way and I'm so glad I get to thank them here.

I actually have to travel back past 2009 all the way to the late 1900s, as my teenage son refers to that time period, for my first acknowledgement. I hope everyone out there has at least one teacher who believed in them so deeply and supported them so wholeheartedly that it changed the trajectory of their life. For me that teacher is Gloria Stumme. She was my English teacher and the director of the drama department at my high school. She helped me discover my love of acting but it was her enthusiasm for the one act plays I penned my senior year that stuck with me. After watching one of those plays, my dad remarked that if I ever got famous it would be for my writing. My dad's belief in my talent and Mrs. Stumme's encouragement sparked a fire in me that, at times though it certainly dimmed, never went out. If it wasn't for her, I never would have attempted writing an entire novel.

The next people I owe a large amount of gratitude to are my early readers: my mom, my sister Kim, my friends Hannah and Sam and first ever critique partner Sheena Boekweg (a talented writer and author herself). Oh, and, Marilyn who very generously printed out *Seeds* and made me a beautifully bound book. They carried me through the next leg of my journey. If they hadn't read that early draft of *Seeds* so enthusiastically and loved it so much, I truly don't know if I would have continued down the long path to publication. Their belief in the book buoyed me through the inevitable rejections that pepper every writer's journey as did that of an editor I hired to help me get the book into the best shape possible. Julie Wright, I don't know if you'll ever see this, but the fact that you told me *Seeds* had the 'it' factor and believed it so much that you refunded part of my editing fee was something I relied on heavily in those hard moments when I almost stopped believing this book would ever see the light of day, so thank you for that.

When I queried *Seeds* the first time in 2010 (back in the day of paper queries and SASEs) I received exactly one partial request that turned into a full request that turned into a revise and resubmit. Though the revision didn't lead to representation, I'm still so grateful to agent Jennifer Weltz for taking the time to provide me her professional insight on how to give the story and characters more depth.

This brings me to the Fort Collins Writers, my first critique group. They read *Seeds* in early 2011 after I incorporated the revisions suggested by Ms. Weltz. Not only did their feedback helped elevate the manuscript, I received perhaps my favorite piece of critique ever which was 'Oh, the magic penis trope. You need to get rid of that.' Their understanding of my passion for writing and my deep desire to get my work out in the world was a pivotal part of my writing journey so thank you Nico, Christopher, Heather, Rick, Abi (of the magic penis comment) and Matt. Wherever you all are in the world now I hope you're thriving.

I took a seven-year hiatus from writing for various reasons so the next person to come on the scene didn't do so until July of 2021. I was querying another project at that time and, though she wasn't interested in that book, literary agent Shannon Snow asked what else I had. I told her about *Seeds* and she requested it. This led to another revise and resubmit, which again didn't end in representation, but her specific feedback about pacing and the use of deep point-of-view helped me get to manuscript closer to the iteration that would land me a book deal. Putting her advice into practice was the hardest edit I did on *Seeds* but the end result was so worth it. Thank you, Ms. Snow, for pushing me out of my comfort zone. Without you *Seeds* wouldn't be the book it is today.

Seeds passed through the hands of one final critique partner before making its way to Rising Action and I would be remiss not to thank that person. Rebecca Danzenbaker, whose debut novel came out the same year as *Seeds*, reiterated Shannon's advice to use deep point-of-view and pointed out some weak parts in the plot (as well as my terrible comma placement). Her feedback was invaluable in getting the book ready for its final phase, so thank you, Becky!

Around this time, I found my current critique group, The Monday Night Writers. The name might not be terribly creative but they sure are. They welcomed me with open arms, listened to all my angst over my unsuccessful query attempts and celebrated with me when I signed my book deal. They also came in clutch on a couple of sections of *Seeds* I was having trouble with during line edits. I appreciated every bit of advice and feedback as well as their willingness to engage in my impromptu pop quiz. Thank you, Amber Laura (if you like romance, go check out her books), Alicia, Hayden, Rachel, Jenn, MB, and Mark!

Now on to the fantastic team at Rising Action. I'm so grateful to them for believing in my book enough to help me get it out in the world! First thank you goes to Alexandria Brown who saw something worthwhile in one of my other manuscripts. While she decided not to acquire it, she did open the door for me to submit *Seeds* to Tina Beier for which I'm so grateful. Tina, thank you for reading through *Seeds* so much faster than you told me you would. Thank you for being so enthusiastic about acquiring it. Thank you for the developmental edit suggestions that ended up becoming some of my favorite moments in the novel. And thank you for loving my book almost as much as I do. To Marthese Fenech, thank you for your meticulous copy edits and all your kind words about my work. I appreciate it so much. And thank you to Natasha Mackenzie for my phenomenal cover.

Last, but definitely not least, I need to thank my family. My husband, Nick, to whom this book is dedicated has been an unwavering support through this entire journey. I would need to write a whole other book to do justice to the ways in which he's shown up for me while I chased my dream of becoming a traditionally published author. I absolutely couldn't have done it without him. I'm forever grateful to have such a loving, patient, supportive partner and father to my children. And to my kiddos, Kymry, Owen, Sylvie and Claire, thank you for teaching me what motherhood means and thank you for thinking it's pretty cool that your mom is a published author. I don't think I'll ever get any higher praise than that.

Oh, and my readers! I can't forget you guys! With all the wonderful books out there in the world waiting to be read you definitely didn't have to take a chance on mine, but I'm so grateful you did. Thank you! I hope you enjoyed reading *Seeds* as much as I enjoyed writing it!

ABOUT THE AUTHOR

Angie Paxton is an American author who writes books that explore complex female family relationships in dark, atmospheric settings. She's a part of the North Idaho Writers' League. Angie is a stay-at-home mom who enjoys reading and research. She'll occasionally emerge from her books to run, hike or boat in beautiful Idaho where she lives with her husband, four kids, and three spoiled cats. *Seeds* is Angie's debut novel.

Looking for more mythology? Check out the next page!

PERILS OF
SEA AND SKY

"A refreshing adventure
with innovative technology
and characters you'd trust
with your life
or your imagination!"
—Shelby Adina,
bestselling author of the
Magnukon Divide
steampunk series

LILIAN HORN

In the early 1700s, the discovery of anti-gravity technology led to the development of the aeroship trade. But there is one area into which no sky captain dares to venture, and that is the Grey Veil: an inhospitable fog threatening the lives and sanity of all who enter. With the Veil under a strict travel-ban, most level-headed pilots circumvent this treacherous place. Captain Rosanne Drackenheart, on the other hand, makes a pretty penny conducting her smuggling operation through the very edge of the mysterious fog.

When she is blackmailed into searching for a lost warship, she is forced to venture into the untraversed bowels of the Veil. Rosanne must protect her crew from mystical creatures, defend against pirates gunning for her ship, and save herself from the creature known as the Forest Devil.

Featuring Scandinavian myths and steampunk elements, *Perils of Sea and Sky* is a thrilling high fantasy adventure.